THE LIVERPOOL NIGHTINGALES

Liverpool, 1870. In the dirty backstreets, housemaid Maud Linklater witnesses an appalling accident. Rushing young chimney sweep Alfred to hospital, she helps nurse the boy on the overcrowded ward — and finds herself with a new job. Maud cannot believe her luck at joining trainees Alice and Eddy at the new Nurses' Training School and they form the closest of bonds. Then one day Alfred is abducted. Maud and the girls know the alleyways and slums of Liverpool are no place for a lost little boy. Can these determined women find Alfred before it's too late?

KATE EASTHAM

◆

THE LIVERPOOL NIGHTINGALES

Complete and Unabridged

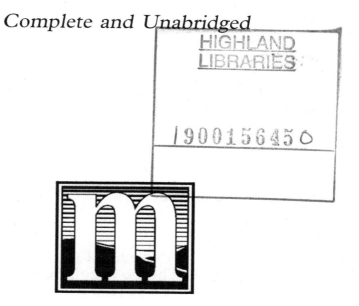

MAGNA
Leicester

First published in Great Britain in 2019 by
Penguin Books
London

First Ulverscroft Edition
published 2020
by arrangement with
Penguin Random House UK
London

A catalogue record for this book is available
from the British Library.

ISBN 978–0–7505–4774–1

Published by
F. A. Thorpe (Publishing)
Anstey, Leicestershire

Set by Words & Graphics Ltd.
Anstey, Leicestershire
Printed and bound in Great Britain by
T. J. International Ltd., Padstow, Cornwall

This book is printed on acid-free paper

Nightingale nurse Miss Mary Merryweather was the first superintendent of the Liverpool Nurses' Home and Training School. She went on to become a member of the Ladies National Association for the Repeal of the Contagious Diseases Acts, which united women from all over the country in opposition to the forcible examination of women suspected of being infected with venereal disease. Her sister, Miss Elizabeth Merryweather, worked with her in Liverpool as an assistant superintendent and the story goes that one of the sisters was never seen without her bonnet and the other never without her gloves. They were known as 'Bonnet' and 'Gloves'; one was very stern and the other gentle and kind.

Prologue

'... plans for a School and Home for Nurses
in Liverpool ... appeared to me so well
considered & laid out — they appeared to me
so much needed, not only in Liverpool
but in all the earth.'

Florence Nightingale

Liverpool, 1 May 1863

Ada Houston stood shivering in her light-grey uniform and starched cap. She hadn't thought to wear a shawl, though she should have known better. She'd lived in this city her whole life and she was aware how quickly the weather could change. Even though it was late spring there was still a cold breeze off the river and she could feel it seeping into her bones. Miss Mary Merryweather had been wiser, however. She was wearing a bonnet and a thick cloak, and her sister had donned the same, plus a pair of leather gloves. The ward Sisters, too, were all wrapped up warm in their shawls. Only Ada was left shivering. It was her own fault: she'd been trying to get through the mound of paperwork that had been left on her desk and she'd rushed out, afraid of being late. Ada was newly appointed to the role of assistant superintendent and hadn't quite got the measure of it yet. But she soon

1

would; she would have to.

She looked over to the doctors standing in line to her right in front of the steps leading up to the main entrance of the Nurses' Home and Training School, the new building that was just about to be officially opened by Mr William Rathbone, patron of the city and the hospital. Next to the doctors, the Mayor of Liverpool stood to attention as Mr Rathbone stepped forward to say a few words. As he opened his mouth to speak the wind gusted more strongly and the bunting that had been hastily draped above the door came untied at one end and started to flap around him. The man was not deterred by it one bit and he continued with his speech.

Ada was trying not to look too carefully at the people that had gathered before them, a fair crowd standing in front of the building and spreading out on to the street. She knew that her best friend, Mary, was there — she had exchanged a smile with her — and she had also seen her brother, Frank, his eyes shining with pride. But then she'd caught sight of another person, someone that she had only ever seen once or twice but never spoken to, and with whom she definitely did not want to make eye contact. It was the woman who'd turned out to be her half-sister, Stella, standing there as brazen as you like with a bright-yellow ribbon in her hair, her hands on her hips and a shawl loosely wrapped around her shoulders covering a low-cut gown.

It was not that Ada had any objection to

Stella's line of work, she simply had no interest in getting to know someone who had been part of her father's other family. She had never met her father, Francis, and she vowed that she never would. All she knew was that he had never shown any care for her or Frank, even after their mother died giving birth to her. Not until her brother was a grown man himself, and willing to be led astray, did his father make any contact with him and that had turned out to be a disaster. Ada wanted nothing to do with Francis or his wife, Marie, and although Frank kept telling her that Stella just wanted to be friends she wanted nothing to do with her either.

Mr Rathbone continued to speak as the bunting lashed around him. He was expressing a debt of gratitude to Florence Nightingale for her abundant advice with regard to the design and the dimensions of the building, even, apparently down to the floor tiles, the special cement, the number of windows and the type of stove. There was no denying that the woman was a genius and it was sad that her health had been so poor since she'd returned from the Crimea that it was out of the question for her to travel to Liverpool for the opening. Ada would never forget the two times — first in Scutari and then at the hospital in Balaklava — that she had met Miss Nightingale. The intensity of her gaze and the intelligence of the woman had left a lasting impression. Alongside Mary Seacole, Miss Nightingale had been Ada's inspiration for continuing her own work after the Crimean War ended. She still found it hard to believe that it was almost eight years since she had started nursing, having set out alone from Liverpool, a young woman searching for her brother. That same young woman who was now standing here amongst the great and the good of the city, cold and shivering, at the opening of a new building.

The wind was now billowing the skirts of the nurses and trying to remove Mr Rathbone's hat as he continued to thank Mr Horner, the architect of the building, for his fine work in making Miss Nightingale's ideas a reality. Ada could smell the varnish that was barely dry on the solid front door and she knew that she was already in love with the building: the galleried landings, the stone stairs that led up to two floors, and the skylight in the roof. It was light and airy in there, somewhere to find inspiration and also respite from the busy work of the hospital. She knew already that generations of nurses would live and learn and play out their own dramas within those walls.

Ada was really shivering now and fighting against the wind to keep her starched cap on her head but she continued to stand resolute with the rest of the nurses. She did hope, however, that Mr Rathbone would bring his speech to a close soon. Even Miss Mary Merryweather, in her thick cloak, was beginning to look cold, and the sky had just turned slate grey. There would be rain soon, a heavy downpour by the look of it.

Just as Ada thought it, the first big spots of rain fell. Mr Rathbone speeded up a bit and then

4

he was thanking the people of Liverpool for attending the opening, but just as he was suggesting that the staff and patrons reconvene inside the building, the heavens opened and rain came at them almost horizontally. The dignitaries and the doctors ran up the stone steps and into the building with their jackets flapping around them, closely followed by the nurses holding on to their starched caps with one hand and trying to restrain their billowing skirts with the other. Who knew what had happened to the people outside, including Ada's family? She could only hope they would quickly find shelter.

Once inside the building Ada felt a moment of pure giddiness overtake her as she stood dripping wet over Miss Nightingale's Minton floor tiles with the rest of the group. She had to work hard to stop herself from laughing out loud when she saw Mr Rathbone and the Mayor drying their bewhiskered faces with large handkerchiefs, and Miss Elizabeth Merryweather seemed completely unaware that she had a large dewdrop at the end of her nose. In the end, just to get back some control, Ada had to suggest that she give a guided tour of the school to anyone who hadn't already seen the wonders of the building. She was very proud indeed to show people around and to be able to tell them that it was the second Nightingale school to be built in the whole of the land. The first was, of course, at St Thomas's in London, which had been sponsored by the Nightingale Fund. This new building, planned so meticulously and built with such care, had been funded by William Rathbone and other Liverpool patrons and it belonged to their city. It was the Royal Infirmary's own Nurses' Home and Training School.

1

'A nurse should be . . . punctual to a second, and orderly to a hair . . . Quiet yet quick; quick without hurry; gentle without slowness; discreet without self importance, no gossip.'

Florence Nightingale

Liverpool, 1870

As Maud Linklater threw a dustsheet over a dining table in one of the grand houses in a newly respectable area of the city of Liverpool, she caught a glimpse of movement in the large, gold-framed mirror that hung above the fireplace. Startled, she glanced up from her work and for a moment, she almost didn't recognize the woman that she saw in the reflection. Her face was quite long and with her dark hair pulled back under her maid's cap she was all face and forehead. Maud thought that if it hadn't been for her big, dark eyes there would have been no saving grace at all for a young woman with such a long, mournful face.

She had a plain face, that's what she'd always been told by her grandmother. But there was something indefinably attractive about Maud — some light in her eyes, the way she held herself — that could only be seen in a flash. No one, least of all Maud, had any idea of what she might be capable of yet.

Maud always worked hard and she never usually gave herself time to dawdle. It was definitely not in her nature to daydream or gaze at herself in a mirror; not like some of the maids in the house who were forever looking at their own faces on any reflective surface, even the backs of the best spoons. Maud saw her reflection only in a flash and then got straight back to the task in hand. The polished wood of the dining table was quite an expanse and it would take two large dust-sheets to protect it completely. Maud made sure that all of it was covered and then went around pushing each chair under in turn to make sure that the yellow silk damask of the seat covers was tucked away under the table.

Without breaking her stride she went over to the side table where some porcelain figures stood, which needed protecting with a special light cloth. This was the one place that Maud always allowed herself a few moments simply to stand there just looking. One of her favourite figures was of a boy in a bright-blue suit holding a little dog; another was an image of the nurse Florence Nightingale, the Lady with the Lamp, standing next to a wounded soldier with his arm in a sling. Maud loved this piece in particular and made sure that she gave it extra care. And before she covered the figures she always kissed the tip of her finger and placed it on the head of the wounded soldier, Florence Nightingale and the little boy, each in turn. She had started out years ago just with the wounded soldier but then she hadn't felt able to leave the other two out so she now gave each one of them her special token. Then, ever so carefully, she pulled the light cloth over the side table, making sure that not one speck of soot would fall on to her favourite pieces.

The Persian rug was next. As she was pulling the thick cover over it she heard the tell-tale swish of a heavy wool skirt and the jingle of keys that signalled the arrival of the housekeeper, Miss Fairchild, in the room.

'Well done, Maud,' said Miss Fairchild, looking around with her eyes narrowed. 'I can always rely on you to get the job done without any messing or frivolity.'

Maud gave her a smile and nodded, grateful for the housekeeper's approval, although for some reason she felt a heaviness inside of her body, as if she were old and tired beyond her twenty-three years. She was glad to know that her work was of the best quality — of course she was — but sometimes she found herself wishing that she could, just occasionally, break away from the fastidious nature at the core of her being, which kept her always correct and always in order. Just sometimes she wished that she could make herself be a little bit frivolous. But she found it impossible. She was Maud and that was that.

When Miss Fairchild had gone, she looked around the room again, checking that all was in order, and then she walked over to the large window that looked out to the street. She gazed up to the sky and saw the blue of a clear sunny day, and for the first time in her ten years of service at the big house she felt as if the world outside that dining-room window was calling to her, trying to draw her away from her safe household routines.

The days were busy here and very long. Sometimes it was growing dark outside before she'd even had a chance to look out through the window or stand at the back door for a breath of air. She was locked into the rhythm of the house and the family that lived there and there didn't seem to be any way of escape.

Most of the staff talked about finding other work outside the house, and in the last few years Maud had been wondering if she should look for something else too. For a start, she wasn't bound to stay in Liverpool. She had no family — her mother and grandmother were both long gone — and beyond one of the footmen who had shown her some unwanted attention years ago there had been no suitors. She knew that it was unlikely that she would ever marry and she also knew that if she didn't make a change soon in another ten years' time she would be just like Miss Fairchild: sleeping alone in a narrow bed every night wearing a starched nightcap, with the keys to every room in the house on her belt but nowhere to call her own home.

As Maud stood staring out of the window she saw a familiar dark figure rounding the corner at the far side of the square. It was the chimney sweep, black with soot, and silhouetted against the clean, white stucco of the houses. She could see that he was looking up at the chimney of the house across the square as he walked. Then he stopped and swung round impatiently to face a much smaller figure struggling to cover the distance between them. At last the small figure, clearly a child, stood before him. The man bent from the waist, spoke some words and then clipped the child, a small boy, hard around the back of the head, knocking his cap to the ground.

Maud gasped and felt the dislike she had for the man swell within her. She continued to watch, making sure that he did not raise a hand to the boy again. If he had done so, she would have been straight out of that front door and across the square.

She continued to watch, feeling the tension in her body, as the man adjusted his grip on the bag and black brushes that he carried on his shoulder before continuing his advance towards them. Then her heart melted a little as she saw the small boy grab his cap up from the ground and move as fast as he could on his short legs, trying to catch the man up, though the large brush that he carried dragged him down and Maud knew that he didn't stand a chance of catching the man, who was striding ahead. As she stood she balled her right hand into a fist, willing the small boy to keep going but also readying herself to step outside the door and protect him if the need arose.

She held her breath as she saw the man stop again just before he turned down the alley at the side of the big house, the one that led to the tradesmen's entrance.

'No donkey today, Mr Greer.'

'Do you see a donkey?' replied the man, turning to face the head groom, who had just stepped out of the stable to lean on his shovel.

'Not one with four legs,' said the groom, laughing too loud at his own joke.

'Ha ha,' said Greer, before hawking up a large gobbet of black phlegm and spitting it at the groom's feet.

He turned and walked up to the back door, his thin shoulders held square and his left hand grinding at the blackened handles of the brushes he carried. He knocked with more vigour than was required, sensing the groom's eyes still burning into his back.

As soon as the heavy door started to open he announced himself in a loud voice, 'William Greer, master sweep.'

'Hello, Bill,' said the kitchen maid, drawing back the door to its widest extent to allow him to enter with his bag of soot and sweeping brushes. She was just about to close the door when Greer held up a hand and asked her to wait for his new climbing boy to enter.

'Bit slow this one,' he said. 'Needs training up.'

Aware of the sweep's arrival, Miss Fairchild had joined Maud in the dining room and they were ready and waiting as the man and his boy entered the room. Maud heard Miss Fairchild take a sharp intake of breath when she saw the boy.

'I see you have a new climbing boy, Mr Greer,' she said.

'I do indeed, Miss Fairchild. This fine lad is

fresh from the workhouse only last week,' said Greer, doffing his cap and baring his teeth in a smile. Yellow, broken teeth almost white against the black of his skin.

'Isn't he a bit young, a bit small for the job?'

'Definitely not, Miss Fairchild. The lad is a full eight years of age, and being small, see, is a real advantage for his line of work.'

'But he is so thin, Mr Greer; he looks so weak.'

'Well, the lad must have worms or summat. He's clearing a big bowl of porridge twice a day. Eating us out of 'use and 'ome he is at present. And besides, no one wants a fat climbing boy, do they now? The buggers just get stuck.'

Maud saw a shiver go through the boy's small frame at the sweep's words and her heart went out to him. She glanced at Miss Fairchild and she knew that she had seen it too, but it seemed like there was nothing either of them could do except wait for the job to get started. Greer had started unpacking his brushes and the boy was standing with his head bowed. Maud couldn't bear to watch any of the preparation so she turned and checked around the room for one last time. Sensing her unease, Miss Fairchild also made a move, nodding to Maud and mumbling something about orders for the kitchen maids and then she was gone, leaving Maud, in her position as senior housemaid, to supervise the sweeping of the dining-room chimney.

When all the brushes were unpacked Greer turned to face the boy, his face tight. With a nod he indicated that it was time to unfold and place

13

the soot cloth that would cover the hearth. Maud saw the boy shudder and wondered if the story that these boys had to sleep under the soot cloth was true.

Maud stood quiet, her right hand balled into a fist once more as she watched the unfolding and the fixing of the soot cloth around the hearth. Greer's last lad had been a sturdy specimen who could stand his ground, the sort who would no doubt go on to be a master sweep himself. But this boy was one that you just wanted to wrap up warm in a blanket and give a drink of milk.

When all was ready the boy removed his tattered coat and mucky boots, and stood for a few moments as if he didn't know what to do next. He was black from head to toe, with ripped elbows on his shirt and the knees of his trousers worn through.

'Get a move on — we haven't got all day,' barked Greer.

The boy glanced up at Maud before entering the hearth and pulling his cap down so the brim would protect his nose and mouth. He then disappeared through a slit in the cloth, holding the flat brush in his right hand.

'What are you waiting for, Christmas?' said Greer, looking over at Maud for approval of his joke.

She was not concerned with Greer or his jokes; she had looked up the flue that morning as she cleared out the remains of the fire. The opening was small, and it was dark and hot up there. How would the boy be able to breathe?

Maud's fears were realized much sooner than

expected when a whimpering cry came from the chimney. A cry that quickly became a terrified wail.

Greer hastily pulled the soot cloth aside and yelled up the chimney, 'What the blazes is going on up there? Sweep that soot and stop messing about.' Glancing back at Maud, he tried to smile but quickly had his head up the chimney again. 'What do you mean you're stuck? You've only just gone up there, you lazy bastard. You'd better look sharp or I'll light a fire under you, mark my words I will.'

The boy went quiet and Maud held her breath, straining for a sign of life. She could feel her heart racing and her fist was now balled so tight her fingernails were digging into her palm. The sign that the child had heard came soon enough, however: a mournful wail that brought tears to her eyes.

'Please, Mr Greer,' she implored. 'You must do something.'

'Do something, do something?' he shouted. 'I'll do something,' he yelled up the chimney again. 'I'll light a bloody fire under him.' And with that he pulled his head from the flue and made a move to the pile of kindling that lay ready by the fire.

Instantly Maud was there, blocking his way. 'No you don't, Mr Greer,' she said with some steel in her voice. 'We're not lighting any fires.'

Greer glared at her, then turned back to the chimney, stuck his arm up and felt for the boy's leg. He could just reach a small foot and, after forcing his shoulder further up the flue, was able to get some purchase and pull hard. The boy was stuck, but not fast, so that with one good yank Greer was able to bring him down, crashing on to the hearth.

He fell hard, then was covered with a soft flump of soot.

Greer dragged him out and tried to stand him up but his legs gave way and he started to sob uncontrollably.

'Please don't send me up again, please don't send me up again . . . ' he wailed, with soot in his mouth and snot and tears running down his face.

Greer was about to start shaking him when Maud placed her hand firmly on his blackened sleeve.

'Don't do that, Mr Greer,' she said with a sure and certain tone in her voice that she had never used before. 'You'll get soot all over the show and if that happens Miss Fairchild won't offer you any more business at this house.'

Greer drew back immediately, shocked by the power in the voice of a housemaid who was usually so quiet. Maud stooped down to the boy. She just wanted to gather him up in her arms but she could see the terror on the child's face and see how he instinctively leant away from her. She could see his breathing coming fast and she felt a pain in her heart as she saw him start to tremble. She had to help him, she had to make him know that she would not hurt him, so she murmured softly to him, 'It's all right, it's all right, I'm not going to hurt you.' Then she held out her hand to him. His eyes widened for a moment and for a split second she thought that he was going to turn away but then he took her hand.

'Try to stand up,' she said gently. 'Try to stand and we'll get you a drink and something to eat.' He looked at her now with the palest blue eyes that she had ever seen. Eyes that would match the finest blue gown that you could buy.

She felt him pulling on her hand as he tried to stand up and she placed her other arm around him protectively but as soon as he was almost upright he began to keel over again. Instinctively Maud held on to his hand and then she grabbed one of the dining chairs from under its protective cover and lifted the boy to sit down on it. She saw the soot from his clothes smear black on to the yellow silk damask but in that instant she knew that she had more important concerns than the soft furnishings.

As the boy sat he rested back and closed his eyes. Maud crouched by him and gently placed the flat of her hand on his tiny chest. She could feel how dreadfully thin he was and how his small heart was beating as fast as a rabbit's in the cage of his ribs. Looking down to his poor knees, now exposed as he sat, she saw how the skin was shredded and matted with fresh blood and soot. Spotting a discarded linen napkin under the table she grabbed it and pressed the clean white cloth gently to his wounds.

'Don't be fussing him now,' said Greer, advancing towards them. 'Nobody has call for a climbing boy who's gone soft. He just needs more salt brine on those knees and a rough

17

brush to harden them up.'

Maud let out a small gasp at the thought of the boy's poor knees being scrubbed with brine. She had heard of this practice but thought it was something of the past. How could this still be happening?

Greer pushed past her, grabbed the boy and tried to haul him up off the chair. But the child screamed out in pain and Maud immediately yelled, 'Stop!'

The sweep froze in his tracks, surprised by the power of the housemaid's voice.

'Let go of him,' said Maud with a voice full of authority, 'or I will ring for Miss Fairchild.'

Greer dropped the boy's arm and Maud lifted him back so that he could be supported by the chair. She could see that the arm looked out of shape. Clearly it had been twisted as the sweep had dragged him back down the chimney.

'He has been injured,' said Maud.

'What?' said Greer. 'It's nothing, just a sprain. I need him today so you'll have to bind it up.'

'I will not bind it up,' said Maud. 'The boy needs to be seen by a doctor.'

'No doctors,' said Greer. 'He needs to be up them chimneys. I've got three more on for today and he hasn't even finished this one yet.'

Maud stood up and turned to face Greer, eye to eye.

'This boy is hurt,' she said with steel in her voice. 'He will not be climbing your chimneys.'

Just at that moment the door of the dining room swung open and Miss Fairchild swept into the room.

'Whatever is going on in here, Mr Greer?' she said, seeing Maud standing in front of the boy with both arms held out to shield him.

'The boy got stuck up there,' Maud explained. 'He was wailing and screaming, and then Mr Greer dragged him back down. His arm is twisted out of shape, Miss Fairchild. He needs to be seen by a doctor.'

Greer stamped his foot impatiently but before he could speak again Miss Fairchild held up a hand to silence him.

'Mr Greer,' she said, 'may I remind you that you are employed to sweep the chimneys of this house and many other chimneys of the houses in Devonshire Square on my recommendation, and my recommendation alone. If I was to inform the proprietor of this home and the other houses that I thought your standards were no longer suitable, then I'm sorry to say there would be no more work for you here ever again.'

Maud saw Greer take a step back and then he bowed his head and muttered, 'Right then, right . . . I'll get him to a doctor if that's what you say.'

'No,' said Miss Fairchild, holding up her hand to silence him yet again. 'You will not get him to a doctor, Mr Greer. I do not trust you to take care of him. My maid here will take him up to the hospital and we will make sure that the boy is properly treated.'

Greer said nothing more. He stooped down and started packing up his brushes, noisily clattering them together and shoving them into the bag. Then he strode out of the room muttering and swearing under his breath.

'Right, Maud,' said Miss Fairchild, 'there is no time to lose. I'll go and get a blanket and organize one of the footmen to go with you up to the hospital. You stay with him there, Maud, and make sure that he is all right. You are excused from your duties for the rest of the day . . . Oh, and I have some money saved up; I will pay for anything that the boy needs.'

'Thank you, Miss Fairchild,' said Maud, almost in tears, and then letting out a small gasp as she spotted the linen napkin in her hand stained with blood and soot.

Miss Fairchild took the napkin straight out of her hand, saying, 'Don't worry about that. Those stains won't come out. I'll dispose of it.'

As Miss Fairchild turned once more to check on the boy before she left the room Maud saw that her eyes were brimming with tears, but when she spoke her voice was firm. 'This stops right here, Maud. I should have done something about this before; there is no excuse. This practice of sending boys up chimneys is barbaric. The sweeps were supposed to stop doing it years ago but it still goes on. They have brushes that can be used to do that job these days, not children. From now on I will make sure that in this house we will only employ a sweep with one of the appropriate systems of brushes. I don't care if it doesn't sweep as well as a boy or it puts more soot out into the room. I don't care. This has to stop.'

'Yes, Miss Fairchild,' said Maud, her heart swelling with pride for the woman.

★   ★   ★

That same evening, in a house near Lime Street Station, Ada Houston's half-sister, Stella, was tending to the needs of one of her regular customers. As the man sat on the bed she pulled his shirt off, seeing once more the jagged wound that ran the length of his right arm, cutting through the distinctive tattoo, tearing apart the name of some person and what looked like the shape of a swan, a black swan. Then, as she leant forward to pull the singlet over his head, she saw the stripes across his back that she knew, for sure, were the marks of the lash.

Unbuckling his belt, she slipped down his breeches, noting once again the muscular left thigh with its covering of pale hair and then the right leg, pitiful and wasted with a big chunk of flesh missing from the calf, the angry skin on that leg pulled tight around the shin. Stella had seen all sorts in her time but the sure knowledge of violence and pain that shot through her every time she saw that particular wound always made her stomach turn. And, as always, no matter how gentle she was, her hand caught the scarred remains of his calf and she felt the man wince with pain.

'Sorry,' she said straight away, hating the pain that the man had to suffer and angry with herself for not being more careful. Then laying the breeches aside, she turned to face him with her hands on her hips. He sat on the edge of the bed with his head bowed and she could see that he was gritting his teeth waiting for the pain to subside. He looked thinner, she thought, and even more exhausted. She had known him for years and knew how he lived, and it looked like things were starting to catch up with him. He lifted his head and she smelt the liquor on his breath. She saw, too, the crease in his brow and the lines around his eyes that told her that he was still in a great deal of pain.

Seeing the sympathy in her gaze he snapped at her, 'Just get on with it, will you? At least I've paid this time.'

'I'm just waiting for you to be more comfortable,' she said gently.

'Get on with it,' he snapped again.

'All right then,' she said. 'Have you got your French letter?'

'In my breeches pocket,' he said, before swinging his legs up on to the bed and lying back on the pillows.

Afterwards, as always, Stella gave the man time to sleep on her bed and she must have nodded off herself because she woke with a start, hearing the shrill laughter of her friend, Laura, in the next room. Feeling a bit sick and groggy, Stella felt her heart pounding as she tried to get some idea of how long she'd been asleep and how many customers would be waiting. She needed to get this man moving. Shaking him by the arm, she tried to rouse him but he was sound asleep and his skin felt like it was burning up.

'Come on, come on,' she said, 'I need to work. Watching you sleep won't earn me any brass.' But she couldn't wake him and when she looked down at his leg, she could see that it was discharging fluid on to her bedsheet.

The walls of the brothel were thin; she didn't

have to knock all that hard to get some attention. So within seconds the door to her room was swinging open and Laura stood there, breathless and worried, with a heavy stick in her hand.

'It's all right,' said Stella, 'he wasn't getting rough or anything. Poor bugger's passed out, that's all.'

Together the women wrapped the man in the sheet where he lay and then dragged him off the bed.

'We'll put him on that mattress in the cellar for now. He'll be warm enough down there with plenty of blankets,' said Stella. 'And if he's still there when I've finished for the night I'll see if I can get him up to the Infirmary.'

'Why not just tip him out on to the street?' said Laura.

'No, I can't do that. He's a regular and I think he must have been in the army. He's fought for Queen and Country, that's for sure.'

'Just looks like a drunk, the same as the rest, to me,' said Laura. 'But it's up to you. Give me a shout if you want and we'll take him up to the Infirmary on the handcart.'

★ ★ ★

The next morning a drunk and delirious man was found sitting on the steps of the new Nurses' Home on Dover Street, right next to the Liverpool Royal Infirmary. Stella and her friend had pushed him in the handcart but decided not to go right up to the hospital itself; they didn't want any questions, they just needed to get back to their beds. So they had left him at the next best place, the Nurses' Home and Training School.

Stella knew that one of the superintendents — maybe even Ada — or any number of probationers would be passing by the man on the steps as they made their way to their morning shift at the hospital. They were bound to find him, she thought.

Before they left him there, propped on the steps, Stella stood with her hands on her hips looking up at the first-floor windows of the fancy brick building, imagining that's where the nurses' dormitory would be.

'Bet they're sleeping sound up there in their clean beds,' she said quietly to herself, thinking of her half-sister again. No love lost there, she thought, but she couldn't help but feel some envy towards a woman who didn't have to share her bed with some lout from the backstreets and would always have clean sheets to lie on. Then again, she wasn't sure that she'd be able to stomach all that cleanliness and discipline and timekeeping, and she felt fortunate in that she hadn't actually been forced to go into the same trade as her mother. Her mother, Marie, ran the brothel and she had told Stella, her only child, to make her own choice. She could have gone into domestic service, she could have probably come up here and worked at the hospital, and there was always work at the docks for a strong, healthy woman. But she had chosen to follow her mother and one day she would take over the running of their place herself. She would make

24

sure that they always had the right standard, keeping the place as clean and as safe as they could for the women.

'So that's that,' she muttered to herself, 'no clean and tidy life for me.' Then she turned from the building and saw Laura, her red hair pulled back from her face, looking exhausted and shivering in her thin gown. She went straight over to her and put an arm around her shoulders, giving her a bit of a rub to try to warm her up.

'Come on, let's get you back and then we can both have some sleep before the next lot of rabble come knockin' at the door.'

Then linking her friend's arm and huddling up to her, she walked away. But before they were out of view, Stella glanced back once more and made a promise to herself to go up to the Infirmary later that day to see how he was getting on.

* * *

The door of the Nurses' Home opened at 6.30 a.m. sharp and the nurse probationers started to emerge into the morning light. They all saw the man on the steps but, as they filed past him in their brand-new uniforms and white starched aprons, none of them stopped to attend to him. They could see that he looked drunk. His head was lolling around, his face was flushed red and he was muttering about Miss Nightingale, he wanted to see Miss Nightingale. And then, as each one walked by, the man reached out a hand to try to touch the long skirts of their clean uniforms, tantalizingly close and brushing the steps as they passed him without looking, each one making sure to keep her distance.

The truth was the young nurses could not stop even if they had wanted to. They all needed to get to the ward on time, but certainly Nancy Sellers, leading the group with her nose in the air and her neatly curled blond hair pinned beneath a spotless white cap, did not want to stop. Nancy should have been beautiful — she had perfect features set in a heart-shaped face, big blue eyes with dark lashes, a narrow waist and perfect feet; she should have been the belle of Liverpool Infirmary — but unfortunately Nancy's nature was such that it seeped out through her face and made her look sour, and when she opened her beautiful mouth to speak her voice came out harsh and her words were usually spiteful.

No, definitely Nancy would never have stopped to help some foul-smelling tramp reeking of drink. And even Alice Sampson — following close behind Nancy with her tentative step, slightly out of breath as always and her face pale that morning — even Alice did not dare stop.

Nor Edwina Pacey, running late as usual, hurtling after the group with her face flushed and her cap askew. Not even Edwina could stop, even though she was the most likely candidate within the group to freely offer assistance to any mortal soul.

Not one of the young nurses dared to stop and risk being late for the ward. Not after Louisa, a well-meaning girl but with no common sense or real purpose in life, had been dismissed by the superintendent in front of the whole group last week for lateness and slovenly behaviour.

In fact, all of the nurses were well into their work on the wards before anyone came close to helping the man on the steps. And in the end it was the superintendent of the training school herself, Miss Mary Merryweather, who attended him. She was, as always, later than the probationers. She'd been checking that they had left their dormitories in the correct order and then she had gone back to the dining room for extra eggs and a slice of ham.

Seeing the man on the steps was no surprise to Miss Merryweather. Since the building had opened they had regularly found sick, abandoned and even dead people on the doorstep. She felt at his forehead with the back of her hand: he was burning up, he definitely had a fever, and she could smell suppuration. He must have some festering wound, she thought. Then he opened his eyes and started talking some nonsense about going into battle and seeing Miss Nightingale. Despite the resident smell of drink on the man, it was easy for the superintendent to tell that the man was delirious from fever and he would need urgent treatment if they were going to save him. Miss Merryweather needed two orderlies with a stretcher to transfer the man to the hospital and she knew exactly where they would be at this time of day. So, leaving the man on the steps, she walked swiftly to the hospital and a quiet corridor tucked away behind the kitchen.

As Miss Merryweather stood at the top of that corridor she could see a cloud of tobacco smoke emerging from a recessed area behind a store cupboard and she knew that she was right.

'Mr Delaney,' she shouted, and heard immediately the sound of scuffling and muttering from the recessed area and then the man in question clearing his throat.

'Yes, Miss Merryweather,' said a red-faced man, stepping into view, slightly out of breath and wiping drops of tea from his stubbly chin with the back of his hand.

'Ah, there you are, Mr Delaney,' said Miss Merryweather, making out that she had no idea where the two men were stationed. 'I need you to find your colleague, Mr Walker, and proceed at once to the steps of the Nurses' Home. We have another patient who has been left there for medical attention. He has a fever and he looks quite poorly. I need you to remove him from there as soon as possible and bring him to the Male Surgical ward. I believe they had a number of deaths overnight so there should be a bed.'

'Yes, miss,' said Michael Delaney, trying to smile but feeling very badly done by. They had only just finished moving the bodies of the deceased out of the wards, they were desperate for a drink, but now there would be no time to finish their tea or their smoke. He knew that Miss Merryweather had the exact measure of everything that went on in the hospital and that she would stand and wait until she saw him and Stephen Walker heading down the corridor with the stretcher. There was no way round it and he knew that they might as well get moving straight away.

★ ★ ★

'Right then, Stephen,' said Michael, as always taking the lead. 'Let's get the blighter loaded up and in that bed as quick as we can, then we can get back to the kitchen for another brew.'

Stephen nodded. He never said much, he simply moved carefully in the direction that he was pointed. They had an easy working relationship: Michael was in charge and Stephen did as he was told.

'Don't like the look of this one,' said Michael, at the head of the stretcher. 'He's not going to make it through the night.'

'He might do all right,' said Stephen at the foot, 'I've seen 'em worse than this.'

'Aye, but this man's got a lot of liquor inside him. I don't mean just from one night, I mean from years and years of drinking. He's pickled in it. If he survives the day then they'll have a hell of a time with 'im on the ward when he comes off the liquor. A hell of a time. He'll be shaking and rattling that bed for days to come, you mark my words. It'll be terrible for them new nurses, those young probationers, it will indeed,' he said, starting to laugh. 'All new on the ward this week, some of 'em look like they've never even nursed a sick kitten, never mind a nasty, full-grown man full of liquor.'

The patient was delivered directly to the Male

Surgical ward where there was, thank goodness, still a free bed. The wards were so packed out that they filled instantly. By rights this man should have gone to the medical ward, but there wasn't even one bed on there that morning. Michael saw that the sheets hadn't been changed after they'd removed the previous occupant. He knew they should have summoned a nurse and made sure the bed was clean, but he was desperate for his cup of tea and this fella they'd picked up from the steps was filthy dirty from the streets anyway, so he had to let it go this time. There was something that they could do, however, to hide their tracks, a tip that he'd picked up years ago. When they had the man on the bed they rolled him about a bit on the bedding to transfer on to it some more of his own grime. Who would know?

Before they could pick up the stretcher and leave, however, Sister called down the ward and the two men stood stock-still, looking at each other, their eyes wide. Sister Law was a fearsome woman. Michael always referred to her as 'the one that must be obeyed'.

'Mr Delaney,' she shouted, 'wait RIGHT there.'

Michael stood as if in a trance for a few seconds and then he pasted a smile on his face and turned to face the woman as she strode down the ward towards them with her starched cap fastened in a tight bow beneath her ample chin.

'Yes, Sister,' he said, managing to maintain the smile as Stephen stood frozen behind him with his head bowed and his jacket hanging loose around his thin frame.

'Right, you two,' said Sister, slightly out of breath as she stood before Michael. 'We need you both at the top end of the ward. We have another patient who needs to be moved: another mortal soul who has passed away, I'm afraid.'

Stephen couldn't help but let out a huge sigh of relief. Sister switched her gaze straight to him and scowled.

'Good that the poor man is out of his suffering,' said Michael instantly, crossing himself.

'Yes, indeed,' said Sister, twisting back to face Michael with a suspicious glare.

Then looking past him she said, 'Miss Merryweather has already spoken to me about this patient — has he been able to give you his name?'

'No, Sister, not yet. He's not making any sense at present,' said Michael, already starting to move up the ward before Sister Law got any closer to the sheets on the bed. 'Get the stretcher, Stephen. We'll move the deceased straight away, Sister, straight away.'

2

'The time is come when women must do something more than the domestic hearth.'

Florence Nightingale

'What is your name?' asked Maud when she saw the boy's eyes begin to flutter open.

She had been sitting by his bed now for some time on the Male Surgical ward of Liverpool Royal Infirmary. Miss Fairchild had given her the full day off again so that she could go back and check on the boy. Maud had accompanied him to the hospital the previous day, when he had been in so much shock, and it had got so late by the time they'd been given a bed that she had only been able to make sure that he had a blanket to cover him before she needed to head back to the big house. And so here she was again, out on a mission for Miss Fairchild. The place was packed with patients and there was a horrible smell, but she hadn't minded waiting there by his bed, watching over him. He was her priority.

The nurses kept passing by the bottom of the bed and glancing at them, sometimes smiling, often walking by fast on their way to rescue some poor soul who was falling out of bed or staggering down the ward or screaming out in pain. Maud could see how some of the young nurses in their new uniforms were flushed in the face and seemed uncertain, and she could hear how the older woman in the grey uniform and starched cap tied in a tight bow under her chin kept scowling down the ward and shouting at them. She needs to give them a chance, thought Maud. This place is so busy and clearly they are new to the job. There seem to be about three of them who look brand new.

One of them was in constant attendance at the bedside of the new patient next to them. Maud had seen the men with the stretcher bring him in, slide him on to the bed and roll him about a bit on the sheets. She'd been keeping an eye on the poor man whilst she waited for the boy to be seen. The man had seemed sleepy at first but now he was shouting and rolling around, agitated and trying to get up. His legs were bad and they couldn't hold him so the nurses kept coming to him and wrestling him back down, then tucking the blanket in around him firmly, well under the mattress in an attempt to keep him safe. But in no time at all, he was off again. There was no rest for the nurses. No rest for anyone.

Looking down to the boy, who seemed to have gone back to sleep or whatever state he had lapsed into, Maud couldn't help but worry about his injury and feel an ache in her chest when she thought about how he had been forced to climb chimneys. His face and his hair — and the rest of him, in fact — were completely black with soot. And the sticky blackness of soot was the blackest of black that can be imagined, especially against the white sheet of a hospital bed.

Maud had held the boy whilst one of the nurses put some kind of sling on his arm, the light-grey cloth of it now drawing attention to the injured part of his body. She still bore the marks of the soot on her skirt from where she had held on to him. She had tried dusting it off but it just smeared more. She would have to wait till she got back to the house; Miss Fairchild would know what to do about the stain.

Then she had an idea. Maybe if she started cleaning the boy up it would be good for him and it would help stop the soot rubbing off on the sheets and any other person who came into contact with him. She kept trying to catch the attention of one of the nurses as they hurried by the bottom of the bed, to ask for a bowl of water and a cloth, but as soon as she saw one coming and opened her mouth to speak, they were gone.

Now the man in the next bed was at it again, shouting out, something about wanting to see Miss Nightingale. Maud wondered at first if the famous lady had actually come to work at the Infirmary in Liverpool but soon realized that the man was delirious. She felt disappointed. She would have liked to be able to go back and tell Miss Fairchild that she had met the Lady with the Lamp. She wondered if the man had met Florence Nightingale at some time in his life. Given the huge scar and the chunk of flesh missing from the leg that he kept thrusting in her direction, maybe he had been a soldier in the Crimean War.

The man sat up again, with renewed energy this time, and Maud could see that he was trying to scrabble out of bed. She leapt up from her seat and quickly went round to steady him as he sat swaying on the edge of the bed. She held on to his arm and managed to balance him, but then he swore at her and tried to wrench his arm free, so she held on to him and as they struggled she noticed that he had an unusual tattoo on his forearm. It looked like a black swan, and it was ripped through by a vicious-looking scar. The poor man, she thought, he must have been through some terrible battle. Then he growled at her and pushed himself up from the bed and she couldn't stop him. He was standing up and lurching sideways. She was determined to hold on to him but frantically looking around for one of the nurses. She could smell the liquor on his breath and his eyes were burning with some kind of fury. She could also feel how strong he was, despite his crippled leg. She stood, just holding him, until one of the red-faced young nurses came to her side.

'Thank you,' said the nurse, a bit breathless. 'As you can see we are very hard-pressed today and this one just won't stay in bed.'

Maud helped the young nurse, who had a very pleasing manner, load the man back on to the bed and then, before the nurse could disappear, she took her opportunity. 'Please can you tell me where to get a bowl of water and a cloth so I can give my boy a wash?'

'Yes, yes,' said the nurse, already on the move.

35

'Go into the sluice room, there, that one,' she said, pointing to a door as she moved off down the ward.

Maud checked that the boy was still sleeping and the man in the next bed was settled before she made her way over. She found some tin bowls and a stack of cloths and, grabbing one of each, she ladled some water into the bowl from a large bucket that sat on the ground. As she went back out through the door she almost knocked into Sister, who instantly scowled at her.

'What are you doing?' she said. 'You are not a nurse . . . what are you doing in our sluice?'

'It's just that one of the nurses . . . ' No, thought Maud, I'm not going to get that young woman into any trouble. 'It's just that I wanted to help and I needed some water to start washing the boy that I've brought in.'

'You needed some water,' Sister almost shouted. 'Do you realize that those tin bowls and cloths are for the use of the nurses, and the nurses alone?'

'No, I didn't know,' said Maud, standing her ground and meeting the woman's gaze.

The woman, who was quite short, pulled her shoulders up towards her ears and pushed out her chest before speaking again. 'I am Ward Sister. All people going in and out of the sluice are answerable to me.'

'I'm sorry,' said Maud. 'I can see that you are very busy on the ward today. Please can I help by using this bowl and this cloth out of your sluice to wash the boy who I am staying with until one of your doctors is free to attend to him?'

Sister's face went bright red and she started to splutter a reply.

'Thank you,' said Maud, turning and making her way back down the ward to her patient.

Maud daren't look back but as she walked she heard a crash from the top of the ward and then Sister's voice shouting, 'Nurse, nurse, go to that patient immediately. Go on, go on, before he knocks something else over . . . oh, for goodness' sake, let me deal with it.'

Feeling safe again by the boy's bed, Maud put the tin bowl on the floor and soaked the piece of cloth in the water. She was so gentle at first with the cloth on his face that no soot was coming off. Then gradually she used a bit more pressure but she was still very careful, treating the boy as if he was the most precious thing in the world. She had never spent much time looking at her own face — she usually just gave it a quick swill with water and a wipe with a towel at the beginning and end of each day — so paying attention to all the different contours of a face was quite a new experience for Maud. She liked the line of the brow and the sweep of the boy's cheekbone. She kept going but in the end the cloth was black, the water was black, the boy's face was still black and there didn't seem to be much to choose between them. But Maud kept on, not wanting to risk a trip back to the sluice for clean water just yet.

Suddenly the boy's eyes popped open. They were so blue, pale blue that again Maud almost gasped at their colour against the black of his skin.

'Hello,' she said. 'Just lie still . . . you will be all right.'

The boy tried to sit up and grimaced with the pain from his arm.

'You've hurt your arm and now you are in hospital,' said Maud soothingly.

The boy looked at her with dread, as if he had just woken from some nightmare. She saw him try to sit up again and she wanted to help him but she could feel him pulling away from her.

'It's all right, it's all right, I'm not going to hurt you,' she said gently, but then he was looking around the ward frantically and when she put her arm around him to offer some comfort she could feel him tense, sitting separate and erect in the bed in a position that was clearly uncomfortable for his injured arm.

She let him look around the ward for as long as he needed so that he could see where he was and try to make sense of things. When he looks at me again, she thought, that's when I'll try to speak to him.

When she eventually saw his shoulders start to relax just a little and he tried to shift himself into a more comfortable position, she spoke, reminding him of what had happened.

The boy looked at her again, for longer this time, and then he, too, spoke, his voice tiny against the background noise of the ward with men shouting out and people clattering up and down.

'Is Mr . . . is Mr Greer coming for me?'

'No,' said Maud firmly. 'He is not coming. Miss Fairchild has made sure of that.'

She carefully placed a hand on his forearm and he looked at her again. She smiled gently at him, her slow smile. He didn't smile back but she could tell that her words had given him some comfort and she knew that he was starting to trust her a little.

'Now let's try to get you a bit more comfortable,' she said. 'See if you can slide down in the bed a bit and try to lie on your back. We'll prop the arm at that side . . . '

The boy cried out with pain as she started to wedge his arm with a blanket. Maud drew in a sharp breath and almost felt the pain herself. 'Ouch,' she said. 'Sorry about that.'

'It's all right,' said the boy, and Maud thought that he was trying to smile at her.

'I keep trying to clean the soot off your face,' she laughed. 'But I don't seem to be getting very far.'

'Mr Greer says I have to keep the soot to protect the skin. And he doesn't want Mrs Greer having to wash and clean for the likes of me.'

Really, thought Maud, the smile frozen on her face as she felt the anger start to rise again. 'Well, you don't need to worry about Mr Greer or his wife from now on,' she said, determined to make sure that was the case.

'But Mr Greer said he needs me to climb the chimneys and get some money back for him, the money he had to pay to get me out of the workhouse,' said the boy with his eyes wide, trying to raise himself back up again in the bed.

'Lie down, lie down,' said Maud reassuringly. 'And don't you worry about Mr Greer or his chimneys. Miss Fairchild and I will deal with Mr Greer. Now just you lie quiet and let's see what the doctor has to say about your arm.'

The boy still looked worried but he nodded his head.

'What's your name?' asked Maud.

'My name's Alfred, miss, but Mr Greer calls me 'boy'.'

'Right, Alfred,' said Maud. 'My name is Maud and I will stay with you today for as long as I can, and then, I hope, I will be able to come back and see you tomorrow.'

The boy tried to smile but then closed his eyes, almost as if the effort had been too much. Maud continued to wipe his face with the cloth and although she could tell that he wasn't really asleep or passed out like before, he didn't seem to mind and so she continued. Then she looked at his small hands, thick with soot, and when she picked one up to give it a wipe she felt the calluses where he had held the sweeping brush. She almost cried as she held each hand in turn and as she wiped them she tried to remove not just the soot but the hurt and the pain that the boy must have endured in his short life.

When the doctor eventually came he told them, thank goodness, the bone hadn't broken the skin. That would have meant amputation and then who knew if the boy would have survived? Maud felt her heart harden further against the chimney sweep when she realized how dangerous his actions had been. She could not believe that with all the progress that had been made in her lifetime with clever machines and steam railways and gas lighting, small boys were still climbing the chimneys of big houses.

Thinking of how badly the boy had been treated, both by the workhouse who had farmed him out as an apprentice and then by the sweep who had used him so cruelly, Maud was more determined than ever to make sure that the boy was cared for properly from now on. She stayed with him whilst the doctor pulled on the arm to straighten it, and held on to Alfred as he screamed with pain, feeling his heart hammering through his thin chest, keeping time with her own. And then she helped one of the nurses to bind the arm and, at last, to put it back in the sling.

As he lay there on the bed afterwards, still exhausted and trying to bear up to the pain, she sat by him and held his hand, praying that he might fall asleep and get some rest. She asked the nurse if the boy could have anything for the pain and she had said no, their supply of laudanum was low and besides, they didn't like to give it to the children because sometimes a drop too much could put them to sleep for ever. But seeing Maud's face the nurse felt sorry for them both and in the end she brought the boy a measure of brandy. He swallowed it down and coughed a bit but it might have helped him a little as within an hour his face began to relax and then he had fallen into a restless sleep.

The doctor had told them that if the bones in the arm knitted together properly then the boy should get some use back in the arm. But not for climbing chimneys, vowed Maud. Greer would have to stride over her dead body if he wanted to claim this boy back.

Maud was shocked at what had happened to the man in the next bed. He'd gone from some poor soul trying to get out of bed to a man possessed by demons, or so it seemed. He spent most of the day shaking and gnashing his teeth and shouting out, and he was still climbing out of bed as well. The nurses were in constant attendance and they kept trying to sponge him down, but he was lashing out at them. She had seen him catch one or two with his punches, and one of the nurses even had a black eye.

Maud could see that he couldn't help it, but the noise of the iron bed rattling and the agitated shouting that came from the man added to the general racket on the ward so that she found the cacophony difficult to manage. One thing that they always had in the big house was plenty of quiet and plenty of calm.

Seeing her worried face, Alfred had reached out his hand to her and said, 'Don't fret. I've seen plenty like that in the workhouse. It's the drink that does it. They're all right when they're drinking but when they stop they get the shakes and they start screaming and shouting.'

'But how could you sleep at night?' said Maud, thinking of the silent room in the attic of the big house that she shared with one other maid.

'I can sleep through anything,' he said. 'You have to in the workhouse, and besides, I was there all my life until I went to Mr Greer's and then I slept in the shed with the donkey.'

'With the donkey!' gasped Maud. 'He couldn't even find you a bed?'

'Well, it was all right because I had some straw to sleep on and it was quiet out there, and I liked the donkey,' Alfred said.

This brought tears to Maud's eyes. How could anyone treat a child no better than an animal?

'No, don't cry,' said the boy. 'The man will be all right. Once he gets through the shakes he will go quiet and he will be able to sleep and then he will be able to eat.'

'I'm not crying about the man,' said Maud, 'I'm just thinking about you and all the things that have happened to you.'

'Oh, I'm all right, miss. I've been lucky. Lucky as a baby to be found on the steps of the workhouse before some wild dog or some bad person got to me, and lucky to be rescued from that chimney by you,' said Alfred, looking at her with his wide blue eyes.

'That's good then,' said Maud, moved beyond words by the trust he was showing in her. She'd never had much to do with children but she knew honesty when she saw it, and the way he spoke was clear and honest. He may have seen all sorts of stuff in the workhouse and had to suffer many things but he didn't seem to have been twisted up by it. The more time she spent with him the more she began to know just how remarkable he was.

Looking again at the man in the next bed as he thrashed from side to side, she thought, I hope he starts to settle soon, not least for the young nurses who keep having to wrestle with him.

Then he started calling out, 'Drink, drink, I need a drink.'

Still the nurses did not come and Maud could see that the man was getting more agitated. Then she spotted a spouted cup by the side of his bed. She had seen one of the nurses giving the man a drink from it. She couldn't see any harm in trying to help him with that herself. So she picked up the cup and offered it to him. He paused in his thrashing for one moment and stared at her, then he took a sip. Instantly his face contorted with rage and he growled, 'Not that drink,' and smashed the cup clean out of her hand.

Maud yelped with shock and stepped back as the man tried to swing his legs over the side of the bed again and get up. She could have run straight back to the safety of Alfred's bed, but she stepped forward once more in an attempt to restrain him. She knew that if he tried to get up he would fall and hurt himself.

So Maud clung to him as she shouted for a nurse, determined to keep him as safe as she could. They must all be busy with an urgent case, she thought, when no one came. She could see the boy looking at her and he seemed to be pleased that she had stepped in to help. Then the man got his arm free and grabbed at her hair, and she wasn't sure what was going to happen next but she knew that she needed to stay calm.

Just at that moment a small woman appeared by Maud's side. She was like an angel appearing from on high, as far as Maud was concerned. An angel with a light-grey dress and dark curly hair piled up and firmly pinned. She had the face of an angel as well. Maud could see she was beautiful.

'Now,' said the nurse, placing a firm hand on the man's arm, 'please let go of this young lady's hair.' Maud heard the man make a low growling sound but then to her absolute amazement he did as he was told and released her.

'Now you stand back,' said the angel quietly to Maud. 'I've got him.'

So Maud moved back and then the small woman looked down at the man who was starting to rant about something again. She said quietly, 'Hello, are you one of the soldiers that served in the Crimea?'

The man scowled at her.

Then she said, 'I believe you met Miss Nightingale.'

He scowled at her again and then he said in a slurred voice, 'I did, and she saved my life. She saved my life and she saved my leg. Not that it's much use to me now, but I've still got it. She saved me, Miss Nightingale saved me.' Then he started to sob and cry while the nurse crouched down by the side of his bed and held his hand.

'I think you're through the worst of it now,' she said. 'Let's get you comfortable in this bed. I think it's time you got some rest.'

'Yes, miss,' said the man, rolling on to his back and allowing the woman to straighten the sheet and pull his pillow into a better position.

When she was satisfied that the patient was

settled, the nurse got up from the side of the bed and turned to Maud to thank her. 'Are you all right?' she asked. 'I can see that you aren't a nurse, so you must be a visitor.'

'I'm with the boy,' said Maud, able to speak at last and pointing to Alfred in the next bed, who was looking straight at them with his eyes wide.

'I see,' said the nurse. 'He is a lovely boy, isn't he? Is it Alfred? The nurses have been telling me about the boy with the beautiful eyes. I can see he's fairly soot-stained — is it true that he's a climbing boy?'

'He is,' said Maud, 'but not any more. I'm going to make sure of that.'

'Good for you,' said the nurse. 'Look, I need to go now but my name is Miss Houston, Ada Houston. I'm the assistant superintendent here at the hospital. What is your name?'

'Oh, sorry, yes, I'm Maud Linklater.'

'Right, Maud, well . . . I don't know what kind of work you do or even if you would consider this, but I think that you would make an excellent nurse and we happen to have a position for a probationer with the new set that have just started. If you're interested, come and see me. Ask one of the girls; they know where to find me.'

Maud was astounded. She stood with her mouth dropping open for a moment and then she stumbled out a garbled thank you, her head reeling with this unexpected offer.

Then Miss Houston turned and started to walk down the ward. Maud watched her go and then looked over at the boy, who was grinning

46

from ear to ear. 'I think you would make a good nurse too,' he said quietly.

Maud looked back down the ward to check that Miss Houston was actually a real person who had just said those things to her, and yes, there she was, and she had in fact stopped just a few beds down. She seemed to have been confronted by some woman with a yellow ribbon in her hair.

Maud hadn't liked to judge, but she had thought from the way that the woman was dressed she might have been what Miss Fairchild called 'a lady of the night'. Again, she couldn't be sure and to Maud, it didn't matter. She seemed like a good person: that's what was important.

Looking at her now as she faced Miss Houston, Maud wondered what was going on. The woman stood with her hands on her hips, her black, curly hair pulled back from her face with the yellow band. She didn't look happy and she could hear Miss Houston starting to raise her voice.

'I can't see you now,' she said.

'Well, when can you see me?'

'You need to make an appointment. Come to my office,' said Miss Houston, her shoulders held square. Maud could see the tension in her body.

And then she saw Miss Houston try to sidestep her, but the woman grabbed her arm and said, 'Look, it wasn't my fault, you know. I had no control over what my father was doing. I was a baby.'

Maud could see Miss Houston's face — it looked like she was in pain — and then her head dropped and the woman let go of her arm.

'Make an appointment,' said Miss Houston as she walked away.

'I will, you can count on it,' said the woman before continuing up the ward to the man in the next bed, who now seemed to be sleeping soundly.

Maud watched her as she stood looking down at the man but she could tell that the woman's thoughts were elsewhere. She seemed to relax a little and Maud saw her straighten the sheet over him and then she looked up, straight at Maud.

Maud felt her face flush a little; her gaze was very direct. She opened her mouth to speak but the woman was already smiling at her and saying, 'You must have wondered what was going on back there.'

'Well, no, it's not — '

'Don't worry,' said the woman, her smile now creasing the corners of her eyes, 'if I were you I'd want to know what was going on . . . some strange woman accosting the assistant superintendent in the middle of the ward.'

'Well, if it's private . . . '

'Don't you worry about that,' said the woman. 'I like the look of you and your young lad, so I'll tell you . . . Well, the thing is, my name is Stella O'Connor, and Miss Houston and me, we are family, but she doesn't want us to be. She's my half-sister; we have the same father.'

'Ah, I see,' said Maud, glad that she had an explanation and aware from the many staff who worked at the big house that families could be complicated. So much so that sometimes she had thought that maybe it was best to be like she was, completely alone in the world. But she knew in her heart that she would like a bit more complication, even if it did cause trouble.

'You look alike,' said Maud. 'She is quite a bit smaller than you, but you have the same hair.'

'And the same temper,' said Stella, laughing. 'That's why we are . . . how we are.'

'I suppose so,' said Maud. 'I hope you can work things out.'

'Oh, I think we will, one way or another. In fact, now he's sleeping it off, I might just go up there and see if I can find where she has her room, appointment or no appointment. See you next time, young lady,' said Stella as she strode down the ward. 'Wish me luck.'

'Good luck,' said Maud, smiling after her.

'Looks like she means business,' said Alfred.

'She does that,' said Maud.

'And, Maud,' said the boy, 'you know what you said to the other woman, that Miss Houston, about me never going back to being a climbing boy? Is that right?'

'It is,' said Maud. 'I will make it right. Don't you worry.'

'Even if you decide to be a nurse, is that still right then?'

'It is,' said Maud. 'I will make sure that it is.'

★   ★   ★

'What do you mean coming in here like this in the middle of a busy day? I told you to make an

49

appointment,' said Ada, glaring at Stella, who'd just managed to get herself shown into the office by one of the clerks.

'Well, Ada, I think it's time we sorted things out and I don't think there's any time to lose. I've tried and tried to speak to you, and your brother has as well. Frank keeps telling me that he's tried, but there's no shifting you.'

'Look, I have no objection to you as a person or your friendship with my brother, but, let me be clear: I do not want to see you. I do not want to know you. I do not want to be your friend.'

'Ada, your father already had a relationship with my mother before I was born, before you were born. It was nothing to do with me. I didn't even know that you existed. What was I supposed to do?'

For once Ada had no reply. She didn't want to have a conversation that stirred up the loss that she had always felt: the loss of a mother who died on the day that she was born.

'I know you don't approve of my profession and that I live in a brothel — '

'That has nothing to do with it,' shouted Ada, surprising herself at the strength of her feelings.

'Well, you could have fooled me,' said Stella, raising her voice to match that of her half-sister, her hands on her hips.

Then the door clicked open and the small face of a worried clerk appeared.

'It's all right, Emily,' said Ada. 'There's no need for concern.'

The door clicked shut and then Ada looked at Stella again.

'I think you need to leave,' she said. 'I can't have my clerks upset. Emily has a delicate disposition.'

'Delicate indeed,' said Stella, starting to smile. 'Does she live in a mouse hole?'

'No she does not,' said Ada, also starting to smile in spite of herself.

'Maybe I should bring her a small piece of cheese next time,' said Stella, picking up on the warmth that was just beginning to show on her half-sister's face.

'Oh, for goodness' sake,' said Ada. 'Look . . . just sit down and let's talk.'

'Well, the thing is,' said Stella, after she'd settled herself on the most comfortable seat that she could find and leant her elbows on Ada's desk. 'The thing is, it's not really about the family stuff that I've come today. Yes, I've always wanted us to be friends — you know that — but I've got another reason for coming that relates to my profession.'

'Really?' said Ada, keeping her voice formal as she tried to stop herself becoming interested in anything that Stella had to say.

'Well, yes,' said Stella. 'Some of my girls have started going missing.'

'Missing?' said Ada, unable to hold back the concern in her voice. 'Are you sure?'

'I'm certain. They're reliable girls, keep out of trouble, and they've got regular work with me and Ma. But they've been gone weeks, two of them, no sign. I've been to the police but they just laughed in my face. You can guess what they think.'

'Right,' said Ada. 'How do you think that I could help?'

'Well, I've been hearing about this Contagious Diseases Act. The police are picking women up off the streets and taking them in, forcing them to be examined for the pox, and then keeping them and making them have treatment for weeks and weeks. Well, my girls are clean — I make sure of that for their sake — but I'm wondering if they've been taken anyway. It doesn't seem to make any difference whether they're infected or not. Ma says she's heard that the girls are set on by doctors with metal instruments; they're held down and forced. It's like an attack. And then they keep them for weeks, treating them for pox. And Ma says that some of the women never come back.'

Ada sat for a moment deep in thought and then she looked up with a frown between her brows. 'Yes, I've heard of the Contagious Diseases Acts and I know that women are being brought in for treatment. We at the Infirmary have always treated women for syphilis — it's a terrible disease — but we've always treated men as well, and if it is true that women are being held against their will then that is completely wrong and it needs to be stopped.'

'It is happening, Ada,' said Stella, standing up from her chair, 'right under our noses, and it's all about the men. They passed the law, they arrest the women, they examine 'em, and they are the ones who bring the pox to the brothels in the first place. They should be the ones held down and have a piece of metal forcibly shoved up their — '

'I know what you're saying,' said Ada, holding up her hand. 'Look, I will make enquiries. If your women are anywhere they will be in the Lock Hospital. I don't have any jurisdiction over there, but I will send word if I find anything.'

'Do you know where . . . ?'

'My brother has your address,' said Ada standing up from her desk and walking over to open the door for Stella to leave.

'Ah, yes,' said Stella with a smile. 'Frank does know where we live.'

'Now if you don't mind . . . ' said Ada, who wasn't smiling.

'Yes, yes, of course, you need to get on with your work . . . but, just one thing: you might want to wear a hat with a veil and not look so la-di-da if you come to see us on Lime Street. It might not suit some of your fine companions here at the hospital if, on their way to the railway station, they spot you dodging into some brothel. They might be reporting you to Miss Florence Nightingale her very self.'

'I'll be careful,' said Ada, pursing her lips. 'Now I need to — '

'Get on with some work,' said Stella, smiling at Ada one more time before slipping out through the door, hoping at last that she was starting to see a chink in her sister's armour.

⋆ ⋆ ⋆

Back on the ward, Maud was watching Sister Law as she marched in their direction. She knew

53

that Sister was coming to Alfred's bed. Despite all her efforts not to be intimidated by the woman Maud couldn't help but feel nervous and she found herself looking down at the floor.

Then she heard the click of Sister's heels stop at the bottom of Alfred's bed. Maud looked up, and was shocked to find that the woman was trying to smile at the boy as he sat up. The glance that she gave Maud was icy, but then she shifted her gaze back to Alfred and spoke gently.

'Now, young man, the doctors are very pleased with the way that the arm has been set and we are all admiring of your calm and pleasant manner on the ward.'

Alfred glanced at Maud and gave her a quick smile.

'We were hoping that we would be able to discharge you home now, or back to your employer, but we would like you to stay here for a while longer so that we can make sure that you have the right diet. You seem very thin — have you been eating?'

'Yes, Sister,' said Alfred. 'My employer, Mr Greer, has been giving me porridge.'

'Is that all you've had?' said Sister with a frown.

'Yes.'

'Mm, was it made with milk?'

'No, it was water, I think,' said the boy tentatively, as if afraid to give the wrong answer.

Sister tutted. 'Well, no wonder your ribs are poking through. A growing boy needs more than that. You should have milk and meat each day, and some greens as well.'

Maud could see that Alfred looked worried.

'This is not your fault, Alfred,' said Sister, immediately switching her gaze to Maud, who sat up straighter on her stool.

'The boy has been apprenticed to a chimney sweep,' said Maud, feeling her face flush red. 'I've only known him since he injured his arm.'

'Mm,' said Sister, narrowing her eyes, 'that may well be the case.'

Maud opened her mouth to make sure that Sister knew it was definitely the case, but the nurse was speaking again already. 'So I think we need to keep you a while longer, young man, not only to make sure that arm heals properly but also to see if we can get some meat on your bones. Is that all right?'

'Yes,' said Alfred and Maud together, exchanging a glance as Sister moved from the bottom of the bed and strode down the ward, glancing as she went to the beds at either side.

Once Sister had reached the end of the ward and Maud could see that she was involved with one of the nurses and a patient, she said quietly to Alfred, 'I'm just going to get some water to see if I can clean up some more of that soot,' and with that she got up from her stool and slipped in through the door of the sluice again.

She was surprised to find one of the young nurses in there and even more surprised to hear the sound of her retching into a bucket.

The girl looked round and Maud saw then that it was the nurse with the pleasant manner who she'd helped earlier that day. Her face was red and she couldn't even speak for the retching.

'Are you all right?' said Maud, fearing that the girl had picked up the typhus or some other deadly fever.

The girl nodded and then tried to speak but she retched again and then she started to cry, tears streaming down her face.

'There, there,' said Maud, pulling out her handkerchief and dabbing at the girl's face.

'I'm not sick . . . I'm with child,' sobbed the nurse, when at last she could speak. And then she was weeping and retching over and over into the bucket.

'Oh dear,' said Maud, putting her arm around the girl and then soaking a cloth in some cold water and sponging her face. She stood with her until she stopped retching and then she helped her tidy up her hair.

'Thank you,' said the girl.

'Should you still be working in your condition?' said Maud. 'Does Sister know?'

'Nobody knows except you,' said the girl. 'Please, swear that you won't tell anyone . . . I need to keep this job.'

'Yes, of course, but you can't keep the baby a secret for ever. Your belly will start to show soon.'

'I know,' said the girl, her eyes still brimming with tears, 'but I have to work for as long as I can.'

'Have you got family?' asked Maud.

'I have, but they live over thirty miles away. My mother is strict — she wouldn't let me back in the house if she knew I was in this condition — so there'd be no sympathy there. I'd be sent straight to the workhouse.'

'And is there a . . . ?' said Maud, not quite knowing how to ask about the father of the baby.

'He's not around. He's gone away, far away,' said the girl, choking up as she started to cry again.

'Don't cry. I won't tell anyone; you can trust me, don't worry.'

'Nurse Sampson, Nurse Sampson? Where is that wretched girl?' shouted Sister from the other side of the sluice-room door.

'That's me,' whispered the girl to Maud. 'I'm Alice Sampson and that's Sister Law, the one who must be obeyed.' Then, straightening her cap, which sagged limply on her head, and smoothing her skirt, she whispered urgently, 'I need to go; *promise* you won't tell?'

'I won't tell,' said Maud as the girl slipped out through the door.

'Ah, there you are at last,' Maud heard through the door. 'I hope you've been cleaning in there, Nurse Sampson, and not skulking out of the way. I don't like skulkers . . . '

Managing to sneak back to Alfred's bed without being seen by Sister, Maud continued to wash the boy as he lay quiet, used now to the gentle pressure and the rhythm of what had become a ritual for both of them. Eventually Maud was delighted to see that the colour of his hair was starting to emerge. Alfred had a fine head of blond hair.

'Your hair is very fair,' she said to him.

'Is it?' he replied. 'Well, I never knew that; I've never been able to see it.'

'Really?' said Maud, smiling at him. She felt

increasingly drawn to this strange child.

'I'll just clean you up a bit more but then I'll have to get going back to the big house,' she said.

Alfred nodded and settled back into his relaxed state. As she wiped away the soot Maud's mind continued to turn over all that had happened on the ward that day. She thought about Nurse Sampson in the sluice and wondered if there was anything at all that she could possibly do to help her; but the thought that dominated her mind was what Miss Houston had said to her: that she would make a good nurse.

And, you know what, she thought: this work, here on the ward, is starting to feel like some kind of calling for me. Surely it would be better, if I was to remain unmarried, for me to spend the rest of my life as a nurse in service of the sick and the poor rather than as a housemaid in service to those with money and entitlement?

However, Maud had never made her mind up instantly about anything ever. So as she finished Alfred's wash she told herself not to rush into anything and to take time to think about Miss Houston's offer. It was a huge decision and she would talk it over with Miss Fairchild. But then, as she poured the grey water out of the tin bowl in the sluice that day, even though she couldn't fully admit it to herself yet, she was already starting to acknowledge which way she would go.

3

'To be a good nurse, one must be an improving woman; for stagnant waters sooner or later . . . always grow corrupt and unfit for use. Is any one of us a stagnant woman?'

Florence Nightingale

'Where will I find Miss Houston?' Maud asked shyly as she sat by Alfred's bed two days later.

Alice looked up, startled, from her checking of Alfred's sling, and spoke hesitantly. 'She does come down to the ward sometimes but she's a superintendent so she's in and out. The best place to find her is up in her office on the first floor. Her room is through where the clerks sit. Why would you . . . is there . . . ?'

Suddenly clicking that Alice might be thinking that she was going to report on her or something, Maud reassured her instantly. 'No, no, don't worry. This is nothing about you. It's just that when I was here the other day, trying to help with the man in the next bed, Miss Houston came and we spoke. She said that she thought I would make a good nurse and, well, if I did want to consider it I was to go and see her. She said that there is a place for another probationer with the new set that have just started.'

'Really?' said Alice, smiling. 'That's my set.

59

You might end up working here, with me.' The smile was now a beam.

'I might,' laughed Maud. 'I've been weighing it up and I've decided I do want to try nursing.'

'I think you will make an excellent nurse,' said Alice enthusiastically. 'I've seen what you've been doing with the boy . . . and the way you were with me,' she added more quietly. 'And if you can stand the thought of working on this ward, where it is so busy and the work is so hard with all of these men, then the other wards will be a doddle in comparison, that's all I can say. But you won't tell anyone about — '

'Of course not,' said Maud. 'That's just between you and me.'

Just at that moment another nurse that Maud hadn't seen before appeared from nowhere behind Alice and tapped her on the shoulder. Alice jumped round, clearly concerned that she might have been overheard. Then Maud saw her face flush red as she tried to stammer out an introduction for the beautiful blond-haired nurse, who now stood completely still as if waiting for something.

'Right, so this is Nancy, Nancy Sellers,' said Alice. 'She's in my set too. And, Nancy, this is Maud, who's thinking of joining us.'

'Pleased to meet you,' said the nurse with a gesture of a smile around her mouth but no sign of it in her eyes as she transferred her gaze to Maud just for a moment. 'I think we need to get on,' she said. 'You know that Sister doesn't like us getting too chatty or too friendly with patients . . . or their visitors.'

60

Maud could swear that she saw the shadow of a sneer on Nurse Sellers' features, but she couldn't be sure because her face was like a beautiful mask.

'All right, yes, of course,' said Alice, her face still bright red as she almost curtsied to the other nurse, who simply turned her back and walked away casually, throwing an instruction to Alice over her shoulder: 'We need to check the sluice room. Sister says it smells like vomit in there.'

Maud saw the look of horror that crossed Alice's face and then she turned and trotted after Nurse Sellers like a puppy.

Alfred said quietly, 'I don't like that Nurse Sellers, Maud. I have seen her before but she usually works up at the other end of the ward with Sister.'

Maud didn't comment. She would never pass judgement on a person that she had just met. She always tried to give herself time before she formed an opinion about anyone and, even then, very often she would keep her view entirely to herself.

She just stood staring after the two nurses for a few moments and then she made a small noise, as if to rouse herself from her thoughts. 'Right then, Alfred,' she said. 'I'm just going to see if I can find Miss Houston and ask about how I can start my nurse training. I shouldn't be long.'

Maud wandered the corridors a bit before she found the stairs that led up to the first floor. She knew that she was on the right track when she saw a couple of desks with the clerks that Alice had told her about. One of them, a woman with a small face, looked up from her work as Maud approached and sat patiently whilst she explained her reason for seeing Miss Houston.

'I'll just see if Miss Houston can speak to you now,' said the clerk with a timid smile. Then, after tapping very gently on the polished wood door and saying a few words that Maud couldn't hear, the clerk showed her into the room.

'Ah, yes. Maud, isn't it?' said Miss Houston, instantly getting up from her desk and crossing the space between them.

'Yes,' said Maud, amazed that the assistant superintendent had remembered her name.

'Sit down, sit down . . . and if you just give me one moment to finish this paperwork you will have my full attention.'

Maud sat quietly on the chair that had been proffered. She could feel her heart beating a little faster than usual but otherwise she was calm.

'Right,' said Miss Houston, at last looking up with a smile. 'My clerk, Emily, tells me that you have been considering the offer to train as a nurse here at the Infirmary and you have decided to accept.'

'Yes,' said Maud, surprising herself at how clear and firm her voice sounded in the large book-lined office.

'What kind of work do you do at present?'

'I am a senior housemaid in a large house.'

'Right, good. I take it you have worked at the same establishment for some time?'

'Ten years now.'

'Well, I can't make any promises to you,

Maud, but from what I saw of you on the ward, stepping forward like that to help a stranger, taking a risk to do that, you have the makings of a good nurse. I will be straight with you, though. The training can be tough. You will work long days on the male and female wards, medical and surgical, and there will be very little time off for a full year. Are you prepared to leave your current position?'

'I think I am,' said Maud, 'but do you think that someone of my age and background will be a suitable candidate?'

'Well, Maud,' said Miss Houston, leaning forward in her chair, 'there are no guarantees, and until you get into the work no one can say for sure. However, bear in mind that there are women of all ages and backgrounds who make good nurses. We need all kinds of approaches in nursing. I was very young and without a penny to my name when I started nursing soldiers during the Crimean War, but I met Florence Nightingale in Scutari and went on to learn many things from her nurses in Balaklava. I also learnt from Mary Seacole, who is an older woman with a completely different approach. There was also someone called Betsi Cadwaladr. I didn't meet her — she had already left the Crimea before I arrived — but she was a Welsh nurse who made a very valuable contribution, and she was sixty-five years old when she started out. In the end it isn't who you are or where you're from that makes the difference, it's the qualities that you have as a person that matter. If, above all else, you want to do good work and you are prepared to fight for your patients then that will make you an excellent nurse.'

Maud sat quietly but her mind and body were fired up by what Miss Houston had just said. She would have taken up a banner there and then and marched through any street of Liverpool to rally the cause, if need be. She felt a bit breathless.

'Do you have any questions?' said Miss Houston gently as Maud sat with her eyes shining. 'This could be a wonderful new beginning for someone like you, Maud. We are lucky enough to be living through exciting times here in Liverpool. When I walk out through the city I can smell change in the air. What with paddle steamers sailing back and forth to New York now, there are more opportunities opening up than ever. Do you know that during the American Civil War hundreds of women volunteered to nurse the troops, all inspired by Miss Nightingale?'

'Really?' said Maud, her attention grabbed by news of a world that she had never even imagined could be open to her.

'Yes, indeed,' said Miss Houston, starting to laugh. 'So are you in, Maud?'

Maud could hardly speak and a simple 'Yes' was all that she could say in the end. But her face was flushed and her heart was pounding.

'So, to practicalities,' said Miss Houston. 'You will live in at the Nurses' Home and you will be supplied with uniform, board and lodgings and be paid ten pounds per year. How does that sound?'

'Yes, that sounds fine,' said Maud. Suddenly she couldn't stop smiling.

Miss Houston matched her smile and then leant forward across the desk again. 'You will see people endure terrible suffering here, Maud, but there will be heartfelt joy as well. All of life is here within the walls of this hospital and there is no better work for a young woman like you. I think you will do very well indeed.'

'Thank you,' said Maud, meeting Miss Houston's gaze.

'Right, if you go back out to Emily, my clerk, she will take some more details from you and fill in a form. On your first day you will meet one of the superintendents, Miss Merryweather, and she will go through more of the rules and regulations and ask you to sign a contract. Have you any questions, Maud?'

'No, I don't think so,' said Maud, standing up from her chair.

'Right, let's get you started as soon as we can,' said Miss Houston, reaching across the desk to shake Maud's hand.

★   ★   ★

When Maud got back to the ward, having sorted out all the paperwork with Emily, she saw the man in the bed next to Alfred's sitting at the side with his back to them, his feet on the floor and a pair of new crutches resting beside him. He was having a smoke, his back curved over it almost protectively. Maud wasn't happy about the cloud of smoke that was wafting over to Alfred's bed but it was good to see him sitting up. The boy had been absolutely right: once the man had come through the shakes and started to sleep and eat he was like a different person. Yes, he still had the nasty injury to his leg and Maud had seen the long scar down his arm, but he looked like a new man.

Alfred smiled at her as she walked back down the ward, a big smile, and she noticed for the first time that his eyes drooped slightly at the outer corners, giving him a slightly sorrowful expression even now. She smiled back at him and felt the glow of connection between them. It was wonderful to see his face open up and look less pinched.

'I can see by your face,' he said, 'even though you haven't told me yet. You will be a nurse, won't you?'

'Yes,' laughed Maud, 'I will. And don't you worry, as long as you are here I'll come and see you, and if I am a nurse I can make sure that you are properly looked after.'

'Sister Law has been to see me whilst you were away and she says that I will be going soon — being discharged, she called it — but only once they've seen me put some weight on. He's going today,' he said, pointing to the man in the next bed.

'Well, I need to speak to Sister about that,' said Maud. 'We have to make sure that you go back to the right place. Miss Fairchild, from the big house, she has been making enquiries and there is a home for boys not far from here. It is a school as well. She knows the gentleman who

66

runs it so she's going to speak to him about you.'

'Sister said that I should be going back to the workhouse.'

'No!' said Maud. 'No, you are not. Miss Fairchild has given Mr Greer the money that he paid for you when he took you from the workhouse so the sweep isn't out of pocket and he has no claim over you now. You are definitely not going back there.'

Maud saw the boy's shoulders relax and then he smiled at her again. 'You say that the new place has a school, so I can learn my letters and numbers. Is that right?'

'Yes, I think so,' smiled Maud. 'That's what Miss Fairchild said. You're going to be much happier there, I'm sure of it.'

'Good,' said Alfred.

Maud melted to see the boy's beautiful, trusting face, but seeing Sister Law moving down the ward in their direction, she and Alfred both stopped short their conversation and almost held their breath until she had passed them by. She halted in front of the man in the next bed, who still sat with his crutches resting beside him.

'It is good to see you looking so much better,' said Sister in a much gentler voice than they had ever heard her use, 'and today you will leave the ward.'

'Yes, miss,' said the man.

'Have you tried the crutches? Can you walk with them?'

'Yes, miss.'

'Good. Well, there is one more thing before you leave us. We know that you are an old soldier and that you fought in the Crimea. We have a small fund set aside for men like you, just a few coins to help you on your way. We have a number of Nightingale nurses working here and one of them served in the war, so they have started the fund to try to help out, in recognition of what you did out there.'

'Pah,' said the man, almost spitting on the floor.

'Here,' said Sister, sounding unsure of her ground now but nevertheless ploughing ahead. 'Take these few shillings to help you on your way.'

He shook his head, 'I don't want your charity,' he said, his voice gruff with emotion.

'Look,' said Sister, 'we understand that the trials of war are not over for veteran soldiers once the last shot is fired on the battlefield. We know that you live with the consequences of war for the rest of your lives. So, please, take it,' she said, pressing the coins into his hand, 'and go to Lime Street Station. Take a train out to the country, to somewhere you can breathe fresh air. You need to find something different from this.'

The man grasped the coins but still sat shaking his head.

'Now,' Sister said, 'remember, you need to get out of the city. If you fall into the path of loose women or you take to the drink again, you will surely die. Do you have any family? Do you have somewhere to go?'

The man sat thinking on the edge of the bed, his crutch propped beside him. Then he nodded and heaved himself to his feet. Sister Law grabbed his arm as he lurched a bit, trying to position the new crutches, and then he nodded at her again and set off down the ward. Sister watched him for a few moments to make sure that he could manage the crutches and then she turned back to the bed. Seeing Maud and the boy staring across at her, she scowled at them before starting to strip off the bed linen. Even before the man had reached the bottom of the ward the mattress was laid bare and ready to be made up again for the next patient.

'Nurse, Nurse!' Sister shouted up the ward with extra venom, just in case anyone overhearing her words to the old soldier had got the impression that she might be going soft. 'Nurse!' she shouted again, heading off down the ward when one didn't instantly appear.

Maud and Alfred looked at each other and, once Sister was at a safe distance, they both started to giggle.

'What are you two laughing about?' said Alice, appearing at the bottom of the bed, out of breath as usual and with no chance of ever catching up on the mountain of chores that needed to be done on the ward each day.

'Nothing,' said Maud and Alfred together, giggling even harder and trying to stop themselves from snorting.

It was infectious, and soon Alice was giggling with them.

Then they heard Sister roaring down the ward, 'Nurse Sampson! Stop that nonsense at once and get on with making the bed. Look sharp and make sure you fold those corners exactly right this time. I will be down there to check.'

'Yes, Sister,' cried Alice, turning her back on Maud and Alfred but still struggling to control her giggles.

When she turned back round her face was straight, which was more than could be said for the corners on the bed linen. Maud noticed immediately that they were crooked but didn't want to say anything to Alice who, as she alone knew, had enough to deal with.

'Well, how did you get on?' said Alice to Maud, almost in a whisper.

'I got in,' said Maud. 'And I start next week.'

'That is so good,' said Alice, beaming at both her and Alfred. 'Which ward will you be starting on, do you know?'

'They didn't say, but even if I don't start out on here I can still call in to see you, and I will keep an eye on Alfred, of course,' Maud said. 'They said that I will need to move into the Nurses' Home at the end of the week. They gave me a list of things I should bring and they said I will be living in a single dormitory . . . what is that?'

'Oh, it's good,' said Alice. 'They are all on one floor, up on a gallery, and they are like very small rooms, partitioned off from each other so you have your own space. The walls are very thin, so you can hear everything, that's the only problem. You soon get to know who snores, who talks in their sleep, everything, but I like it. They'll probably be putting you in Louisa's dorm. She left — well, she was told to leave — last week.

It's right by the door, so that means you only have somebody on one side. The trouble with that room, though, is that you're first in line for any inspection.'

'Inspection?'

'Yes, when the superintendent comes down to check that your room is tidy and you are keeping yourself clean. The rest of us get some warning, but that room or Nurse Sellers, Nancy's room, which is opposite to yours, is usually the first.'

So she's opposite, thought Maud, relieved at least that though uncomfortably nearby, she wouldn't have the presence of that particular nurse immediately through a thin partition. And being near the first in line for inspection was all right. Maud had always been a person to keep herself in order, so that should be fine.

'And the other thing about that room is that you are next to Nurse Pacey, Edwina. Edwina is lovely but she doesn't know how to do anything quietly. I should know; I'm at the other side of her. She keeps me awake and distracts me many a time, but then again, sometimes I need some noise to cover up my . . . ' Alice didn't say the word but gave a small imitation retch.

'Nurse Sampson!' shouted Sister down the ward. 'We need a mustard poultice to bed two . . . '

'Best get going,' said Alice, and then with a wry smile to Maud, 'Are you sure that you know what you're doing, choosing to leave your life in service to come to this madness?'

'I do, or at least I think I do,' said Maud.

Later that afternoon, just as Maud was

71

preparing to leave, she saw Stella striding down the ward. There was already another patient in the man's bed, an old man with long grey hair, who seemed very sick and hadn't made a sound since the men with the stretcher had brought him in. Maud had been a bit upset when she had overheard the orderly at the head of the stretcher say something like, 'This one won't last long. We'll soon be back to clear the bed again.'

Sadly, looking at the old man after they had left him there lying flat on his back with his mouth gaping open, Maud had to agree. His skin was white and pulled tight across his thin face and his breathing seemed shallow. Maud hadn't seen many sick people until she had become a regular visitor on the ward, but she had sat with her grandmother when she was dying and she had enough sense to know that the old man looked like a corpse that was still breathing.

'Has he gone then?' said Stella, not realizing the patient she'd come to visit was not on the bed until she reached it.

'Yes, he went earlier this afternoon,' explained Maud. 'Sister spoke to him and gave him a bit of money from a special fund for army veterans and she told him to make sure that he got out of the city into the country where he could breathe some fresh air.'

'Well,' said Stella, 'to my old friend that probably would mean the taproom of his favourite public house, especially if he has some money in his pocket. I think I know where I might find him. What's happening with you two then? When are you off home, young man?'

'He's going soon,' said Maud, 'and we are trying to get a place for him at the Blue Coat School for orphans. And I'm, well, I'm going to start here at the hospital as a probationer.'

'Are you indeed?' said Stella. 'So you must have passed muster with that battle-axe of a sister of mine, then?'

'I have seen her, yes,' said Maud, 'and she was very encouraging.'

'I'm glad for you, I truly am. But you wouldn't catch me here, not with all those rules and regulations and all that stuff those nurses have to see. It's enough to make you gag.'

Maud smiled in return and then looked down at her hands. She didn't really know if she would be up to it herself yet. After all, she'd always been a bit squeamish.

Seeing Maud's discomfort Stella offered, 'No, but that's good, though. You have all the makings of a good nurse, from what I've seen. In fact, I like you so much that if my sister hadn't stepped in and offered you a job I'd 'ave asked you to come and work at my place.'

Maud had some idea of what kind of 'place' Stella ran and she couldn't help but laugh as she lifted her eyes to meet Stella's smiling face.

'Now, lad,' said Stella, looking at Alfred, 'I've heard a lot about that school they want you to go to, and boys like you can do very well there. You could end up being the captain of a ship or anything if you work hard at your lessons. So you make the most of it. Don't end up like the poor fella who was in this bed. You make something of yourself.'

'I will,' said Alfred solemnly.

'That's my boy,' said Stella. 'And if either of you ever need anything, come and find me on Lime Street. Ask anyone round there where you can find Stella and Marie's place — remember, Stella and Marie — and they'll point you in the right direction.'

'Thanks for that,' said Maud. 'We won't forget. And I hope you manage to get something sorted out with Miss Houston. Are you friends yet?'

'Not yet, but I'm working on it and I won't stop until I succeed. You know what they say: life's too short, and blood's thicker than water — all that kind of thing.'

Stella looked down at the old man with the long grey hair lying on her friend's bed. Then she lightly touched his hand. 'Hope he goes peacefully,' she said to no one in particular. Then she was striding past the bottom of the bed, wishing them well. And then she was gone.

'I like her,' said Alfred. 'She is a good person.'

'I think so too,' said Maud, 'although there'd be plenty in this city that would not agree with that opinion.'

'Is that because she works in a brothel?' said the boy.

Maud gasped at his knowledge. 'Let's say no more on that score,' she said. 'You need to be thinking about going to school, not knowing about suchlike.'

'It's just that some of the pauper nurses who were at the workhouse, they talked about working in a brothel and I didn't know what one was so I asked them and they told me.'

There was nothing that Maud could say in return that would make any sense so she just shook her head. It seemed that Alfred knew all there was to know about most things, and anything new that he encountered he took on board in a very open way and dealt with it. It was almost like her grandmother used to say about people sometimes: 'He's been here before, that one . . . he's an old soul.' Thinking about her grandmother, Maud could picture her looking directly at her, then gazing back up over her shoulder at someone else — could it have been her mother? Maud couldn't remember her mother, but she could remember the words because they were oft repeated: 'She's as deep as the sea, this one, as deep as the sea. You never know what she's thinking. She's one to watch all right, is our Maud.'

4

'I have rarely known a nurse worth the bread she ate . . . who has not been trained under hospital discipline.'

Florence Nightingale

Maud walked up the stone steps to the Nurses' Home and Training School with her heart racing. She hadn't felt at all nervous when leaving the big house and saying goodbye to Miss Fairchild. But now, for some reason, as she ascended those steps her heart was pounding and her mouth felt dry. There was no going back now, although walking up those steps, in front of that tall building with its big front door, carrying a bag containing her few clothes and the copy of Florence Nightingale's *Notes on Nursing* that Miss Fairchild had given her a couple of days ago, Maud could not quite believe what she was doing.

She knocked on the impressive wooden door and stood there waiting, but nobody came and she wasn't sure what to do. In the end she was saved: someone else, who looked like she knew exactly where she was going, came straight up the steps and pushed open the door. Then, turning to Maud, she signalled for her to go inside. Maud didn't even get a chance to thank the girl, who had raced off, a busy look about her, but thankfully a door to her left swung open and a woman wearing a bonnet appeared.

'Welcome,' said the woman. 'I am Miss Mary Merryweather, superintendent of the Nurses' Training School. Miss Houston told me to expect you. Come through.'

Maud didn't have a chance to speak; she could only trot along behind the woman who led her directly into the building. It was immediately wonderful to Maud. So much so that she would remember for ever that moment when she walked across the coloured floor tiles and stood there for the first time. The space was open and when she looked up she could see all the floors above and the galleries that Alice had told her about. Looking right up to the top, Maud saw a huge skylight where the light flooded down. She had never been anywhere so light. She couldn't move; she was completely transfixed. And there was a new smell, a smell of varnish. It was amazing.

'Ah, well,' said Miss Merryweather, pleased by the impression that the building had clearly made, 'Miss Nightingale always makes sure that there is plenty of light and air coming in. These things are very important. I must say, I never tire of gazing up to the skylight myself, and I've been here since we opened. It must be seven years now, yes, seven years. The Training School was set up eight years ago and we were in another building to begin with but then we came here and well . . . isn't it wonderful?'

'Seven years,' said Maud. 'This has been here all that time and I didn't even know about it.'

'Come along,' said Miss Merryweather, 'I'll show you to your dorm. The uniform is already waiting for you in there.'

'Thank you,' said Maud, struggling to keep up with the woman who was already half-way up the stone stairs.

When they reached the next landing they had a choice of galleries right and left. Maud was shown to the left and then they stopped immediately in front of a varnished wooden door. Looks like Alice was right, thought Maud, I am to take the first room. Then she leant over the balustrade and looked down to the floor below and realized that you could see everything from up there, and you could probably hear what was going on as well. The place was open and at this time of day it stood so still and so quiet.

Turning around, she saw that Miss Merryweather had the door to the room open and so she went in. It was small but it looked like it had everything she would need: a single bed, a small chest of drawers and a hanging space. There was also a little window that Maud went straight over to, and as she looked out she felt very high up in the world, higher than she'd ever been. In fact, her attic room in the big house had been much higher, but it had no window, that was what made the difference.

'I'll let you get sorted,' said Miss Merryweather, preparing to leave the room. 'When you have the uniform on, come down to my room, the one by the front door. We will have a chat and then I will escort you around the hospital. Your duties on the ward will start tomorrow.'

Once Maud was left alone she sat on the bed listening to the silence and staring at the uniform that was hanging up in front of her. It was, of course, just like Alice's — dark-grey with a full skirt and a fitted bodice. It looked huge, hanging there; it seemed to dominate the room. On top of the chest she saw the snowy white lace cap, almost identical to the one she had worn as a maid, so at least that looked familiar, and she had been instructed to bring some hairpins to secure it — again, very familiar. As was the white starched apron that lay folded beside it.

I'd best get cracking, she thought, opening up the bag and unpacking her few belongings, finally taking out the book, her own copy of *Notes on Nursing*, and running her hand over the cover before setting it down square and neat on top of the chest.

The uniform felt a bit stiff when she pulled it from the hanger and it seemed to resist her every move as she wrestled with it to dress. But at last she had it on and after she had run a firm hand down the skirt to straighten out the last crumples it felt reasonably comfortable. When she fastened the white apron tight round her waist the whole thing felt even more familiar and she knew that she was ready for work. Even as she descended the stairs, she felt like a housemaid still, but she relished the thought that, when she tapped on the door to Miss Merryweather's room, she wouldn't be answering a bell or required to stand with her eyes lowered and to repeat 'Yes, ma'am' and 'No, ma'am'.

The chat that she had been invited to attend turned out to be more of a lecture, but Maud was glad of the time that was taken to try to explain the important requirements for being a nurse and what kind of duties she would have to undertake. It felt like Miss Merryweather had learnt them off by heart and that she was eager to demonstrate her knowledge as she whistled through all of the detail very fast indeed.

'So, Nurse Linklater . . .' she said, and Maud felt surprised and pleased to be given her title straight away, so much so that she found herself sitting up a bit straighter in the chair across the desk from the superintendent.

'So, Nurse Linklater, let me just fill you in a little on my own background. I am proud to be able to say that I spent some time at St Thomas's Hospital in London, which is where Miss Nightingale's first training school is situated. The training here follows the same pattern as that of St Thomas's. You will be with us for twelve months, working in the hospital. Miss Nightingale is very clear that all nurses must be trained in a hospital and nowhere else. At the end of that time you will then choose whether you stay in the hospital, work in the district, or work as a private nurse in the homes of those who can afford to pay.

'I don't know if you are familiar with any of Miss Nightingale's writing or her thoughts on the requirements for a nurse . . . ?'

Maud tried to say that she had read and reread Notes on Nursing, but Miss Merryweather was unstoppable.

'Well, all applicants need to be sober, honest, trustworthy, truthful, punctual, quiet, orderly, clean and neat. Are you all of those things?'

Not waiting for a reply, she continued, 'Miss Nightingale is clear that women who come to train as nurses *must* have a vocation and *must* be ready to learn. Can you read and write to a good standard?'

Again, not waiting for a reply she ploughed ahead, 'The sanctity of our calling is paramount, *paramount*. And if you are found to be lacking then I, as superintendent, have been given the power to dismiss any of you probationers. You will have experience on all the wards of the hospital, medical and surgical, male and female. You will also attend a series of lectures given by one of our renowned surgeons, Mr James Fawcett. You have missed the first of the lectures but you must attend all others.

'Miss Nightingale has deemed that all probationers should acquire fundamental nursing skills including the application of dressings and leeches . . .' *Leeches*, thought Maud, oh no, I didn't think leeches would be involved. I thought the doctors would be doing that. ' . . . the administering of an enema . . . ' Maud didn't know what 'anenemas' were but felt sure that she would soon find out. ' . . . the making and applying of bandages . . . ' That should be all right, she thought. ' . . . and, of course, every nurse must ensure the *constant* flow of a clean air supply.'

Maud knew about the importance of air supply and light from her reading of *Notes on Nursing*.

81

'Any questions, Nurse?' said Miss Merry-weather, sliding a piece of paper across the desk to her before Maud could open her mouth to speak. It will have to be all right, she thought, taking the pen that was proffered so that she could sign the contract.

'Before you sign,' said Miss Merryweather, holding up her hand, 'I need to let you know that there will be no examinations. Miss Nightingale regards them as little more than memory tests. However, your performance on the ward will be assessed and reported monthly, and let me be clear right now, Nurse Linklater . . . ' and then she paused to give Maud a solemn look, 'Miss Nightingale considers that the most important consideration is a nurse's *personal* and *moral* character, so, do understand that this will be monitored alongside the practical tasks that you will be required to perform on the wards. And one thing that will *not* be tolerated is *drunkenness*. It will result in instant dismissal. All nurses are given full board and a daily allowance of beer. We can't trust the water round here to be clean enough, not now we know for sure that it's linked to cholera. And there was a cholera outbreak in Liverpool last year. So you have your allowance of beer, but if you exceed the allowance then there will be consequences. *Drunkenness* has been the most frequent of reasons for dismissal of probationers over the last five years and it will *not* be tolerated here in the training school,' Miss Merryweather reiterated. 'Are you clear?'

'Ye — ' Maud tried to say but in fact she felt far from clear.

'Now sign,' said Miss Merryweather. And Maud did as she was told.

'Right, first,' said Miss Merryweather, standing up from her desk as soon as Maud had signed the paper with as much of a flourish as she could muster, 'I will let you meet my assistant, Miss Elizabeth Merryweather, and then we will go on a tour of the hospital.'

Miss Merryweather was gone from the room only moments, not even enough time for Maud to catch her breath, before she was back with a small woman in tow.

'This is my sister, Miss Elizabeth Merryweather,' she said, and Maud saw instantly the contrast between the two women. Miss Elizabeth stood with her eyes lowered and a faint flush on her cheeks, her voice was very quiet as she introduced herself and then she looked up at Maud and held out her hand. Maud couldn't help but smile at the woman as she saw the warmth and the kindness in her eyes. She readily took Miss Elizabeth's hand, to find to her surprise that she was wearing a soft leather glove.

'Pleased to meet you,' said Maud, feeling very strange indeed to be greeted so warmly by someone who was indeed a lady, and then wondering why Miss Elizabeth Merryweather felt the need to wear leather gloves indoors. Clearly the woman had not just come in from outside and she was certainly not on her way out.

'Pleased to meet you, Nurse Linklater,' said the small woman very quietly.

'Now,' said Miss Mary Merryweather, turning her back on her sister, 'let's get you shown around the hospital. There are so many things that I still need to do today.'

Finding herself trotting along behind Miss Merryweather on a tour of the hospital seemed peculiar to Maud after all the time that she had spent as a visitor, and as they moved speedily through all of the wards she began to feel disorientated. There were so many new faces, so many patients, what seemed like miles of corridor, and all the time she just wanted Miss Merryweather to slow down and let her take things in at a much gentler pace, or at least let her try to get her bearings. But there was no chance of that. She had to do her best to keep up with the superintendent and in each new area she was introduced to ward Sisters, probationers, a few doctors, enough to make her head spin. She saw Miss Houston in passing as they whisked along one of the corridors, but there was no time to speak although Maud saw her smiling at them.

Then, finally, they were on the Male Surgical ward and she was being introduced to Sister Law, who looked her up and down with the usual scowl on her face. Maud didn't think she even recognized her at first, but then she made some comment about how at least she would be able to legitimately use the sluice room and she knew that Sister knew exactly who she was. She saw Alice's smiling face in passing, and Alfred was sitting up in his bed watching everything that was going on. He didn't smile, but she had told him not to. She had said that she wanted to maintain a serious face and if she saw him grinning at her she wouldn't be able to help herself from smiling or, worse, laughing out loud.

And then Miss Merryweather made a point of introducing Maud to Nurse Sellers. She introduced her as 'our leading probationer in this intake' and Maud felt a small shudder go through her as she saw Nurse Sellers smile with her mouth but not with her eyes, which she then lowered in what looked like mock humility. Despite Maud not wanting to jump to any judgements too quickly she was increasingly uneasy around Nancy Sellers. Just give her a chance, she reminded herself. You don't know her properly yet.

By the time they had got through a full tour of the hospital, including the boiler room, the coal store and the mortuary, some of the nurses were getting ready to come off shift and it felt like the day was coming to an end of sorts. Miss Merryweather turned abruptly to Maud and told her that she had some business with Miss Houston, so she asked Maud to make her way back to the Nurses' Home and wait for the other probationers to arrive.

Maud, of course, went straight back to the Male Surgical ward to find Alfred. It had seemed strange not being able to make her usual visit to him that day, the first time that she had missed chatting with him since he had been admitted.

She was still buzzing with excitement and information from her rapid tour of the hospital and wanted to share some of it with Alfred, but when she got back to the familiar place on the ward she found his bed standing empty. What? Could he have gone already? She had seen him that afternoon — how could he have been moved so quickly? And how could she be sure he'd made it to the Blue Coat School as planned? Her heart sank and in that moment she knew how important he had become to her. It had crept up on her without her even realizing it.

Then she saw that the bed had not been remade, and when she felt the sheet it was still warm. How odd. Just as she was starting to wonder, she saw him down the ward, walking along beside Alice. As soon as they saw her they both waved and Alfred began to trot towards her, his arm still awkward in the grey sling.

'What are you doing up?' Maud said at the same time as he asked, 'How did you get on?'

They both laughed and he stood in front of her admiring the brand-new uniform that was just the same as Alice's. 'What are you doing up?' repeated Maud.

'Well, the doctor came along and he had a look at my arm and he said the swelling is going down and it is looking all right, so he suggested that I get up and about a bit and do some walking, ready for when they send me out.'

'Did they say when that might be?'

'Soon,' said a voice from behind.

Maud turned to find Nancy Sellers, standing there looking like she hadn't done a stroke of work all day even though they must have been busy on the ward, as they always were. There was no flush on her face, not one strand of hair was out of place and her uniform lay perfectly clean with the white cap straight and neat perched on top of her blond head.

'I was with Sister today when the doctor made his round,' said Nancy. 'The boy is doing very well and he has put weight on. There really is no need to keep him any longer than a day or two. I hope he has somewhere to go, otherwise it will be the workhouse.'

'He has somewhere to go,' said Maud straight out though not sure of her ground. 'He will be going to the Blue Coat School.'

'Well, I hope you are sure of his place at that school. I've heard that it's very difficult to get in there and they don't accept any rag-tag.'

Maud wasn't able to reply. From what she understood the place wasn't confirmed yet so she had to keep quiet and witness the flicker of triumph in Nancy's eyes as she picked up on the uncertainty. Then she watched with slow fury starting to burn inside her as Nancy walked down the ward, stopping by Sister and saying a few words to her, and then both of them looked down the ward in Alfred's direction.

Maud tried to smile at Alfred but her face was tense. Seeing the worried look on his face she had felt anger swell inside her. She wanted to walk straight up the ward and punch Nancy Sellers right on the nose. Looks like that's the end of me giving her 'a chance', thought Maud. I think my mind is made up.

Turning back to Alfred, she could see that he was still worried.

'Look, I will go and see Miss Fairchild this evening,' she said, trying to smile, 'and make absolutely sure that the arrangements are in place. It will all be all right.'

'You will need to be back by ten o'clock,' said Alice, who had remained within earshot of their conversation, 'otherwise the door will be locked at the front and you will be in for some trouble.'

'That's all right,' said Maud. 'It won't take me long to get where I'm going. But I do need to go.'

'Of course,' said Alice. 'We need to make sure that Alfred will be all right. We don't want to see him coming back in here again, do we? Just one other thing as well: you will need to go back to the Home and change out of your uniform. If you're seen out and about in it there will be hell to pay.'

★   ★   ★

It felt extraordinary to Maud to be knocking on the back door of the big house on the evening of the same day that she had walked out of there with her bag packed ready for a new life.

The door was opened by Cook. 'Changed your mind already, Maud?' she said with a puzzled smile.

'No,' laughed Maud, stepping into the warm kitchen. 'I need to see Miss Fairchild, that's all, about Alfred.'

'Alfred?' said Cook, looking even more puzzled.

'The climbing boy . . . '

'Of course, of course. Poor little mite. Best thing that was ever done in this house was rescuing him from that Bill Greer. How is the boy doing today?'

'He is just fine.'

'Well, that's good,' said Cook, heading over to the range where a number of pans were starting to boil over on to the plate all at the same time. 'Don't mind me. I'm battling with the range as per usual. You go straight through and see Miss F. She's been missing you already.'

'Maud!' cried Miss Fairchild, opening the door fully as if greeting a long-lost relative.

Maud was taken aback — she had only said her goodbyes that morning — but as Cook had said, it seemed like the housekeeper was missing her.

'Sit down,' said Miss Fairchild, and then instantly a shadow of concern darkened her smiling face.

'Is everything all right, Maud?'

'Oh, yes, yes, everything's all right with me, but they are asking questions on the ward about where Alfred will be going. It sounds like he will be discharged soon and one of the nurses thought that he was going back to the workhouse.'

'What! But that is ridiculous. I went into the ward only this morning to speak to that Sister. I told her that he was definitely going to the Blue Coat School.'

'Did you?' said Maud. 'That's strange, so . . .' and then she remembered who had been questioning her about the school. It hadn't been Sister but that Nurse Sellers. Maybe she hadn't known, maybe Sister hadn't told her, but for some reason Maud began to feel fairly sure that Nurse Sellers had known full well that Alfred had a place at the school and for whatever reason she had just wanted to cause trouble.

'So is it confirmed then?' said Maud, slumping back in the chair as relief started to wash over her.

'Yes, the gentleman that I know there managed to put Alfred's name to the top of the list, he will be going . . . definitely. But Sister said that they would be keeping him another couple of weeks anyway. She wanted him to put even more weight on — did that nurse not say?'

'No, there must have been some kind of mix-up, that's all,' said Maud, suddenly feeling tired out by the strangeness of the day and now, being back here, having to bat away the longing for her familiar bed in the attic and easy companionship of the people that she knew so well. In that moment she knew that it was not going to be easy for her to say goodbye and go back to the Nurses' Home for the second time in one day.

'Now, let me get us some tea,' said Miss Fairchild. 'You look exhausted already by that hospital. And I want you to tell me everything about everything.'

★ ★ ★

Maud did get back through the front door in time, but only just. She raced up the stone stairs and managed to get into her dorm just before the evening inspection. Alice was straight in to see her.

'That was close,' she said, closing the door quietly behind her, a bit breathless. 'Is everything all right?'

'Yes, it is,' said Maud, still heavy with emotion but also heady with relief, both that Alfred's plans were all in place, and that she had made it back in time.

'I need to go now,' said Alice, 'but don't worry, I will watch out for Alfred on the ward. And don't worry about this inspection. They just do a quick look round at this time of day. Edwina's not even back yet. She has a big family near the docks and she's always down there and in trouble for being back late. Just listen out, you'll know when she's in; we all will.'

Maud must have been much more exhausted than she thought because after changing into her nightgown, then making sure that her uniform was ready for the next morning before she climbed into bed, she fell asleep with *Notes on Nursing* open at the first page. She did briefly wake to the sound of some bumping around from the room next door, but was soon back to sleep and dreaming that she was in the big house trying to stack the best china. But no matter how careful she was, every time she picked up a plate it slipped from her grasp, fell to the floor and smashed into pieces. She was still sorting and piling crockery what felt like minutes later when there was a loud knock on her door and the sound of a woman's voice shouting, 'Come on, you nurses, time to get up. Rise and shine.'

Maud sat up in bed and looked around her, momentarily terrified by the huge uniform hanging above her. Then she realized where she was and knew that it was time to make a start. Here I go, she thought to herself. Here I go . . .

5

A nurse who rustles . . . is the horror
of a patient.

Florence Nightingale

'Nurse Linklater,' shouted Miss Mary Merryweather from the floor below.

'Yes,' shouted Maud, amazed at how clear the
superintendent's voice sounded in her room.
Then she had her door open and was leaning
over the wooden balustrade of the gallery to see
Miss Merryweather looking up at her.

'You will go to the Male Medical ward today
with Nurse Pacey, Edwina Pacey. They are short
of staff; two of the nurses have gone down with a
fever. You might not stay on there but, for now,
that is where you will be working. All right?' she
said, as Maud just carried on looking down at
her.

'Yes, yes, of course,' said Maud.

'So,' said Miss Merryweather, 'team up with
Nurse Pacey — she is your neighbour — and
GET CRACKING.'

'Right, yes, miss, yes, thank you.' But Miss
Merryweather had already gone.

When Maud looked up she saw Nancy Sellers
on the opposite gallery, leaning with her elbows
on the balustrade, looking at her with an almost
but not quite blank expression and the trace of a

smile on her face. Maud pulled herself away from the balustrade and turned around, bumping straight into another nurse.

'Hello,' said the nurse. 'I just heard what Miss Merryweather said. I'm Nurse Pacey, Edwina. Everybody calls me Eddy,' and then in a whisper she added, 'Don't take any notice of Nancy over there — she's not right in the head. Don't let her intimidate you.'

Maud glanced across to Nancy again but she had slipped back into her room.

'Thank you,' said Maud, 'but I can look after myself.'

'Good,' said Eddy. 'You will need to.'

'Nice to meet you,' said Maud, sticking out her arm to shake Edwina's hand.

'It's a pleasure,' said Edwina with a broad smile and eyes that shone with good humour. Straight away Maud thought, I'm going to be all right here with Eddy. She knew immediately that Nurse Pacey was a very good sort indeed.

As they walked to the hospital Eddy told her that the Male Medical ward was very busy and the work was hard but the Sister — Sister Cleary — was kind, and that meant a lot. In fact it was the thing that mattered most on the wards. If you had a good, kind, sympathetic Sister it made a whole world of difference. Even if she was strict and a real stickler, it made things so much easier for the nurses and the patients.

Maud had already seen what impact Sister Law had on Alfred's ward and knew that Eddy was probably right, but the thing about Eddy was — and anyone meeting her for the first time

94

would pick up on this immediately — she never stopped talking. She talked so fast about any number of things all at the same time that it was difficult to follow her many trains of thought. Yes, Maud got the gist of what she was saying, but all of the extra detail around it made her head spin.

Of course, Maud had taken to her instantly, but Maud was a natural stickler herself and she really just wanted to tell Eddy to stand still for a minute so that she could tidy up the strands of curly hair that were falling across her face. She definitely wanted to straighten up her cap, which was not only crooked but looked like it had been sat on, squashed flat and then hastily pulled back into shape. Maud had to try to stop herself looking at the cap, but as Eddy chatted on and on she couldn't help her eyes being drawn to it and the horror of its disarray.

Eddy had been right about Sister Cleary, though. She was strict but she had very kind eyes, and although the ward was packed out with patients and clearly very busy, she took time to speak to the nurses individually as she advised them of their duties.

'Right, Nurse Pacey, you have been here a couple of weeks now, haven't you? And I know that you have applied leeches under supervision.' Maud felt her skin crawl immediately as she heard mention of the creatures. She had seen them used by the physician who attended the family at the big house, and she couldn't bear the things, especially after they were removed from the skin and placed back in a jar, swollen with a patient's blood. It made her shudder just thinking about it.

'So do you think you would be able to apply some leeches to the man in bed four, Mr Hollingsworth? He was admitted last night with congestion of the lungs and a suspected kidney ailment. The doctors want to try bleeding him first to see if that makes any difference. Do you think you could apply two leeches to his sternum for me?'

Maud saw Eddy already nodding enthusiastically, her eyes shining.

'And then can you keep an eye on them, keep checking and call me when they are ready for removal?'

'Yes, Sister,' said Eddy, turning to Maud, who had gone very pale indeed.

'Are you all right?' said Eddy. 'I know some people don't like them at first but you'll soon get used to it.'

Maud nodded carefully, feeling her stomach starting to churn but she knew that she had no choice. She would just have to get used to it — to all of it, leeches included. She could hear Sister's voice but it sounded like it was at a bit of a distance. Maud took a deep breath to stop herself from feeling faint and Sister came back into focus.

'So if you could show Nurse Linklater the procedure, I would be very grateful indeed. As you can see, with all the new cases that have been admitted overnight we are going to be really pushed for a few days. Some of the medical cases have had to be accommodated on the Male Surgical ward, yet again. There just aren't enough beds, or enough nurses, to go round.'

'Right, Sister,' said Eddy with a glint in her eye, and then to Maud: 'Let's get it done. First we need to collect the leech jar and then select two lively ones.'

'Lively ones?' said Maud, taking another deep breath.

'Yes,' said Eddy. 'Do you not remember — Oh, I forgot, you've only just started. We did enemas, leeches and mustard poultices in the first lecture that Mr Fawcett gave, but you missed that one. Well, I've done leeches a few times with Sister so I can show you. And I've done enemas as well, so I can show you that in due course, but for now we'll stick to the leeches.' Then Eddy cracked up laughing. 'Just realized what I said: 'stick to the leeches', ha ha ha, do you get the joke?'

But Maud just felt bewildered.

'Come on, Maud, no time to lose,' said Eddy, clapping her on the back and nearly knocking the wind out of her.

'This is where we'll find the little blighters,' she added with relish, leading on.

Maud watched as Eddy removed a large jar from the ward store cupboard, tucking it under her arm, and then she seemed to be looking along the shelf for something else. 'Now they usually have some smaller pots so that you can put the selected leeches into them to take to the patient's bedside, but I can't seem to find any here and we don't really have time to go looking,

97

so just this once, I'll take the big jar with us.'

'Are you sure that's a good idea . . . ?' said Maud, her voice trailing off as Eddy was already half-way down the ward.

She needed to walk briskly to catch up and by the time that she did Eddy had already found bed four where Mr Hollingsworth had just shot upright after Eddy greeted him in quite a loud voice and told him that she had come to apply some leeches to him.

'Well, I don't really like those things that much,' he was saying as Eddy set the large jar down next to him on the bed. 'They give me the shivers, but if the doc thinks they might help me chest then you need to have a go, I suppose.'

'Right, thank you, Mr Hollingsworth. I will select two and apply them to your sternum.' When he looked puzzled Eddy added, 'The sternum is just another name for the breast-bone,' and Maud could see her smiling, probably at her own newly acquired medical knowledge. Maud was also impressed; she had never heard that word so she tucked it away in her memory for future use.

In moments Eddy was unscrewing the lid of the jar. 'Darn,' she said, 'we usually use a long pair of forceps to pull them out but I must have left them in the cupboard . . . never mind,' she muttered, plunging her hand into the jar and fishing around inside. Maud simply could not look. She knew that she should — she knew that she would have to in due course — but right there and then she could not look at Eddy or the jar.

She heard Eddy say, 'Ha-ha, that's a good one,' and that's when she made herself look up to see Eddy with a large leech in her hand. Maud felt her stomach heave but she was determined to focus on what Eddy did with the leech. Mr Hollingsworth already had his shirt open and Eddy simply held the leech in place on his breastbone until it had fastened itself there. It seemed easy, if you could bear to touch a leech.

Then Eddy was back to the big jar and fishing around in there again until another specimen was removed and applied in a similar way to the middle of Mr Hollingsworth's chest. Maud could see the patient looking down at the two leeches, his eyes wide, and then Eddy gently pulled his shirt over to cover them and told him she would be back every half-hour to check that they were still safely applied and doing the job. Mr Hollingsworth gulped and then tried to smile, but Maud could see that he was almost as troubled by leeches as she was. But at least that seemed to be it for the time being, and Maud started to relax a little when she saw Eddy putting the lid back on the big jar.

Eddy was straight off down the ward with the leeches, leaving Mr Hollingsworth sitting bolt upright in the bed, his face rigid. Maud went to him and patted his arm, keeping an eye on his shirt front, just in case.

'You will be all right,' she said, trying to smile. 'They use leeches all the time on the wards and they will do the job for you. Just try to keep still and relax a little if you can.'

He looked at her and nodded, still holding his

shoulders square but she could see in his eyes that he appreciated her words and he tried to smile in return.

'Thank you, Nurse,' he said. 'I'll manage, I'll still be sat here when you get back, don't you worry.'

'I'd best go and catch up with Nurse Pacey, but we'll both be back soon.'

⋆ ⋆ ⋆

'Now,' said Eddy, closing the door of the cupboard where she had jostled around any number of containers and pieces of equipment to replace the jar of leeches, 'let's go and find Sister and see what other duties she has for us.'

Before they could even begin to find Sister Cleary, however, they heard a blood-curdling scream from the direction of Mr Hollingsworth's bed and when they turned as one they could see him dancing up and down by the side of the bed very vigorously indeed for a man with a bad chest.

'Jesus Christ, Jesus Christ,' he was shouting. 'Get them off me, get them off me!'

Eddy was straight there, closely followed by Maud.

'Get them off me, get them off me!' shouted the man again, as Maud saw Eddy pull aside the man's shirt to expose the leeches still firmly attached.

'Not those, not those! Bloody hell, bloody hell!' yelled the man, and then Maud saw what the issue was. Poor Mr Hollingsworth had three more leeches attached to his lower leg and he was frantically trying to shake them off.

'Whatever is going on, Nurse Pacey?' shouted Sister as she steamed down the ward. 'I told you to apply two leeches to the sternum, not three to the leg.'

'I did,' said Eddy. 'They must have got out of the jar.'

'What!' said Sister. 'Nurse Pacey, you know that we never take the big jar to the bedside. One of the reasons why we do not take all of the leeches is that they are naturally drawn to any warm body.'

By this time Maud had managed to grab hold of Mr Hollingsworth, who had started to cough and wheeze, and persuaded him to stop dancing about and get back on the bed. Then Sister was apologizing and neatly removing the three rogue leeches from his leg.

Eddy stood by with her head down whilst Sister Cleary and Maud soothed the patient and made a thorough check of his bed to make sure no more leeches were lurking in the sheets. Then Sister came over to Eddy and gave her the three leeches, which were firmly wrapped in a handkerchief.

'Why exactly did you take the big jar to the patient's bed?' she said.

'Well, there were no small pots. I knew we were busy and I just wanted to get on with it, and then we could come and help with the rest of the patients.'

'Well, Nurse Pacey, your rushing has caused unnecessary distress to this patient and on this

101

ward. Even at the busiest of times — *especially* at the busiest of times — I do not want any rushing or cutting of corners. What do I keep telling all of you nurses? What is Miss Nightingale's first rule? The first rule is that we do our patients *no harm*. Now take these leeches straight back to the jar and make very sure that the lid is on tight.'

'Yes, Sister,' said Eddy quietly, and Maud's heart went out to her.

'Look, Nurse Pacey,' said Sister in a gentler voice, 'I know you mean well and you have the makings of an excellent nurse, but you just need to slow down. Do you understand? Now go along and get a bandage to apply to Mr Hollingsworth's leg. There will be some blood seepage from those unexpected puncture wounds on his lower leg.'

'Yes, Sister,' said Eddy, starting to get some life back into her voice.

After the incident with the leeches, Sister Cleary asked Maud to work with one of the more experienced nurses for the rest of the day and although Maud did feel a little sad for Eddy, she was glad of the decision. She needed to move at a slower, more considered pace, especially since, on this her first day on the ward, she was exposed to sights that were not commonplace for a single woman with a careful upbringing like Maud. She was exposed to the body parts of men. She had never seen so much as an exposed chest or thigh before, but in one day it was all out there on display. So much flesh. Most of the patients were old men, but there were some young ones and they were the worst. They had so much firm flesh and so much hair, it made her blush just to think about it.

As Maud moved alongside the nurse from bed to bed and task to task, she almost felt dizzy with the pace of the work. And with each new case, she tried really hard to become accustomed to their state of undress. The nurse that she was working with kept saying, 'Don't you worry, you'll get used to it,' but it was strange: she had been worried that she was squeamish and wouldn't be able to manage the gory stuff, but she had seen any number of deep, festering ulcers and a severe burn with no problem at all. It was the flesh of the men she was struggling to cope with. Maybe she would only enjoy working on women's wards. That's if she got through the training.

Later that day she caught up with Eddy and they teamed up together again. Sister had asked them to replace a dressing, one that Eddy had done before and she was trusted to do again.

'This is a bit of a nasty one,' said Eddy over her shoulder as they hurtled down the ward. 'The patient has a large bed sore — do you know what that is?'

'No,' said Maud, slightly out of breath and thankful that Eddy seemed to be slowing up as they approached the store cupboard.

'Well,' said Eddy, turning to face her with a solemn expression, 'Sister is quite cross about this because these sores can be prevented by making sure that a patient moves position in the bed every two hours. The man, Mr Latimer, was admitted with congestion of the lungs and that has been improving, but the nurse assigned to him on his first day left him sitting in the same position all day and he has a nasty sore now on his sacrum — that's at the bottom of his back. It's quite deep and it's started to suppurate. We are packing it each day but it doesn't look good for him. Sister thinks that he probably won't do well.'

'That's terrible,' said Maud, feeling for the poor man who had been admitted to hospital for one thing but now sounded like he was dying from another.

Eddy collected the dressings tray, a big wad of lint, a bottle of iodine and some bandages. When they got to the bed Maud was shocked to see how poorly the patient looked, lying on his side, his breathing quite laboured and a very bad smell emanating from under the bedclothes.

Maud stood by as Eddy spoke gently to the patient and explained what they were going to do. Then she carefully removed the big dressing from his back. Next she soaked the lint in iodine and pushed it into the deep hole, asking Maud to help with the bandage that needed to go all the way around the man's torso to hold it in place.

'Now, Mr Latimer,' said Eddy, for once her voice quiet, 'that's all done for you. Let's get you moved over on to your other side.'

As the man nodded and tried to smile, Maud could see that his eyes were watering but she didn't think he was crying, he was just so very poorly. Without being told she stood at the opposite side of the bed and helped the man

104

over. She pulled the pillows that propped him up in the bed into a better position, making sure that the cloth was straight under his face. He tried to smile again and murmured, 'Thank you, Nurse.'

Maud felt her heart tighten and she smiled back at him, but already his eyes were closed and he was drifting to sleep.

'Why didn't he scream with pain when you did that?' asked Maud as they walked together back down the ward.

'I wondered that as well the first time I did the dressing. Sister said that when the wounds are deep like that the nervous connections don't seem to be there, whereas if it's near the surface people can scream blue murder with something much smaller.'

'Right,' said Maud, glad at least that Mr Latimer was without pain.

'Might it still heal up?'

'That's the thing,' said Eddy, her voice falling quiet again. 'There is no way that a huge hole like that can heal. It is bound to be fatal.'

Maud took a sharp intake of breath and felt her heart flutter. So that was it; that was the everyday reality of this work that she had decided to undertake. This was going to be hard, she knew that now, but she would do her absolute best.

Before Maud could ask any more questions Sister was calling down the ward with further instruction and immediately they were assigned another task.

'Nurse Pacey, Nurse Linklater, please take two

bowls of soup and two cups of tea into the side room. We have a couple of patients in there who have been isolated due to some fever that has flared up since they were admitted.'

Eddy and Maud went straight to the kitchen and prepared the trays, and then Eddy led the way to the side room and used her hip to open the door whilst she held the tray with both hands. She was a bit vigorous with the swing of her hip and the door opened with a crash into something inside the room. Then as Maud approached, at a much slower rate, she heard more rattling inside as Eddy seemed to be jostling her tray. Aware that Sister was fast approaching down the ward Maud slipped quietly into the room with her tray perfectly balanced.

She could see Eddy trying to clear some space on the table between the men's beds with one hand whilst she held the tray in the other. The cup was rocking on the saucer and some tea was spilling.

As Maud assessed the situation — about to put her tray down temporarily on top of some papers so that she could help Eddy — the door swung open and Sister Cleary appeared.

'Sorry, Sister,' Eddy said. 'I seem to have got myself — '

'Shhh!' said Sister, and then in a whisper: 'No noise around fever patients, remember.'

'Sorry,' said Eddy again, unable to use a quiet tone of voice.

Sister helped straighten things up and Maud sorted out her own tray. Once outside the side ward, she took time to speak to them both, but mainly Eddy.

'Do you remember what Miss Nightingale advises about noise in the sickroom, Nurse Pacey?'

But despite standing there frowning, Eddy could not recall what had been written by Miss Nightingale. She had no idea.

Maud knew, but she would never have said, not when Eddy was racking her brains to find an answer.

'Remember, Nurse Pacey,' said Sister Cleary, ' "Unnecessary noise is the most cruel absence of care which can be inflicted either on sick or well. Even the fidget of silk or crinoline, the creaking of stays and of shoes, will do a patient more harm than all the medicines in the world will do him good.' Do not be the nurse who cannot open a door without making everything rattle, or carry a tray without shaking the tea cup and spilling half the drink into the saucer. Try, do try, to not be that nurse because 'a nurse who rustles is the horror of the patient.' '

'That's it,' said Eddy, 'Of course, I remember it now.'

'All right then, you two,' said Sister, 'it's about time for you to go off shift. I'll let you off a bit early today so that you can look through the chapter on unnecessary noise in *Notes on Nursing*. See you both in the morning; on time, please, Nurse Pacey.'

'Yes, Sister. Thank you, Sister,' they said as they made their way off the ward before Sister Cleary could change her mind.

Maud walked away from the ward in some kind of trance. She didn't know what to think. It felt like everything had happened in a whirl that day and now she was relieved to be getting away from all those men. Hurtling along the corridor, trying to keep pace with Eddy, she began to realize that it would take her a long time to get used to the new routine and all the detail of the work. Until she understood all the basics, and more besides, she knew she would not feel entirely comfortable. All she could do was keep going day by day, slowly and steadily, until things started to make sense and fall into place.

Then she saw a woman whom she recognized but couldn't quite place immediately walking down the corridor towards them. It was only as she got nearer that she recognized Stella, who was heading down towards them at quite a pace. She looked preoccupied with something and didn't see Maud at first. Ordinarily Maud would have let a person in that much of a rush pass by, but for some reason she felt an urge to connect with her. She felt she needed to speak to someone who had got to know her before she was a nurse probationer, when she was just a housemaid visiting a hospital ward — when she knew exactly what she was doing.

So as Stella drew level with them Maud stepped in her direction and said a bright 'Hello', stopping Stella in her tracks. Eddy carried on walking and when she glanced back Maud gestured for her to continue, telling her that she would catch up later. Stella had stopped, and looked up, surprised.

'Oh, hello. It's Maud, isn't it? I didn't recognize you in that uniform and with that little starchy cap on your head. You look quite different . . . but it suits you, it really does.'

'Thank you,' said Maud, starting to relax. 'Just had my first day on the ward.'

'Crikey,' said Stella. 'Hope it was all right. I mean, personally, I don't know how you nurses do what you do. Not everybody could do it. You need something special, I think. I couldn't bloody do it, that's for sure.'

'Well, your job can't be easy either,' said Maud, without even thinking about what she was saying and definitely not wanting to get into any conversation about the workings of a brothel whilst she was stood in the hospital corridor.

'Well, you know what they say, it has its ups and downs,' said Stella, starting to laugh. Then, seeing Maud's uncomfortable expression, she moved on to another topic. 'I'm just off up to see the half-sister again; we seem to be getting on all right at present.'

'That's good,' said Maud, warmly. 'Did you find your friend, the man who was in the next bed to Alfred?'

'No, I didn't,' said Stella. 'I thought I knew where he'd be but he seems to have vanished off the face of the earth. He'll probably turn up sooner or later: they usually do. I've known any number of men who were injured in the Crimea, some with terrible injuries. Life has been very hard on them since that war finished. Usually they turn up again, but sometimes they just disappear for ever. And speaking of disappearing, that's the reason I'm on my way to see my half-sister, see if she can help. One or two of my girls went missing a few weeks back and they still haven't turned up. I think they might have been taken into the Lock Hospital. Have you heard anything about that sort of thing?'

'No,' said Maud, 'but I'll listen out and let you know if I hear anything. You're on Lime Street, right?'

'Yes, that's right,' said Stella. 'What an excellent memory you have. And don't worry, if you need me, or the boy does, come any time. We will give you a welcome and try to help in any way we can.' Then Stella put her arm around Maud in her brand-new uniform and gave her a squeeze, whispering in her ear, 'And remember, Maudie, if things don't work out for you here on the wards you can always come and get a job with me.'

Maud knew that Stella was joking but she felt her face start to flush red. After all the naked flesh she'd seen on the ward today, it seemed a bit much for someone to start talking about her working in a brothel.

6

'All nurses and Probationers will be provided with a sufficient allowance of beer or porter to take at mealtimes.'

Florence Nightingale

After two weeks Maud was finding life at the hospital much harder than she expected. She had held on to the plan of just keeping going day after day with the work on the ward but there were some things that she hadn't taken into account whatsoever. Maud was used to hard work — very hard work — and she was used to feeling tired at the end of the day, but the work at the big house involved cleaning or supervising or answering the bell for a tray of tea, not dealing with people who were desperately ill, and often in tragic circumstances. Coping with that, the patients, the diseases, the sheer workload, and managing her own feelings at the same time, was exhausting. She was still working on the male ward, and it was the nakedness of the men that she was struggling to cope with as well. Having grown up in a very small household with just women, she had never had brothers or fathers strolling around with their shirts off or getting a wash at the sink. And then at the big house, she had shared a room with another woman. So now, to be fully exposed to men in all states of

111

undress, well, it was very difficult indeed for Maud. She was just hoping that she would get used to it, but there was no sign of her getting used to any of it yet. If anything, she was feeling even more overwhelmed.

The other thing that was becoming increasingly difficult for her was to stomach the beer that they were given to drink. She didn't like the taste of it, it made her feel sick and she didn't like the fuzzy feeling in her head that it gave her during the afternoon shift. Prior to coming to the hospital she had never touched any liquor, but now she had to drink it. Well, she didn't have to, exactly, but she didn't want to risk catching the cholera or some other horrible disease from the water. It hadn't been a problem at the big house. Their water supply was good, or so they were told. It had been fed in when the new houses were built and there had been absolutely no cases of cholera in that area that she knew of. Also, they always drank tea, so the water was boiled.

She was hoping that she would get used to drinking the beer, but even the thought of it now made her feel sick. For a start, she couldn't manage her daily allowance of three pints. Some of the nurses could manage it, but she was struggling to get one pint down.

Eddy seemed to be all right with it — she could knock it back — but Maud had noticed Alice sipping at it and not able to take her full amount, probably on account of the sickness she had from being with child. The one that she couldn't work out, though, as usual, was Nancy

Sellers. She just seemed to sip at it smoothly but when you looked across it was gone. Maud had seen Alice, who always sat next to Nancy at the table, passing hers over as well, but Nancy never looked any different, having drunk so much, not even the slightest slurring of her speech. Maud was beginning to wonder if the woman was a real person or some kind of machine.

Anyway, it looked like she was going to have a chance to find out. Miss Merryweather had told her to report to Alfred's ward, Male Surgical, for duty that morning, so she'd be back with Alice and Nancy. The nurses on Male Medical who had been off with the fever had unexpectedly pulled through and were returning to duty, so Maud was leaving that ward just as she was starting to get used to the staff and Eddy crashing and banging her way through the duties.

She was glad, in a way, because she would see more of Alfred before he left the hospital, even if it did mean being back under the eagle eye of Sister Law. In the meantime, Miss Fairchild had sent Maud a note: everything was in hand, she had spoken to Sister and would be taking Alfred up to the Blue Coat School herself.

That morning Maud left the Nurses' Home with Alice and Nancy, and made her way back to where it had all begun.

As they entered the ward she broke away from the other two and nipped down to see Alfred. He did look fine, there was no mistake. They had kept him a bit longer than expected after he'd started with some mild fever. But she could tell

113

that he was recovering by the way that his eyes were shining and he was sitting up in bed bright and alert.

'I can't stay,' she said, 'and I don't know if I'll be working down this end, but I'll give you a wave in passing.'

'That's all right,' said the boy. 'They are really busy on here. You need to get on with the work. And I'll be going tomorrow or the next day, going to the school.'

'I know,' said Maud, 'Miss Fairchild sent me a note. That is good, very good. I'll — '

'Nurse Linklater,' bellowed Sister Law down the ward, 'you are not a visitor now. Get up here at once.'

'I have to go,' she said, feeling her face turning bright red as she walked away from Alfred's bed.

Sister Law scowled at her and then set about reminding her that now she was an actual nurse and legitimately able to use the sluice, then she would have to make sure that she remembered that she was there to work on the ward and therefore prioritize her duties over fraternizing socially with the patients. Then her beady eyes scanned the whole of the group and she said, 'Right, you two, Sampson and Linklater, get down to the bottom of the ward, to the end bed. There's a man who was admitted last night badly beaten. We don't know his name and he's been unconscious. Check on him, give him a bit of a wash if he needs it, and report back to me. Once he comes round we want to get him discharged as soon as possible. He's been checked over, no bones broken, apart from his nose.'

'Yes, Sister,' said Maud and Alice in unison, heading straight down the ward. Maud was so relieved that she hadn't been partnered with Nancy and determined that she would stick right by Alice's side.

Neither of them had been prepared for the man that they found lying on that bed. They had never in their lives been up close to any man that looked so beautiful. There he lay, still completely out of it, but like some prince from a storybook. He had a mop of black curly hair and yes, his face was bruised and swollen, but they could see the shape of his cheekbones and his nose was a bit crooked but it only seemed to add to his beauty, the slight imperfection making him more real and more desirable. His clothes were far from new, but he had on a dark-green jacket that had obviously been very splendid indeed in a past life.

'Right, well,' said Alice. 'I suppose we'd best get him cleaned up.'

'Now wait a minute,' said Maud, starting to feel uncomfortable and not able to cope with seeing the naked flesh of such a handsome man just yet. 'He looks clean enough, on his body. I think we should just give his hands and face a wipe and see if he rouses up and then we can report back to Sister.'

Maud could see the disappointment on Alice's face.

'You're probably right,' she said. 'I'll get the water.'

Whilst she was away Maud crouched down beside the bed and spoke a few words to the

115

man. 'Hello, are you awake?' But there was no response. She could smell the beer on him, but she could also smell something else, something musky and very male, something she had never smelt before on any man. And she had been very close to quite a few over the last couple of weeks. This was some kind of particular man smell and for some reason she really liked it. And then she saw that he had a small gold loop through his ear lobe. She'd never seen anything like that before.

It seemed all too soon before Alice was back with the water and handing it to Maud. 'Sister wants me to move along to the man in the next bed and check his dressings. I'll be just there if you need me.'

Maud nodded and immediately started to wash the man's face. Then she gently dried him, patting his closed eyes, then his sore nose and then wiping his mouth. Then she took his hands each in turn and soaked them in the bowl of water. They were dirty with what looked like fresh muck from the streets, and the knuckles on both hands were skinned raw.

'He's been fighting all right,' she said quietly to herself.

As Maud was just finishing she caught a piece of raw skin on a knuckle and it started bleeding, fresh red blood soaking into the towel. She was leaning down to have a closer look when the man shot straight up in bed and grabbed her by the front of her uniform, pulling it tight around her neck and swinging his other arm up as if to punch her.

116

Maud gave a scream — she couldn't help it — and Alice was there instantly, grabbing the man's arm, shouting, 'No!'

There was a moment when Maud didn't know which way it would go. He was holding her tight with one hand and they were face to face. She could feel his breath in her face and see his eyes, almost black, with dilated pupils. She hung there, suspended and completely helpless for what seemed like a long time but in fact was probably only seconds. Then Alice pulled on his arm more firmly. 'Let her go,' she instructed. And he released Maud and fell back on his pillow with a groan.

Maud reeled back and caught her breath, then immediately straightened the bodice of her uniform and made sure that her cap was set square on her head. She could still feel the strength of his fist and the stinging of the skin on her neck where he had held her, and she was breathless.

'Are you all right?' said Alice, her face full of concern. 'Do you want me to take over here?'

'No, no, I will be fine,' said Maud, taking a deep breath. 'You get on. Honestly, I will be fine.'

'All right then,' said Alice reluctantly, 'but you shout for me straight away if this fella starts any rough stuff again.'

'I will,' said Maud, anxious now to get on with the work and surprised at how quickly she was able to collect herself.

For some reason, she was not fearful of the man. Cautious, of course, but not afraid. After all, if he had wanted to hurt her he could have done it there and then. Clearly, although he was still drunk from the night before or delirious as a result of the beating, he had some restraint. She was able to take account of that, and now that he was laid back on the bed and seemed to have slipped once more into some kind of sleep she felt in charge again. In the next moment she was able to kneel down by the side of the bed and speak to him very calmly.

'You've been injured and you're in hospital.'

'I bloody well know where I am,' snapped the man, wiping a hand across his eyes before twisting his head to the side and looking Maud full in the face.

His eyes were green. Maud couldn't speak.

'I need to get going,' he said. 'Where's my dog?'

Maud tried to speak but no words would come out.

'I need to find it,' said the man, propping himself up on his elbows.

'I haven't seen a dog,' said Maud. 'No one mentioned a dog.'

'Where's my dog?' said the man again, this time pushing himself up and swinging his legs over the side of the bed.

Maud leant out of his way. She could tell by the look on his face that he was determined and he was very strong. So she let him move and gave him some space.

But as he heaved himself up from the bed and on to his feet, he immediately lurched to one side. Maud was there in a flash, steadying him and firmly guiding him back to the safety of the bed.

'Let go of me,' he said, looking at her with such intensity she felt her own legs might give way.

'You can't go yet,' said Maud. 'We need to report back to Sister. She's the only one who can discharge you.'

'Report away,' said the man, 'but I'm leaving right now.' With that he started to walk up the ward, unsteady but finding his legs the further he went. Maud was quick to catch up with him and gently took his arm, trying to reason with him, but he wrenched free and strode out through the door. She knew by his behaviour that any further attempt would only antagonize him and he was set to leave the ward whatever she said or did, so she let him go.

Moments later she heard Sister Law shouting down the ward, 'Where's that man? Where is he? Doctor wants to see him.'

'He's gone,' Maud called back apologetically. 'I tried my best to stop him but — '

'Gone? Oh, for goodness' sake,' shouted Sister. 'Well, don't stand idle. Move along to another patient. And make sure you strip that bed and get it ready for the next admission. No, wait a minute, Nurse Sampson can do that. You come here and work with Nurse Sellers. I want to make sure that you are shown the proper way to do things on the ward.'

Maud's heart sank instantly but there was nothing she could do. An order from Sister was an order. 'See you later,' she said to Alice as she

119

lifted her chin and walked up the ward.

Working with Nancy was the last thing that Maud wanted to do that day but there was no way that she would let any of the staff or patients know how she was feeling. She would get on with her work in the best way that she could. Maud had not spoken about her feelings for Nancy to anyone, not even Alice. It wasn't in her nature to engage in tittle-tattle but there was something about Nancy that made her feel that she had to be very careful about what she said to anyone. Alice always seemed to be in Nancy's thrall — she could see that — and although she trusted Alice, whom she knew for sure was a kind soul, she sensed the power that Nancy held over her.

So, she would just have to make the best of it. She had no choice.

'Sister wants me to show you how to lay out a body,' said Nancy haughtily. 'Do you think you can manage that?'

'Yes, of course,' said Maud, making sure that Nancy had no inkling that her condescending attitude, probably deliberate, was making her feel riled already.

'Right then,' said Nancy, setting off up the ward to the top bed where a table stood ready with a bowl of water, some towels and a stack of clean linen.

Maud stood looking at the body for a few moments. She had seen a few in her time, including one of the family who had died at the big house, but this was the first time that she had helped lay anyone out. Although there had been a number of deaths on Male Medical, Sister had said that she wanted her to feel more comfortable and get a grip of nursing the living before she moved on to the dead, so she had not been allocated this particular duty. She stood now looking down at the dead body of a man that she had never known, not even as a patient, feeling that she just needed to take a few moments to collect herself and say a few words in her head out of respect for him.

She heard Nancy tut as she threw a towel across at her. 'Are you ready?'

'Yes, of course,' replied Maud, setting her mouth in a determined line.

'First we wash the body,' said Nancy, setting to with the cloth like she was wiping down a sideboard. There was absolutely no tenderness in her touch, none at all. 'You dry,' she ordered, pointing to the towel.

Maud did as she was told, but with much more sensitivity for the poor soul. She knew that he deserved to be treated with the same tenderness and respect as the living. Who knew what he was leaving behind and who was mourning him now?

'Now we've done the front we can slip on the shroud. It opens down the back,' said Nancy, holding it up for inspection.

Once the shroud was slipped over the man's arms Nancy continued her instructions. 'Right, we need to roll him over so I can wash his back and then fasten him up behind. You roll him over towards you and then hold him, all right?'

'Yes,' said Maud calmly, not wasting any time

and pulling the man over towards her. But as she rolled him he let out a low groan, an unearthly sound. Shocked, Maud couldn't help but let go of him. 'He's alive,' she said. 'He must be.'

'No, no, silly,' said Nancy with a small smile on her face. 'Of course he isn't alive. It's normal for them to make that noise when you roll them over. It's just the air coming out of the lungs.'

Well, you could have told me, thought Maud, beginning to see the sense of it and knowing that she would be prepared the next time she was asked to perform last offices.

After they had finished the laying out, the orderlies were summoned to remove the body from the ward, and then Maud got on with the job of washing the bed down with soap and water before making it up again with clean linen. She hadn't seen Nancy for a while, not since she had headed into the sluice with the bowl of water, and she had been glad to be left to work alone. Checking that the corners on the bed linen were perfect, she noticed one of the cloths that they had used lying discarded on the floor. She picked it up and headed into the sluice with it.

As soon as the door opened she saw that Nancy was still in there and she switched round instantly to face Maud. As they stood suspended in the moment Maud drew in a sharp breath as she saw Nancy slipping a small bottle or flask of something into her pocket, as quick as lightning. There was a faint smell of strong liquor in there as well; she was sure that's what it was.

So that's what you're up to, thought Maud,

remembering a maid with a nasty temperament that they'd had at the big house who had been dismissed in the end for secret drinking. I've got your measure, Nancy Sellers.

Maud smiled at Nancy and held out the cloth to her but she did not take it straight away. Instead she held Maud's gaze and in those few moments a clear message passed between them. Nancy knew that Maud was fully aware of her secret drinking and Maud knew for sure just how ruthless and defiant Nancy could be. Then Nancy took the cloth with a small smile and turned her back on Maud.

Maud went straight out of the sluice, feeling that she needed to breathe. It had been suffocating in there. She was shaking inside and needed to take a few deep breaths to try to settle herself. Then she felt some inner strength start to unfold and she lifted her chin and walked down the ward, anxious to find Alice and wanting to be back down at the other end of the ward where she could check on Alfred and keep well out of Nancy's way.

Alfred had a visitor, someone that Maud hadn't seen for a while. Miss Fairchild was sitting by his bed, and Maud could have hugged her, she was so pleased to see her familiar face.

'How are you doing?' said Miss Fairchild warmly.

'All right, I think,' said Maud, trying to smile. 'It's still early days, of course, and there is so much to learn and get used to, but, yes, all right.'

'As you know, we still miss you at the house,' said Miss Fairchild. 'I know I've said this before but someone like you can't be replaced easily. So if it doesn't work out here, you know that you can come straight back to us. You do know that, don't you?'

'I know that, and thank you,' said Maud, feeling her stomach tighten as Nancy sauntered past the bottom of Alfred's bed.

'I was just telling young Alfred here that they are expecting him up at the Blue Coat School tomorrow. I know you are busy here and your shifts are long, but if I take him up there in the afternoon, do you think that you could check on him later in the week or just as soon as you can?'

'Are you sure he's ready to go?' said Maud, suddenly feeling worried about the boy leaving and going somewhere that she couldn't readily keep an eye on him.

'Yes, yes, I've spoken to that Sister. She says he needs to wear the sling for a few more weeks but he is definitely ready to go.'

'I will be fine,' said Alfred, sensing Maud's concern. 'You get on with your nursing. There is no need to come up there to check on me, not if you're busy.'

'Of course I will come. I will try to see you every week if I can,' said Maud, not really knowing why she felt so anxious when she should be happy and relieved that the boy wasn't going back to the workhouse or, worse still, returning to Mr Greer's house. She hadn't thought about Greer for ages and now that she did she felt a small shudder go through her body.

As if she was reading her mind Miss Fairchild said, 'It's all straight with Mr Greer — I've made sure of that — and what's more I've heard that he has purchased one of those mechanical sweeping brushes.'

'Really?' said Maud. 'So no more climbing boys, then.'

'No more climbing boys,' said Miss Fairchild, glancing at Alfred.

Thank goodness, thought Maud, thinking about what state the boy had been in when she first laid eyes on him and how afraid he had been at first on the ward. And look at him now — what a change! A change for him and for me, she thought. We have moved together.

'Walk back with me this evening,' said Miss Fairchild. 'I know you are finishing your shift soon so come for tea.'

'I'd love to,' said Maud, feeling a surge of relief at the thought of such easy and welcome company. 'I will have to go back to the Home first to change out of my uniform but, yes, thank you, that's a lovely idea.'

As Maud strolled away from the Infirmary that evening with Miss Fairchild she saw the man who she had tended to on the ward that morning, the one who had tried to grab her. She was certain it was him; she wouldn't have been able to mistake him anywhere. Even as she was telling herself that was because of his unusual dark-green jacket she knew if she was honest that it was much more than that.

He must have found his dog, she thought, seeing a thin brown beast with long legs and a tail like a whip trotting beside him. She had seen dogs like that before with the tinkers and pedlars

125

who sometimes called at the big house. The man and the dog were walking at quite a pace but she admired the way the dog was moving with him, steadfast by his side.

She was glad to see the man walking steadily and not showing any sign of his injury. He must be all right. Looks like he's heading somewhere in a hurry, probably back to the pub, she thought, remembering the smell of beer on him. Which reminded her of that other, musky smell, that special smell that made her skin tingle even now just thinking about it again.

'Seen any interesting cases on the ward today?' said Miss Fairchild.

'One or two,' said Maud vaguely, glancing after the man once more before he rounded the corner to follow his own route, which seemed to be in the opposite direction to theirs.

7

'The most important practical lesson that can be given to nurses is to teach them what to observe . . . '

Florence Nightingale

As Maud and Alice stripped the bed the next day after Alfred had gone with Miss Fairchild, they found a brown, woollen sock between the sheets that must have slipped off the boy's skinny foot.

Alice picked it up, holding it out to her. 'Look at that, Maud. He's left his little sock. You'll want to keep that, I know you will.'

Maud took the sock and shoved it in her pocket. 'Thank you. I'll take it up for him when I go to visit. Then he'll have a matching pair.'

'You are so practical,' said Alice, bundling up the sheets and taking them over to the laundry basket. 'I would want to put it in a special box and keep it for ever.'

'Maybe,' said Maud, turning her back on Alice to look up the ward, seemingly for another bed to strip. In fact, seeing the sock lying there had given her an ache in her chest and she knew that she had to move on quickly to stop Alice from going on about the sock and making her feel worse.

'Right, next bed to strip over there,' she said, moving across the ward with Alice following.

127

Then they both stopped in their tracks as they heard a sharp voice shouting down the ward, 'Nurse Sampson, Nurse Sampson, we need you up this end.'

'That's Nancy,' said Alice. 'Best go. Sorry, Maud.'

'That's all right,' said Maud, giving her a tight smile. She knew that Alice would never challenge Nancy but why, exactly, thought Maud, does Nancy think that she can give orders and tell people what to do? She is at the same stage of training as Alice, they are both in the same set, there is absolutely no reason why she should think herself superior in any way. Nancy is not 'in charge' of anyone.

There was nothing that Maud could do about the situation yet — she was those few weeks behind Nancy — but she had the measure of her already and she knew that when the time came she would not be taking any orders from Nurse Sellers.

So she busied herself at the other end of the ward. Maud never worried about working on her own. She had no problem checking on the patients who needed poultices, and she had even become adept at applying leeches. She had always been capable of getting on with work and quietly using her initiative. She would only need another person, not Nancy if she could help it, to assist her moving a patient. Otherwise she was fine.

However, the time when she might need to call for assistance came sooner than she expected as the two orderlies, with whom she was

128

becoming increasingly familiar, came in through the door with a man on a stretcher. Maud knew as soon as she saw the head of black curly hair who the patient was and she had to be firm with herself to stop her knees going slightly weak.

'What's happened?' she asked Michael, the man at the head of the stretcher.

'Oh, he'll be all right,' Michael Delaney assured her. 'It's the other fella you need to be worrying about: he's knocked out cold. The docs are still workin' on 'im.'

'What do you mean?' said Maud. 'Have they been fighting?'

'They have that,' said Michael. 'These fellas are always at it. In fact, I 'ad a bet on the other fella to win. He's a real big bugger. I've no idea how this fella managed to knock 'im out — he's only half the size — but he's wick, is this one, and quick on his feet. He's not been beaten yet.'

'What?' said Maud. 'Are they always fighting? Do they have a quarrel or something?'

'Nah,' said the man, looking at her as if she was daft. 'These lads are bare-knuckle fighters. They're set up in matches — have you never seen 'em?'

'No, I haven't,' said Maud grimly, helping the men as they unloaded their patient on to what had been Alfred's bed.

'Must not move in the best circles like us,' said Stephen, and both men starting chuckling, and then Michael was coughing and wheezing.

'Right, Nurse,' said Michael when he had his breath back, 'you make sure you get him fixed up good. He's due back for another bout tomorrow.'

129

'Tomorrow!' said Maud, horrified. 'He could get killed.'

'That's the risk they take and they get paid good money for taking that risk, more than we earn in a month shifting the sick and the dead in and around this place.'

Maud looked down at the man on the bed, exasperated by the acceptance of such barbaric practice. He had his eyes open and he was trying to focus on her but he didn't seem able to speak.

'What's his name?' she called after the orderlies.

'He's Harry Donahue,' the man at the head of the stretcher shouted back, 'the now famous Harry Donahue. Who would have thought that he had a punch like that, knocking out the reigning champion with one blow?'

'Harry Donahue,' said Maud to herself, as she noticed that he was starting to close his eyes. She had no idea what to do with somebody who'd been in a fight and got punched about the head but she didn't think it was a good idea to let him sleep so she gave him a gentle nudge. 'Harry, Harry Donahue, open your eyes,' she said, seeing him give a slurry smile in reply.

Well, at least his nose didn't look any more crooked than it was last time he was in, she thought, so no more damage done there, but she could see some new bruising on his face and a small cut above his eye. She looked at his hands and saw the knuckles were raw and bleeding again, and this time the left hand looked quite swollen. She thought that getting a bowl of water and trying to clean some of the muck off him might be a good start so she made for the sluice.

Turning round to check on him, she could see that he was trying to get up out of bed and she knew that he would fall. She ran back to him and spoke firmly. 'You need to lie down, Mr Donahue, really you must.'

For some reason as she leant over him and put light pressure on his chest she saw him take on board what she was saying. There seemed to be a light of recognition in his eyes, some kind of connection, and he nodded and swung his legs back up on the bed and then lay very still on his back with his arms straight by his sides. Not quite what I had in mind, she thought, given that he looked like he was ready for laying out.

'Stay there and don't move,' she said firmly. 'I'm going for some water. I don't want to see you trying to get out of bed again before I get back.'

Harry nodded and didn't seem to have the energy to put up any more resistance. When she came back he was asleep. As she washed him, she decided this time to let him sleep, having reassured herself that he was responsive. His breathing was regular, his skin was a good colour, and when she leant down to gently wash his face and tend to the worst of the grazes, she felt overcome again by that special smell, which made her feel rather light-headed.

But she continued her work, deftly moving on to his swollen left hand, sponging it gently over the bowl and trying to get as much of the muck off as possible. She was engrossed in her work, being so careful not to hurt him and set him off like she had done last time that she didn't hear the footsteps as they approached.

'He's my patient,' said Nancy sharply, appearing by Maud's side and almost pushing her out of the way. 'I've nursed him before.'

'What the — ' Maud started to say, but then hearing Sister's voice calling for her from up the ward, she had to give in. She let go of Harry's hand and put the cloth in the bowl of water. As she moved away from the bed she did at least have the satisfaction of hearing the man groan and when she glanced back she thought she saw him stretch his arm out in her direction, though that might just have been a fancy.

'Nurse Sellers knows the patient well,' said Sister Law. 'She is the one best placed to assess him. Now I want you to go into the sluice and make sure that the sink is scoured and that all the sputum pots have been emptied.'

Maud's stomach turned. She didn't mind any amount of cleaning, but emptying all the sputum pots full of the thick phlegm that had been hawked up by the old men on the ward overnight, that was something that made her heave. And she never saw Nancy being given any of the sluice duties. It always seemed to be her and Alice. It didn't seem fair, but she also knew that she would rather that than be the favoured one, the chosen one who got preferential treatment but was disliked by the rest of the staff. When she had been working at the big house she had known that Miss Fairchild liked her and through the years that they worked together she had probably become a favourite,

132

but she respected Miss Fairchild for always, always making sure that no one, not even Maud, was aware of her preferences, and she knew that she always tried to treat everyone equally and give each individual some chance. Clearly Sister did not have the same ethos and it was, thought Maud, very much to her detriment.

The sluice door swung open behind Maud and she felt her stomach tighten. She thought it was Nancy but, looking round, she saw Alice, thank goodness.

'Have you been sent to clean the sluice as well?' said Maud.

'What? Oh no, no,' said Alice, her voice tight.

'Are you all right?' said Maud, immediately noticing that Alice sounded strange and not the same Alice that she had worked with just an hour before. 'Are you feeling sick again?' said Maud, placing a hand on Alice's arm.

To her surprise Alice glared at her and pulled away, then almost shouted, 'No I am not, and what is it to you anyway . . . traitor?'

'What?' said Maud, completely bewildered.

Then Alice was gone and when she looked out of the door after her she could see that she was heading back down the ward to Nancy.

Maud drew back into the sluice and then stood feeling shaken, trying to make sense of what had just happened. She held on to the sink and then, pulling herself together, returned to the task in hand, taking the scouring powder and a cloth and scrubbing the sink with fury. She nearly took the glaze off it but as she scoured she kept thinking over and over what had just happened, and by the time she had finished she thought she had a good idea. Could Nancy, somehow, have found out that Alice was pregnant? And if she had then Alice might naturally assume that Maud had told her. The more she thought about it the more she thought it could be the only explanation.

I will have to speak to her later, not here on the ward, when we get back to the Nurses' Home. And what's more, thought Maud, after I saw Nancy in the sluice yesterday taking a nip from her flask, it's obvious she's just trying to stir up trouble between me and Alice. It's nothing more than a game of power to her.

Well, she won't get far with that, thought Maud as she emptied the pots of phlegm with some vigour into the slop bucket. Plop, plop, plop. Emptying each one in turn, tipping all the nastiness straight out, all in one go, then washing out each pot and cleaning her hands in a fresh bowl of water. When she had finished she went back out on to the ward.

She could see Alice standing at the bottom of Harry's bed with Nancy still fiddling about with something there. But she didn't care about that. All she cared about now was that Alice was in some distress and her heart went out to her as she saw her friend standing there with her head slightly bowed, waiting for Nancy.

Maud knew there was nothing that she could do there and then, and she was overtaken by events as the ward door swung open again and the orderlies staggered through, barely able to walk with a huge man lying on the stretcher.

134

'Here's the big fella we were telling you about,' grunted Michael. 'We need to put him down, quick, quick.'

'Over here,' said Maud, seeing an empty bed next to Harry Donahue.

The men lurched across the ward, their knees buckling, and they just got the stretcher on to the bed in time. They both stood gasping for breath as the giant of a man gave a groan and tried to roll over. The pair of them used the opportunity to pull the stretcher out from under him.

'Now then, champ,' said the man at the head of the stretcher, 'you just lie quiet and let this young lady, this nurse, look after you.' Then they were both gone, scuttling out through the door with their stretcher.

Maud was straight there and starting to take a close look at the man, making sure he was breathing, which thankfully he was. She could sense Nancy's cold eyes on her but it didn't put her off her stride. She did, however, slip round to the other side of the bed, where she could have her back to her.

The man's shirt was ripped open at the front and she could see his huge expanse of chest, full of black hair, rising and falling like an enormous pair of bellows. His forehead looked like a battering ram but there was a huge bruise coming up around one eye and his mouth looked like it had been smashed with something heavy. He probably doesn't have any teeth left in there, Maud thought, but she dared not try to open his mouth to have a look in case she woke him. She couldn't believe that a slim man like Harry Donahue could have floored this big fella. Like the orderly had said, Harry must have a hell of a punch.

Reassured that she had done all she could for the patient for now, she was taken aback to see Sister Law steaming down the ward towards them with her short legs covering ground at an extraordinary rate, and the bow of her cap tied so tight it made her face red and her full chin bulge.

Expecting a tirade, Maud braced herself, but none came. Instead Sister came to the other side of the bed and laid a careful hand on the man's forehead, a gesture of gentleness that did not fit with the view that Maud had of the woman.

'How long has he been here?' she said quietly, her face full of concern.

'Only about five minutes,' said Maud.

'You've checked him over, Nurse?'

'I think so,' said Maud, puzzled by this sudden change in Sister's demeanour.

'I know this patient well,' Sister explained. 'He's been coming in for years. I know he's a fighter — I know all that — but he is the gentlest man on earth.'

Maud was amazed by this other side to Sister. Could she trust it? No doubt it was just a brief interlude and Maud would find herself running for cover again any time soon.

'What are you still doing with that patient, Nurse Sellers?' snapped Sister, looking over to the next bed as her usual self began to re-emerge.

'Just checking, just — '

'Enough justs,' said Sister. 'I think that patient has had more attention than the rest put together on the ward today. Go to bed three. There is a man there desperate for a wash down and you will need to roll him and change his draw sheet. Take Nurse Sampson with you.'

'Yes, Sister,' said Nancy, and as she passed the bottom of the bed Maud saw that her face was flushed bright red and her mouth was set in a sulky line. Maud tried to catch Alice's eye as she followed along behind Nancy but she was looking at the floor.

'This man will be all right,' said Sister after she had completed her own assessment. 'He'll sleep it off and then we'll send him out to fight another day. You can leave him now, Nurse Linklater. Oh, and I've been into the sluice and inspected the sink . . .'

Uh-oh, thought Maud, here we go.

' . . . And I have to say,' said Sister Law, drawing her shoulders up and puffing her chest out, 'I have to say that I have never, in all my years on this ward, seen that sink in there . . . so clean.'

What? thought Maud. Can she actually be giving me praise?

'Cleanliness on the ward is a priority and you have shown that you are committed to that principle. We have to keep clean to stop the spread of contagion and the festering of wounds. So well done, Nurse Linklater. I will recommend you to go through and assist our surgeon, Mr Jones, the next time that he takes a patient to theatre.'

'Thank you,' said Maud, still not quite able to believe or fully trust what she was hearing.

'Now,' said Sister Law briskly, 'you just need to bathe that small cut — it won't need a stitch — and he has some nasty-looking grazes on his knuckles. See to them as well. When you've finished get back up the ward and see if there is anything that needs doing.'

'Yes, Sister,' said Maud, feeling her head start to buzz as she pieced together what Sister had just said to her about being allowed to go into theatre. She began busying herself with the cut, bathing it in clean water, as gently as she possibly could. It felt like she was tending a sleeping giant and, despite what Sister Law had said about him being a gentle man, she wasn't sure that she wanted to be there when he woke up.

Then she lifted his right hand to bathe the cut. His fist was huge and full of calluses, some of the fingernails were broken and they looked sore. Each finger had a mane of black hair running to the knuckle and all his knuckles were skinned raw like Harry's. Moving round to the other side of the bed to bathe the cuts on his left hand, she pulled up his sleeve a little so that his shirt didn't get wet. She saw the edge of what looked like a tattoo and, interested in what it might be, she slid his sleeve up further to reveal a big heart shape with an arrow stabbing through. There was a name in the heart: it said 'Daphne'.

'That's his wife,' said a voice from the next bed.

Maud let out a small gasp. She felt like she had been caught sneaking a peek at something

138

that was out of bounds. She looked over to see, of course, Harry Donahue leaning up on his elbow, looking straight at her with his eyes twinkling.

She was unable to muster a response.

'He worships her,' Harry said. 'He worships Daphne all right and all of his six children. Everything that he does is for them. He works down the docks like some mountain of a man, unloading cargo from as many ships as he can get near, and then he fights: he fights for extra money for her and the children. He is an honest, hardworking man and I am sorry that it was him that I had to go and beat.'

'You two are friends, then?' said Maud, trying to get her head round what it must feel like to step into a match with another man and beat the living daylights out of him, especially when you like him and admire all that he stands for.

'Yes, we are friends,' said Harry. 'We've travelled the same path, me and him. Well, he's older than me but we've come from the same people and we've worked the same jobs.'

'How can you beat each other senseless then?'

'Just makin' a livin'. He wallops me and I wallop him back. Just makin' a livin' like everybody else. Can't believe I knocked him out, though. I was more shocked than him, I think. I just caught him in the right place under the chin and that was it: he went down like a huge tree being felled. God, I was so worried at first that I might have killed him.'

'Well, I still can't understand it,' said Maud, as she finished tending to the wounds and then pulled down the big man's sleeve to cover the tattoo. 'What would have happened to Daphne and the children if you had killed him?'

Maud saw Harry stare down at the sheet on his bed. He had no answer for that. Then just as he was about to speak the ward doors burst open again as the orderlies almost ran in with their stretcher. A thin man lay there screaming his head off, clearly in absolute agony and clutching his belly.

'Up to the top of the ward,' instructed Sister Law, who had appeared from nowhere. 'He needs to see the surgeon straight away.'

The men swiftly found an empty bed with the sheets drawn back.

'Nurse Linklater,' shouted Sister, 'this is your chance. If Mr Jones is taking this man to theatre, you can go in there with them.'

Maud saw the hostile look on Nancy's face when she heard Sister's direction but it only made her more determined than ever to make full use of this opportunity. And so with a glance back to Harry, who gave her a small salute, she made her way up the ward, quickly returning her equipment to the sluice, and arriving at the bed of the new admission just in time for the man to lean over the side of the bed and vomit all over the floor.

Then a door that Maud had never even noticed before at the top of the ward sprung open and a tall man with a long face came through, straight to the bed.

'Right,' said the man, deftly stepping around the pool of vomit and signalling to one of the orderlies to clean it up before moving to the side of the bed and trying to pull up the man's shirt. But with the patient's knees up to his chest it was impossible.

'Sister,' called the tall man, and Maud watched carefully as her supervisor spoke to the patient in the gentle voice that Maud now knew she used sometimes.

'Now, sir,' she said, 'I know that you are in terrible pain but we need you to try to straighten your legs for just a minute so that the doctor can have a look at you. Can you do that?'

It took a moment for the man to respond but then Maud saw him make what looked like a huge effort to push his legs down straight and he lay there for just a few seconds, his face contorted with pain whilst Mr Jones pressed on his belly in a few places. Sister gestured to Maud to hold the patient's hand and she immediately moved to the side of the bed. He was squeezing her hand so tight that it was hurting, but she stood firm and never flinched. Maud stood almost holding her breath until Mr Jones was finished and he straightened up from the bed. The man instantly drew his knees right up again to his chest and rolled on to his side groaning with pain.

Mr Jones looked across the bed to Sister Law, grimly. 'I believe you're thinking what I'm thinking,' he said to her. Sister nodded and then Mr Jones said, 'An abscess of the appendix.'

Sister Law nodded again and Maud thought she caught the inkling of a sorrowful look on her face.

'Almost certainly,' continued Mr Jones. 'Acute pain in the abdomen, centred on the lower right quadrant, he is vomiting, his breath is foetid and he has pallor of his skin. This man almost certainly has an abscess that might have already ruptured.'

Maud saw the terrified look on the man's face and took hold of his hand again.

'But if we are in time,' said Sister Law placing a hand on the man's shoulder, 'we might just be able to drain it, cut out the inflamed appendix and save his life.'

Maud saw the orderlies standing ready; they hadn't even removed the stretcher from under the man. They seemed to have known exactly what would be required.

'Right,' said the surgeon, 'take him straight through to theatre. Let's see what we can do.'

Maud thought that the poor man looked like he was going to expire anyway with the pain and the shock at what had just been said over him. But she had no more time to think. Sister muttered into her ear, telling her to go in with them, observe everything and do anything that was instructed.

Maud felt her heart racing — she wasn't sure if it was from terror or the thrill of being asked to help — but in she went with the whole party and as the door swung to on the orderlies after they'd left the patient on a high wooden table in the centre of the room, she knew that this was a huge opportunity for her. She would sink or swim.

The poor patient — she didn't even know his

name — was still screaming and drawing his knees up to his belly in pain. Her heart went out to him but she had seen so much pain on the wards in her few weeks at the hospital that she knew that the kind of agony that he was in could not be treated with anything that she had seen so far. It was pure pain, so deep inside the body and so unrelenting. It was terrifying.

Her heart was still racing so she took a few deep breaths to try to steady herself and make sure she took everything in. Mr Jones was over at the sink scrubbing and washing his hands with plenty of soap, and another man had quietly slipped into theatre, a slim man with dark hair, bright shining eyes and a quickness about him. Maud had never seen him before. He was at the head of the table and he had opened a bottle of something and was putting some drops of it on to a wad of lint. And there was a nurse wearing the same uniform as Sister but with a full bib apron. She was arranging knives and instruments on to a small table and then she placed a bucket and an enamel bowl on the floor. Then the surgeon looked round from the sink and nodded to the other man. He went over to the window and opened it, saying something about letting in some more light and some air.

'First things first,' said the nurse to Maud. 'Go to the sink and wash your hands with plenty of soap.'

'Quite right, quite right, Sister. Unlike many, we here at the Liverpool Royal are devotees of Dr Joseph Lister and his new ideas,' said Mr Jones as Maud went straight to the sink and

143

rolled up her sleeves, scrubbing at her hands as the sound of the patient screaming behind her seemed to fill her whole body. When she turned and walked back she felt again the shock of seeing the man on the table in such pain and she went to him and grabbed his hand, doing her best to try to soothe him.

Maud was fascinated by what happened next. The man holding the lint with the drops came to the other side of the table and spoke soothingly as he applied the lint over the nose and mouth of the screaming patient. Within seconds there was silence in the theatre. The man was knocked out cold or dead. Maud really wasn't sure which, and given the colour of him it could have been either.

Maud instinctively moved closer to the table to get a better look, and the doctor smiled at her, noticing her interest.

'Never seen it before?' he said.

'No,' she said, still amazed.

'It's chloroform,' he said. 'We use it to put the patients to sleep so the surgeon can operate. It's an anaesthetic.'

An-aes-thetic, repeated Maud in her head, desperately wanting to remember the name of something so incredible.

'We have to be careful, though,' said the doctor. 'If we give too much we can kill them; if we give too little, the blighters wake up.'

Maud nodded, taking it all in eagerly.

She glanced over to Mr Jones, who had taken the opportunity to have a quick smoke by the open window. She saw him turn and then

144

extinguish the remains before slipping it into his pocket. Then he cleared his throat and looked straight at the man with the anaesthetic. 'Are we all set, Dr McKendrick?'

'We're ready,' said the man, glancing up from the patient for just a moment.

Mr Jones then strode over to the theatre table and gestured for the nurse to help him move the patient fully on to his back with his arms and legs straight. Once he was satisfied with the patient's position he took up a knife from where they had been laid out on the small table and without any hesitation he cut through the skin of the man's belly.

'Abdominal incision,' he announced, and the nurse took small pieces of lint in her hand and dabbed at the wound. Maud could see that her hands were immediately covered in blood. It made her legs feel a bit weak to see it but she felt that she wasn't going to wobble.

'Next layer,' said Mr Jones, cutting again, and then Sister dabbed some more, throwing the pieces of lint soaked with blood into the bucket on the floor.

'And the next,' said the surgeon, cutting again, and there was more bleeding and more swabs going into the bucket. All the time the nurse's and the surgeon's bare hands became covered with more and more blood.

Then the surgeon pulled open the wound and asked Sister to hold it at one side so he could have a good look inside. He put his hand in and fished about a bit and that's when Maud did start to feel a bit dizzy, seeing the man with his

145

hand inside someone's body. But she took some deep breaths and managed to stay upright.

'Ah, there it is,' said Mr Jones. 'There it is, look,' he said, indicating for Maud to come closer.

She peered inside the hole in the man's body and saw some red, angry, swollen mass that looked like it was full of pus.

'It's as we thought,' said the surgeon, 'and if I can drain off the pus, I will try to remove the appendix and then our man might just stand a chance.'

To Maud's horror the patient gave a groan at that moment and started to shift a little on the table. It looked like he was waking up. Dr McKendrick at the head of the table was straight there with the dropper, immediately putting a few more drops of the liquid, the chloroform, on to the lint and then checking very closely on his patient's condition. All those gathered in theatre were waiting for the patient to settle but not until Dr McKendrick had nodded to Mr Jones were they able to proceed.

Maud was in awe of the man with the chloroform. Without his skill and his careful attention none of this would be able to happen. She had never been so captured by anything before and this whole experience felt like a revelation.

Working swiftly, Mr Jones placed his hands back in the wound. Maud couldn't see what he was doing but within moments he was using lumps of gauze as he soaked up and mopped out the man's insides.

Maud could see that it wasn't just blood coming out. It was yellowish fluid and what looked like yellow pus. Then Mr Jones looked very intently inside the wound for a few moments before going back in with the knife and immediately bringing out a piece of blackened gut with his hand. Sister quickly took it from him with a swab and placed it in a basin. 'Suture,' called the surgeon, and Sister was already handing it to him. Then he called for a suture again and he was, at last, sewing up the wound.

Maud didn't realize how still she had been and how caught up she was in what was going on until it was all over and the nurse was applying a dressing to the wound. Maud watched avidly.

'She did well, our new nurse, didn't she, McKendrick?' said Mr Jones. 'Most of the probationers and even some of the medical students hit the deck on their first time in theatre. You did well,' he reitereated to Maud, giving her a warm smile.

'You did very well,' added McKendrick more quietly, and Maud noted how refined his accent was.

'Thank you both. I am so grateful for the opportunity to work with you in here,' she said, 'but I have a great deal to learn.'

'Haven't we all?' smiled McKendrick, and then his attention shot back to his patient as the man began to groan and to move a little.

'I will speak to Sister Law,' said Mr Jones. 'I will ask her to send you in again, as often as she

147

can spare you. I think you have the makings of a fine theatre nurse.'

Maud couldn't believe what had just happened and she was thrilled at what Mr Jones had said.

'I would like that very much,' she said eagerly, smiling her thanks to the surgeon, but he was already going out through the door back on to the ward.

When she was back out through the door again herself she realized that it was way past the end of her shift. She had lost all track of time. Sister Law told her to get herself off the ward straight away and she must have agreed to that because it felt like she only started to come back to reality when she was out in the open air walking the short distance back to the Nurses' Home.

She remembered the whole sequence of the procedure in theatre and it was still playing in her head as she made her way home. Even small details of what McKendrick had told her about the chloroform and what to watch out for: the colour of the patient's skin and any blueness of the fingertips. It felt like it was ingrained on her mind and might well stay there for ever.

As Maud came in through the now familiar door of the Nurses' Home she could hear the sounds of their evening meal in the dining room so she headed in that direction. As she entered the room she saw Nancy look up immediately and continue to stare with dead eyes as she crossed the room. Maud also saw Alice glance up as she sat pale and silent with Nancy's little

148

group of nurses, and the pain on her face made her stomach tighten. She started to go over to Alice — she needed to sort things out — but as soon as Alice spotted her she got up from the table and left the room.

Maud's heart sank and she suddenly felt the tiredness from all the events of the day starting to catch up with her. She knew that she would have to find a way to speak to Alice but she also knew that she must leave it for now. She didn't have the strength, she needed to eat and she needed to get some sleep.

Seeing Eddy's smiling face beckoning her from another table, she went over, grateful in the knowledge that she could let Eddy talk and talk, the words would flow over and around her and there would be no need at all to make any response.

8

'No training is of any use, unless one can
learn 1) to feel, and 2) to think things
out for oneself.'

Florence Nightingale

'Maud, Maud,' said a voice in a loud whisper
and then someone was shaking her arm.

'Maud, wake up.'

'What? Is it time?' said Maud, not knowing
where she was.

Opening her eyes she saw Eddy's concerned
face looking down at her. Not used to seeing
anything but a smile on Eddy's face she was
instantly worried, even in her sleepy state.

'What's wrong?' she said. 'What's going on?'

'Shhh,' said Eddy.

Even stranger, thought Maud. Eddy doesn't
usually even think to be quiet.

'It's . . . ' said Eddy, pointing to the dividing
wall between their rooms, 'and Nnn,' she said,
pointing to Maud's door and across the gallery.

'What?' said Maud as quietly as she could.

Then Eddy whispered, 'It's Alice. I heard her
crying on and off all night and I think it's
something to do with . . . ' She pointed in the
direction of Nancy's room.

Of course, thought Maud, of course that's
what it was.

'Ah, right,' she whispered. 'I need to speak to Alice somewhere private. She won't see me, she won't speak to me. You need to bring her, but where can we go?'

Eddy thought for a moment then whispered, 'The back yard is the best place, where they keep the coal. I'll take her there after breakfast. Nancy always goes back up to her room to primp and preen before she leaves for the ward, so she won't be watching. So when you see us go, you follow, all right? There's a back gate so you can go straight out to the hospital from there.'

Maud nodded and gave Eddy's hand a squeeze.

Breakfast seemed to go on for ever that morning and whilst Eddy tucked into her fried egg and extra bread, Maud was struggling to eat anything at all. Maud hated this atmosphere. The sooner she could get things straight with Alice, the better.

As Eddy wiped the egg yolk up off her plate with a piece of bread Maud was beginning to think that she might well have forgotten all that they'd said in her room that morning. But it was almost remarkable in the way that Eddy reacted as soon as Nancy slipped away from the table. She must have been sensing exactly what was happening the whole time. The moment Nancy was gone she was up out of her seat and across to Alice with the remains of the bread in her hand. Maud watched as Eddy spoke to Alice and they both kept glancing in her direction and then Alice looked at her for a longer time and Maud's heart tightened when she saw how unhappy she was. Then Eddy said something else and, with relief, Maud saw Alice give a single nod of her head and get up from the table to follow Eddy towards the door at the far side of the room.

When Maud opened the door to the yard she found Alice standing with her back to her, facing the wall.

'I'll leave you to it,' said Eddy, slipping by and closing the door behind her, the piece of bread still in her hand.

Maud waited for a moment to see if Alice turned round but she was showing no sign and Maud could see that her shoulders were held very square.

'Look, Alice,' she said at last, to Alice's back, 'please turn round so that I can speak to you properly.'

But Alice just sighed and continued to look at the wall.

'All right then,' said Maud, 'I'll just talk to you like this then. Look, I have an idea about what must have happened for you to be like this with me all of a sudden.' Not sensing any reaction from Alice and seeing her shoulders were still held square, Maud had no choice but to continue. 'I think Nancy knows about the baby and I think that you've assumed that I am the one that must have told her.'

Alice still didn't speak.

'Alice, please, you have to listen, you have to believe me. If Nancy has found out about the baby then it has nothing — nothing — to do with me. I promise. I would never tell anyone, least of all her.'

Alice still stood with her back turned.

'Look, if you don't believe me then that's that, there's nothing I can say or do. But Alice, please, *think* about it. Why would I tell her? You are my friend and I promised to keep your secret.'

'Well, how would Nancy know then?' said Alice, turning to face her at last and folding her arms across her chest. 'You are the only one that I've told.'

'I have no idea,' said Maud, looking her straight in the eye, 'but you have to believe me. I did not tell her.'

Alice bowed her head for a moment and didn't speak.

'Maybe she noticed something about you; maybe she guessed. Think back over the last couple of days — could she have seen anything that might have given her a clue?'

'Not that I know of,' said Alice quietly, then lifted her head with a look of realization in her eyes. 'But there was the fried egg thing yesterday morning — that could have been it I suppose. I can stand all the smells on the ward — they never seem to bother me — but the smell of a fried egg first thing in the morning can sometimes really turn my stomach. Well, the girl opposite me had one and instantly I started to heave inside and I had to leave the table. I always sit next to Nance on that table. Sometimes I want to sit next to you and Eddy on the other table but she always looks up when I come into the room and pats the seat next to her. It's like she draws me to her every time. I didn't really think anything of it at the time. I mean I've got so used to feeling sick all the time, I just jumped up and went straight up the stairs to my room.'

'That could have been it, it really could. Because, you have to believe me, Alice, I have not told anyone, not even Eddy,' said Maud.

Alice stood silent again for what felt like a painfully long time, until Maud heard her speaking very quietly. 'I believe you, Maud. I believe you didn't say anything to Nancy. Sorry about that.'

Maud let out a sigh of relief. 'You don't need to be sorry,' she said. 'I'm just glad you believe me. And that we are friends again. That's all that matters.'

Alice lifted her head and gave her a small smile. 'We are friends, Maud. I think you are my best friend ever. And I am so sorry, I should have realized that it wouldn't be you. I should have known straight away.'

'Look, Alice, please don't worry about any of that. We are friends and that's all that matters.'

'Thank you, thank you,' said Alice, 'I don't know what I'd do without you. I've been so worried because Nancy started saying things like, 'Well, you know they'll find out, you know you'll have to leave,' and all that kind of thing, and it made me panic. I've got nowhere else to go, Maud, nowhere. I can't tell my family, I can't go home, and Jamie, the father of the baby, well, I really like him, Maud, and we've been friends from childhood, but you remember I told you he's gone far away? He's in Australia. And you know what makes me really mad as well? We only did it once, just once, on the night before he left.

154

And look at what happened!'

Maud stood quiet, not knowing what to say for the best. But seeing her friend looking so desperate, she knew that she would have to do something other than commiserate. She had to try to lift the mood somehow.

So she reached for Alice's hand, took a deep breath and brought her voice up a notch, 'Australia, hey, Australia. Did you not have any other childhood friends who were just nipping back to Ireland or going on a trip to France or even America? But *Australia*! You know how to pick 'em, Alice Sampson, you certainly do!'

Alice looked up and started to smile with the tears still in her eyes. Maud caught the smile and expanded it with her own.

'Look, Alice, I have no idea what we are going to do about your situation yet but I will help you in any way I can. You've got me working with you on this. As for Nancy, well, I just want to say one thing: do not trust her. Tell her you don't want to talk about the baby and if she comes back to you with anything else or starts talking about people finding out, you come straight to me, you hear?'

'Yes,' said Alice, 'I will.'

'Another thing,' said Maud. 'I didn't feel that I could talk to you about this when we first met, but, well, do you want to keep the baby? I mean, I have no idea what women can do in your situation but have you any idea?'

'I've not been able to think straight,' wailed Alice. 'And at first when my courses didn't come and I began to know what had happened I felt absolutely sure that I wanted it. It was his baby and I could still feel his kisses on my lips and his breath on my skin. But now, now that he's gone, he feels long gone, and I'm trying to do my work here, and I love the work, but I'm so tired all the time and I'm puking in the sluice, and once I had to be sick in my hands. And then Sister saw me with it in my hands and I had to tell her that I'd caught it for a patient when I saw that they were going to be sick, and Sister said, 'My goodness, Nurse Sampson, you have amazed me. I would never have thought it from your performance to date, but you have the makings of a nurse after all. I've never seen any nurse do that for a patient before ever,' and then she said I might one day make an excellent nurse . . . '

'Sorry, Alice,' said Maud, starting to giggle. 'Sorry, I just can't help laughing. It's just that I can see Sister Law's face, sorry . . . ' Then Alice began to giggle as well, and she tried to pull a stern face to look like Sister but she couldn't stop giggling. Maud put a hand on Alice's arm and managed to sober up. 'But seriously, Alice, things must have been so difficult for you all these weeks and I can understand how confused you must feel about the baby. How many months are you, do you know?'

'Well, I must be about three months gone by now. And I really don't know what I want any more, Maud. I haven't felt it move yet. I don't know when that happens but I think as soon as it does then that'll be it, I will have to keep it. But how can I keep it? I know that they won't let me have it at home. We live in a small town in the countryside over thirty miles from Liverpool.

Everyone would know and it would bring too much shame on my family. And I'm terrified, Maud, terrified, not just about what I'll do about here and the work, but two women from my town have died already this year giving birth. What if I'm going to be the third?'

'Don't talk like that,' said Maud firmly. 'Yes, it's a risk that every woman takes, even those who've birthed before, but you have to try to manage the fear, Alice, and try to think that it won't happen to you or your baby.'

'It's not easy,' said Alice.

'I'd like to say I know,' said Maud, 'but I've never been in your situation and a spinster like me probably never will be, so I really have no idea how you must feel. But like I said, I will help you in any way that I can. Just come to me any time. Always talk to me, Alice. I can't stand it if you stop talking to me.'

'Thanks, Maud,' said Alice, reaching out a hand to her. 'You really are a good friend, the best.'

Maud just gave her a smile and then said, 'Right, come on then, we can't stand in the coal yard for the rest of the day. We'd best get off to the ward or we'll be even later than Eddy.'

'Does Eddy know?' said Alice, her eyes wide.

'No,' said Maud. 'All she knows is that you were crying on and off last night and you weren't speaking to me. She knows nothing else, as far as I'm aware, but if Nancy's guessed then it's possible Eddy will have done, too. Anyway, it's up to you if and when we tell her.'

'All right, thanks,' said Alice. 'I think I will tell

her but I don't want to just yet.'

'That's fine,' said Maud. 'And for now at least she's working on another ward so she won't see you making a bowl out of your hands and puking into it.'

'That's true,' said Alice, starting to giggle again. 'The things you have to do, honestly.'

★ ★ ★

They arrived on the ward with seconds to spare. Maud could see the group of probationers around Sister Law at the top of the ward as they gathered, as always, before they commenced the morning's work. They were in luck it seemed: Sister was speaking directly to another probationer and hadn't yet done the head count to make sure that they were all there. Maud saw Nancy glance round just as she and Alice slipped in at the back of the group. She couldn't tell what Nancy was thinking but that one glance had made her feel very protective of Alice and she felt her body tighten and her right hand ball into a fist. She smiled to herself: she felt like she could be turning into one of those bare-knuckle fighters just like Harry Donahue, whom she'd glimpsed sitting up in his bed as she'd flown in through the ward door.

As the group dispersed, Sister Law gestured to Maud to come forward. 'Nurse Linklater,' she said, and Maud thought, uh-oh, she has seen me after all. But then Sister Law said, 'Mr Jones told me how well you did in theatre yesterday and he has requested that you are allowed to observe

158

again, as often as we can spare you.'

'Thank you, I would like that very much,' said Maud, delighted but instantly checking to make sure that Nancy wasn't in earshot. 'And the man with the appendix, how is he doing?'

'Ah, sadly,' said Sister, 'he died during the night. It's often the way with those cases. If they come in too late there is very little chance that they will survive.'

'But he seemed all right after the surgery,' said Maud, struggling to believe that there could have been such a change.

'Yes,' said Sister, 'but if the poison has already entered the bloodstream then it affects the whole system and within hours the patient is overwhelmed and there is nothing more that can be done. We lose many, many patients with the same thing year after year.'

'I see,' said Maud, bleakly, wishing there was more she could have done for the poor man. Aware, too, of how much she had to learn about everything.

'Now, Nurse Linklater, there is no more that could have been done for the man. Going to theatre was the only option and very few survive an appendectomy . . . You go with Nurse Sellers to the bottom of the ward. Nurse Sampson can work up at this end. The man you attended yesterday has already been discharged but Harry Donahue is still waiting to see the doctor. His left hand is very swollen. Once he is checked he will be going on his way also. Nurse Sellers is best placed to assess him; she seems to have taken a special interest in that particular patient.

159

I need you to go directly to Mr Clifford in the opposite bed. He hasn't been able to pass urine all night and he needs urgent assessment. Report back to me.'

Maud walked quickly down the ward. She could see straight away that Mr Clifford was thrashing around and looking very uncomfortable.

She grasped his hand and started to speak gently to him. 'Tell me — '

But the words were hardly out of her mouth before he was crying out for a urinal. The poor man looked desperate so she rushed to get him one as quickly as she could. By the time she got back his face was bright red and he was breaking out into a sweat.

'Thanks, Nurse,' he said, grabbing the urinal. 'I've been trying to pee all night but nothing will come.'

She left him with the urinal but could soon see by the effort on his face that there was nothing doing and he seemed to have a real problem. Glancing up the ward, Maud could see that Sister was busy but she thought it likely that she would need to report back to her very soon.

Turning back to the man she said gently, 'Is there anything I can do to help?'

'Leave me be, Nurse,' he almost shouted. 'There is nothing that will help me. I'm in agony here.' And then he started crying, tears of pain and frustration running down his face. She asked if she could see what he had managed in the urinal and he thrust it at her from under the bedclothes. There was just one small drop of very dark urine in the bottom, a tiny amount. No wonder the man was in agony.

Right, thought Maud, this is no good. I need to report back to Sister immediately.

'What is it, Nurse Linklater?' said Sister, back to her usual snappiness and seeming to have forgotten her previous instruction to Maud amidst the busy morning ward. 'Out with it,' she ordered when Maud seemed stuck for words.

'It's just that Mr Clifford is still unable to pass urine. He seems to be in a great deal of pain and he's getting distressed.'

'Why didn't you say so?' said Sister. 'Right, yes, I'll be down there directly, Nurse Linklater, directly. You go back to him.'

And she was true to her word, arriving at the man's bed soon after Maud with Mr Jones in tow.

'Lie on your back, flat on your back,' said Mr Jones calmly to the patient. Then he turned briefly to Sister Law. 'So, he was admitted yesterday and he had leeches applied to the perineum overnight, is that correct?'

'Yes,' said Sister. 'He has been in a great deal of pain and we have given him numerous doses of laudanum but to no avail.'

Mr Jones nodded and then he leant over the bed and pressed on the man's belly. Mr Clifford screamed out in pain but Mr Jones did not desist. 'Lie still,' he said and then he pressed again. The man screamed again.

'The bladder is very distended. It feels as though it might be about to rupture,' said Mr Jones. Maud saw the look of horror on the patient's face and reached down to hold his hand.

'There must be some obstruction to the bladder neck. It could be a large bladder stone or a soft growth of some kind. We need to remove the obstruction as soon as we can.'

Maud squeezed the man's hand tighter as she saw his face crease with fear and pain.

'Take him straight to theatre,' said Mr Jones. 'I will see what I can do.'

'You will be all right, we're going to look after you,' soothed Maud. The poor man clung on to her hand like his life depended on it and all she could do was keep by him and pray that everything would be all right.

'You stay with the patient,' said Sister Law, 'and go into theatre with him.'

'Yes, Sister,' said Maud, feeling that even if she hadn't been given official permission she would have found some way to keep by his side.

The orderlies were called, the man was moved on to the stretcher and then up the ward and in through the door of the theatre. Maud caught her breath as she saw the high wooden table in the centre of the room. She stood back a little as the orderlies placed the man on the table and then she moved in by the side of him, grabbing his hand as the waves of pain kept hitting him, a spiral of pain that seemed to have no end. He was squeezing her hand so tight that she was almost crying out herself sometimes, but she stood firm beside him. She found herself looking around, impatient to see Dr McKendrick. When would he come and perform his magic with the drops? He needed to come soon.

Mr Jones was over at the sink, scrubbing his hands, Sister was laying out instruments and Maud heard the clank of the bucket and the enamel bowl on the floor, but there was no chloroform yet. Maud just wanted the man to be knocked out, to not be in pain any more. She felt she couldn't wait.

And then she heard the door open and with a wave of relief she saw Dr McKendrick coming through with a determined look on his face as he immediately started asking questions about the patient.

'What do we have here, Jones?'

The surgeon filled him in on the man's history. Maud was too impatient to listen; she just wanted the conversation to be over and then McKendrick could put her patient to sleep and out of his pain.

Then she smelt the drops of chloroform as they came out of the bottle and she felt her whole body relax a little, knowing that the man would soon be out of his agony. Or maybe it was the whiff of the chloroform itself that relaxed her. She did like the smell of it.

Within moments Dr McKendrick had spoken to the patient and then put the lint over his nose and mouth, and in seconds there was quiet in the theatre. The man wasn't completely asleep, he was still groaning a little, but at least he was no longer screaming out in pain. And then with one or two more drops of chloroform, Maud could see that the patient was sound asleep and just for a few seconds there was a ringing silence in the theatre.

Maud went straight over to the sink to wash her hands as Mr Jones stood drying his own and silently nodding approval of his new recruit.

'Right then,' said the surgeon, waiting for Maud to finish at the sink, 'let's have a look at this fine fellow.'

Maud almost held her breath as the surgeon moved towards the theatre table, stopping on his way, as before, to open up the window and let some air in. Then as he stood over the patient Maud braced herself for the sight of an abdominal incision, like last time. But this time the surgeon did not take up the knife. Instead, he lifted the man's shirt. 'Let's have a feel at his belly now that he is relaxed,' he said, placing his hand on the man's abdomen. Maud noted to herself how long his fingers were and she saw how carefully he pressed around all areas, sometimes with quite firm pressure.

At last Mr Jones said, 'Right, yes, his bladder is distended above the umbilicus . . . that's the belly button,' he said, looking across at Maud. 'It is difficult to tell but there is definitely an obstruction to the urethra . . . that's the tube that connects the bladder to the end of the penis,' he said, looking at Maud again. She felt a red flush start on her neck at the mention of a man's anatomy, but she was so interested in what might happen and how they might be able to help the man that she didn't feel embarrassed.

Mr Jones pulled the sheet further down and picked up the man's penis, looking closely at it, scrutinizing it.

164

Oh dear, thought Maud, this might be a step too far.

'Right, no obvious sign of any venereal disease, so most likely the obstruction is a stone, or it could be some growth in the bladder. There is only one way to find out. Sister, do you have a probe?'

'Yes,' said Sister, handing him a long, thin metal tube.

Taking the man's penis in one hand and the probe in the other, Mr Jones slid the tube up what Maud now knew was the urethra.

'Right, everyone,' said the surgeon, 'complete silence.'

So they all stood holding their breath, and there was complete silence in the theatre, apart from the buzzing of a single fly that must have come in through the open window.

Maud watched Mr Jones move the metal tube gently in and out and she could hear a faint chinking sound, like the distant sound of a teaspoon on a china cup . . . chink, chink, chink.

'It's a stone,' said the surgeon, breaking into a smile. 'It's quite a size, but we should be able to have a go at it.'

Then withdrawing the metal tube he asked Sister for 'the box' and she lifted a large wooden cask up off the floor and opened it on a side table. Maud glanced in: it contained a collection of what looked like instruments of torture.

Mr Jones selected one of the instruments and brandished it in front of Maud's face. 'This wonderful instrument is a lithotrite. It has been designed to crush up the stones in the bladder.

165

Clever thing. It grasps the stone and then we can use it as a drill. This bit here,' he said, touching the end of the metal instrument, 'this ingenious device drills into the bladder stone and breaks it up, and if we can break it up fine enough then it can be expelled from the body when our man here passes urine.' Mr Jones spent a few moments gazing almost lovingly at the instrument and then he said, 'This piece of metal has revolutionized the treatment of bladder stones and the outcome for the patient. Many patients used to die when we had to cut into 'em to get the stones out.'

Maud could only hope that he was right and that the new instrument would produce the miracle that her patient needed.

'We used to have to cut them open and fish around to get the stones out; now we just slide the lithotrite up the urethra and crush them up. So much better for the patients. They used to haemorrhage or die from poison to the blood, and before anaesthetics the procedure was very painful.'

Maud was relieved when she saw Mr Jones stop brandishing the instrument and use it in the way that he had described. It took some time before he was satisfied that the stone had been broken up into small enough pieces to be passed out of the bladder and at one stage there was a gush of dark brown urine that showed that at least now Mr Clifford could pass water. Maud felt so relieved for the man her legs momentarily went weak.

'Are you all right?' said Sister as Mr Jones

withdrew the prized instrument.

'Yes,' said Maud firmly, pulling herself together and watching intently as the surgeon finished his work, taking it all in.

'Right, Nurse Linklater,' said Mr Jones, 'you have impressed me and Sister again very much. I know you feel like you aren't *doing* anything in here just yet — I know what you nurses are like — but let me tell you, the foundations of a good theatre nurse are her powers of observation and her ability to keep absolutely still.'

Maud saw Sister smile and nod, and she began to feel a glow of satisfaction.

'For example,' said the surgeon, leaning over the patient on the table towards her, 'Sister Law sent in one of your compatriots the other week, the blonde one who always looks neat. A disaster. She didn't seem to understand that one needs to watch carefully to learn in here and that you can't just take over and assist. Sister, here, was up in a spin and I needed a stiff drink as soon as I was out through those doors. Granted the woman might be suited to other branches of nursing but you, my dear, seem to have the makings of this.'

★   ★   ★

Maud was still glowing when she emerged from the theatre with the orderlies as they carried Mr Clifford back to his bed. She couldn't help but smile, but then she saw Nancy stop and turn, just for a moment, with such a look of pure hatred burning in her eyes that it almost made

167

her feel sorry for the woman.

She knew that it was best to completely ignore Nancy, though she couldn't help but feel her stomach tighten just a little. When, however, she was busy settling her patient in bed and she could see how comfortable he was, that moment with Nancy was forgotten. He was still quite sleepy and seemed slurred in his speech but she could tell how much easier he looked straight away. She saw him reach down and press his belly, and then he smiled because even when pressure was applied there was still no pain.

'Right, Nurse Linklater,' said Sister Law, appearing by Mr Clifford's bed, 'we need to make sure that he has plenty to drink. Go to the kitchen and get him some beer or some boiled water and get him to drink as much as he can. That way we'll flush out the remains of the stone. Make sure you leave a drink by him at all times. This is very important to the patient's recovery.'

'Yes, Sister,' said Maud, quick to follow her instructions. And so pleased to have been part of the whole thing and to be able to see the transformation of the man. He looked like a different person.

Whilst she'd been away in theatre Maud had forgotten about everything else: about Alice and her worries, and Nancy and . . . oh yes, the man in the opposite bed, Harry Donahue. Looking over there now she saw the bed was empty. He must have gone, she thought. But as she moved up the ward she was startled to see him walking in the opposite direction with a bit of a swagger.

She tried not to look at him, to keep her eyes to the ground, but she just couldn't stop herself. He was smiling at her.

'You're back,' he said as they met half-way.

'Yes,' she said, puzzled by his familiarity: had he mistaken her for someone else?

'It's Maud, isn't it?'

'Nurse Linklater,' said Maud immediately.

'Well, Nurse Linklater,' Harry said, 'I asked your friend, that lovely girl . . . what's her name?'

Here we go, thought Maud.

'Alice, she said her name was Alice. I asked her where you'd gone. I wanted to say thank you for what you did for me yesterday. And she said you were in theatre with that fella. Poor bugger was awake and in agony all night long and now look at him. It's like a bloody miracle. It is for sure.'

Maud was shocked by the direct way he spoke to her and even more so that he had taken the time to find out her name. What with all the excitement of the theatre and not having had any breakfast and now this — this ridiculous man with his twinkling eyes looking straight at her — she started to feel a bit swimmy in the head and she had to take a firm grip of herself there and then.

She took a deep breath and said briskly, 'Thank you, Mr Donahue. Just doing my job.' She made to move away but he grabbed her hand. She looked wildly around, expecting Sister Law or Nancy to come by at any moment and find him holding on to her hand in the middle of the ward. Such inappropriate behaviour. She tried to pull away.

'Now just a minute, Nurse Linklater,' Harry said, 'I want to say, you might just be doing your job, but I've seen how you do your job: your dedication to that man over there and the way you try not to show your feelings on your face but they come out through your eyes.' He was staring into her face now. 'Your eyes are like deep, warm pools.'

'Now that's enough,' Maud said, pulling her hand free and walking away before he could see the red flush on her cheeks.

'I'll be seeing you again, no doubt,' he said to her back as she retreated up the ward.

Maud continued to walk and pretended not to hear him. She continued to walk with her heart pounding and her face bright red. When she got to the sluice door she made a *humph* sound, saying to herself that she knew his type and that was how a man like him was with all women, even the plain ones like her. I can't let myself fall for the tricks of such a man, she thought, too handsome for his own good and with the gift of the gab. Then, shaking her head, she thought, well, anyway, I wouldn't stand a chance with someone like him, ever.

9

'Ward training is but half the training . . .
The other half consists in women being
trained in habits of order, cleanliness,
regularity and moral discipline.'

Florence Nightingale

Miss Merryweather had shown Maud where
the pigeonholes for nurses' mail were on the
first day and she had checked dutifully every
day, just in case there was a letter. Only once
had she had a note from Miss Fairchild and
nothing since, but she still checked each
morning and evening. She shared a pigeonhole
for the letter L with a Miss Lord and a
Miss Langtry. At least, theirs was the only
mail that she had seen. Miss Langtry seemed
to get a great many letters and sometimes a
postcard, whereas there had been only one
for Miss Lord, the same as for Maud. No
surprise really: who else but Miss Fairchild
would send her mail? With her mother and
grandmother both dead and gone, there was
no one else.

So when she saw a letter that day in the same
cream vellum envelope she knew at once who it
was from and she was right. It was a letter from
Miss Fairchild and, as before, it was about
Alfred.

Dear Maud,
Alfred is settled at the school and he has
started his lessons. He is enjoying them. I
have bought him some new clothes and he
looks very smart. I told him that you
would be visiting when you can. I know
that you are very busy and I hope that the
nursing is going well. Just to let you know
there is no need to worry, I will keep an
eye on things.

Kind Regards,
Constance Fairchild

Maud couldn't help but smile when she saw
the name. Even after all the years that she had
worked with Miss Fairchild she had never known
or thought to ask what her Christian name was,
but seeing the name now, she thought how
'Constance' sounded just right for Miss Fairchild. In the same way, she had always thought
that 'Maud' was just right for her. She was Maud
and that was that.

It was good to hear news of Alfred and she was
planning to go up there to see him as soon as she
could. She felt a niggle of guilt in the pit of her
stomach that she hadn't been able to go yet, but
at least Miss Fairchild — Constance — was
keeping an eye on him. She was just trying to
work out when would be the best time for her to
take a trip up to the school when she saw Alice
come in through the door of the Nurses' Home,
looking tearful and in a terrible rush.

Maud stuffed the letter in her pocket and

headed after her, just catching up as she was about to climb the stone stairs to the first-floor gallery.

'What's wrong?' she said, slightly out of breath.

Then Alice grabbed her and clung to her like a child, sobbing on her shoulder.

'Alice, Alice,' said Maud, 'look, just try to calm down and tell me what's wrong.'

But still Alice couldn't speak.

'I know you've been working all day with Nancy so I'm thinking that she's been saying something else to you,' said Maud quietly.

Alice nodded and continued to cry, her nose running. Maud produced a neatly folded linen handkerchief from her pocket and Alice took it to wipe her eyes and then her nose. Then she was able to speak but only in a whisper.

'I wanted to come down the ward to help you when we finished — it wasn't all that busy at the top end of the ward — but she started ranting on at me, saying that I preferred to work with you, saying that I wasn't a good friend and then she said that it was probably time that she told Sister Law about me, told her about the baby . . . Oh, Maud, I've been so worried all day and I couldn't come to you on the ward; she was watching. I don't know where she is now. Where is she?'

'Right,' said Maud, suddenly feeling absolutely furious, 'I don't know where she is but if she's up there in that room I will deal with her.'

'No, no,' Alice almost shouted, 'it will make things worse. Please, please, Maud, don't say anything to her,' she begged, bringing her voice right back to a whisper.

Seeing her fraught face, Maud took a deep breath and got a hold of herself, saying in a quieter voice, 'It's all right, I won't say anything. I won't do anything that you don't want me to do,' but all the time her heart was pounding and her right hand was balled into a fist. 'Come up to my room,' she said. 'We can't talk here.'

Alice nodded and then Maud led the way up the stairs. As she reached the top she couldn't be sure but she thought she saw the door to Nancy's room click shut ever so quietly and when she looked at the door she sensed the too-heavy silence that lay behind it. She didn't say anything to Alice; she didn't want to lay even more worry on her.

'No, let's go to my room,' said Alice, also glancing at Nancy's door.

Once they were behind the closed door of the room Alice collapsed on to the bed, lying flat on her back and staring up at the ceiling. Maud sat herself down at the bottom of the bed and waited, not saying anything, just giving Alice some time.

After a few minutes Alice sat up, swung her legs over the edge of the bed and said, 'I'll have to get this uniform off. It's getting so tight, I can't breathe.'

'All right,' said Maud, 'just do what you need to do.'

So Alice pulled the bodice of her uniform off and let it drop to the floor, unfastening the stays that held her tight before undoing the skirt of her uniform and slipping out of it, handing it to Maud, who got up to hang it straight so that it would be respectable for the next day.

Then Alice stood by the bed, just in her shift and her undergarments, running her hands over her belly and having a scratch under her breasts.

'Sorry,' she said, remembering how Maud was about seeing naked flesh, 'I always do this as soon as I get back from the wards. I just feel so confined in that uniform and it's getting so tight. This belly of mine is really starting to grow now,' she added, lifting up her shift to show Maud the full extent of it.

And then she started crying uncontrollably again. 'Look at it, Maud, just look at it. It's growing so fast, soon everybody is going to know. Everybody.'

'There, there,' said Maud, holding on to her friend's hand, a bit shocked herself to suddenly see a full expanse of bare belly and to see how big it was. 'But it looks beautiful. Yes, it's big and you know there's nothing in the world anyone can do to stop it growing, but, Alice, you look so fine.'

'It doesn't feel fine,' wailed Alice. 'What am I going to do?'

'Hush now,' said Maud, gently pulling Alice's shift back over her belly, 'Sit down on the bed and let's both have a think about things.'

So Alice sat on the bed and Maud snuggled up next to her, soothing her and stroking her arm until her friend had got back some control.

'I bet it's a relief to get those stays off,' said Maud at last.

'It is,' hiccuped Alice, and then she cradled her breasts one in each hand and said, 'These are so tight and sore all the time, honestly, they feel like they might just explode.'

'Poor you,' said Maud, putting an arm around her shoulders. 'Are you still being sick?'

'Only once a day now, so that's much better . . . but I don't know how much longer I can carry on like this. I just don't know what to do. I don't even know what there is that I might be able to do. I sometimes think I want to find out if I can do anything about the baby, if there is some way that I can make it all go away. But at other times I can't even think of that as a possibility. I'm in the middle of it all and if it wasn't for you I'd be on my own, absolutely all alone, with everything. What can I do?'

Maud sat thinking with her arm around her friend's shoulders, determined to sit there until she made the beginnings of an idea start to form in her head.

'We could go and see Stella,' she said at last.

'Stella?' said Alice, turning her face to Maud.

'The woman who visited that army veteran, do you remember? He was in the next bed to Alfred. You know, Stella: she was — she is — well, she works in a brothel.'

'Oh, that Stella,' said Alice. 'Does she? Oh, I didn't realize. I thought she just liked to dress in bright colours. Yes, she was nice, I liked her.'

'Well, she told me that I could go and see her if I needed to, about anything.'

'Really?' said Alice. 'Well, I don't think we have any other choice, do we? I'm completely stumped and there's nobody else that I can talk to. How can we find her?'

'She told me she lives on Lime Street, near the station. She said to ask anyone round there for Stella and Marie's place.'

'Mmm,' said Alice, lost in thought for a few moments. 'I don't fancy trailing round the streets of Liverpool looking for a brothel, but there might be another way. Why don't we tell Eddy about the baby and ask her for help? She knows all parts of the city, and I mean all. She could find Stella's place for us, I'm sure she could.'

'Yes,' said Maud, 'good idea.'

★ ★ ★

That evening the door of the Nurses' Home opened and Maud, Alice and Eddy filed out wearing their own clothes. All were dressed in sober colours. They could almost have been mistaken for a party of Sunday school teachers or young women heading for the convent if it hadn't been for the bright-red silk flower pinned to the large hat that Eddy was wearing. But Eddy had insisted that she wear the hat to lead the way, so they wouldn't lose her in the crowd, and it did make sense. However, both Maud and Alice knew that she always wore that hat anyway, a particular favourite, on her 'goings-out' into the city.

'Right,' said Eddy, 'follow me and try to keep up. I know, I know, I do walk fast but try not to lose me. Lime Street is busy. I've already made enquiries about the place we need to find and it might be difficult if you don't know exactly where it is. So stick with me and you can't go wrong.'

Maud and Alice followed that red silk flower on Eddy's hat through streets, past shops and carts and horses and stray dogs, threading their way through the people of Liverpool crowded into groups or walking alone: talking, shouting, laughing and sometimes crying. They followed along behind their friend, steadfast in her mission, dodging past all obstacles. Sometimes Maud had to push her way through so that they didn't get lost, and other times she was at risk of being distracted by a child in ragged clothes holding a hand out to beg. But they kept going.

Then, abruptly, the red flower stopped moving and Maud and Alice almost ploughed into the back of Eddy.

'I just need to get my bearings,' she said, raising her chin in an attempt to see over the heads of other pedestrians and almost sniffing the air.

Maud stood quietly looking around and checking for herself on their position in the city. It was easy: they were right outside the entrance to Lime Street Station and she could feel the buzz of excitement around her as people headed into the station. She almost wished that she was going there as well, with the prospect of travel to some unknown destination, and then she nearly got her wish as a clump of people moving together and in a rush to catch a train almost swept her along with them. Disentangling herself just in time, Maud straightened her skirt and

178

stood ready for further instruction but Eddy was still looking around, her eyes narrowed; she looked like she was on the brink of a decision.

Then, as the sounds of the clanking of metal wheels and the hoot of a train came out of the station, and a huge cloud of steam rose up into the air above Liverpool, Eddy gestured for them to move, shouting over her shoulder, 'Right, you two, this is the tricky bit. Stay close.' Then, walking at speed straight past the front of the station and a little way beyond, she turned right abruptly down a narrow alley.

Alice followed with Maud behind, and as Maud entered the alley she was surprised at how quiet it was. They were still so close to the main thoroughfare, but here was almost a secret passage, nestling up to the high walls of the railway station on one side and some red-brick buildings on the other. She would have liked to have taken a moment just to stand and listen to the muffled sounds of the station but Eddy was unrelenting as she kept up the pace. Already she and Alice were taking another turn into an even narrower alley and disappearing out of sight. Maud picked up her pace a little so that she wouldn't lose them, but as she turned the corner herself she saw that they had already stopped in front of a house. When she drew level Maud could see that the house had a newly painted blue door with an impressive letter box and a stone step scrubbed so clean that it was almost white. This wasn't what she had been expecting at all and she wondered if they had got the wrong property. But Eddy stood firm on the step

179

and rapped confidently on the door as Maud joined Alice standing in the alley.

In moments the door was opened by an older woman with dark-grey hair tied back with a ribbon. She appeared familiar in some way but Maud couldn't be sure. The woman looked at them without smiling, her bosoms filling out the top of a bright-blue gown. In that moment Eddy seemed to become transfixed and although she opened her mouth to speak no words came out.

'Yes?' said the woman, starting to scowl.

Maud stepped up beside Eddy at the door. 'Is this Stella and Marie's place? We're here to see Stella.'

The woman gave Maud a good going-over with her eyes and then said, 'Who should I say is asking?'

'Tell her it's Maud, the nurse from the Infirmary. She'll know who you mean.'

Then the woman turned her head and shouted over her shoulder, 'Stella, you have some visitors.'

'Thanks, Ma,' shouted Stella from the back somewhere, and then she was there at the door. 'Maud, you have come! Did you change your mind about that job after all?'

Maud felt that familiar flush on her neck but she completely ignored Stella's jokey remark and said, 'We need some advice.'

'Is it about Alfred, the boy on the ward?'

'No, no, Alfred's fine. He's settled now up at the school. It's something else.'

'Come in, come in,' said Stella, sensing that the matter was of a delicate nature. 'Let's get a brew of tea on and then see what we can do for you.'

Maud turned to Alice, who was still in the alley, looking down at her feet. 'Come on, Alice. It will be all right, I promise.'

Stella showed them into the first room off the hall as they came through the door. It was quite a large room with some women sitting on chairs or sprawling on settees. 'Just wait a minute in here,' said Stella, 'and I'll find us a private room.'

Instantly Maud felt uncomfortable and she chose to stand with Alice at the door.

'Sit down, sit down,' said the women, all of whom seemed to Maud to be in various states of undress.

'No, thank you,' said Maud, trying to smile and then pursing her lips.

'We're fine here,' said Alice, 'thank you.'

'Cheers,' said Eddy, who had quickly regained her composure and was now throwing herself down on to a purple velvet settee next to a woman wearing nothing but a loose-fitting shift.

'So . . . ' said Eddy, removing her hat and placing it on her lap and then turning to the woman next to her, 'hello. I'm Eddy. Pleased to meet you.'

'Pleased to meet you too,' said the woman, stretching out a slim arm to stroke one of the flowers on Eddy's hat. 'Nice hat.'

'Thank you,' said Eddy, clearly pleased that someone at last was able to appreciate her fashion sense. Maud stood stiffly by the door, envious of Eddy's easy way with people but also intrigued by the woman who sat next to her.

Maud had never seen any woman who had so much paint and powder on her face. It was like a work of art.

'How are you girls doing at the moment?' said Eddy, looking around the room and then running a hand over the soft, purple velvet of the settee.

'Oh, we're doing all right,' said one of them. 'We're lucky to have this place with Stella and Marie. They run a good, clean house and the work is very steady. So we're doing well, thanks for asking. Where are you lot from?'

'Oh, we're all nurses at the hospital — well, we're probationer nurses. We will be trained by next year.'

'Crikey,' said a woman with red hair, 'I wouldn't like your job. You must see all sorts.'

'We do, don't we?' Eddy said, turning to Maud and Alice, who were still standing straight-backed by the door. 'But we like that, don't we?'

Maud nodded, and Alice said, almost too loudly, 'We do, we do.'

Maud was just clearing her throat to speak when the woman with red hair got up from her seat and walked over to where they were stood by the door, putting her arm around Maud's shoulders. Maud felt her face start to flush and then she turned to the woman. She smelt lovely, some kind of perfume that Maud had never smelt before, and close up her skin looked so clear and so beautiful. And even though her lips were painted red they were soft and when she began to speak Maud couldn't take her eyes off them. She felt like she was being hypnotized.

'Look,' said the woman, 'I know you must be feeling a bit worried coming to this place, but remember, we are all women together, just like you and all the nurses and the thousands and thousands of other working women in this city. We all need to make a living.'

Maud bowed her head slightly, starting to feel ashamed that she felt so uncomfortable around the women, but it had been drilled into her so many times by so many people, the worst thing that can happen is that you will get mixed up with some man and then end up being disgraced and then out on the streets. A fallen woman. But these women seemed to be at ease with themselves and not desperate. In fact, they were nice, from what she could see.

'Don't worry,' said the woman, 'I can understand what you are thinking and you are right, there are some desperate cases out there on the streets: women who have no other choice. That's what people see and that's what ordinary women are fed as they grow up: you stay pure or else. But all I ask is that you look around here and then make your mind up. Try to get to know us a bit.'

'I already know Stella,' said Maud, smiling.

'There you go,' said the woman, giving Maud's shoulder a squeeze. 'You already know the boss's daughter, you're 'well in' here already.'

'Thank you,' said Maud, sensing the genuine warmth that came from the woman and wanting in her heart to make some connection with her,

183

but unable to find any other words to say.

'Tea up,' said Stella, reappearing at the door and almost bumping into Alice. Then seeing Eddy sprawling on one of the settees she said, 'I see you've made yourself right at home. I was going to offer a job to Maud but I think you might be a better candidate.'

Eddy smiled, grabbed her hat and jumped up, saying, 'It was nice to meet you all,' to the women, and then followed Maud and Alice, who had left the room straight away, close on the heels of Stella.

The room they were led into looked like a small dining room; it had a polished table and velvet drapes to the window. Maud was surprised at how clean and tidy it was. Stella gestured for them each to take a seat around the table where a tray of tea and what smelt like freshly baked biscuits stood. When they all had cups of tea in front of them she looked around the table at each of them in turn and then directly at Maud. It was time to speak.

'First,' said Maud, 'I need everyone here to swear to secrecy. None of this can go beyond these four walls.'

Stella nodded her understanding.

'Right,' said Maud, placing a hand on her friend's arm. 'We're here about Alice. She's with child — about four months, we think — and she has no idea if there is anything that can be done about it or what she should do.'

'I see,' said Stella, shifting her gaze to Alice, who slumped back in her chair and then, to Maud's horror, began to sob.

'Alice, Alice,' said Maud, 'I'm so sorry. We are just trying to help.'

'It's all right,' said Stella. 'Just let her cry if she needs to.' Then to Alice: 'I bet you've been keeping this secret for a long, long time.'

'Yes,' hiccuped Alice, tears streaming down her face.

'Well,' said Stella, 'if it's any help at all I've sat here with dozens of women in your situation. I take it there is no father of the baby on the scene?'

'No,' said Maud gently, when Alice couldn't reply.

'Well, as you can imagine, some of the women who sit here are in my line of business and often they have no idea who the father of the baby is anyway, never mind if he is on the scene or not. So you are very far from the only person to be in this situation. The thing is that most of those women who have sat in this very room — some of whom have gone on to have their babies and some of whom have not — the important thing is, they have all come through the experience . . . and, Alice, you will too.'

'But sometimes I think I want to get rid of it. I don't want it now, I just want it gone.'

'I can fully understand how you are feeling,' said Stella. 'Many of the women I've known have said exactly the same thing. But the truth is, yes, there are things that you can take — powders and pills, gin, hot baths — and then there are the women in the backstreets with their sharp needles. My girls have tried all of them over the years and what we have found is that mostly the pills and powders don't work. It's up to you, but please, please, think carefully before you visit the women with the needles because that is very dangerous indeed. Many women die that way; some of mine have died.'

Alice had stopped crying, just at the point when Maud fully expected that she would have cried even more. She seemed to be calming down and she had been really listening to what Stella had said.

'I see,' said Alice at last. 'It's very much as I thought then: there is little that I can do about it. I just can't stand the thought of somebody sticking a needle up inside me. I'm scared enough of the birthing as it is, but the thought of that is terrifying. I think I would die from shock, if nothing else. But how on earth can I have a baby? I have no family that will help me and I love my nursing. I don't want to have to give that up.'

'I know there are no easy answers. If it was safe to go to the women with their needles then that would be a different matter. It's all down to you making a choice — and you're right that there isn't much of a choice — but, as I say, I've known many women go through it and come out the other side. I mean you're not showing that much yet. You could carry on working for longer, for as long as you can, and then, well, if you want, we can always do with someone to help with the cleaning and tidying round here. If you wanted to come to us then we could provide you with food and shelter whilst the baby comes. We couldn't pay you but you could have board and lodging. We've delivered many a live one here in this very house. Some women keep their babies, some women don't. There is no way that you will know what you will want to do yet, no way. But let me say this to you, Alice. Even though this feels terrible right now, you have good friends around you and that means a great deal. And you know what? Over the years I've seen a surprising number of women go through all kinds of tragedies and I have seen them emerge victorious. We women are strong, Alice, we are very strong. We have to be.'

Maud had been almost holding her breath all the time that Stella was speaking to Alice. Now she had a warm glow running right through her body. She had never heard anyone speak like that before. It was inspiring. She took a deep breath and then reached for Alice's hand and gave it a squeeze. Alice turned to her and they both smiled.

Maud could see that Eddy had been listening too and, for once, she was sitting still and not interrupting. Then she piped up, 'And, Alice, if you come here to Stella's I could come and help too. I can't wait to be given the chance to deliver a baby. I would love to help.'

'See,' said Stella, 'there's help coming from all sides now. It will take time, but what you need to do is try to get a grip of your situation, accept it and get on with it. That's all I can say.'

'Thank you,' said Alice, standing up from her chair and reaching over to Stella. 'Thank you.'

'You are more than welcome,' said Stella. 'I said to Maud when I met her on the ward, if you need anything come to me. Who knows what we women have to deal with in life? And when I saw how Maud was on that ward, and what she was doing for that young lad who is no kin of hers, I thought how wonderful, how generous, and so I made the offer, expecting she might need some help with the boy or her love life.' Maud felt her face flush instantly. 'But it turned out to be you and your baby. And if we can help we will. Now let's have a look at you before you go. I've seen so many pregnant bellies I seem to be getting a bit of a name for myself round here. Lie yourself down on that settee there in the corner and let's have a look.'

So Alice lay down and pulled up her skirt, bunching it up and barely able to see over the top of it.

'Right,' said Stella, with Eddy leaning in very close, breathing down her neck. 'Let's see if we can tell how far on you are. What I need to do is feel for the top of the womb, see how much it's grown. Right, yes, I can feel it right there between that bone low down, there, and your belly button. Put your hand down, Alice, press in a bit, can you feel it?'

'Yes,' said Alice, 'I can.'

'Right, so that means you must be about four months gone.'

'That sounds about right,' said Alice.

'Can I have a feel?' said Eddy, unable to contain herself any longer.

'All right,' said Alice, starting to laugh as Eddy pressed a hand firmly into her belly. 'I can feel it too,' she said, breaking into a grin. 'Do you want to have a go, Maud?'

'No, that's all right,' said Maud, thinking that Alice had been prodded and poked quite enough already for one day.

'So you should feel some 'quickening' soon then,' said Stella.

'What's that?' said Alice, feeling with her hand again for the top of her womb.

'The first movements of the baby. Women say it feels like a butterfly inside, very light and fluttery at first, then as the baby grows it will get stronger.'

'I have felt something a bit like that, I think . . . and I can feel it now; it's fluttering. I can feel it, I can feel it,' said Alice, breaking into a smile and then starting to cry. Then they were all smiling and crying in a mixed-up way together as the new life inside Alice's belly made itself known for the very first time.

'That's the baby,' said Alice, 'my baby.' And there was no need for anyone to ask any more questions about what decision she would make.

10

'If you are a Nurse, Nurses ought not to be dressy, whether in or out of their uniform.'

Florence Nightingale

'I've thought of something,' said Maud to Alice as they walked to work together the next day. There had been no Nancy at breakfast that morning, no sight or sound of her, and Maud could tell that Alice was dreading having to see her again and still saying that she didn't want Maud or anyone else to speak to her about what had been going on.

'What?' said Alice, looking even paler than usual that morning and seeming distracted.

'Why don't we go to Miss Merryweather or Miss Houston together and tell them about your situation? Then there would be nothing that Nancy could hold over you, nothing at all.'

Alice glanced at Maud, horrified. 'No,' she said, 'not yet, it's too soon. And they will just tell me to leave straight away, you know they will.'

'Not necessarily,' said Maud. 'They might well be much more understanding than you think.'

'They might not,' said Alice. 'They might well give me my marching orders and I want to work — I *need* to work — for as long as I can.'

'I suppose,' said Maud, still thinking. 'Well, what if we tell Nancy that we have already told

Miss Merryweather, that she knows all about it?'

'That's lying,' said Alice.

'So?' said Maud, linking her arm. 'So what, if it keeps Nancy off your back?'

'I suppose . . . ' said Alice, still sounding very unsure.

In the end it seemed that, for the time being, they didn't have to say anything else to anyone. Nancy was already on the ward when they arrived and she smiled in their direction. Straight away Maud wondered what she'd been up to, but Alice just seemed relieved. It made Maud worry about the hold that Nancy appeared to have over her friend and other people too. Was it just her who could see those cold, blue eyes above that smile?

'Maybe you're right,' said Alice, anxious not to cause any more trouble. 'If she mentions it again I'll tell her that the superintendents know and see what she thinks about that.'

'All right then,' said Maud, not trusting Nancy for one minute and wondering what exactly she was up to.

'Now, you new probationers . . . ' said Sister Law, glancing around the group with an eagle eye. 'Alice Sampson, why are you so pale and can you not do something about your cap? It always looks so limp.' Maud saw Alice go even paler.

'Ah, Nurse Linklater,' said Sister, 'I'm afraid I need to have a word with you and I will do that now in front of the group because it will be a reminder to others also.' Maud felt her stomach tighten as she racked her brains for what she could have possibly done wrong. In that split second she looked up and saw how Nancy's eyes were shining, and she knew that she had been meddling.

'Nurse Linklater, did I or did I not ask you specifically to leave a drink by the bed of Mr Clifford, the patient whom you escorted to theatre yesterday?'

'Yes, and I — '

'No ands or buts please, Nurse Linklater,' continued Sister, riding over what Maud was about to say in her own defence, knowing full well that she had followed the instruction and not only had she left the drink there but she had been back to help Mr Clifford take more fluid a number of times.

'Can you explain why there was no drink on the man's bedside table as instructed? Can you tell me why I had to get the drink myself and ensure that Mr Clifford took enough fluid to wash out the remains of his bladder stone? Thank goodness that I was extremely late off the ward and the patient had started to groan with the pain that alerted me to his plight. I got the fluid in straight away and prevented him going back into obstruction. Do you realize what could have happened, Nurse Linklater? Do you realize that your inattention may even have proved fatal for the poor man? If it wasn't for your exemplary conduct so far I would have been forced to bring the issue to the attention of Miss Merryweather. As it is, you are new and you have a lot to learn, and we will leave it at that.'

Maud couldn't speak, even though she knew

for certain that she had done all that she could for Mr Clifford. She still felt ashamed and her face was flushed red. She stood in the group with her head down, knowing that it would be worse to try to contradict Sister. Clearly someone had moved the drink to get her into trouble and she knew, of course, exactly who that person was. So she let Sister's words wash over her and she stood there and took it.

When the tirade was finished Maud lifted her head and simply said, 'I will make sure next time, Sister,' and then she looked straight at Nancy, staring into her glinting eyes until Nancy was forced to look away.

'Just one more thing,' said Sister, continuing to glance around the group. 'All of you, take note of Nurse Sellers' appearance today. Of course she is always neat and tidy, but today she is particularly well turned out and her cap is perfect. You, Nurse Sampson, take note in particular.'

Maud's hand balled into a fist as she saw Nancy look over at Alice and then she felt her stomach tighten when she saw her friend try to smile at Nancy.

'One more thing,' said Sister Law. 'Let me remind you that this afternoon you will all be required to attend Mr Fawcett's second lecture. Make sure that you are assembled on the ground floor of the Nurses' Home at four p.m. promptly, are you clear? Four p.m.'

'Yes, Sister,' chorused the nurses before they got on with their duties.

⋆ ⋆ ⋆

Maud and Alice arrived back at the Nurses' Home just in time for the lecture to find all probationers assembled, apart from Eddy, of course, and they quietly slipped in at the back, hoping that they hadn't been seen.

'Right, you nurses,' called Mr Fawcett over the heads of the group, 'let's get started on our topic.'

'Sorry, sorry,' shouted Eddy, arriving breathless at the back and sliding into position next to Maud.

'Right then, nurses, just a reminder,' said Mr Fawcett, glaring at Eddy on the back row. 'Lest we forget, let me remind you all of the importance of being ON TIME. Being on time is an important part of ward routine. If we were all late then nothing would get done, would it now?' he added, looking straight at Eddy again, who just smiled back at him. 'The best Sisters on the ward are never late and never flustered. Bear that in mind, nurses, bear that in mind . . . Now last time we talked about the application of leeches and the administration of enemas. I hope you've all been practising.'

Maud and Eddy exchanged glances.

'Just a reminder, in relation to the leeches, and this has been brought to my attention by a number of ward Sisters: please, please be very careful where you apply them. DO NOT apply them to the very vascular places, the ones that have a good blood supply, or your patient will continue to bleed. Can anyone tell me what the favoured sites for application of leeches are? Yes, you there, on the front row . . . '

'The sternum, the instep and behind the ear.'

Maud and Alice raised eyebrows at each other as they instantly recognized Nancy's voice.

'Yes, very good: the sternum, the instep and behind the ear. Other places may be used but only if directed by a doctor. And for some reason, and I cannot understand this, some of the younger doctors are no longer in favour of using leeches; they have other ideas. But in my view there is nothing to be lost and everything to be gained from bleeding a patient. Now, always remember to pick a lively leech, not one that's half dead, and remember that if the patient won't stop bleeding there are things that can be used. What are these? Does anyone know what can be used to stop bleeding from the site? You there at the back, the one that was late . . . '

Eddy looked dumbstruck, opening and closing her mouth in silence.

'Well,' said Mr Fawcett, 'come on, dazzle us.'

Maud was muttering at Eddy's side, 'Flour, cobweb or fur from a beaver hat, flour, cobweb or fur from a beaver hat . . . '

'A floured beaver!' said Eddy in desperation, and the whole room, including Mr Fawcett, broke into laughter.

'Well, Nurse, I don't think we'd find many of those in the corridors of the Liverpool Royal, but flour can be used and is a good haemostatic, as is the fur from a beaver hat, or cobweb. Anyway, the important thing is that you keep the leeches away from the more vascular areas unless directed by a doctor and only use the leeches once. Chuck 'em out once they've been used;

195

that way we can keep the supply fresh and lively. And another thing: don't put the blighters in your pocket. We don't want any more unfortunate incidents, do we now?' he said, gazing around the room as if they all knew exactly what he was talking about. 'Any questions?'

There was complete silence in the room as Mr Fawcett continued to stand at the front and stare straight ahead.

'All right then, today I am going to talk about what we mean by health and introduce you to what sickness can do to the body. Clearly, however, with all your recent experience on the wards you will all have a fairly good idea about that already.

'So, what is health? Health is the natural condition of the body when it is free from pain and disease. And our job here at the hospital is to restore the body, whenever we can, to a state of health and, if we can, to prevent the body from becoming sick. And I agree with Miss Nightingale on this matter: when we nurse a patient we must nurse the room. Ventilation is a key issue in caring for the sick. It is a key factor in aiding recovery and in preventing diseases such as cholera, typhus and consumption . . . '

Having read *Notes on Nursing* so many times already, Maud found her mind drifting to other matters as Mr Fawcett spoke at some length about what Miss Nightingale had written and she only came to when he said emphatically, 'Nursing is the special province of women. They have a natural tendency for it, and all of you nurses must take heed of the fact that your moral character is very important indeed. Sobriety, honesty, chastity — these have to be upheld. Do not stray from your chosen course.'

Maud glanced to the side to see Alice with her head bowed. What does he know about these things? thought Maud. What does he know about what women have to deal with in their daily lives?

At the end of the lecture Mr Fawcett told them that next time they would be starting on the systems of the body and they would work their way through digestion, the skin, bones and muscles, respiration and the nervous system, and more besides. Then he walked over to a table where he had what appeared to be a row of jars covered by a cloth.

'And just to give you a taster, and again, a reminder of where the sins of the flesh can lead, I have here some specimens that were removed from the bodies of men and women alike, bodies that bore the marks of syphilis, commonly known as the pox. As you can see,' he said, removing the cloth, 'this is where indulgences of that kind can lead.'

Maud felt her stomach heave and there was a gasp from the women in the room as they all stood and tried to leave without looking at the jars but they had all looked at the specimens as they were uncovered — a row of pickled body parts in jars, mainly male anatomy bearing horrible ulcers or twisted out of shape by disease.

Maud saw one girl at the front stand up and then faint, and Mr Fawcett stooped down to attend to her. Maud grabbed hold of Alice's hand and led her out of the room as she heard Mr Fawcett's voice saying something about the Contagious Diseases Acts and that's why the women on the street have to be brought in and treated. At that point Eddy got up from her seat and followed them out without saying anything.

Alice turned to them before running off up the stairs, saying, 'That's it, I'm definitely not going near a man ever again. I need to be sick.'

'Are you coming in for tea?' said Eddy, heading for the refectory with one other girl as the rest of the group moved in the opposite direction.

'Give me ten minutes,' said Maud. 'I need to check on Alice.'

It took a bit longer than ten minutes before Maud and Alice had settled their stomachs but then they were able to go and get something to eat. After tea they sat with Eddy on a few chairs that had been left behind from the lecture. Most of them had been cleared along with the jars of pickled specimens, but there were enough left to form a small group. The evenings were starting to feel cooler and one of the large stoves on the ground floor had been lit. It gave a welcome glow as the girls sat together in happy companionship, not needing to say much to each other, just glad to be at the end of another day and able to spend time together. Maud was glad, but also suspicious, that Nancy never even bothered to make much attempt these days to speak to Alice and she rarely looked in their direction. She had another small group of probationers in her tow. Maud should have been happy that Nancy's attention had shifted but after what had happened that day on the ward with Mr Clifford she knew that she had been right not to trust her. People like Nancy never forgot, never really moved on, and Maud knew for sure that inevitably Nancy would be back for something else as well.

Anyway, for now they were cosy, and the stove had just been lit so they had the crackling and the spitting of the wood as they watched the flames flaring and licking at the kindling sticks, working their way up to the shovelful of coal that had just gone on. Maud felt a shiver go down her back as the fire began to draw air through the stove and she pulled a wool shawl that she had brought from her room around her shoulders.

'The nights are definitely drawing in,' she said to no one in particular, remembering what Cook used to say to them as they all huddled round the kitchen stove in the big house at this time of year. 'And, of course, I understand the importance of ventilation in any building from all my readings of Miss Nightingale's *Notes on Nursing*, but sometimes, don't you think, we could do without a draught round the back of our necks?'

Alice and Eddy laughed.

'Well, at least us nurses shouldn't get the typhus or the cholera or the 'orrible consumption,' said Eddy in a growly voice.

'Stop, stop,' said Alice, still sensitive from the jars of diseased organs on show at Mr Fawcett's lecture. 'Let's talk about something else, not disease, nothing horrible.'

None of them could think of anything to say, and they all laughed again. 'Looks like we're stumped if it doesn't relate to horrible or life-threatening disease,' said Maud.

Then they fell silent again until Eddy could stand it no longer. 'What do you all think about when you're tired like this? When you can't do anything or think straight, what's going through your head?'

Alice looked at her and groaned. 'Eddy, why do you have to start talking about something that nobody else would think of, something strange?'

'It's not strange,' said Eddy, her eyes wide, 'is it, Maud?'

'It might be,' said Maud, 'but I suppose you could say that it is also interesting.'

'There you go,' said Eddy. 'Maud says it's interesting . . . so what do you think about?'

'Nothing at all,' said Alice with another groan. 'I can't think about anything other than what's going on inside me, all the fluttering and moving around, and my back is killing me at the end of each day . . . there's no room for anything else.'

'No other thoughts on anything else at all?' said Eddy.

'No, not really,' said Alice.

'Crikey,' said Eddy. 'What about you, Maud, what's going on in your head?'

Maud didn't reply straight away. She just gazed into the fire. Eddy was used to her and liked the way that Maud took her time to consider things without rushing in with an answer. At first it had driven her mad — she

200

always wanted an instant response to everything — but by now she knew that Maud would answer eventually.

'Right now, I was thinking about some music that I heard playing when I worked at the big house. I don't know what it was called but they had someone in to play the piano and I had never heard anything like it before. It was so beautiful and it stayed in my head for days afterwards, and now it comes and plays in my head whenever it wants. I think it will be with me always. Oh, and I was wondering if I will have the energy to climb those stairs and get into bed.'

'I'm with you there,' said Alice, sounding sleepy. 'I think you two will have to carry me.'

'What about you, Eddy?' said Maud. 'What do you have in your head?'

Eddy didn't even pause to think before she replied, 'Well, I've always got a tune playing in my head — something from the music hall — and then on top of that I'm thinking about hats and gowns, bright colours, new babies, singing songs and boats on the river, all at the same time.'

'Why does that not surprise us?' said Maud, and they all laughed again.

Then they sat for a while longer, with the warm glow of the coal in the stove flickering over their faces. Alice's eyes were starting to close and even Eddy looked a bit sleepy. They heard someone coming down through the hall and Miss Merryweather walked past them on her way to the dining room.

'Wonder what she thinks about,' said Eddy quietly, after she had gone past. Nobody even tried to answer that, and then Eddy pulled a wicked witch face and they all giggled.

'Stop it,' said Maud. 'I really like Miss M. And her sister, the assistant superintendent, is lovely too.'

'Oooh, Miss M and her sister, me and Miss M and her sister,' said the other two at the same time before they all got comfortable again and continued to enjoy the fire before the coal was burnt right down. They knew that there wouldn't be any more fuel going on to keep it in overnight, not at this time of the year.

They were still sitting by the stove and starting to doze when they were roused again by the sound of loud, sharp heels clopping down the stone stairs and then the same heels tap, tapping over the coloured tiles in the hall. They all looked up together and saw Nancy crossing the space in front of them and heading towards the front door. She was wearing a yellow dress with a low-cut front and as she tripped past them with her back very straight and her head held high she left a thick trail of flowery scent.

'Well, look at her all la-di-da,' whispered Eddy. 'That dress makes her look like she might have got the yellow jaundice.'

'Shush,' said Maud, feeling anger burn inside her but not wanting the others to know about it. She didn't want Alice to be worrying or Eddy to come out and say something that would make matters worse. 'She looks very beautiful, you know she does.'

'And doesn't she know it,' said Alice sleepily.

'Looks can be deceiving,' said Eddy. 'I wonder where she's heading dressed like that, smothered in lily of the valley scent. Bet she's going to find a man.'

'You don't need to be a genius to work that one out,' said Alice.

'Shush, you two,' said Maud, feeling uncomfortable at the very thought, especially after the lecture they'd had that afternoon. And there was something else that unsettled her, something she couldn't put a finger on but it was like a bat squeak of a feeling as Nancy had passed by. She was probably just imagining it, but she thought that she knew exactly where Nancy was heading that evening and exactly who she would be seeing.

11

'I do not expect that love passages will
be frequent in her life.'
(F. N.'s mother, writing about
Florence in 1838)

After work the next day Maud was sitting up in
bed reading her way through *Notes on Nursing*
for the umpteenth time, when there was a light
tap on her door.

'Come in,' she called, knowing by the pressure
exerted in knocking it definitely wasn't Eddy,
and hoping she was right in thinking that it was
very unlikely to be Nancy. So it could only really
be Alice. And it was Alice, breathless and tearful.

'Come in,' said Maud, putting her book aside
and swinging her legs over the side of the bed.
'Are you all right?'

'No,' said Alice, and Maud could see that she
was holding back a sob.

'Come and sit down,' she said, patting the bed
next to her and then putting an arm around her
friend as soon as she sat down. 'What's up then?'

'Oh, I've been worrying,' Alice said, 'and I
don't even know if it is something to worry
about or not, so that's making me worry even
more. It's just that I've been feeling so tired
today on the ward and we are so busy, as you
know, and so I had to keep going, but when I got

back to my room after tea I started to feel really dizzy and I needed to sit down. Then I realized that I hadn't felt the baby moving at all today. I don't think I've felt it even once. So I thought: just rest up, Alice, just rest up . . . and then I needed to use the chamber and when I did I saw some spots of blood on my underclothes, just tiny spots, and then that really worried me. What if I'm going to lose the baby? What if it's going to come? I don't know what to do.'

Maud sat for a moment with her arm around Alice's shoulders before answering, 'Well, to be honest, Alice, I have no idea but to me, from what you've said, it doesn't sound really bad. I think you should rest, and in the meantime I will go over and see Stella again. She'll know what's what.'

'No, no, don't be going all that way, not to a brothel at this time of night.'

'Look, I will be fine, Alice, don't worry. And it isn't all that late yet.'

Alice looked at her gratefully. 'If you're sure, Maud. Only if you're sure . . . '

'I'll be fine,' said Maud, already standing up from the bed and getting herself ready to leave. 'You just go and lie down, and I'll get back to you as soon as I can. Try not to worry.'

Alice nodded. 'So long as you're sure, Maud. But do you know the way? Eddy isn't in; she can't go with you,'

'I know the way,' said Maud, 'and even if I get lost I know how to find Stella and Marie's from Lime Street Station, and everybody in Liverpool knows where Lime Street is.'

'That's true,' said Alice, 'but you be careful. The later it gets, the more people of all types you see out on the street.'

'I'll be careful. Now stop worrying, go back to your room and lie down.'

As soon as Maud set out she started to wonder almost straight away whether walking through the city at this hour was a good idea after all. Alice was right: there were all kinds of people out — it was even busier than during the day — and more of them were drunk. And there was a sense of something in the air, a tension, as if a fight could break out at any minute. Always able to rely on her common sense and usually able to stay calm, Maud put her head down and walked, telling herself just to keep walking and imagine that she was following the red flower on Eddy's hat just a little way ahead.

She was at Lime Street Station much sooner than she expected, and again she could hear the buzz of the passengers as they moved through the station or waited on the platforms. This time steam was rising up into the air above and out of the front of the building as a train prepared to leave. For a moment she was enveloped in it and she felt a moment of panic as she lost her bearings and found herself bumping up against some rough-looking men. If it hadn't been for her excellent sense of direction she would have been sent completely off track, but as the mist started to clear she was able to make out where her route lay and she marched ahead with her heart pounding unusually fast.

Relieved at first to be in the alley and

approaching the house, she was in for a shock. This was not the same quiet place next to the station that she had found last time with Eddy and Alice. This was a whole different place, full of shadows and people talking loudly in small groups bunched against walls. Maud averted her gaze instantly as she saw the shape of a woman with her back against a wall and a man . . . She walked past as quickly as she could but just as she turned into the second, narrower alley a man's hand grabbed her arm and a voice said, 'How much?'

'Let go of me,' Maud almost shouted, pulling the man's hand off her. Then she almost ran to the house with the blue door, which seemed to her in that moment like some kind of sanctuary. She could still hear the drunken laughter of the man who had accosted her in the alley as she knocked, out of breath and with her heart pounding, feeling at any moment that someone might grab her from behind. After what felt like an age the door opened and a man lurched out, or maybe he was pushed from inside — it was difficult to tell. He knocked into Maud, who had to grab the door frame to steady herself, and then he fell flat on his face in the alley. Maud watched as he pulled himself up from the ground and then walked away unsteadily, weaving along, using anything he could find — the wall of a building or a lamppost — to steady himself. Turning back to the open doorway, Maud found herself looking into the stony face of the woman with the dark-grey hair, Stella's mother, Marie.

The woman didn't say a word, she just stood

waiting and then made to close the door in Maud's face.

'I'm here to see Stella,' said Maud just in time.

'Thought so,' said the woman.

'Is she in?' said Maud, when the woman didn't say anything else.

'What do you want 'er for?'

'I just need to ask her something,' said Maud. 'It won't take long.'

Marie looked her up and down and then sighed. 'Well, she did say that you and the others were all right, so I suppose . . . '

'Is she in?' said Maud, beginning to feel impatient despite herself.

'No, she isn't,' said the woman.

Maud frowned, trying to stop herself from losing her temper.

'But you can see her if you want.'

Maud's frown deepened as she wondered how that would be possible.

'She's in the pub,' said the woman abruptly and then started to close the door again.

'What pub?' said Maud, blocking the door just long enough for Marie to tell her that it was the public house directly opposite the station.

Then the door clicked shut.

'Thank you,' said Maud to the blue painted wood. 'Thanks for that.'

She turned, and from her vantage point on the stone steps she could make out the shapes in the alley and plan her way through. She knew she would have to go fast and not stop and she knew she would have to go now, straight away, whilst she had the nerve. Her heart was pounding but she thought that she could do it.

She could hear the noise from the pub before she could see it. There seemed to be many people singing very loud, drowning out the tinkle of a piano. She had never been into a pub before in her life, having always been told that it was no place for women. If it hadn't been for her need to do the best for Alice there is no way on earth that she would have gone into such a place but there she was, standing outside the door, knowing that she had no choice.

Whilst she was waiting the door swung open and a man staggered out, giving her a glimpse of the interior. It was so full of smoke that she could barely make out who was standing at the bar. It looked like they were all men. With the opening of the door the full volume of the noise hit her for a few seconds, not just singing but people shouting and laughing. And the smell that wafted in her direction was pure tobacco smoke overlaying the odour of beer and unwashed bodies. Maud's stomach tightened instantly but she knew that she had no choice, particularly since the man who had just come out of the place was sidling up to her with a strange look on his face.

She took a deep breath, said to herself, 'Here I go', pushed the door open and then she was in. It felt like hell on earth and she hadn't accounted for the press of bodies around her. She would need to push her way through if she wanted to find Stella. So she pushed and squeezed past some of the men until she came up against one who would not budge, even though she used all of her power. Then through the noise she could hear the sound of a man laughing and when she looked up she saw that the man she was trying to move out of the way was looking down at her and laughing his head off.

'Excuse me, please,' said Maud, giving another push, determined to get past.

'Whoa, whoa,' said the man. 'Steady on, Maud. What the blazes are you doing in a place like this anyway?'

Maud looked up sharply to find Harry Donahue grinning at her.

'What the . . . ?' she said, thinking to herself: well, that's all I need, having him here as well.

'I need to get past,' she said, meeting his gaze and trying to seem as if she did this kind of thing every day of the week.

'But why are you here? Do you need to get to the bar? Do you want me to buy you a glass of ale?'

'Don't be ridiculous,' said Maud.

'What then?'

'I'm looking for someone.'

'Well, here I am,' he said, holding both arms out to her.

'Don't be ridiculous,' she said again. 'Not you.'

Harry pulled his mouth down in mock sorrow. 'If not me, who then?'

There didn't seem to be any way round it so Maud said, 'I'm looking for a woman called Stella.'

'Stella?' said Harry. 'Why on earth would you

be looking for a woman like her? I mean, don't get me wrong, most of the men in here are looking for a woman like Stella, especially the brilliant, beautiful Stella O'Connor. But why are *you* looking for her?'

'It isn't really any of your business,' said Maud, feeling impatient and drawing herself up to her full height.

'Well now, if you want me to help you find her, which I'm taking it you do, then it has to be my business,' he said, smirking at her.

'Oh, for goodness' sake, I just need to ask her something, that's all,' said Maud, knowing by now that she wasn't going to get anywhere unless she told Harry something and even enlisted his help.

'What kind of thing?'

'Look,' said Maud, 'I've had enough of this. Don't just stand there like a ninny, show me where she is right now.'

'Like a what?' said Harry, laughing his head off.

'Now,' said Maud, starting to raise a hand to him.

'Whoa, whoa, right, I can see you mean business . . . I know exactly where to find her. Come with me,' he said, catching hold of her hand and dragging her through a group of men to a space by the end of the bar.

'There she is,' he said, pointing to the person playing the piano. 'There's our Stella.'

'Thank you,' said Maud. 'That will be all.'

Harry cracked up laughing. 'That will be all, will it? That will be all.'

Maud did not smile. The man was infuriating, yet she was shocked to register that there was something inside — a very strong feeling — that made her want to smile and even have a beer with him. But she locked it deep down. She could not possibly give someone like him any encouragement, especially in a place like this. She could not, she would not, and that was that.

Harry stood by as Maud tried to catch Stella's attention by waving, and then she called out to her, but her gesture and voice were drowned out by the smoke and the noise. Seeing her vain attempts, Harry picked up his pint and shouted out, 'Let's raise a glass to all here now, and those we've left behind . . . And to Stella, lovely as always, and who needs to have a word with someone here at the bar.' Maud saw Stella look up from the piano and she knew that she had seen her in the moment before the whole pub shouted, 'Cheers!' and everyone took a swig of ale. The man next to Maud missed his mouth and it slopped down his front and on to her sleeve. She brushed at it with her hand but knew that she would reek of beer for some time to come.

'Shorry,' said the man, sloshing more of his ale on to her as he leant forward to apologize.

Maud turned her back on him and waited. This meant that she was face to face again with Harry Donahue. He didn't say anything but just kept smiling at her.

She tried not to look at him but she knew that he was looking at her. She could feel him examining every tiny detail of her face and she had to fight hard to keep her poise.

Maud was so relieved to feel a tap on her shoulder and she knew that it was Stella.

'All right there, Maud?' she said. 'This is the last place I thought I'd see you.'

'It's the last place I would have come if I wasn't desperate,' she said, having to shout above the noise of a group of men who seemed to be having some kind of banter, or maybe they were starting a fight.

She felt Harry push past her and heard him say, 'Now, you lot, calm down. There's nobody goin' to start throwing punches inside here. Just you wait for me to do that later . . . outside. Have you placed your bets?'

For goodness' sake, thought Maud, does he never learn? And, struggling to hear Stella, she saw her indicate that they should go outside. As they passed by the group with Harry, Maud saw her pat him on the shoulder and he turned and smiled at her and then gave Maud a small salute. She looked away immediately, pretending that she hadn't seen, but she could feel her heart racing.

Maud was so relieved to be back on the pavement with the door to the pub closed behind them that she felt like she needed to sit down. Stella stood with her hands on her hips and took in some deep breaths of air. 'It gets a bit stale in there at times, and a bit loud,' she said. 'Sorry about that. I'm used to it, but I know that you aren't. Now, there must be some good reason why you've come all the way here to see me — is it about Alice?'

213

'It is,' said Maud, still feeling like she had been chewed up and spat out by the pub, but so relieved to speak to Stella, who instantly understood what was going on without even being told.

'We're just a bit worried,' said Maud, needing to catch her breath and slow her heart before she could continue. 'She's really tired, she doesn't think that the baby is moving and she's seen a few spots of blood. I have no idea about these things. I've told her to rest tonight, but what do you think? Will she be all right?'

Stella thought for a moment then said, 'Has she been working today?'

'Yes,' said Maud, 'and we've been really busy.'

'And you say a few spots of blood, fresh blood? And only a few drops?'

'Yes, yes, I think so,' said Maud, wishing that she'd taken a bit more time to get the precise details from Alice before she hurtled off across town.

'Well, it sounds to me like she's just overdone things at work and, being so busy, she probably hasn't had time to feel the baby moving. As for the blood, well, it might be nothing or it might get worse, and if it does it might mean that she will lose the baby. That's nature's way and there isn't anything we can do to stop that, not us working women at any rate. The better off, they can stay in bed resting, but us lot, we need to get on, don't we? No time to be lying about for us.'

That's true, thought Maud, also thinking that if Alice did lose the baby in the long run it might well be the best thing for her anyway.

'So tell her to rest overnight. She needs to rest as much as she can now, and she's not to worry about the bleeding but to keep an eye on it. And tell her that the baby is probably still moving, she's just been too busy to feel it.'

'I understand. Thank you so much for that, Stella. I know you need to get back; I don't want to keep you from your . . . ' said Maud, not able to find quite the right word for what she thought Stella might be doing.

'No, that's all right, any time. And, yes, I do need to get back in there to that rabble,' said Stella. 'Bye for now, but like I said, come and see me any time. Cheerio.'

'Cheerio,' said Maud, turning to walk back as fast as she could to the Nurses' Home before they closed the door. But her way was blocked. Two men wearing dark suits had instantly stepped out of the shadow of a building and now they were in front of her.

'Evening, miss,' said one of the men. 'We've been observing this public house all evening and me and my partner here, we saw you going in earlier and we have just seen you waiting outside. Not only that, you have been in the company of a woman we suspect is of ill repute. Would you like to tell us who you are waiting for out here? Are you waiting for a customer?'

'What do you mean?' said Maud, having no understanding whatsoever of why she might be being questioned. Not only that, but one of the men had moved to her side and had taken hold of her arm.

'Let go of me,' she said, instinctively taking her

215

arm out of his grasp.

'I think you need to be answering our questions, young lady,' said the other man, who still stood in front of her. 'Until we know exactly what is going on here, we will not be able to let you go.'

'What do you mean?' said Maud again. 'Who are you?' She was trying to stay calm but beginning to feel panic rising inside her now.

'We are gentlemen of the law who have been given jurisdiction under the Contagious Diseases Acts to manage the likes of women like you who prowl our streets looking for men — looking for men and looking for money. And then infecting our men with venereal diseases.'

'How dare you?' said Maud, fully realizing exactly what they were saying. 'I can give a full account of myself. I have nothing to hide.'

Then she heard Stella's voice: 'She has nothing to hide, gentlemen, it's true. She's telling the truth.'

Maud looked round, as did the men, to see Stella in the doorway of the pub. She must have been watching to make sure I got away safely, thought Maud.

'This lass is a nurse at the hospital. Go up there tomorrow if you want to check, and you will find her on one of the male wards, tending the sick and dealing with men . . . the likes of you. How dare you even think that this woman could be working the streets? Look at her: she isn't dressed right, and even if she was choosing to earn a living like that, so what? What business is it of yours? You should be speaking to the men, not picking up women off the streets.'

'It's all right, Stella, really,' said Maud, seeing how the men were looking at Stella, and sensing that they were only a hair's-breadth away from latching on to her instead and taking her with them. 'You go back inside and play the piano. I'm going to make my way back to the hospital.' With that, she stepped away from the two men and left them staring at Stella, who now had the benefit of a couple of rough-looking men from inside the pub standing by her side.

'We won't take the matter any further this time,' said one of the men to Maud's back, 'but make sure we don't find you out here again.'

Maud didn't turn round. She just kept walking as fast as she could, a cold shiver running down her spine and a feeling that someone was breathing down her neck.

She didn't feel safe until she was in through the heavy wooden door of the Nurses' Home. And as she entered the space inside she smelt the varnish and gave thanks for the solid tiled floor beneath her feet and the skylight reaching up to heaven above her. In her absolute relief at being home safe she realized just how special this place had become to her. It was like some kind of sanctuary, and the feeling was so powerful, she knew that everything would be all right. She was safe now; she was back.

She moved further into the space and then stood in her favourite spot looking up at the skylight. She heard the door to Miss Merryweather's room click open and in moments she was aware of the superintendent standing right next to her.

'I love it too,' Miss Merryweather said, almost able to read Maud's mind, 'even now, when it's dark outside. I always hope to see the stars. There is no better place than standing right here, exactly where Miss Nightingale meant us to be. This place was built to stand for ever and be used by generations of nurses who will come after us, when we are long gone. Who knows what the world of nursing and medicine will have to offer by then? With the changes that I've seen already in my lifetime I sense that there is so much more to come, so much to look forward to.'

'Yes,' said Maud, 'I sense that too, standing here. It feels like we are at the beginning of something very special. I wonder if those nurses in generations to come will stand here and think about us.'

'They will,' said Miss Merryweather. 'Miss Nightingale has already laid such a strong foundation, I think that even in a hundred years' time she will still be known and still talked about. And the rest of us can make our mark as well in the work that we are doing now. We can do our bit to progress the profession.'

Then they both stood quiet for a few more minutes, lost in their own thoughts, before the front door opened again and someone else returned, brushing through the entrance quickly with her head down and going straight up the stairs. Must have caught sight of Miss Merryweather, thought Maud, realizing that she was still standing in comfortable companionship with the superintendent and she hadn't yet got back to Alice to tell her what Stella had said.

'Good night then, Miss Merryweather,' said Maud as she turned to make her way to Alice's room.

'Good night, Nurse Linklater,' said the superintendent, still staring up to the skylight.

Maud tapped lightly on Alice's door and then went straight in as soon as she heard a response. 'How are you, Alice?' she said, finding her friend lying on her side, trying to look relaxed but still seeming quite stricken.

'What did Stella say?' Alice asked immediately.

'She said you were not to worry, it is probably just that you have been overworking. Have you had any more bleeding?'

'No, nothing else.'

Maud felt relief settle inside of her. 'Well, that's good then. There is no need to worry unless the bleeding gets much worse.'

'Are you sure? Is that what Stella said?'

'Yes, that's what she said, and she also said that sometimes when you are busy you don't notice the baby moving. Has it been moving?'

Alice smiled. 'Yes, just as soon as you went out through the door the little blighter started moving all over the place. Sorry, Maud, that you had to go out across the city at this time of night.'

'So long as you're feeling better everything is all right and, well, I've had an interesting time,' said Maud, not wanting to disclose any of the details to Alice.

'This all seems so ridiculous, doesn't it, Maud? Not many weeks ago I wanted to start bleeding, I wanted to lose the baby, but now . . . now I am absolutely terrified that something will go wrong. How ridiculous.'

'It's not ridiculous,' said Maud. 'That's life. And no wonder you didn't relish the idea of carrying a child and bringing it up with no father, and going through what women have to go through to deliver it. No wonder, Alice!'

'Will you stay with me, Maud?'

'Of course I will. I can squeeze into your bed for one night.'

'No, no, I didn't mean tonight — I'll be all right now — I meant stay with me throughout all of this, stay close.'

'Of course I will,' said Maud, leaning down to give Alice a hug so she didn't need to get up off the bed.

'You stink of beer and tobacco,' said Alice, wrinkling her nose. 'Whatever have you been doing out there, Maud?'

'Oh, nothing,' said Maud. 'I had an interesting time, that's all. Nothing to be concerned about.'

'Mmm,' said Alice, narrowing her eyes. 'Well, don't go running off like that again. We both need to get a better grip of things, I think. Everything will be fine.'

'It will,' said Maud, giving Alice a kiss on the cheek. 'Now get some sleep. We're back on the ward tomorrow and Sister Law will be on the warpath if we're late.'

12

' . . . the superintendent should be able to
go to all parts of the hospital under her
charge without its being known where
she is, nor when she is coming.'

Florence Nightingale

Maud kept an eye on Alice for the next few
weeks, making sure that she got as much rest as
she could. Overly anxious at first, she drove her
friend mad with constant questions. In the end
she had to be told not to keep asking and so then
she had to rely on how Alice looked. Fortunately
for both of them, Alice was looking well. Her
colour was good, she seemed to have an air of
contentment, and slowly Maud started to put
her anxiety aside. In fact, far from being pale,
Alice even seemed to be getting a bit of a flush
on her cheeks. But time was going by and Maud
knew that it wouldn't be long before the shape of
Alice's belly would start making itself known to
other people.

It was time for the probationers to move wards
and to Maud's absolute relief she was going to
Female Surgical. Yes, she had started to get used
to the male bodies, but she knew that she would
be instantly more comfortable on a female ward.
She was really looking forward to it and she
would be with Eddy again. Alice would be

moving to Male Medical and they hadn't heard from Nancy yet but they were praying that she wouldn't be given the same as Alice. Alice had enough to deal with, without that. For Maud the move was good because the ward was still surgical. Despite her ups and downs with Sister Law, the Sister had kept her promise to make sure that Maud spent as much time as possible in theatre and she had been in there so often now that she was able to help with laying out the instruments, dressing wounds and even on one occasion had been allowed to administer the drops of chloroform under Dr McKendrick's close supervision. Sister Law had said that she had spoken to Mr Jones and he would make sure that Sister Pritchard on Female Surgical allowed Maud to go into theatre as often as she could be spared so that her training would continue.

For some reason Maud had expected that the female patients would be operated on by a female surgeon but Eddy had said, 'Don't be daft, there aren't any women doctors, never mind surgeons.'

'Well, I think there should be,' said Maud firmly.

'I agree,' said Eddy, 'and I have heard that there is one in America. Sister Cleary told me about a Dr Elizabeth Blackwell. She is the first woman ever to graduate from medical school and she had to fight to get in there. Anyway, now she's opened her own infirmary, just for women, in New York.'

'Just women, in the whole hospital?'

'Yes!'

How wonderful, thought Maud, to work with a female doctor and in a whole hospital with no male patients whatsoever. I would love to work in a place like that.

★ ★ ★

It was their final week on Male Surgical and the time had gone by quickly, though to Maud it seemed like a lifetime ago since she had been sitting by Alfred's bed as a visitor. She was so glad that she had at last been able to get up to the school to see the boy. She'd gone up there on an afternoon off only to be told by a man at the door that the school was closed to visitors that day. She had stood there outside the stone walls of the grand building straining her ears for any sound of the children but there had been nothing but silence. And the man at the door must have seen the look on her face and taken pity on her, so he shouted over and said he could let her into the courtyard for just five minutes so that she could see the child.

'What is the orphan's name?' he had asked and Maud had felt ridiculous tears springing to her eyes as she'd said, 'Alfred.'

'Right, miss, you wait there,' said the man, and after what seemed an absolute age Maud heard the sound of Alfred running across the stone flags. Then he launched himself at her and she was so overwhelmed she could hardly speak. Alfred led her over to a wooden bench where they could sit and then he rummaged for a handkerchief in the pocket of his blue uniform jacket and handed it to her so that she could dry her tears.

He told her about the lessons in maths and English and the reading that he was doing, and he was so full of excitement with everything. He slept in a dormitory and the discipline was strict but he hadn't been beaten once yet. The food was good, too, much better than at the workhouse. Maud felt her heart swell with pride as she sat and listened to him and she would have loved to have been able to go in and see one of the classrooms, but the man was soon looking at her and it was time to leave.

'I'll see you again soon,' she said to Alfred, blowing him a kiss as he marched steadfastly back inside the building.

Once Maud was outside the gate she smiled to herself and knew for sure that the bond she had with Alfred would survive whether she was able to visit him regularly or not. As she walked away she put her hand in her pocket and felt the brown sock, still sitting there. With all the rush to see him she'd forgotten to give it to him. Never mind, she'd thought, I'll take it next time.

Maud found that she had been standing in the middle of the ward gazing at the bed that had been Alfred's and now that her mind was back on the present she glanced up the ward to make sure that she hadn't been caught dawdling by Sister Law. It was a good job they were quiet that afternoon — unusually quiet — or else she'd have been in trouble for sure.

But as she walked away to start the extra

cleaning that she and Alice had volunteered to do at the bottom of the ward, Maud's head was once more full of what Eddy had said about that female doctor in New York. She was wondering if, when Alfred had finished his schooling, and she was a qualified nurse, she could take him. They could go to America together and she could find work at that infirmary for women.

Maud and Alice had volunteered to do the cleaning mainly because they wanted to keep out of the way of Sister Law and, of course, Nancy, who were both up at the other end. For Maud, the cleaning was easy but she could see that Alice was starting to have a bit of trouble bending over so she did all the hard to reach places. As she was crouching down, cleaning the legs of a bed, she saw Miss Merryweather come marching through the door into the ward. She was glad that she and Alice were busy: Miss Merryweather was an absolute stickler and did not take kindly to seeing any nurse standing idle. As she cleaned, Maud watched the superintendent walk up the ward, glancing from one side to the other, at the men in their beds. She was definitely on the prowl; anyone could see that. Then she disappeared from view and in moments they could hear the sound of her raised voice.

'Nurse Sellers, why are you standing idle, tucked away in that corner when there is a patient in this bed needing attention? Well?'

Maud could not hear Nancy's response but she could hear Miss Merryweather saying, 'Not good enough, Nurse Sellers. Get over there at once and sort that patient out. That's what we are here for.'

Then there was silence, and moments later Miss Merryweather was coming back down the ward. Maud saw Alice try to duck down behind the bed they were cleaning, but it was too late: they had been seen.

They both held their breath as Miss Merryweather stood in front of them, looking over the bed that they were cleaning, but they could read nothing from her stern face. Maud glanced behind Miss Merryweather to the beds on each side of the ward, visually checking where she could, trying to see if any of the patients were in need of something. There was one man looking forlornly in their direction. Uh-oh, she thought, now we're for it.

Then Miss Merryweather took a step closer to them and said, 'Well done, girls. Your patients this end are tended to, the beds are orderly and you are even getting on with some cleaning. Well done.' Then she was gone, vanishing through the door as quickly as she had appeared.

Maud and Alice looked at each other and started to breathe again. 'I was going to say that was a close shave,' said Maud, 'but, you know what? Me and you are a good team and we always keep ourselves busy, so well done us.'

When Maud looked up the ward again she could see Nancy heading into the sluice with a urinal, and the moment before she pushed the door open Maud saw her glare down the ward and give her and Alice a look of pure rage. Clearly she had heard everything that Miss

Merryweather had said to them.

'Oh dear,' said Alice, 'we're in for it now.'

'Don't you worry,' said Maud. 'I'll deal with her if she starts threatening you again.'

After the cleaning was done Maud was heading up to the sluice room to empty a bowl of water when she heard a 'Psssst' from the ward doorway. She couldn't see anyone, but then she heard it again: 'Psssst.' This time when she looked she could see a man with a dog in his arms, a dog with long, dangly legs and a rough-looking coat, quite a big dog for somebody to carry. That's when she realized that she had seen the dog before, and the man who was carrying it was, of course, Harry Donahue. The dog was bigger up close than she thought it would be but he had it bundled up in his arms as if it was a baby.

She marched over to the door. 'What are you doing here?' she said. 'What do you want?'

'I want to see you,' Harry said, and this time there was no twinkle in his eye. In fact, he looked a bit upset.

'Are you all right?' asked Maud.

'I am, but me dog isn't. She's been crying out in pain and she can't put weight on her front paw.'

'Oh dear,' said Maud, seeing the look of pain in the dog's eyes and the way its ears were laid back flat against its head. And when she touched it she could feel that it was trembling. 'Oh, poor thing,' said Maud, stroking the dog's head.

'Is there anything that you can do?' said Harry.

'I don't really know about dogs,' said Maud.

227

'You have to have a look at her,' said Harry, and she could see that he had tears in his eyes. 'I've already asked a horse doctor and all he said was I should just knock it on the head and put it out of its misery. I can't do that. We've been together seven years; she's the only family I've got.'

'I see,' said Maud, very surprised by the genuine heartache that was showing on Harry's face. She had thought that he was all show and gab, with very little substance, but she could see just how much he cared about his dog, and it made her realize that there was another side to Harry Donahue. That was very unexpected.

'Well, I can't do anything just now,' she said, 'but I'm finishing in an hour or so and I'll meet you out at the front of the Infirmary, if you like, by the big gate. I'll have a look at the dog then. I can't make any promises — I don't know anything about dogs — but I'll bring some lint and a bandage with me, see if that will do any good.'

'Will you?' said Harry, sounding grateful. 'I'll go and see if I can find a drink for her. Thank you.' And he staggered off with his dog.

As Maud turned she was almost trampled by Nancy Sellers. 'Who were you talking to?' Nancy said. 'Was that Harry Donahue?'

Maud was shocked. Nancy hadn't spoken to her for weeks so to be confronted by her now, and so earnestly, was very unexpected indeed. For a moment she couldn't speak. She was just opening her mouth to form some kind of reply when there was shouting outside the ward and they both had to stand back as the orderlies ploughed through with a man on a stretcher screaming his head off.

The man was covered in soot and, to Maud's horror, she knew exactly who it was straight away. It was Mr Greer. Nancy took one look at the man and turned away, moving far enough off so that she wouldn't need to get involved with the new admission, but not so far that she wouldn't be able to hear exactly what was going on.

'You see to that admission, Nurse Linklater,' shouted Sister Law from the top of the ward, 'and then report back to me.'

'Yes, Sister,' said Maud as she tried to fight off the feeling of dread that had crept over her like a heavy blanket.

The orderlies dumped Greer on to the nearest bed and didn't even pass any comment. They were out through the door before anyone could say anything. Except Greer himself, of course. He was screaming after them, 'I am William Greer, master sweep. I need to see the finest surgeon. I need to be back at work immediately. I have left a full set of brushes — those damn new-fangled brushes — jammed up a chimney.'

Maud took a deep breath. There was no way round it: she would have to stride up to the bed and do her duty and hope that he didn't recognize her in a nurse's uniform.

'Please try to calm down,' she said. 'As you can see, we have many patients on the ward and most of them are much more poorly than you.'

Greer switched round, remarkably lively for a

229

man who had just been admitted. 'Don't you speak to me like that,' he said. 'I will not see some slip of a nurse about my injury. I need to see a surgeon . . . NOW.' Then she heard him catch his breath and she saw his eyes register who he was speaking to. 'YOU,' he said. 'It's you! It is your fault that I've ended up in here. You forced me to hand over my climbing boy. You took him from me and told Miss Fairchild a bunch of lies. AND THEN none of them on Devonshire Square, my best customers, would have me back until I got some of those newfangled brushes. They are useless, *useless*, and my back is just about broke from fitting 'em together and shoving 'em up chimneys. And I have to do all the work, turning 'em, sweeping 'em, and they bring down clouds of soot. That can't be any good for my chest. They will be the death of me, the death of me . . . ' His voice trailed off and he hung his head.

Just for a moment Maud felt sorry for him. He seemed like a man from a different age, rapidly being left behind, and she wasn't sure if he would recover.

Then he lifted his head and spat at her, 'You will pay for this. You are nothing but a cheap housemaid.'

That was the end of Maud's sympathy. She caught her breath. Then she felt her mouth form into a hard line and when her voice came out it was controlled. 'Right then, Mr Greer, could you give me some account of what has happened today?'

'Happened, happened? This has not just

'appened, it has been done to me, and now look at me.'

'Where is your injury?' said Maud.

'Injury? You stand there and ask me about my injury. Me whole self is injured, body and soul.'

'Look, you need to tell — '

'I will not tell you nothing!' yelled Greer at her face and she could feel a spray of spittle landing on her cheek and on her lips. She took out her pocket handkerchief and wiped her face with it. When she looked at him again, his eyes were wide and white against the black of his skin, his mouth set in some kind of snarl.

'I will ask you again,' she said, keeping her voice steady.

'You will not,' he yelled, then grabbed hold of the front of her uniform, pulling her roughly towards him, right up to his face. Maud was terrified but she would not let him see.

'You will tell me where my climbing boy is,' he said.

'Never,' she said.

He pulled her tighter and she gasped, not able to breathe properly. She could hear some of the other patients shouting, 'Sister, Sister,' up the ward.

And then Maud saw Greer's face change and he leant back away from her. At the other side of the bed she saw that someone had laid a hand on his shoulder and was hissing into his ear, 'Let go of my nurse *now*.' He did so instantly.

It was Miss Houston. Where had she come from? Maud couldn't speak. She couldn't even thank her as she stood trying to regain her balance and collect herself and then, seeing the marks of soot on the front of her uniform, she took out her pocket handkerchief and tried to wipe it clean.

'Now tell me what your problem is,' said Miss Houston to Greer. 'I want you seen by the doctor and out of this ward as soon as possible.'

Greer seemed momentarily stuck for words and then Miss Houston looked over to Maud and said in a gentle voice, 'Are you all right, Nurse Linklater?'

Maud nodded.

'Right, you get yourself off duty. Go now. I will see to this patient and I will let Sister Law know.'

'Thank you,' said Maud, tears starting to spring to her eyes, not so much at what had happened but at the kindness in Miss Houston's voice.

'Please can I take a bandage and some lint with me?'

'Yes, of course,' said Miss Houston, not even asking what they were for.

As Maud moved away from the bed she saw Nancy by the sluice door. She seemed to have been watching and listening to everything that had been going on. There was nothing to read from her face but as Maud went by Nancy muttered something like, 'Trying to get yourself well in with her as well, are you? Well, you'd better watch out, you and that pregnant friend of yours. You'd both better watch out.'

Maud was still rattled from what had just happened so she was quite numb to what Nancy was saying, but when she mentioned Alice she felt anger rise inside her. She turned and looked straight at Nancy without saying anything, just looked at her until Nancy looked away. Then Maud moved on, feeling fierce and very strong.

As Maud approached the gate outside the Infirmary she didn't see Harry or the dog at first. She thought that Harry must have changed his mind and gone back to the horse doctor after all, but then she saw them sitting on the ground leaning against the wall and she couldn't help it, her heart soared. Harry had a protective arm around the dog and it was leaning against him, but as soon as he saw Maud he stood up and the dog let out a pitiful yelp. She saw the look of pain on Harry's face as he instantly crouched back down to try to soothe the dog.

Maud knelt down beside them and gently stroked the dog's head. It was easy to see which paw was injured because the dog was holding it up off the ground.

'Poor thing,' said Maud to the dog. 'Poor, poor thing. Now what have you been doing?' She looked at Harry and, seeing the concern on his face, her heart almost melted.

'She just started limping all of a sudden. She jumped down from a banking. It was when we were in the park, when I was sparring with a mate. She'd been running around and then she jumped down and she was yelping like she was being murdered or summat. And she couldn't stop. It was terrible. And then she was trembling and panting and she couldn't put the front paw down, so I've been carrying her round everywhere ever since.'

'Right,' said Maud, starting to smile inside at the thought of this tough bare-knuckle fighter lumping a dog around the streets of Liverpool. 'What's her name?'

'She's called Rita, after a woman I knew once,' he said.

Maud raised her eyebrows but didn't pass any comment.

'All right, Rita,' she said, 'let's see if there is anything we can do to help you, just let me have a feel at this paw . . . ' But as soon as she touched the paw Rita yelped and Maud jumped back, feeling the noise like a knife going right through her.

'This is a bit harder than treating a human person,' she said, starting to feel a bit flustered. 'You can't really talk to a dog and explain things, can you? And I do need to have a feel at the paw if I can.'

'It's all right, Rita, it's all right,' said Harry. 'Just let the nurse have a look at it. She knows what she's doin' and she might be able to help. Now you keep still and just let her feel. She will be gentle . . . ' Then he nodded to Maud and quietly said, 'Now just tell her what you're goin' to do and have another go.'

That's exactly what she did and, remarkably, it worked. It was like he'd hypnotized the creature or something. Maud was gentle and now she was able to feel the length of the dog's paw.

'Well, I can't feel anything obviously broken or out of shape,' she said, remembering what Alfred's arm had looked like, 'so that's promising.' Harry and the dog both looked at her hopefully.

'But the leg is definitely swollen. Can you see here, and compare it to the other?' Maud was aware of the closeness of Harry as their heads moved together to look at the paw. She could smell that special smell that he had again — what was that; was it in his hair? — and it was a good job that she was kneeling down because she was sure that her legs were starting to feel a bit weak.

'It could just be a sprain,' she said, taking a deep breath to try to control the racing of her heart. She'd started to feel a bit dizzy too.

This is ridiculous, she said to herself, trying to get herself in order.

'Right, I have a piece of lint and a bandage,' she said, gently letting go of the dog's paw and rooting in her pocket. 'What I'm going to do is wrap the lint round the whole lower leg, just below the knee. Is that what you call it on dogs, the knee?'

Harry nodded and she could hear his breath coming fast.

'Now, could you hold her fast? She will probably find this painful but we need to be firm. All right?'

'All right,' said Harry, looking very serious indeed.

Maud was able to apply the lint around the leg with no more than a small yelp from the dog, but when she took the bandage and started to fix it firmly the creature yelped and howled like they were killing her and Harry had to use all of his muscle to hold her still.

'That's it, that's it,' said Maud, bandaging fast

235

as if her life depended on it and then expertly ripping down the ends of the bandage and tying it securely around the leg.

'There,' she said, sitting back on her heels, her face flushed and her breath coming quickly.

Harry was still holding the dog but she had stopped yelping and trying to struggle free. He was talking quietly to her and they both seemed to be in some kind of trance. Maud stood up from her work and continued to watch them.

'Do you want to see if she can put the paw down?' she said at last when they didn't move.

'Oh right, yes,' said Harry, gently lowering the paw to the ground and then holding his breath.

Maud was holding her breath too, expecting at any moment to hear that piercing howl of pain again, but the dog seemed comfortable. Maud looked at Harry with her eyebrows raised and they exchanged a 'so far so good' smile.

'Now, carefully,' said Maud, 'let's see if she can stand.'

Maud could see Harry hold his breath again as he stood back a bit and called to the dog, who was sitting quite comfortably, 'Come on then, Rita, come on.'

The dog stood and yelped. Maud thought, here we go again. But it was just one yelp and then when Harry tried her with a few steps she was limping and her ears were still flat back against the sides of her head, but at least she could walk.

'It seems to be helping,' he said, turning to Maud with a triumphant smile, 'don't you think?'

'Yes,' said Maud, completely amazed, 'it does.' She was so pleased that she had been able to help the animal. She looked at Harry and they both smiled again, and then she realized that they were standing just outside the grounds of the Infirmary and she was still wearing her uniform so she cleared her throat and said, 'Now just go easy with her and make sure she gets some rest. If the bandage starts to loosen, you saw how I applied it, just put it back on the same way.'

'Or I could bring her back to you,' he said, starting to get a bit of a twinkle back in his eye.

'No,' said Maud, 'you will be quite capable of putting it back on yourself.' Then she straightened her uniform skirt and prepared to leave.

'Thanks, Maud,' he said, very genuine. 'I will find some way to pay you back for sure. In fact, do you want to come to the fight tonight? We'll be in that small park as usual, just down the road from here . . .'

But Maud was already shaking her head. 'No, no, I can't,' she said. 'I couldn't. I just couldn't stand by and watch people set out to hurt each other. It's just too, too brutal.'

'I suppose you're right there,' he said, 'but if you change your mind, you know where I am.'

Maud smiled and then looked down at the ground. It was time to get going.

'Thanks again,' Harry said, stooping down to pick up the dog. 'I'm not letting her walk just yet. I'm not risking anything. I can't stand to hear her in pain. She can go and stay at Stella's place.'

'Good idea,' said Maud, watching him settle the dog in his arms and then set off walking. She stood and watched him go, the dog looking back at her over the shoulder of his dark-green jacket. Then she thought, come on, Maud, snap out of it. Even if you were looking for a man — and you are definitely not looking for a man — he is absolutely the wrong type for you. Then she looked at him again as he carried the dog, and she smiled before turning in the opposite direction and heading back to the Nurses' Home.

13

Ward management is only made possible
by kindness and sympathy.
                              Florence Nightingale

'Have you heard about Nancy?' said Eddy.

'No,' said Maud, anxious to be off and wishing
that she hadn't agreed to wait for Eddy so that
they could walk to the ward and arrive for their
first morning on Female Surgical together.

'She's been given Female Medical and she's
furious. They've all got apoplexy on there, and
that's just the staff from working with Sister
Fox. She's even worse than Sister Law. And
what with all those patients with bad chests
coughing up buckets of phlegm all day long, it
isn't a good placement for anybody, let alone
Miss Nancy Prancy,' said Eddy, clearly relishing
the news.

Maud glanced at Eddy, for once just wanting
her to speed up a bit, and she definitely wanted
to straighten up the nurse's cap that sat
squashed and askew on her head. She was only
half listening, and even though there was no love
lost between her and Nancy, she still always
hoped for the best for everyone. She was glad
that Nancy was away from Alice, and for Maud
that's what really mattered.

'Well, we'll have to do our time on there as

well in due course,' she said. 'Our turn will come.'

'Hadn't thought about that,' said Eddy, 'but she's got it first,' and she was almost rubbing her hands together with glee.

They arrived on the ward with moments to spare and Maud made a silent promise to herself that she would tell Eddy that it was best for them to make their own way to the ward in future. She just found all that rushing too stressful first thing in the morning.

Ward routine was much the same on all of the wards so Maud felt instantly at home, as she knew that she would on a ward full of women. The whole sound and smell of the ward was different. It felt cleaner and lighter in some way, even though the shape and layout was exactly the same. Sister Pritchard was nice too. She was tall, thin and very softly spoken, the complete opposite of Sister Law on Male Surgical, although over the weeks Maud had to admit that she had started to warm to Sister Law in a strange way. But Sister Pritchard felt like the right sort from the start, and Eddy had told her that nobody had a bad word to say about her.

They weren't far into the morning's work when Maud found out that the same two orderlies, Michael and Stephen, whom she had become familiar with on the male ward, served this one as well. They came running through the door with a young woman screaming in pain and clutching her abdomen. Sister Pritchard was straight there and she called Maud and Eddy over to observe how they dealt with an admission on Female Surgical.

'They say she's been like this for about three hours,' said Michael, at the head of the stretcher. 'It doesn't look good.'

Sister gave him a sharp glance as if to say 'let me be the judge of that', but Maud could see that she was also looking a little perplexed by the new admission, especially when every time she tried to ask the woman anything she just screamed her head off.

'Bring those screens from over there, please, you two,' said Sister.

'They never had these on the men's ward,' said Eddy as they picked up the folded wooden screens and brought them to the bed.

'Now put them one at each side,' said Sister, 'just to give us some privacy.'

Maud and Eddy did as they were told and then squeezed in at the opposite side of the bed to Sister.

'Now,' said Sister to the patient, 'I need you to try to be calm.' The woman screamed again but not quite as loud. 'I need you to try to tell me what has been happening today. Tell me where the pain is.'

'It's all 'ere,' said the woman, 'and it comes and goes,' clutching again at her belly as a new wave of pain hit her.

Maud saw a glint of recognition on Sister's face as she let the woman ride out the pain before she spoke again. 'Have you been losing any blood from down below?' she said before the pain came back again.

'I 'ave, but I thought it was just me monthly

241

courses coming, but there's been much more than usual and I 'aven't seen anything for months and months.'

'Could you be with child?' said Sister.

'No, no,' screamed the woman as another wave of pain hit her. 'It can't be that, it can't be.'

'Can I just have a little feel at your belly, please?' said Sister, and the woman nodded, tears starting to stream down her face.

Sister Pritchard pulled up the woman's nightgown, which was all that she was wearing, having been carried in straight from her bed that morning. Then she placed the flat of her hand on the woman's abdomen and had a feel around. The woman was soon screaming with pain again and whilst that was happening Sister kept her hand resting there until the pain had gone. The poor woman seemed to be in a constant ebb and flow of pain. Maud felt so sorry for her.

Then Sister removed her hand and leant down to the woman, taking her hand. 'I think you are with child,' she said quietly.

'No, no, I can't be,' said the woman but Sister persisted.

'You are with child,' she said. 'You might be about five or six months gone and the baby is coming early. That is what's happening: you are in labour.'

The woman started to cry quite loudly.

'I am sorry,' said Sister. 'Truly I am sorry, but there is nothing we can do to stop the baby from coming and it is far too soon for it to be born. I am so sorry.'

'I didn't even know about it,' sobbed the

woman. 'I told 'im we shouldn't do it but he kept saying, 'Don't you worry, Lil, we'll be married in spring. What does it matter?' And now look at — Aaargh!' she screamed out. The pain was getting stronger and to Maud, who was standing tense by the bed, completely caught up in what was happening, it seemed like she could feel it too. Her heart was beating fast and she was hoping that they would be taking the woman to theatre so that she could have some chloroform, but there didn't seem to be any sign of that. She glanced at Eddy, who stood transfixed, her eyes wide.

Then the woman gave another scream and her face changed in some way. Sister pulled down the sheet and glanced between the woman's legs.

'The baby is coming now, Lil,' she said. 'You will feel like you need to push. Just push, push as hard as you can.'

Maud saw Eddy grab hold of the woman's hand and she heard her tell the woman to squeeze her hand as hard as she needed to. Then Lil pushed and pushed as some kind of dark mass started to emerge and then she stopped pushing. When Maud looked down at the bed, there lay a tiny baby. It was the saddest thing that Maud had ever seen: ugly and yet beautiful all at the same time. It had all its arms and legs and a tiny face, and then, to her horror, it started to open its little mouth and it gave some kind of gasp. It was trying to breathe. Maud felt the sorrow of the world inside her as she gazed at that poor scrap of life that didn't stand any chance of survival. She had never seen anything so awful. When she looked at Eddy she could see that tears were streaming down her face and she reached out and took her friend's hand.

Sister Pritchard took off her apron and folded it neatly and then she picked up that tiny scrap of life and laid it on the clean cloth. There was still a thin, twisty cord attached to the baby's belly so she took a pair of scissors out of her pocket and cut through it, so that it was free.

Wrapping the baby very carefully in her clean apron, Sister Pritchard went up to the head of the bed and stood holding the bundle. 'Here is your baby,' she said gently. 'It's a girl, but she is too small and has been born far too soon so she wasn't able to breathe. All we can do for her now is to hold her and pay our respects.'

The new mother started to cry and then she held her arms out for the tiny bundle that Sister gently gave to her.

Then Sister went back to the other end of the bed and said, 'When you feel you need to push again, just do that, will you? The afterbirth still needs to come and it's important for you that we get it all out.'

Lil nodded, tears streaming down her face. Maud fished in her pocket and handed her a handkerchief, and then she gave her spare handkerchief to Eddy, who was still crying at the bedside. As the two nurse probationers stood and watched they saw the woman touch the face of the tiny baby and then she loosened the apron that Sister had wrapped her in and looked at the baby's body. Maud was fascinated by the tiny fingers and toes that it had, all absolutely perfect. Then the woman looked at them both and said, 'She is so lovely.'

'She is,' said Maud and Eddy together, both transfixed by the tiny bundle that the woman held close to her heart.

'That's it, push the afterbirth, that's good,' said Sister, paying full attention to what was going on down at the other end. Then Maud saw her scrutinize what had been delivered. When she saw her looking, Sister said quietly, 'It is very important to check that everything comes away. Afterbirth left behind can cause a fever and make the mother very sick or worse. We are hoping that this woman will be able to go on and have other children.'

Maud understood instantly and nodded her head.

Satisfied that all was in order, Sister Pritchard then straightened up from the bed and said, 'Right, Nurse Linklater. Please can you get me a bowl from the sluice?'

Maud was gone in an instant, relieved to be away from the bed behind the screen for a few minutes. Grabbing one of the bowls she headed back down the ward, slipping behind the screen to find Eddy was now kneeling by the bedside and holding the woman's hand as she sat cradling the baby in the crook of one arm. She's good at this kind of thing, thought Maud as she placed the bowl on the bed for Sister to put the afterbirth in. Sister stood for a moment longer by the side of the bed and then she gestured for Maud to leave and Eddy to continue doing whatever it was that seemed to come absolutely naturally to her.

'We'll leave you now,' said Sister Pritchard quietly, gazing with sadness at the mother. 'Everything has come away. You will be all right, though I'm so sorry about your baby. Nurse Pacey will stay with you for as long as you need.'

When they stepped out from behind the screen, Sister headed up the ward and Maud was about to follow her when she heard the sound of a woman sniffing. It was the woman in the next bed, at the other side of the screen, and she had tears streaming down her face.

'I'm sorry, Nurse,' said the woman. 'I'll pull meself together; I'll be all right.'

'Please, please don't worry,' said Maud, guessing the woman's tears were about what had just happened at the other side of the screen.

'You carry on with your work, Nurse. You keep going. I know how busy you are.'

'No, no,' said Maud, 'that's all right, honestly. Sister told us to take as much time down here as we needed. Tell me what it is. Please tell me.'

'No, no, I'm just being a sentimental old woman. I will be fine.'

But Maud persisted, crouching down by the side of her bed and gently putting a hand on her arm.

'What is it?' she said. 'You can tell me.'

The woman looked at her with such sorrow that Maud felt a pain go right through her body. She knew that sorrow like that must have taken a whole lifetime to grow.

'It's just that, what happened just now to that

246

young lass behind that screen . . . it happened to me over fifty years ago when I was first married. I lost one as well.' Then she started to cry again and her chest sounded tight, like she was holding on to something deep inside.

Maud took hold of the woman's hand and continued to crouch by the bed.

'And, do you know what, I never forgot that little baby. Even though I went on to 'ave six more, I never forgot that little one. And when it happened to me, the woman who was with me, she just bundled it up and took it away. She didn't even let me look at it. I don't even know if it was a boy or a girl.'

The woman cried harder then, really letting her feelings come out.

Maud squeezed her hand a bit tighter, not knowing what to say, but needing to show that she felt something for her and understood that she was still grieving. Even though it had happened such a long time ago, for her it was still fresh.

'This is the first time that I've ever been able to tell anybody what 'appened to me, apart from me mother, and she said best not to speak of it. 'Least said, soonest mended,' she told me. I never could tell my husband. He was working away at the time and he never even knew that there'd been a baby. I kept all of it to meself for all of these years. I'm glad I've told you now, though, Nurse. It's made me feel a bit lighter in some way. I might be dying now. I've got this big lump in me belly: I think it's a cancer. The doctor hasn't said but I can tell that he's thinkin' the same and he's askin' if I've got anyone at home to look after me. I will probably be dying soon . . . '

Maud shook her head and she started to say, 'No, no, don't — ' but then she saw the woman smile.

'No, it is all right. I mean, I've had me three score year and ten, and then some more, and that husband of mine — he went thirty years ago. No, I've lived longer than anybody in my family has ever, so I'm content with that. I've still got three of my six children. Two got caught by the diphtheria when they were little and another drowned at sea — he left five children of his own. So I'm lucky I've still got three of my children and they're in work; they'll look after me. And now that I've told you about the baby, it's like I said, a weight seems to have lifted off me.'

Maud smiled. 'I'm glad that you told me. Thank you for that,' she said.

'No, thank you,' said the woman. 'Thank you, Nurse. I know it's your first day on the ward — I've been here two weeks and I've never seen you before — but with your lovely face and your kind eyes you have really helped me today. Some people think that old women like me have lived so long we don't feel anything any more. But they're wrong. We feel all the sorrows of the world, and we have all got so many of our own to bear as well. So I thank you, Nurse, for listening to me today. What is your name? Then I can remember you.'

'Nurse Linklater,' said Maud.

248

'Well, I'm Martha,' said the woman, 'and I can see Sister Pritchard coming back down the ward, and I know that she is one of the kindest people on God's earth but she is a real stickler, so you'd best get moving and get on with the work.'

'Thank you,' said Maud, with a conspiratorial gleam in her eye. 'I'll come back and see you later.'

Martha smiled at her and then Maud saw her rest her head back on the pillow and close her eyes.

'Nurse Linklater,' said Sister Pritchard, 'is Nurse Pacey still with Lil?'

'Yes, she is,' said Maud. 'Do you want me to —'

'No, no,' said Sister, 'leave her for as long as the patient needs.'

And in fact it was an hour or more before Eddy emerged from behind the screen to say that Lil was ready for them to take the baby away. Sister Pritchard had given strict instructions to Maud that they must let the woman hand over the baby to them, not to take it from her, and that's exactly what they did — well, what Eddy did.

'She called the baby Florence, after Florence Nightingale,' said Eddy.

'Really?' said Maud, looking at her friend with raised eyebrows. 'Is that a good idea, to name her? Will that not make it harder for her to forget?'

'I don't think so, Maud,' said Eddy straight out. 'The thing is, she won't ever forget what happened here today. It's important to remember these things, and having a name for the baby will make it easier for her to remember, that's all. She will be glad that she at least gave her a name and was able to spend some time with her.'

Maud understood instantly what Eddy was saying and, in that moment, as she looked at her friend standing there in the sluice with her nurse's cap skew-whiff on her head and that look of wonder that she always seemed to have on her face, she knew that Eddy was very probably one of the wisest women on earth.

'Well, you've both had quite an introduction to Female Surgical,' said Sister Pritchard later that day. 'You did well. Something like that is not easy to deal with and it isn't something that every nurse can manage. But, Nurse Pacey, the way you were with that woman, I think that you managed it all very well. I'll see if you can spend some time on the lying-in ward. Is that all right?'

'Yes,' said Eddy, breaking into a smile. 'Yes, indeed.'

'And Sister Law has already told me about you,' said Sister Pritchard, turning to Maud. 'We will make sure that you are given the opportunity to work in theatre as often as you can.'

'Thank you,' said Maud, grateful that she was not going to be sent to the lying-in ward. She wouldn't relish witnessing something like today's birth again.

As they walked back at the end of the shift Eddy was all excited and full of what had happened that day but Maud just felt numb. She wished that she could be more like Eddy, who seemed to be able to feel for people — really to feel for them — but then get herself back to normal as well afterwards. Maud had been thinking about that baby all day long and then she'd been worrying that Alice's might be about the same size by now, and what if something happened to her baby? What if it, too, was born too early? And so she told Eddy that she wouldn't be coming for tea, she wasn't all that hungry.

'Come on,' said Eddy. 'At least try.'

Maud shook her head but then seeing the look on Eddy's face, with her big eyes pleading like a puppy, she couldn't say no to her.

Even though she knew that she should eat something she could manage only a nibble of bread and couldn't even face a sip of beer. She had to give it all to Eddy. She sat through the whole meal, listening to Eddy chatter on while the stuff from the ward was still playing in her head and she knew that she would need to do something to shift it or she wouldn't be able to sleep that night. She realized, although she tried to resist even thinking about it, that there was only one thing that she could do that might distract her: something that had kept coming and going in her head all day long, something that she knew for a fact was absolutely the wrong thing to do, but she was desperate for distraction. *Desperate.*

So after Eddy had put on her hat with the red silk flowers and gone into the city that evening, Maud got herself changed and set out on her own mission. She knew exactly where she was going, even though it wasn't anywhere near the right thing to do. She was going along to the park to find Harry and watch him fight. As she walked she kept trying to talk herself out of it. Why would she want to see two men battering each other, especially since one of them was someone who, despite herself, she was starting to have feelings for? But it seemed like the more she tried to talk herself out of it, the more determined her feet were to keep walking in that direction. She could not stop. But when she reached her destination, the place was deserted. Just empty grass with some patches worn to bare earth and some handbills blowing around in the gentle breeze.

She picked up one of the handbills and there was the answer. Scrawled writing on the piece of paper read, *'TONIGHT'S EVENT CAN-CELLED. WILL TAKE PLACE ON . . . '* and the date was the following day. Maud couldn't be totally sure the event referred to was the one that she'd been hoping to attend, but she'd heard that these fights weren't really meant to take place, and might even be illegal, so it was very likely. Well, that just shows you, Maud, she thought. It was not meant to be and you have been saved from yourself so that is that. Promising herself there and then that come the next evening she wouldn't even be thinking about Harry Donahue or his dog, she wandered back to the Nurses' Home at something of a loose end. On a whim, having not checked her pigeonhole for mail for a few days, she walked over to have a look as soon as she was back through the door. It was stuffed full of things for Miss Langtry as usual, but sticking out from all of that was a cream vellum envelope for her. A letter from Miss Fairchild.

Maud pulled it out with excitement, she was desperate for news of Alfred, anything that would distract her, so she tore at the envelope to get at it as quickly as possible. But as she read, she felt her legs buckling underneath her.

Dear Maud,

I called to see you, only to be told that you had gone out. I am so sorry to tell you this news by letter and not in person but I needed you to know straight away. Our dear Alfred has gone missing from the school. When I went up there today I was told that he had disappeared without trace yesterday. No one saw him go, no one has any idea where the poor boy is. I am so sorry.

All I can suggest is that you and I make enquiries where we can. Please would you ask anyone that you know to be on the lookout in the city? I hate to say it but I fear the hand of Mr Greer in all of this. I have been down there today to see him and he denies all knowledge. He said that he has been ill recently and in hospital and he had seen you, so I wondered if you had any thoughts. I don't trust him one little bit.

I am in despair, Maud. Please come and

see me as soon as you can.

Ever yours,
Constance Fairchild

Maud crumpled the letter in her hand and leant forward with a hand against the wall, supporting herself. She felt as if the wind had been knocked out of her by a single blow. Thoughts spun through her head. Where could he be? Who has done this? And all the time a feeling of crushing anxiety bore down on her until she almost cried out in pain.

'Maud,' said a voice behind her, and then Alice was there, cradling her. 'What is it? Please tell me.'

Maud couldn't speak. She just turned to face Alice and then clung to her friend with tears streaming down her face. Then, after a few minutes, knowing that she had to take control of herself, she stood back from Alice and handed her the crumpled letter to let her read for herself.

'Oh, Maud,' said Alice, a hand coming up over her mouth, 'whatever are we going to do?'

Maud wanted to go to see Miss Fairchild there and then, and she was heading for the door before she heard Alice pleading with her to wait: it was far too late now, she would never be back in time before the door was locked and she didn't need a strong reprimand to deal with alongside all the anxiety over Alfred.

'Besides, look at the state of you. You're not fit to go off walking through the city at this time of night,' said Alice. 'You need to stay here for now. Go and see Miss Fairchild tomorrow.'

Maud reluctantly turned back from the door. Of course Alice was right. So she climbed the stone stairs to the gallery with her legs feeling heavy and her head bowed. Alice wanted to take her arm to help her along but she insisted that she could manage and was even able to go along to Alice's room and sit on the bed with her for a while before being forced to admit that she needed to get to bed and try to get some rest.

Meticulous as always, Maud removed her nurse's cap and placed it square on the chest of drawers. Then she took off the uniform and hung it straight, before at last sliding into bed and burying her face into her pillow so that she could have a silent cry. She could almost sense that Nancy was listening to her every move from across the corridor. There was no way on earth that she wanted to give her the satisfaction of knowing that she was in absolute despair over the disappearance of Alfred.

14

'People often say to me you don't know what a
wife and mother feels. No, I say, I don't and
I'm very glad I don't.'

Florence Nightingale

Alice must have spoken to Eddy because she
bounded straight into Maud's room the next
morning telling her that she was sorry to hear
the news, and she would help her to get dressed
and take her to the ward.

As soon as they got there, however, Sister
Pritchard took one look at Maud's face and
demanded to know what was wrong. Sister
listened carefully and then said she had an idea.
She wanted Maud to go to see Miss Houston,
not in her office, but in her quarters, which was
where she would be at this time of day.

Afterwards Maud would not even remember
finding her way there, but somehow she
presented herself in front of Miss Houston,
whose companion was a little white dog with a
brown patch over one eye, wagging its tail and
making a fuss.

'Go on, Bob, go on,' said Miss Houston,
shooing the dog back into her room and then
walking over to the bed and patting the bottom
of it for the dog to jump up and lie down.

'Sorry about that, Nurse Linklater,' she said.

'He's getting very old, but he still likes to make a fuss.'

Maud asked why Miss Houston had a little dog in her room and the superintendent told her about it belonging to a friend that she'd had out in the Crimea. Something like that — Maud couldn't quite remember all the details afterwards.

She did remember Miss Houston taking her hand and leading her over to an armchair next to the fire and giving her a cup of hot tea, placing it on a small table next to the chair. And then she was telling Miss Houston everything, before falling completely silent.

Maud wasn't sure how long she sat but eventually she looked up at Miss Houston and said, 'I had a dream that I could find work at the Infirmary for Women in New York, and I'd planned to take Alfred with me.'

'I can understand just how worried you must be,' said Miss Houston, 'but hold on to that dream. It's a good one and it might still be possible. Alfred could have wandered off somewhere. It is much more likely that he is safe than not. We just have to work out how to find him. There are many places that a boy could be in this huge city. What you need is a plan.'

Maud lifted her head but, despite Miss Houston's attempts at reassurance, she remained desperately anxious. She knew Alfred: she knew that he loved his lessons at the school and she knew that he wouldn't just wander off into the city. There was someone responsible for all of this. It was too much of a coincidence that Greer had been admitted to the ward and he had confronted her about the boy. Someone had told him where the boy was, and she knew almost certainly that person was Nancy.

Miss Houston listened very carefully to everything else that Maud had to say and in the end she agreed that Mr Greer probably had a hand in Alfred's disappearance and he may well have asked about the boy and enquired if anyone knew where he had gone. Maud didn't mention Nancy's name. She knew that she would have to deal with that issue on her own for now. Nurse Sellers always presented as someone completely beyond reproach and as far as most of the senior staff were concerned she could do no wrong. Maud didn't want to be seen to be making unfounded accusations.

'What you need is some time to go up and see your friend, this Miss Fairchild, and then take it from there,' said Miss Houston. 'Take the rest of the day off. I will clear it with Sister Pritchard.'

Maud opened her mouth to protest but Miss Houston insisted and in the end Maud had to accept. She needed time to start the search for Alfred.

Maud was very grateful for Miss Houston's understanding and, not wanting to take any more of her precious time, she stood up to leave. The little dog lifted his head and she went over to the bed to give him a quick scratch behind the ears and then she thanked Miss Houston before leaving, clicking the door shut behind her. As soon as Maud heard that click it was as if something snapped inside of her and she knew that there was no way that she would be able to stop herself from seeing one more person before she made her way to Devonshire Square.

None of the nurses batted an eyelid as Maud marched on to Female Medical. It was common for probationers to be sent with messages or to pick up equipment. She walked straight in and down the centre of the ward and luckily she spied Nancy heading into the sluice. Maud followed her in without hesitating.

Nancy turned around instantly and Maud registered the shock on her face and then the glint in her eyes.

Maud held her gaze and there was silence for a few moments. Then she saw that Nancy was about to speak so she cut her short. 'You know exactly why I'm here, don't you?' she said, still holding Nancy's gaze.

'I have no idea what you are talking about,' said Nancy, starting to smirk.

'Oh, yes you do,' said Maud. 'You know full well that Alfred has gone missing from the Blue Coat School. I can see it in your face.'

'Tut tut, Nurse Linklater, it sounds like you might be losing your very small mind. I know nothing of the sort. Why would I know anything about that rag-tag boy? I do, however, remember telling you that the likes of him would do no good at a place like that.'

'Well, we'll see about that,' said Maud, not deterred in the slightest by Nancy's outright lies.

Nancy glanced down to the floor and then looked up with another smile. 'Oh, there is one more thing. A patient who was on Male Surgical

259

recently — a man I know you are acquainted with, a Mr Greer — has made a complaint to Sister Law that some money of his went missing when he was on the ward and I am about to tell Sister that I saw what happened that day . . . I saw you take that money, Maud, and Sister will believe me. I can make sure that she believes me and — '

Maud stepped forward and grabbed Nancy, pushing her back against the sink and then ruthlessly patting her down to find the pocket in her uniform. She was right: she felt the hard outline of the flask straight away and she was so quick and Nancy was so shocked that Maud had it in her grasp and pulled out of that pocket and she was stepping back before Nancy knew what had hit her.

Maud unscrewed the lid and there was no need to even take a sniff. The smell of the liquor hit her nostrils straight away.

Nancy growled at her and tried to grab the flask and they were locked close together again, so close that Maud could see Nancy's dilated pupils and smell the remains of her floral scent from the night before, but Maud had the flask held fast and there was no way that she was letting go.

'Make one more move, Nancy Sellers, and I will yell for Sister Fox to come in here right now. There may even be some traces of that paint you put on your lips on the neck of this flask as well.'

Maud could see with some satisfaction that Nancy's breathing was rapid and her face was flushed. For once she had lost her composure.

'Right,' said Maud, 'now I have your attention I will ask you a question. Did you tell Greer where Alfred was going when he was discharged?'

Nancy stood silent, her lips pressed together, but Maud had the satisfaction of seeing that her eyes were dull and she had an air of defeat. She knew straight away that she wouldn't get an answer from Nancy, but she stood there for a few moments longer before walking over to the slop bucket and emptying out the contents of the flask before pushing it back into Nancy's hand.

'There, you might need that,' spat Maud. 'I know exactly what you've done, Nancy, but don't worry, we will not rest till we find the boy and bring him home. And another thing: stay right away from Alice.'

Nancy opened her mouth but no words would come. For the first time ever she had been silenced.

As Maud headed back to the Nurses' Home she started to feel lighter than she'd done for some time. With every step she felt a bit stronger and she knew that she was ready to get on with the search for Alfred. Now she felt like she could conquer the world.

★　★　★

Maud was soon changed and stepping out of her room as quietly as she could, almost on tiptoe, even though there was nobody else in the dormitories at this time. Or at least that's what she thought, but she was almost sure that she could hear some noise coming from across the gallery, from the room opposite. It sounded like someone crying. Yes, she was sure that's what it was. Was it possible that Nancy had made some excuse to come off the ward and followed her out? Well, if that was the case, then she was glad. Maybe something had at last struck a chord with Nancy. Maybe she had realized what she had done and she was actually feeling sorry. But these were just passing thoughts. Maud felt absolutely nothing for Nancy, so she turned away from her door and headed quietly down the stone stairs.

Maud hadn't been back to the big house for weeks and it felt very strange indeed standing outside on the back step, rapping on the door. It made her realize how settled she had become in the new world of the hospital. For the first time she felt like a visitor coming back to a place that she had once known so well. She stood for a while before she gave the solid wooden door another knock. She knew how busy they always were in the kitchen, but this second time the door opened instantly and a kitchen maid she had never seen before showed her in. Before she knew it she was standing next to Cook in front of the huge black-enamelled range.

'Maud,' Cook said, grabbing hold of her shoulders and hugging her so hard that Maud could hardly breathe, 'have you decided to come back to us?'

'No,' said Maud, leaning back to escape Cook's mighty grasp. 'I've come to see Miss Fairchild. Is she in her room?'

Cook glanced at the kitchen clock. 'She will be at this time. She's a creature of habit, as you well know. Let our new maid show you the way. It's only her second day. She can't find her way around the kitchen yet, never mind the rest of the house, so the practice will do her good.' Cook called across the kitchen at the maid, who was polishing the best knives with a cloth.

Maud saw the fear in the girl's eyes when she looked up instantly.

She seems really nice, thought Maud, and she wished that Cook could be more patient with the new maid. She remembered her own first few days, how hard it was, and the girl was so young.

Cook must have seen Maud's sympathetic gaze because she gave a sigh and then softened her voice as the maid came over. 'Go on then, you flibbertigibbet,' she said, setting off the giggles from the girl, who had at least started to move and then followed Maud out of the kitchen.

'I'll let you lead the way,' said Maud as they came out into the passageway, 'then you'll start to get used to it. I know what it's like: it seems like a maze of rooms at first.'

The maid smiled at her again and then slipped in front.

'I'm all right now,' said Maud, 'thank you,' as the new maid walked her straight past the door to Miss Fairchild's room. 'You'd best get back to the kitchen . . . that way,' she said, pointing in the direction that they had just come. 'And don't worry, underneath all of that bluster Cook has a heart of gold.'

The kitchen maid smiled her thanks and Maud turned to the door, tapped on it and went straight in. She found Miss Fairchild sitting behind her small desk by the window and as soon as she saw Maud she stood up and came over to embrace her.

'I know, I know,' said Maud, 'I came as soon as I could. I'm sorry it wasn't sooner.'

Miss Fairchild nodded and then went back over to her desk and sat down heavily on the chair, gesturing for Maud to sit opposite. She seemed thinner than Maud remembered and the starched white cap on her head was slightly askew. Maud could see that she had dark smudges under her eyes and, leaning back in her seat, she looked weary. Seeing this woman who had always been so straight-backed and strong look so troubled triggered a surge of strength inside Maud that she had never known she had. I will sort this out, she thought. I will make this all right.

'So, Miss Fairchild,' she said, mustering all the energy that she could into her voice and leaning forward in her seat, 'tell me everything you know.'

'Well, I've been up to the school and the man on the door said that Alfred was missing after the weekly visiting time. The children had all been out in the courtyard and it was very busy so it was difficult to say, but he thought that a woman had visited him that day. He had remarked on it because although Alfred seemed to know her he was looking a bit subdued. Anyway, the place was so busy and there had been other children

264

visited that day as well so it was only when they were doing the register in the classroom that they realized that he was missing.'

Maud reached a hand out to Miss Fairchild when she gave a sob, determined to hold back her own tears, which weren't that far away. She held the housekeeper's hand until she was able to carry on with the story.

'They didn't worry too much at first, the doorman said, because sometimes the rascals do go missing for a few hours, but Alfred didn't come back and that's when they sent word to me. The thing is, Maud, from the description that the man gave of the woman who visited Alfred I thought that it could be Bill Greer's wife. I'm not certain but my suspicions were strong enough for me to go straight over to Greer's place on Market Street and ask them if they knew anything. He was there and she was busy out in front of the house selling pots and rags on that stall that she runs. I've met her a number of times. She knows who I am but she never even looked at me. Anyway, of course Greer said he knew nothing but he looked shifty as hell. Mind you, he often does so that's not really anything to go on. He showed me all through the house and even out to that infernal shed at the back where he keeps the donkey. There was absolutely no sign of the boy. But I've known Greer for years and I'm sure he wasn't being straight with me. Him and that wife of his are behind all of this.'

Sadly, Maud had to agree. As she sat there

nodding her head she was surprised at how calm she was feeling.

'I suppose what we have to think about is this,' she said steadily. 'If it is our Mr Greer who has taken Alfred, he wouldn't have gone to the trouble to do that unless there was some profit to be gained. So, if that is the case then maybe we can assume that Alfred will be kept safe somewhere?'

Miss Fairchild didn't look too sure but she said, 'I suppose you're right, Maud, and of course I've known Mr Greer for years. He isn't all that savoury, if you know what I mean, but I don't think he would set out to deliberately harm the boy. I mean, in his day, the man was the best sweep for miles around — I wouldn't have kept him on for so long if that hadn't been the case — and at that time all the sweeps were sending small boys, and sometimes girls, up the chimneys. So we had no choice. Thank goodness that at last, in this modern world of ours, things are changing. We did the right thing rescuing Alfred that day and now we need to make sure that he is safe yet again.'

'We will,' said Maud firmly.

'I hope that you are right,' said Miss Fairchild quietly. 'He is such a dear boy and he was doing so well at the school. The teacher there said that he was one of the brightest boys that they'd ever had.'

'So what shall we do?' Maud said practically, looking over at Miss Fairchild with a determined expression.

To Maud's relief she saw Miss Fairchild

straighten her back and a bit of a glint was coming back into her eyes.

'Well,' she said, 'I've already commissioned some handbills with a full description of Alfred and a drawing of him, which are now circulating around the city. I'm hoping that someone might recognize him. I made sure that I mentioned his bright blue eyes, which are quite distinctive. The problem we face, however, is that there are so many missing children in Liverpool and so many living on the streets. It is just terrible, Maud, to think of all those poor children out there with no proper beds, freezing cold at nights and at risk of all sorts. I can't bear to think of Alfred — or any of them for that matter — without homes to go to. If only we could rescue them all.'

Maud could feel the ebb and flow of Miss Fairchild's emotion and tried to reassure her dear friend. 'All we can do for now, Constance, is look for Alfred. When he is safely back at the school, then let's think about what we can do for the other children.'

'Yes, you are right — of course you are — Maud. I knew that you had a level head on you. You always seemed so quiet and wistful when you were working here as a housemaid, but now, with your work at the hospital, I am starting to see the strength in you.'

Maud reached over and gave Miss Fairchild's arm a squeeze. 'Now look, I will walk every street in this city and speak to every person on every street corner if I have to. I will do everything in my power to find Alfred.'

Miss Fairchild looked up and offered Maud a small smile. 'I know you will, Maud. I know you will . . . ' she said.

'Now I need to get going,' said Maud, standing up from her chair. 'I'll start by having a look at Greer's place and then I'll walk out through the city and try to get some idea of where a missing boy might go. I know some people I can ask,' she added.

'That's good,' said Miss Fairchild. 'Thank you, Maud. I will send a note to you directly if I hear anything at all.'

'I will do the same,' said Maud.

As soon as Maud was back in the kitchen Cook glanced round from the stove where any number of shiny copper pans stood bubbling and, as always, there sat the kettle singing away next to them.

'You done now?' said Cook.

'Yes,' said Maud.

'Right then,' said Cook, shoving her sleeves further up her meaty forearms. 'Before you go I want you to sit down at this table and have a cup of tea and a piece of cake.'

'No, really I need to — '

'Sit,' said Cook.

It was the first time that Maud had sat at that scrubbed, deal table since her last day at the big house all those months ago. She slipped tentatively into one of the chairs, sitting a bit sideways, feeling almost like the thirteen-year-old girl that she had been all those years ago on her first day in service.

Cook brought the tea and cake over. 'Swivel

your legs under, lass,' she said. 'Make yourself comfortable.'

Cook urged her to drink, saying, 'Don't worry, this doesn't mean we're expecting you will be coming back to work with us. Miss Fairchild has been telling us how well you are doing up there at the hospital and we are all very proud of you.'

Maud looked up and gave a small smile. She felt a warm glow inside her. She had no idea that her progress was being followed so closely. She'd thought that once she had left then she would be forgotten. She continued to smile at Cook as she picked up the china cup by its delicate handle and carefully sipped the hot tea. As she lowered the cup and felt it clink on to the saucer she knew for certain that although this was still the finest tea that she would ever taste, and she really missed drinking from a fancy cup, there was no way that she would choose to go back into domestic service.

★   ★   ★

Maud went straight to Market Street. She knew where Greer's place was because she'd once been sent by Miss Fairchild with a note. The place was packed out with people buying and selling and she had to elbow her way through to get a closer look at the house. She could see Mrs Greer at her stall full of pots and grimy rags. She always wore black and her skin was grey. She didn't look up from her work and, in amongst the crowd, Maud could take some time to study the closed windows and the door of the house. It looked empty and gave nothing away.

Disappointed, Maud turned away at last and went further down the street, looking for clues and determined to check the whole area. She walked until her feet hurt, scanning the crowds for stray children, trying to get some idea of where children gathered. They seemed to be everywhere and by the end of that day she knew how vast this task she had set herself actually was. She had been heartened to see a few of Miss Fairchild's 'missing boy' handbills on lampposts and in shop windows and she took one, folding it carefully and putting it into her pocket. But what she became aware of immediately was that the notices about Alfred were set amongst many such notices: missing boys, girls, women and men. It felt like half the city had gone missing. Towards the end of the day, when she saw some of the bills with the drawing of Alfred on them scattered in the street and trampled underfoot, she began to feel desperately sad.

She called by Stella's. She needed to know her little friend had gone missing and she might even have some idea where a missing boy might be. But Marie told her that Stella was 'out all day'; she would have to wait to speak to her. As Maud walked away from the blue painted door with which she was becoming increasingly familiar, she knew that there was only one other option if she wanted to feel that she had made some progress that day. The one person who, of course, had come to mind first as a source of help would, she knew, be in the park that night.

Harry Donahue was her only hope now. She would go out that evening after Eddy had gone into the city and Alice was resting on her bed. She would go back to the park and seek him out. As she walked back to the Nurses' Home she was telling herself over and over that there was no way on earth that she would even be thinking of doing that if Alfred hadn't gone missing.

★ ★ ★

Maud was stunned by the number of people crammed into the small park. She couldn't see properly what was going on but she could hear a man's voice shouting out. He seemed to be standing in the middle of it all. As Maud stood on tiptoe she saw the head of the big fella, the one that she had nursed on the ward, Daphne's man. He must have been knocked down on the ground because it looked like he was just getting up. Maud could see that he was swaying around and there was blood coming from his nose and, my, did he look fierce. He looked like he could rip someone limb from limb. She felt a tightness in her chest when she realized who the big fella's opponent must be although she couldn't see him. Was he already laid out on the grass? Was he injured . . . was he dead?

No, he can't be, thought Maud. The people squashed up next to her were alive with excitement as they watched and she sensed that they were waiting for something. So there must still be two men standing, at least for now. She knew that she needed to get much closer if she was going to have some chance of seeing Harry so she started to push and shove her way through. The more she pushed and the more people were still in front of her, the more desperate to see Harry she became. She began to wish that she was huge like the big fella and that she could just scream and roar and send bodies flying to either side until she got to him.

Then she could see a gap near the front as a woman turned away with a groan and Maud pushed through. She was at the ringside just in time to see Harry, facing her, blood streaming from a small cut above his eye. He was breathing fast, his face contorted and dripping with sweat, and stripped to the waist so she could see the muscles in his arms and his chest as he stood ready to deliver the next punch. The crowd seemed to be holding its breath as one.

Bang! Harry punched the big fella and he swayed but didn't go down. Then Harry looked in Maud's direction and caught her eye. She saw the fleeting surprise on his face and then, in that instant, the big fella cracked Harry square on the chin and knocked him flat. There was a groan from the crowd and the other man in the ring stood over Harry counting: one, two, three, four . . . Harry started to struggle up from the grass, leaning up on his elbow . . . five, six, seven, eight . . . There was blood dripping from his nose, and Maud made a move to go to help him, but the man next to her grabbed her arm and wouldn't let go.

'You stay where you are,' he said, his voice gruff.

Maud's heart was pounding, but she could feel the man's hand digging into her upper arm. She couldn't move; all she could do was watch.

'Nine, ten,' said the man in the ring, and Maud saw Harry's head drop straight back down. There was a cheer from some of the crowd as the big fella held both hands in the air to signal his victory. Then he went straight over to Harry, who was still lying on the ground, and Maud saw with horror that he didn't seem to be moving.

She pulled her arm free from the man and threw herself forward in an effort to move towards Harry but she stopped as if frozen when she saw Nancy appear from the other side of the crowd, walk straight across to Harry and crouch down by his side. Maud could see that she had a cloth in her hand and she was sponging his face.

Of course, thought Maud, of course she is here. She is probably always here, hanging around. Maud wanted to turn away immediately and push her way back through the remaining crowd but she knew she had to stay for Alfred's sake. She had to see if Harry was in any fit state to help her.

She could see that Nancy was still crouching beside him on the ground and the big fella was looking down, his brow furrowed. Maud marched straight up and went round the other side of Harry, but he was out cold. She wouldn't be getting any information out of him this evening, that was for sure. She knew that Nancy was looking at her. She didn't want to show that she was shocked at seeing Harry's poor battered face and bloodied nose — surely it was broken yet again — so she muttered something along the lines of it being his own fault and then strode away with her head held high. Once she was at a safe distance she felt her knees go weak. She was so anxious about Harry — what if he died there on the grass? Then anger started to build inside her. What a stupid man, she thought, furious now with him and with the feelings that she had for him, and for the sheer frustration of not being any nearer to knowing where Alfred could be.

15

'It seems a commonly received idea among
men and even women themselves that it
requires nothing but a disappointment in love,
the want of an object, a general disgust,
or incapacity for other things, to turn
a woman into a good nurse.'

Florence Nightingale

Maud got up extra early the next morning. She
was always 'up with the lark', Cook used to say,
but she had started to soften a bit since she had
come to the hospital. Well, now was her chance
to get back to her usual standards. First up, first
ready, first to work, she thought as she marched
down the stairs to the dining room with her
mouth still set in the firm line that had
persisted from when she left the park the
evening before. She was first there and sitting in
an empty dining room, waiting for the kitchen
staff to catch up with her requirements, which
were not great: a meagre bowl of thin porridge
and a cup of tea, that's all she would be having
from now on.

She was up from the table and heading back
up the stairs to her room before Eddy and Alice
were out of their rooms. She had already told
Eddy that she would be making her own way to
the ward. Eddy understood. She knew that her

275

rushing and lateness didn't suit other people and she was used to running along to the ward on her own each morning. Maud wanted to get to the ward extra early because above all she did not want to have to see Nancy Sellers coming out of her room or sitting in the dining room with that smug expression on her face. She most certainly did not want to see her at all.

Sister Pritchard was already on the ward, taking report from the night staff, when Maud arrived. Sister looked up and smiled at her probationer before putting her head back down into conversation with the night Sister. Maud walked down the ward, ready to make a start. She could see a couple of empty beds that needed stripping. One of the beds had been occupied by Lil. She must have gone home, thought Maud. She was glad to get back to work and felt that she needed to throw herself into it, lose herself. She swore to herself that there would be no other life from now on, apart from helping her friends and finding Alfred. She would work hard — harder than anyone else — and that would be it. There would be nothing else.

True to her word, Maud went straight over to one of the empty beds and starting stripping off the sheets with some vigour. She was just tackling the pillowslip when she heard a voice calling to her quietly. She knew instantly it was Martha. Maud had walked past her bed, thinking that she was asleep so she hadn't said good morning, but now she could see she was wide awake and trying to sit up in bed.

'Are you all right?' said Maud. 'Do you want me to help you?'

'No, no, I'm fine, I can sort myself out . . . but what's happened to you since I last saw you? You look like you've been well and truly through the mill.'

'What? Oh, nothing really, no,' Maud tried to say but Martha was having none of it.

'Look,' she said, 'I saw you leave the ward yesterday and I asked your friend where you were, and she said you weren't well, but I could tell by her face there was more to it than that. Now, seeing you looking like you've seen a ghost, well, I know that for sure. Do you want to tell me? You know what they always say: a trouble shared is a trouble halved.'

'No, honestly, I'm fine, and you've got enough troubles of your own.'

'Now then, I'm not having that from you nor nobody. I've always had troubles — every family I know has troubles — but I've always wanted to try and help other people as well. I know there are some as only look to their own, but I'm not one of 'em and even though I'm in here and probably going to be dying soon, I still want to do what I've allus done and that's give a helping hand if I can. All I can do is listen, but in my experience being willing to give a good listen to anybody is a sure way of helping. Now the others won't be here for a bit yet so spit it out.'

It didn't seem that she had any other choice, so Maud crouched down by the side of Martha's bed and started quietly to pour out all that had happened with Alfred.

277

When she was finished Martha reached out a hand and gave Maud's arm a squeeze. Then she said, 'Well, I know it is a big worry. Even though the lad isn't your own kin, it does sound like you've really taken to him. And there is nothing I can say that will make you feel much better. I can't give you any guarantee that the lad will come back safe. But there are many people in this city of ours who are good people. Yes, there's some wrong 'uns as well, but there's more good people who might help a youngster who is lost or needs help. And from what you've told me about the boy, he is a special one. He has an old head on young shoulders. He will be thinking things through as well. Young as 'e is, he will get back to you and that Miss Fairchild if he possibly can. There is a chance he might be being held somewhere. One of mine went missin' when he was a lad. He was gone for weeks. I thought he was dead, but he'd been picked up off the street. He was about nine or ten, and he'd got a job as a messenger boy for the Cotton Exchange. He was doing right well with it and then one day he was out running an errand and he was grabbed by a gang, who wanted him to go climbing into houses, robbing stuff. He was locked up for weeks before he managed to escape. But he was a lad with a level head, a bit like your Alfred. He bided his time and then he got away. I'll never forget that day he came back and he bobbed up outside the window when I was peelin' the potatoes. Best day of my life when he came back. So your lad might well just turn up one day. Have you got somebody who can help you look?

Somebody who knows all parts of the city?'

'Oh, yes, yes, I know a woman who lives near Lime Street Station, and there's a man that I know as well who might be able to help, and I'll never stop looking,' said Maud.

'Good girl,' said Martha. 'Now I'm glad that you told me all of that. You look more like yourself already, and I want you to remember summat. I won't always be sat on this ward ready to push you into talking — in fact Sister says I might be able to go home today — so you think on: always talk about things if you can. Don't keep it locked up inside. Now then, you'd best get yourself shifting. I can see Sister Pritchard looking down the ward and she's wondering what us two are up to down 'ere.'

'Thanks,' said Maud quietly. 'Thanks, you have really helped me.'

Martha smiled and then lay back on the pillow and closed her eyes.

'Leave that bed, Nurse Linklater,' called Sister Pritchard. 'We have a patient going into theatre. I want you to go in with her and assist.'

'Yes, of course,' said Maud, feeling an instant sense of purpose as she walked back down the ward, glad to be asked to do a job that she was increasingly confident with. It was an orderly kind of work, which she liked. Following a procedure was very satisfying to her and she knew that once she was in through the door of that operating room she would be able to stop thinking and worrying about everything in the outside world. That was exactly what she needed right now.

It was well into the afternoon before Maud emerged from theatre. The first case had been complex and then they'd had another one to follow, and they had just started using some new techniques to try to keep the operating room clean. There was more washing down and scrubbing to do and they were using a spray of something called carbolic acid. Mr Jones had read somewhere that using it helped prevent the wounds from festering and it might help keep more people alive. It was too soon to know if it was making any difference but Sister Pritchard had already been keeping a record of the patients who had operations and what the outcome had been for them. She had showed Maud where she had drawn a thick line in the book at the point where they had started using the carbolic acid. That way, they would have some idea whether it helped. Maud was, of course, all in favour of improving cleanliness. She loved to give anything a good scour, particularly if she had some worry on her mind.

Coming back on to the ward always felt to Maud like coming back into the real world. She was instantly more aware of the patients crowded in, the activity of the nurses and the noise. It was visiting time as well. Only one person was allowed in at once on this ward and Maud could see the broad back of a man sitting by Martha's bed. That must be her son, she thought.

'Maud,' shouted a familiar voice from the far end of the ward. It was Eddy, smiling away and gesturing, a bit too dramatically in Maud's opinion, for her to go down the ward.

'We're stripping the beds down here,' she shouted again. 'Some patients are being discharged.'

Before Maud could move, she felt someone quietly place a hand on her arm. It was Sister Pritchard. 'Yes,' she said with a note of gentle amusement in her voice, 'Nurse Pacey can always be relied upon to let everyone know exactly what we are doing at any given moment. She is always enthusiastic, I'll give her that. I lent her out to the lying-in ward. They said she was excellent there with the women in labour: she just got on with it. The patients are, as you would expect, fairly noisy on there so our Nurse Pacey fitted right in. She will make an excellent midwife — I have already told her that — she is an absolute marvel.'

Maud was already smiling at what Sister Pritchard had just said. She knew that Eddy was a very special person, but she also knew that it was an exhausting experience to spend too much time with her all at once.

'Yes, she is amazing with the new mothers,' said Maud. 'I'll go down and help her with the beds, then, shall I?'

'Yes, but you might want to take a few minutes first to say goodbye to Martha. I know you have a soft spot for her. I've just spoken to her son. She is going home today. Sadly, there is nothing more that we can do for her here. She has a huge cancer in her abdomen; it's just a matter of time.'

Maud felt her stomach tighten. So Martha had been right: there was nothing that could be done; she was dying. 'Thank you, Sister,' Maud said, mustering as bright a voice as she could. 'I'll go and say goodbye.'

She was just in time. Martha was busy directing her son to put all her bits and pieces of belongings into a small bag. Maud stood by the bottom of the bed until they were finished and when Martha saw her she said, 'Maud, Nurse Linklater, this is my son. This is Gordon, the one I told you about, the one who went missing.'

'Mam, that was a long time ago,' said Gordon. 'What else has she been tellin' you?'

'Nothing else, I promise,' said Maud, matching the warm smile on Gordon's face. She could see the affection he had for his mother right there on his face.

'Now then,' said Martha, 'Sister has probably told you that I'm going home today, and I'm going to stay with Gordon and his lot for a few weeks.'

Gordon gave Maud a glance that told her he fully understood what was going on with his mother, and she wondered if he knew that Martha understood just as well — in fact had worked it all out some time ago.

'So I just want to say thank you again, Nurse Linklater, for all you did for me the other day. And you remember, don't keep things bottled up, talk to somebody,' said Martha when she was at last sure that Gordon had packed everything to her satisfaction.

'I won't forget,' said Maud, leaning down to

Martha as she beckoned for her to come closer so that she could speak in her ear.

'Don't you worry about me,' she whispered. 'Gordon told me what they said, I know what's happening and it's as I thought, but I will be fine. Sister gave me some of those drops to take if the pain comes back. So don't worry, I will be well looked after.'

Maud felt tears springing to her eyes but she fought to keep them at bay. She knew that it wouldn't help Martha or Gordon if she started crying. So, instead, she gave Martha a kiss on her cheek and said, 'Goodbye. I won't forget what you said.'

Martha stretched up a hand and gently stroked Maud's cheek, and then she whispered, 'I hope you find the lad and I hope that things work out with that young man that you mentioned. He will be a lucky man indeed if he ends up with someone like you.'

'But he's not my — '

'Maybe not yet,' said Martha, 'but an old woman like me knows stuff. I saw your face when you spoke about him and I knew.'

Maud shook her head but she couldn't help but smile.

'Right then,' said Gordon, 'let's get you back home. We've got some stone flags that need scrubbin' and a batch of bread to make.'

Seeing the look of surprise on Maud's face Gordon immediately explained, 'Of course not. She's going straight on to a bed near the fire, is this one, whether she likes it or not.'

Then Gordon slipped the small bag over his

shoulder, stooped down to wrap a blanket around his mother and then he swept her up off the bed. He picked her up as easy as anything and not until that moment did Maud realize how thin the woman was. She was tiny.

'Are you going to be able to carry her all the way home?' said Maud, concerned.

'Well, I carried her here,' he said, 'and that was in a bit of a rush, so I can take her home. She's as light as a feather and we only live two streets away.'

'All right then,' said Maud. 'You take care, Martha.'

'I will that,' she said. 'I just need to be with the family now, and don't you be worrying about me, Maud. You've got enough to worry about.'

And then Gordon nodded a goodbye and Maud watched as he turned his back and strode down the ward, carrying his mother. He carried her so steadily but with such tenderness, as if she was the most important thing in the world, that it brought tears to Maud's eyes. She stood there wondering if she would ever have anyone in her life that would care for her so much.

Feeling a hand on her arm, Maud turned to find Eddy. 'They are a good family, aren't they, Maud?' she said quietly.

Maud nodded and quickly wiped the tears from her eyes with the flat of her hand. 'Right then, Eddy, let's get on. Where do you want me?'

Maud and Eddy worked together for the rest of the day: stripping, cleaning and making beds, dressing wounds, bandaging, giving bedpans, administering an enema and applying two poultices. Being so busy really helped Maud. She had no time to think about anything else. Then, towards the end of the shift, she saw Miss Houston appear at the top of the ward, look down in their direction and then gesture for her to come. Yes, it was definitely her and not Eddy.

'Hey up,' said Eddy, 'what've you been up to now, Nurse Linklater?'

Maud had no idea, although she was hoping that Miss Houston might have some news about Alfred. She couldn't read anything from the superintendent's face; she would have thought that she would at least have something of a smile if Alfred had been found.

'Nurse Linklater,' said Miss Houston, 'just step out of the ward with me for one minute, will you? I have a delicate matter to discuss.'

Maud still didn't have any clue what the matter might be.

'There is no need to look so worried,' said Miss Houston, 'but I will come straight out with it. It has been brought to my attention that one of your close friends is with child.'

Maud gasped and felt her face flush. Nancy has told her, she thought instantly.

'No, please don't worry. The reason I have come to you and not Nurse Sampson is that we want to manage this in the best way we can. It's just that someone — and I can't disclose who — has reported your friend out of concern for her condition. I don't know how far along she is, but there really is no way of hiding the fact that she is with child. She is getting so big that Sister on Male Medical says that she can hardly bend

285

down to make the beds.'

'So, it was Sister who noticed then?'

'Well, yes, but to be fair, only after she was given a tip-off by an anonymous member of staff.'

Nancy, thought Maud again, the name hissing in her head.

'And now, of course, any number of staff have legitimate concern for her.'

'Of course,' said Maud, keeping her voice steady. 'I understand.'

'We just want Nurse Sampson to have the support of a friend at this time and your name has been given to me as that friend. Are we right in thinking . . . ?'

'Yes, yes, of course.'

'In that case, please could you break the news of our knowledge of her condition to Nurse Sampson and bring her along to see me, in my room, this evening? Tell her not to worry. We only want to do what's best for her and for the child.'

Maud took a deep breath to calm herself and nodded: of course she would. Now that Maud was rapidly calming down she decided it would be best if neither she nor Alice were to give Nancy the satisfaction of showing any reaction to the news, not if they could help it. After all, it had always been just a question of time before the baby made itself known. Maud had got used to seeing Alice's big belly straining at her uniform, but it would be easy for a group of nurses to tell that she was with child. And at least it seemed that they were in the right hands.

Miss Houston had a reputation for being fair and kind in that strict superintendent sort of way. She only hoped that Alice would see it like that.

★ ★ ★

'Look, Alice,' said Maud, sitting next to her friend on the narrow bed in her room as she cried and cried, 'with that belly of yours growing so much in the last few weeks, everybody in the hospital was bound to notice sooner or later. And yes, of course it was probably Nancy who told in the end, but let's not give her the satisfaction of knowing how upset you are.'

'But I am upset,' sobbed Alice. 'I saw Nancy in the corridor this morning and she was on at me again about watching my step and all of that, and I told her — like you said — I told her that we had already told the superintendents, and she said, 'I don't believe you. You or that mealy-mouthed Linklater wouldn't have the guts to go and tell a superintendent. You are lying.' That's what she said to me. She must have gone and told Miss Houston herself and now I'll have to leave straight away.'

'We don't know that yet,' said Maud, her blood boiling when she heard what Nancy had said about her and Alice. She could feel her heart beating faster and a flush on her neck but she needed to stay calm for Alice, who still had tears streaming down her face. She fished in her pocket for another handkerchief and passed it to her friend, removing the sodden one from her hand. Then she took a deep breath and said, 'Look Alice, I trust Miss Houston . . . and it doesn't matter now anyway, does it? The fact is that Miss Houston knows and she has said that all they want is to do the best for you and the baby.'

'I know what that means,' howled Alice. 'It means she will definitely tell me to leave straight away and I will be disgraced.'

Maud put her arm around her friend's shoulders.

'Look,' said Maud gently, 'just look down at your belly. How much longer did you think that you could keep that secret? Even when you were working with me on Male Surgical you were having trouble bending down — how much worse must that be now?'

Alice went quiet, apart from gentle sobs, and she ran a protective hand over the curve of her belly. 'I know, you are right, Maud. This thing is huge now. I even had to ask for a bigger uniform. I told them the food is so good in the dining room that I can't stop eating it and I've put such a lot of weight on since I started my training.'

Maud couldn't help giggling. 'They would never have believed that, Alice, not with some of the stuff that we get served up.'

'I know,' said Alice. 'I just couldn't think of anything else to say.'

'Alice, let's face it, this baby is only going to get bigger. Now is as good a time as any for everybody to know and for you to stop having to make up stories. You know what Stella said that day, that you could go there when the time came, and if the time has come, if Miss Houston says you must stop work straight away, then so be it. But first we need to go and see Miss Houston and make things straight.'

'You're right, Maud, and I am sick of telling lies and keeping secrets, but you know what?' said Alice, looking around her room with more tears in her eyes. 'I am going to miss this place . . . and you and Eddy . . . so much.'

Maud put her arm around her friend's shoulders again. 'Well, you won't be getting rid of me or Eddy just yet. We will still be seeing you wherever you go, Alice, I promise. Now dry your eyes, get your boots back on and come with me to see Miss Houston. I am right by your side, Alice Sampson, and I will stay by your side every single step of the way.'

16

Poetry and imagination begin life.
Florence Nightingale

Maud held on to Alice's hand as they stood outside Miss Houston's door and then she knocked gently on the polished wood. They heard a soft rustling sound and a light step as someone came to the door and Maud squeezed her friend's hand a bit tighter as the door opened and Miss Houston stood there with a smile and a real welcome on her face.

'Come in,' she said.

Maud felt Alice relax her grip a little and they both walked through, still holding hands. As Miss Houston was closing the door, Maud glanced at Alice's face. She looked very worried and her head was down. Maud wanted to try to ease her friend in any way she could and, seeing the little dog lying on the bottom of Miss Houston's bed, she guided her over in that direction.

'Alice, you like dogs, don't you?' she said as they stood, still holding hands, by the side of the bed where Bob lay sleeping.

Maud hadn't realized just how worried Alice must have been. All the time since she had found out about the baby she must have been dreading this moment, and now it had come. She must feel like the world's falling in on her, thought Maud as they both stood by the bed and Maud stretched out a hand to stroke the little dog. He just raised his head and put it straight back down, seeming to go back to sleep instantly.

Miss Houston came over and stood next to Alice and spoke softly to the dog. Then she said, 'Bob seems to have been very tired indeed these last few days. He can't even get himself off the bed.' Maud saw the dog lift his head once more at the sound of Miss Houston's voice, and then he gave a weary sigh, almost as if the effort had been too much for him.

'Poor old thing,' said Alice, reaching out to give the dog a stroke. 'He does look tired.'

'Are you used to dogs?' asked Miss Houston.

'Yes, we've always kept a dog at home, small ones like this, terrier types . . . He looks like he's a good age.'

'He is,' said Miss Houston wistfully. 'He was out in the Crimea with us. He belonged to a friend of mine.'

Alice stood by the bed still stroking the dog as Miss Houston bustled over to the fire to pour hot water into the teapot. 'Right, anyway, you two sit there, either side of the fire, and I'll pour us a cup of tea.'

Maud had been right. She had known that Miss Houston was absolutely the best person in the whole of the hospital to handle Alice's situation. She soon had them both sitting by the fire and Alice looking far less stricken and almost even starting to relax as she rested back in the armchair. Miss Houston insisted that they call her Ada, but only whilst they were visiting her quarters, not of course when they were out in the hospital.

'Now, Alice,' said Ada, 'is there anyone out there in the city who you can turn to?'

'Well,' said Alice, looking at Maud, 'there is one person who has offered help but it is all a bit unusual.'

'Can you tell me?' said Ada.

'The thing is . . . ' said Alice, clearly struggling to say that she'd had an offer of help from a brothel.

'The thing is,' said Maud, 'you already know her.'

'Do I?' said Ada. 'Who is it?'

'It's Stella.'

Ada looked stunned for a moment and then instantly she pieced it all together.

'Of course, she was there on the ward visiting that man, that army veteran, and she was there after I helped you get him back into bed. That was when I first saw you, I think, wasn't it, Maud?'

'It was,' said Maud, pleased that Ada had remembered everything.

'But I still don't understand, how has all this come about?'

'I got to know Stella a bit and she said that if me or the boy ever needed anything that we should go and find her at her place near Lime Street Station. Well, Alice here needed some advice about the baby, so we went to see her and she said that if Alice wanted she could go there until the baby comes. She said they always need help with the cooking and cleaning and they've delivered many a baby there in the house as well.'

'And is that all right with you, Alice?' asked Ada. 'You do know what kind of establishment Stella runs?'

'Yes, yes,' said Alice. 'I mean, it might take a bit of getting used to but when I met Stella, well, I really liked her and she seems to be an honest and genuine person.'

'Yes, yes, she does, I'll give her that,' said Ada, again a little wistful.

'She told me that she is your half-sister,' said Maud, jumping in, not wanting anything to be left unsaid.

'She is,' said Ada. 'I never knew her until I came back from the Crimea and then, well, we haven't exactly been all that well acquainted until very recently. And that hasn't been Stella's fault. It has all been me, on my side. I have taken a long time to want to get to know her . . . From what I know of Stella, though, this seems like a good offer. I mean, it's probably your only offer so there isn't much of a choice, but I feel that you will be well looked after there and I will fully support that as a plan. In fact, Miss Merryweather told me to make sure that we gave you some money to help try to ease your situation.'

'Miss Merryweather knows as well?' said Alice, her voice sounding small.

'Yes, she does. Miss Merryweather knows everything,' said Ada, getting up from her chair and walking over to a tall polished wood cupboard. 'That's the way it goes around here.'

She took a small key out of her pocket. 'There is no need to worry, Alice. Miss Merryweather is full of sympathy and concern for all of the nurses here and she is very aware of most issues that can affect us women.'

Then Ada unlocked the cupboard and pulled out a wooden box that she brought over to where they were sitting and laid it on the table. She opened the lid of the box to reveal a number of banknotes and a small collection of items, including a mother-of-pearl brooch, a yellowed piece of paper and a lock of hair that looked soft and fine. Having counted out some of the banknotes, she closed the box lid and took it straight back to the cupboard, locking it away carefully where it belonged.

'No, really,' said Alice as Ada stood over her with the notes in her hand.

'I insist,' said Ada. 'This is money that we senior staff at the hospital put aside for times like these. We only give to chosen ones: probationers like you with good conduct, who find themselves in circumstances beyond their control. Nurses who leave for other issues like drunkenness or stealing or bad behaviour, well, they don't get anything from the fund, but you are going to have a baby, Alice, and this is for you. Please, please take it.'

Alice was still shaking her head so Maud stood up and took the money for her. 'Thank you,' she said. 'We will make sure that it is used properly.'

'And another thing,' said Ada, 'when you come through everything, there will be more decisions to make, but you will be welcome back here at the hospital to finish your training and continue your work if that's what you want to do.'

'Thank you so much,' said Alice, almost in tears again. 'It makes such a difference to know that might still be possible.'

'It is possible. And once you have your qualification then there are no end of opportunities. Maud here has even been thinking about work in New York.'

'Have you?' said Alice as she started to haul herself out of the chair.

'I have, but only if and when Alfred comes back,' replied Maud, helping her friend to stand up.

'Mmm, it is about time you finished work, I think,' said Ada, smiling.

Then Alice got her balance and stood a bit awkwardly for a moment and Maud had a fleeting impression that her friend was going to curtsy to Miss Houston or something, but in the end she just bowed her head and went over to give the dog, still sleeping soundly on the bed, one last stroke.

'Thank you so much,' said Maud. 'This has made such a difference . . . '

'The dog's breathing doesn't seem quite right, Ada,' said Alice, turning from the bed with concern on her face. 'He seems to be struggling to breathe.'

Ada was straight there, checking him. Alice was right, the little dog was panting.

'What's the matter then, old lad?' said Ada, gently stroking Bob's head.

The dog didn't even lift his head, and Maud and Alice could see that his mouth was open, he was panting, and his eyes were wide open but unseeing. Ada continued to stroke the dog's head and then she ran her hand down along his body, speaking softly to him all the time. Then the dog started to tremble. Soon every bit of his body was trembling.

Ada took a sharp breath. 'This doesn't look good,' she said, turning to the probationers with tears shining in her eyes.

'Is there anything we can do?' asked Maud.

'Not really,' said Ada, her voice sounding small. 'He's been failing for weeks now. He is so old, I think he's just dying of old age.'

'I'm so sorry,' said Maud, not really able to understand, never having owned a dog. Having seen how close Harry was with his, though, she realized that people must grow to have very strong feelings for the creatures.

'It's sad to see them go,' said Alice, reaching out a hand to stroke the dog again.

'Yes,' said Ada, sounding forlorn, 'Yes, it is . . . particularly when you've had them so long. And you know what dogs are like: they are so straightforward, they try to please no matter what. He has kept wagging his tail at me every time I've come close to the bed and he's so weak now I have to lift him off and stand him up, but then he wags his tail again. It breaks my heart.'

Maud and Alice could see that Ada now had tears streaming down her face and a hand across her mouth, reaching her other hand out to give Bob another stroke as he tried to lift his head.

'It's all right now, it's all right,' she said. 'You get some rest . . . you rest . . . You can't go yet, you need to stay a bit longer. John will be back in a few months.'

Maud and Alice exchanged glances, both of them understanding in that moment that they had glimpsed something from Miss Houston's past, something very private. As Ada continued to gently soothe and stroke the little dog he closed his eyes and seemed to slip into a deep sleep. Then they could see his legs going, as if he was running, and he kept trying to bark but the sound wouldn't come out properly.

'He must be dreaming,' said Alice.

'Yes, he does have this dream sometimes,' said Ada quietly, and then she turned to them with tears still streaming down her face.

'Do you want us to stay?' said Alice.

'No, no, that's all right, girls,' said Ada, wiping her eyes with the flat of her hand and then squaring her shoulders. 'I will be all right. I'll just sit with him.'

'Are you sure?' said Maud.

'Yes, yes, you two go. Go and see Stella. Tell her that I will support the move to her place and, both of you, take the day off tomorrow so you can get everything sorted out. I have cleared it with Miss Merryweather. We both agreed that there was no need for you to go back to the ward, Nurse Sampson. Sister Cleary is fully aware, and we have also spoken to Sister Pritchard for you, Maud, as well, so that you can take the time.'

'But I've only just been off after — '

'It is absolutely fine, Maud. Sister Pritchard is very pleased with your conduct and your hard work and she will look forward to having you back on the ward, but tomorrow you need to assist Alice with the move and make sure that she gets settled at Stella's place.'

Maud nodded. It felt so good to have the reassurance and the support of all these senior staff. 'Thank you,' she said. 'I will work extra hard when I get back on the ward.'

'I know you will, Maud,' said Ada firmly, and then she turned back to the little dog. But as they moved away towards the door she called, 'I'll look forward to hearing news of you, Alice.'

'Thank you, Miss Houston,' said Alice, smiling. Then the two girls opened the door quietly, almost holding their breath, and stepped out of the room. Once they had clicked the door shut they looked at each other. Maud saw the relief on Alice's face and she knew that everything was going to be all right.

'That is so sad, though,' said Alice as they walked back to the Nurses' Home. 'Poor little dog, poor Bob.'

'Yes,' said Maud forlornly, 'but I suppose he has had a good life and a very long one as well for a dog.'

'True,' said Alice. 'It's just that you wish that a dog — your own dog — could live the same length of time as a human so that you could always have it around.'

'I see what you mean,' said Maud, 'but it's time for him to go. I mean, if he was out there in the Crimean War with Miss Houston that was,

298

what, fifteen years ago? He must be at least sixteen years old, probably more.'

'Mmm,' said Alice, thinking things through. 'I heard from some of the nurses that Miss Houston's dog had got blown up in the war and she saved its life. Or did it save her? I can't remember which way round it was now . . . and somebody else said that the dog, Bob, had belonged to a soldier, her one true love, and he had been in the Charge of the Light Brigade. I wonder if that was the John she was talking about?'

'I don't know. I think that just slipped out,' said Maud. 'I have no idea who that is. He might be somebody else, and I wouldn't believe any of those stories if I were you. You know what this place is like for stories: there's always any number of different accounts about one thing. People just make things up the whole time.'

Seeing Maud's serious face, Alice smiled. 'There's nothing wrong with a bit of imagination though, Maud, is there? Or a bit of romance.'

'Yes, but let's not go telling any stories about Miss Houston. What she said to us was private, so it goes no further.'

'Of course,' said Alice, taking her friend's hand.

'Right then,' said Maud, 'so that's straight. Now, about tomorrow: I'll go over to Stella's place in the morning after breakfast to check with her that it is still all right for you to go and stay there. While I'm away you get everything packed. And let's put our uniforms on in the morning and go to the dining room as usual so that Nancy doesn't cotton on. We'll tell Eddy tonight, of course, and I'm sure that the rest will soon find out, but let's keep it to ourselves for the time being.'

In the end Maud decided to help Alice sort out her room after breakfast. They had told Eddy that evening, as planned, as soon as she got back from her outing into the city. She had gone quiet for a bit, not worrying about the baby, she said — she was excited about that; she was excited about the whole thing — but she was sad to see Alice leave. She had got used to her being in the next room and she knew that once she was living at Stella's place, then it would feel different and they would all miss her. That set Alice off crying again, and then Maud started until they were all crying together and there was nothing else to do except start to laugh.

'We'll be all right, though, us three,' said Eddy. 'We'll always stick together.'

'We will,' said Maud and Alice together.

★ ★ ★

So come the next morning Eddy went in after breakfast to say goodbye to Alice. They had to try to keep quiet as they didn't want Nancy to come sniffing round. She was out every evening. They often saw her go, all dressed up, but they never saw her come back. Did she even come back? She just turned up each morning in her uniform like she had been tapped out of a mould, all perfect and ready to go to the ward. Eddy thought that she wasn't a real person, she was some kind of machine and if you tapped on Nancy's head there'd be a hollow sound as if it was an empty copper pot.

Anyway, Maud stayed with Alice in her room until the rest had gone to the wards and then Miss Merryweather knocked on the door. For some reason, they both knew that it was her as soon as they heard the sound, and they looked at each other, their eyes wide, till Maud got up and opened the door.

'Miss Houston has told me everything,' said Miss Merryweather rather stiffly as she swept into the room, wearing her bonnet as she often did, even inside the building. 'I am sorry that you are having to leave us so abruptly, Nurse Sampson, but there is no way round these things. I know that Nurse Linklater will keep in touch with you and let us know how things are going. Please let us know if there is anything you need.'

'Thank you, Miss Merryweather,' said Maud and Alice together. And then the superintendent withdrew from the room with a solemn expression and clicked the door shut behind her.

Maud and Alice looked at each other with their eyebrows raised and then Alice smiled and started to shake her head. 'Well, I never thought that. I thought she was coming up here to tear me off a strip good and proper.'

'I told you she was nice,' said Maud.

'Not sure that 'nice' is the word that I'd use, Maud, but she is . . . honourable, is that the right word?'

'She is honourable and stern, but I like her,'

said Maud. 'Now let's get your stuff sorted out and then I'll go out and see Stella.'

★ ★ ★

Walking out again towards Lime Street on her now familiar route Maud made sure, as always, to look at all the children, just in case there was one with a particular shade of hair, one that might be Alfred.

As she got closer to Lime Street Station she felt that buzz of excitement and the people were packed closer together. Then she heard the whistle of a train getting ready to leave. She felt a thrill go through her and the crowd of people around her as well. She had learnt to walk through this part of the city in a determined way, to hold her ground and so she pushed her way through in order to avoid being taken up with the surge of folk making their way into the railway station.

Then, through a small gap within a group of people moving towards the entrance to the station, she saw a small boy. Although she could see only the back of him, he was the right height and colouring. Could it be Alfred? She felt a surge of excitement as she pushed through the group of people. She couldn't lose sight of him, not now.

'Oi, watch it,' said a red-faced man with a scowl and the smell of liquor on his breath, but Maud pushed past before he could catch his breath. She could still see the boy and she called his name but he was moving quickly and, being small, he could easily dodge around and through people's legs. Maud was determined, however, and she fought her way through to keep up with him. But suddenly he had disappeared completely from view. She spun around, scanning the people milling around her. Where could he have gone? She had lost him despite her dogged pursuit. Instantly tears sprung to her eyes and she felt her heart pounding.

She took a deep breath and tried to calm herself. Looking around again, she knew that there was only one place that he could have gone. To her left was a large stone building with a huge wooden door standing open. There didn't seem to be anywhere else that he could be so Maud walked in that direction.

The small boy was sitting forlornly on the steps of the building. He was so small she couldn't see him from the street and he didn't come into view until she got right up near the door. But he was there, all right . . . only it wasn't Alfred. Maud stood in front of him feeling like she had been winded. She felt such a fool. To cover herself she put her hand in her pocket for a coin, gave it to the boy and then continued walking up the steps and into the building.

Once through the door she heard the hollow sound of her own feet as they walked across some marble tiles. She stopped and then the sense of something in that building came over her: a stillness and calm . . . real calm. It felt to Maud like the feeling that she'd had the first time that she'd walked through the door into the

Nurses' Home. It was as if she had entered some hallowed place, with its high ceiling like a church, and it was so still and quiet. The stillness instantly calmed her. She felt as though she was breathing it in. When she looked around she saw there were paintings on the walls. Most of them seemed to be of rich people, mostly men, but there was one to the side, near the door. A sign above it said something about new work, modern painters, and something called 'Pre-Raphaelite'. Maud had no idea what that meant but she had never seen colours like that anywhere in real life. The brightness of them, the yellows and greens and the earthy brown and red — they felt real. The painting was of two sitting figures, a woman and a girl. The girl had the same blond hair as Alfred and both of them were working people: they wore tattered clothes and heavy boots. There were two rainbows behind them, and even though the sky was dark and menacing the rainbows shone out. Maud felt as if she was holding her breath as she stood there in front of the painting. She felt transported and filled with hope.

In the end she had almost to tear herself away from the painting. She decided if the boy that she'd mistaken for Alfred was still sitting on the step outside, she would try to take him somewhere to safety, or at least give him the rest of the coins she had left in her pocket. But when she got to the door, the boy was gone and there was only a man with a stiff brush sweeping up the dead leaves that had collected by the step.

'Have you seen a boy?' said Maud.

'What boy?' said the man, stopping in his work for a moment.

'The one who was sitting on the step just five minutes ago.'

'Nah,' said the man, shaking his head, 'there's always waifs and strays coming in 'ere and sitting on them steps. Even if I 'ad seen one, they all look the same to me. I wouldn't 'ave been able to say if it was one in particular.'

Maud just looked at him, knowing straight away that of course he had seen the boy and he had probably chased him off the step with his brush.

'Right,' said Maud, and the man went back to his sweeping, muttering something like, 'Damn nuisance these leaves, collecting 'ere every day. Takes me all my time to make sure this place is clean and tidy.'

Maud put her head down and walked on, aware she needed to get to Stella's place as quickly as possible and make arrangements for Alice. She felt a bit numb inside still, but that painting had lifted her out of her ordinary life and her worry over Alfred. She had never known that an object could do that to a person, but now that she knew it was there she could come back as often as she needed. All right, she was no nearer finding Alfred with every day that went by, but she wouldn't give up. She would never give up hope.

17

I attribute my success to this--I never gave or took any excuse. Florence Nightingale

'Look, Maud, I'm a woman of my word,' said Stella. 'Of course your friend can come and stay with us here, so long as she's willing to pitch in and help Ma with the kitchen duties. I think it's a bit of a shame that half-sister of mine couldn't keep her on a bit longer at the hospital, though. Surely they need all the help they can get on those wards, packed out with patients and all sorts going on.'

'Well, to be fair,' said Maud, 'it isn't just Miss Houston's decision. There's all the other senior staff as well.'

'Frosty-faced, strait-laced lot,' laughed Stella. 'It's time they started to live in the real world. Women get pregnant all the time through no fault of their own. It just happens.'

'I know,' said Maud, 'but rules are rules, and Miss Nightingale has set the standards and made the rules.'

'Mmm,' said Stella, clearly not convinced. 'Anyway, bring the lass along and let's get her settled. By the sound of it, the sooner you get her out of that place the better.'

* * *

Once Maud had Alice safely installed at Stella's and Alice was making herself at home, Stella invited Maud into the warm kitchen before she went back to the hospital. Sitting around the freshly scrubbed table with a cup of tea, Maud felt able to shift her focus back to finding Alfred.

'Stella, I need to tell you something about Alfred. You know I said he was settled at the school? Well, he's gone missing.'

'Has he? What, from the Blue Coat?'

'Yes,' said Maud, filling her in on all the details of the boy's disappearance and their theory about Greer's involvement.

'I'm so sorry to hear that, for the boy's sake and for yours. I know how close you were to him, Maud. Even on the ward I could see that. So what's the plan?'

'We've put out handbills and made some enquiries, and I regularly walk by the sweep's house on Market Street just hoping that I might see something. But there has been no sign, and you know how vast this city is: it feels an almost impossible task to start a search. Is there anywhere at all that you think a missing boy might be?'

'There are so many places,' said Stella. 'They often congregate around here, near the station. It's a regular place for begging. You see some desperate cases . . . and then there's the Irish quarter. Those poor people are forced to live in bad conditions and I've heard tell of gangs of street children round there. The thing is, Maud, a lass like you can't just roam off into those areas of the city on your own. You need some kind of guide. I know a few fellas who could help you look for the boy. They've been helping me when some of our women have gone missing. You met one of them in the pub that night when you came to find me — '

'I know who you mean,' said Maud, cutting her short, and not wanting to tell her that she had already known Harry Donahue before that night. 'I was thinking of asking him. He has a dog as well. Maybe it might be some use in finding a missing boy, I don't know.'

'Good idea,' said Stella. 'I know the dog too. It was at my place for a bit when it had an injured paw. Do you want me to ask Harry?'

'No, that's all right,' answered Maud. 'I know where to find him. He's usually in that same pub, isn't he?'

'Well, he's been in there regular this last few weeks, with that nurse, that one with the prissy face and the blond hair. She's been tagging along with him.'

'I know who you mean,' said Maud instantly, not wanting any further conversation. 'I will go in there and look for him this evening.'

★   ★   ★

Maud did find Harry that evening, but she didn't even have to go into the pub in the end. As she approached he was rolling out through the door with Nancy on his arm. Swaying around like some hopeless drunk, he didn't seem to know where he was. She couldn't speak to him in that state and she felt something harden inside her as she saw Nancy stare across at her and then move in closer to Harry's side, making sure that Maud saw how she could snuggle up to him. Maud could see the man was blind drunk and he would have snuggled up to anybody in that state, but she still had to struggle to keep herself calm. She would never have let Nancy be able to tell that she was troubled by seeing them together in the street, and she would still ask Harry to help her, which she knew would rile Nancy.

There was no point talking to Harry in that state, but tomorrow after finishing on the ward, she and Eddy would visit Alice in her new quarters, and then she'd take her friend with her to track down Harry. She hoped he would have had time to sober up by then.

*   *   *

As she made her way swiftly along the corridor between wards the next morning she almost walked straight into Stella, who was coming in the opposite direction with a worried look on her face.

'Is everything all right?' Maud asked, her voice full of concern.

'Oh, hello, Maud. Sorry, didn't see you there . . . No, not really. Well, Alice is fine, but another of my girls has gone missing. She hasn't been seen since last night. I need to see Ada about this right away.'

'Sorry to hear that,' said Maud, then calling

after Stella as she hurried on her way, 'I'll see you later.'

★   ★   ★

'What's up with Miss Mouse?' said Stella, coming in through Ada's door after going by the desk of the small-faced woman who was trying to stop herself from crying.

'I assume you mean my clerk, Emily,' said Ada, looking up from her paperwork.

'Yes, Emily, that's the one. She appears to be crying — what's up with her?'

'She was very fond of my little dog, who died yesterday. She used to walk him.'

'I'm very sorry to hear that,' said Stella, her face falling. 'And are you all right?'

'Yes, yes, of course, the dog was very old,' said Ada a bit too quickly.

Stella gave her a look. 'It's all right to be sad, you know. Yes, it's a dog and not a person, but it was still a living creature. I mean, not that many weeks ago I would have been telling you not to be daft, there's far worse things in our world, all you need to do is take a walk through the streets and see the tiny kids in rags begging for food or the poor women on the street. But, you know what? I've just been looking after a mutt that some fella left at our place. I didn't think much of it at first but in three days I fell in love with that thing with its scraggy coat and its dangly legs. So, yeah, I can understand a bit now how you must be feeling, Ada. You might need to cry.'

Ada just nodded and then looked up at this

half-sister of hers, whom she hadn't wanted to get to know and swore that she would never like. And now look at them. All that she could feel was warmth and admiration. How ridiculous life could be, she thought. You think you know what's best, you think you've got things sorted, but then — and this is even more important the older you get — you realize that in fact you haven't even begun to know or understand much at all.

'Anyway, the thing is,' said Stella, 'another of my girls has gone missing. She went out last night — it was her evening off — and I know for sure that she was in the pub across from Lime Street earlier on but then she didn't come back. She's been with me and Ma for years. She's trustworthy and reliable; she's my friend. She's got red hair and she's called Laura. I know that this isn't right, Ada. She must have been taken by those men. They must have got her as well.'

Ada could see that this woman really meant something to Stella.

'I'm sorry to hear that, Stella,' she said, frowning. 'I did make enquiries about the Lock Hospital. One of the doctors here, a Mr Fawcett, he works over there as well and he assured me that they had appropriate reasons for taking all admissions related to the Contagious Diseases Acts. But clearly you are concerned and it sounds like you have good reason to be. It's difficult to get in there and get the full information, but I'll have another go. I have a friend, another superintendent, who knows how to get access. You leave it with me and I will come to you at your place if and when I have any news.'

Stella nodded and then tried to wipe away her tears without Ada seeing.

'I thought you said it was all right to cry,' said Ada, getting up from behind her desk and, small as she was, reaching up and giving her half-sister a hug.

'It is all right for you to cry, but I usually try not to,' said Stella, starting to laugh and then holding on to Ada for as long as she could before they would both need to pull away and get on.

★ ★ ★

Maud did not hesitate outside the door to the pub later that evening, after she'd reassured herself that Alice was settling in really well at Stella's. She pushed her way straight in with Eddy following close behind. The pub was packed full of men and full of smoke, but she ploughed her way through, knowing that he would be in there somewhere. Sure enough, she eventually spotted the dark-green jacket and she could hear him ranting on to the other men. Did he never shut up?

She tapped him on the shoulder and he whirled around smiling, until he saw her face.

'Can I talk to you outside?' she said, before turning on her heel, grabbing Eddy, who had started chatting to some fella, and making her way straight back out through the door. She knew that Harry would follow; she had seen his shocked face and then the instant gleam in his eye.

When she turned to face the pub door, still holding Eddy's arm, she saw it swing open and he was there with the dog beside him. They both looked up at her expectantly and then they walked over side by side.

'I'll leave you to it,' said Eddy. 'I'll see you later.'

Maud saw Harry and the dog look after Eddy a bit wistfully, as if he thought that she might be an ally, someone who might be able to save him from whatever was coming from Maud. She waited till he was up close, until he was looking her in the eye, and then she had to lay aside all of the things she wanted to say about his drunken, disgraceful behaviour, rolling out of the pub with Nancy, and not smile exactly but at least be civil. Because she needed his help.

'I need to ask you a favour. You remember you said that I could, if I ever needed help?'

'Of course,' said Harry, his face full of concern but showing a little fear too, as if he was picking up on what was inside Maud's head, the things that she wasn't going to say but which were still screaming out at him anyway.

'Well, I need to find someone, a boy who is under my care. He has gone missing and I need someone to help me look. I can pay you.'

'You will not pay me,' Harry said, 'not after what you did for my dog. You will not pay me a penny.'

'Well, we'll see . . . Can you help me?' asked Maud stiffly.

'Of course,' Harry said. 'We could use the dog as well. She hasn't got much of a nose on her, but it might be worth a try.'

'I wondered about that,' said Maud, sticking a hand in her pocket and pulling out the small, brown sock that Alfred had left in the bed that day he was discharged from hospital. When Maud had brought it out of the drawer where she had carefully stashed it after forgetting to give it to Alfred when she visited him at the school, she had felt very sad. Now, seeing it again, out here in the street with Harry and the dog, she felt even worse as she handed it over. Harry let the dog have a sniff at it before he pushed it carefully in his pocket.

'We could have a look now,' he said, 'but it's a bit late. You can't see much by gas-lamp. But I'll keep the sock, and me and the dog, we'll keep trying. There are so many youngsters living on the street it would be good to be able to rescue at least one of 'em. What does the boy look like?'

'His name is Alfred. He's about this high,' Maud said, indicating with her hand against her own body. 'He has blond hair and blue eyes, pale blue eyes.'

And then, remembering that she still had Miss Fairchild's handbill in her pocket she fished it out and gave it to him. He straightened it out and had a quick look at it.

'And we have good reason to believe that Alfred might have been grabbed by the sweep who he was apprenticed to, a Mr Bill Greer. Him and his wife have a place on Market Street. You can't miss it. They have a sign in the window:

314

'William Greer, Master Sweep', and she has a stall outside selling pots and rags. I've been down there a few times but they know me so it's difficult to spend enough time. Also, he was a patient on the ward and he threatened me — '

'He did what?' growled Harry.

'No need to be concerned. It was all dealt with.'

'I'll deal with it all right if I lay my hands on him,' said Harry, raising a fist.

'Look, there is no need to get riled up over him. All I want is that you keep an eye on that area because that's where we think Alfred is most likely to be.'

Harry growled again and then lowered his fist. 'All right then, Maud, and if we find the boy, where do you want him?'

'It's best if you bring him straight to the hospital. Take him to Male Surgical, and they will come and find me. Or if you want, take him to Stella's place, where he'll be safe. My friend Alice is living there now.'

Maud saw Harry raise his eyebrows. 'Really?' he said. 'Your friend is living there? You do know what goes on at Stella's place, I take it?'

'Of course I do,' said Maud, and Harry cracked up laughing.

'Maud, you never fail to amaze me. Do you want to come out with me and the dog now? We can have a look straight away if you want.'

'I can't. I need to get back before they lock up the Nurses' Home,' said Maud, her face tight. 'And besides, I know you've got people to see at this time of night; I know that you are busy.'

'Well, not that busy that I can't have a look for a lost boy.'

'No, really,' said Maud, 'you probably need to go back in the pub, get some drink inside you.'

'Oh, I get you,' he said, starting to smirk. 'You're talking about Nancy, aren't you? You must have seen us somewhere. We have been out together a night or two.'

'What if I have seen you with Nancy?' said Maud. 'That has nothing to do with me or anything that I might be asking of you. Who you see is up to you. She is your type, obviously.'

'Now just you wait a minute. Let's not be getting ahead of ourselves here. I have seen her a few times — she is good to look at, I'll give you that — but she is not 'my type'. What do you know of 'my type', anyway?'

'None of this is my concern,' said Maud, raising her voice. 'I don't care who you see.'

'Well, I don't believe that for one minute,' he almost shouted back at her. 'If that is the case then why are you getting into a lather about it?'

'I am not getting into a lather,' shouted Maud before she could stop herself. Then she stood silent, shocked at her own reaction, her breath coming quick, her heart racing and Harry just smirking away. Her hands were balled into fists and she felt she could have punched him.

'Oh, so you're not in a lather then, are you not, Nurse Linklater? Quiet Maud, with her big, dark eyes and her ladylike ways, you're not in any kind of a lather, not at all.'

Maud couldn't speak, she was so furious. She made some kind of noise, dismissing him, and made to walk away but he grabbed her arm.

'Let go of me,' she spat at him.

'Now let me tell you, Maud, let me tell you here and now, I am not some kind of saint. I'm not anywhere near as good and worthy as you would like me to be and, yes, I like the women and I like the drink, but I am not looking for a woman like Nancy. I am definitely not looking for that sort of woman. I am looking for someone like you, Maud, someone who can make me a better person, the kind of man me mother would have been proud of.'

Maud stood in front of him breathing heavily. She could feel his eyes burning into her, but she couldn't move. Her mind was racing over what he had just said and she didn't like the way that he seemed to think he was qualified to put women into neat boxes. What did he know?

'Women like Nancy are ten a penny. Like soap bubbles, they come and then they go, pop, just like that. What I want is someone like you, Maud, someone solid and real and good and kind. I want you. I want to marry you. Will you marry me?'

'No, of course not!' spat Maud, aware that he was still holding her by the arm and she was rooted to the spot. What was he talking about? None of it made any sense and they needed to find Alfred before she could even think about anything else.

So she looked him straight in the eye, twisted her arm out of his grasp and then said, 'Just find the boy,' before marching away without even wanting to glance back.

317

The next day on the ward Maud was restless. Alfred's disappearance was pressing on her increasingly, and with Alice moving to Stella's where she couldn't readily check on her it felt as if her worries were piling up and something would have to give. Maud could tell that Eddy had some concern about her because she kept looking over and asking her if she was all right. Maud was all right in that she was still performing her duties on the ward to her usual high standard. On the surface she was still Nurse Linklater and every detail of her work was correct, but she wasn't exactly herself. There was an edge to her that only someone close like Eddy could detect.

As soon as the evening meal was over Maud went straight to her room and changed, then headed out into the city, making her way to Stella's to check on Alice. She walked quickly through the streets and then she sped past the door of the pub opposite Lime Street Station, just in case Harry was coming out of there again with Nancy on his arm and some ready excuse, no doubt, some easy explanation of how, even though Nancy wasn't his type, he just bumped into her in the pub and one thing led to another . . . But just as soon as she was past the door, she had to stop. Cursing under her breath, she knew that there was no way round it, she would have to go in and see if Harry was there. Her need to know whether or not there was any news about Alfred far outweighed her drive to avoid that

318

ridiculous man. So Maud turned briskly and marched back and into the pub before she could change her mind. It was packed out and full of smoke, but she checked all corners of the place. There was, however, no Harry, and, thankfully, no Nancy either.

Once Maud was back outside she lifted her chin, took a deep breath and continued on her way. She was soon past Lime Street and then down into the alley and through the door of the brothel in no time. She was almost breathless when she came through into the kitchen to find Alice sitting on a large wooden chair with her feet up on a cushioned stool. Alice smiled at her as soon as she saw her face but Maud could see that her eyes were a bit red-rimmed, as if she'd been crying. Maud understood without asking. She had cried again herself that morning when she'd seen Alice's door standing open and the bed stripped, waiting for a new occupant. She would probably always miss having Alice at the Nurses' Home. After all, they had been together right from the start, from that first day when she had taken Alfred up to the Infirmary.

Anyway, now Alice was sitting in the kitchen of a brothel, with a hand resting on her belly and looking just a bit sorry for herself. Maud went straight over and gave her a hug and a kiss on the cheek.

'So nice to see you, Maud. Is Eddy with you?' said Alice, sounding a bit forlorn.

'No, not yet. She's gone to see her folks but she'll be along later. You look comfortable,' said

Maud, pulling a kitchen chair up right next to her friend.

'I am,' said Alice, 'well, as comfortable as I can be with this one kicking around in there and giving me heartburn. And my back's been aching all day long and now I keep getting a pain in this bump of mine as well. It's what you'd expect, I suppose.'

'I would think so,' said Maud, feeling completely out of her depth but wanting to try and reassure Alice. They could always ask Eddy when she arrived, although Maud didn't know how much longer she would be.

'Is Stella around?' Maud said casually, not wanting to cause Alice any alarm but feeling that she would like to ask Stella about Alice, make sure that everything was all right.

'No, she's had to go out on some mission or other. They were all a bit hush-hush about it. Anyway, I did mention that my back was aching and she said that's what you'd expect from a woman at my stage of pregnancy.'

That's all right then, thought Maud, starting to feel a bit more relaxed and able to rest back on her own chair. It was nice to be in the warm kitchen, sitting by the range, the smell of baking in the air and a scraggy black cat stretched out next to the stove, soaking up the heat. Although it felt strange to be in the heart of a brothel, Maud had started to feel very much at home. She reached over to Alice and took her hand. They didn't need to talk sometimes, she and Alice, they were so at ease in each other's company.

After a few minutes Alice needed to shift her position. Her back was still aching and she stood up for a bit of a stretch. Then she sat back down again and turned to Maud. 'Right, I wasn't going to tell you this, I was going to save it until you and Eddy were going to the next lecture for nurses, but, well, I can't keep it to myself.'

'What?' said Maud, intrigued.

'Guess who I saw in here this afternoon, and you should have seen his face when I called him by name.'

'Who?' said Maud, completely mystified.

'Mr Fawcett,' said Alice. 'Mr High and Mighty 'it's all about moral standards for you nurses' Fawcett!'

'Mr Fawcett!' said Maud. '*The* Mr Fawcett?'

'Yes, *the* Mr Fawcett, the man who had the nerve to show all of us probationers those horrific specimens in jars and lecture us on that Contagious Diseases Act, telling us that it was a good thing that women are rounded up off the streets and inspected for disease. That Mr Fawcett.'

Maud was completely shocked. She couldn't speak for a minute and then she said, 'I wonder if he's going to put that into his next lecture — his visit to a brothel. Oh, no, when I go to the next lecture I'll have to sit there and listen to him going on about moral standards, it makes me squirm just thinking about it.'

'Wish I could turn up as well,' said Alice. 'I'd love to see his face, the hypocrite, the bloody hypocrite.'

Then Maud started to giggle and that set Alice

off again, and in no time at all they were crying with laughter and Alice was trying to do Mr Fawcett's voice: 'Now, you nurses, make sure that you all visit the brothel once a week . . . '

Maud hooted with laughter and Alice couldn't get her breath properly. They were laughing so hard that Stella's mother, Marie, stuck her head through the door to check that everything was all right.

'Oh, Alice, that is so funny,' said Maud when she could at last speak. 'Wait till we tell Eddy.'

But Alice didn't reply. Her face had changed, she looked at Maud like she had seen a ghost and then she doubled over, clutching her belly.

'I think the baby's coming,' she shouted, as a gush of what looked like water burst on to the kitchen floor.

18

'I am of certain convinced that the greatest
heroes are those who do their duty in the
daily grind of domestic affairs whilst
the world whirls . . . '

Florence Nightingale

'It's too soon, it's too soon for the baby to come,'
yelled Alice. She was standing now, clutching her
belly, her face bright red.

Maud did her best to remain calm. She ran
over to the kitchen door to call for help before
returning to Alice, who was leaning forward on
the kitchen table, her breath coming fast as
another pain swept through her body.

'It's too early for the baby to come,' said Alice
again, her voice thick with emotion. 'What are
we going to do? It can't come yet, it might not
survive. Where is Eddy? When is she coming?'

'Soon,' soothed Maud as the realization of
what was happening began to settle on her
shoulders. 'She will be here soon, but I don't
know exactly what time.' And I need her here
now, right now, she thought, gritting her teeth.

Maud was a mess of panic inside but she knew
that she could not show any of that to Alice. She
had to take control of herself, take control of
everything.

'Now, Alice,' she said, as steadily as she could,

'if you are in labour, and I think you are, I don't think that there is anything that we can do to stop it.'

Alice started to cry and ran a hand repeatedly over her belly as if trying to soothe the baby. 'No, no, it can't come yet. It's too soon. I can't — '

'You have no choice, Alice,' said Maud quietly. 'If the baby is coming we will have to manage as best we can.' All the time she was speaking, Maud was trying to rack her brain for any bits of information that Eddy had given when she had been talking about her experience on the lying-in ward. Eddy talked constantly and Maud couldn't possibly listen all the time, but how she wished that she had paid more attention. She knew that labour pains came in spasms and that these were spaced out at first but then got closer together when the baby was about to come. And she'd witnessed that terrible premature birth on the ward . . . She would just have to use her wits.

'Alice, if you are in labour you will get another pain in a few minutes and then the pains will keep coming. I'm here and I will help you.'

'I have nothing ready. I have nothing yet, not even a crib,' wailed Alice, the panic rising in her voice.

'You need to take a deep breath and calm down,' said Maud, 'and I'll go and call for help.' There must be someone else here, she thought, whilst frantically looking around the kitchen for things they might need, but all she could see were pots and pans and a bucket of coal.

'Now, Alice, maybe you should sit down before the next pain comes.'

As she spoke, to her intense relief, Marie appeared at the door. 'What's up?' she said, her face impassive as always, something that Maud usually found disquieting. Seeing the woman now, however, Maud could have hugged her there and then.

'We think the baby is coming,' she said, trying to stay calm but finding herself almost shouting.

'What!' said Marie, instantly frowning and moving over to Alice's chair faster than Maud had ever seen her move before. 'It's too soon for the baby to come — are you sure?'

'I know it's too soon,' said Alice, starting to cry again.

'Now then, I want you to tell me what's been happening.'

Seeing that her friend was incapable of speech, Maud filled Marie in.

As Maud held Alice's gaze she saw her face change again as she clutched her belly and leant forward in her chair and then, *whoosh*, another gush of water came on to the floor.

'Well,' said Marie, placing a calming hand on Alice's shoulder, 'I don't know much, but from what I can see, that baby is comin' all right.'

Alice started to wail and cry, and then she stood up and leant forward on the table again, sobbing her way through the remains of her pain. Maud held on to her, trying to soothe her.

'Is there anybody here who knows what to do?' said Maud, hiding her desperation.

'None of the women in tonight have that kind of experience, as far as I know, and I'm not much good. I only 'ad one of me own. But you're a nurse, aren't you? Don't you know?'

'Well, I am but . . . ' Maud could see the way that Alice was looking at her, the pleading in her eyes.

'Yes, I've seen one or two delivered, so I think I can manage,' she said, trying to smile and putting a firm hand on her friend's shoulder, but inside it felt like an empty space was opening up inside of her and her legs started to feel weak. She had no idea what she was doing. She had only seen the one delivered on her first day on the ward: Lil's baby.

But she would just have to get on with it and do her best. So she took a deep breath. 'Right then, Marie, could you find some towels and, and . . . something to put the baby in, a drawer lined with a blanket, something warm? We will need to keep the baby warm . . . And I need to wash my hands,' remembering what she would do if she was in theatre.

'Right you are,' said Marie. 'I'll go and organize that lot. There's a bucket of cold water down there with a ladle and we always have hot in that big kettle on the range, and an enamel bowl there,' she said, pointing. 'And some carbolic soap and a brush right next to it.'

'Thank you,' said Maud, going straight to the bowl and washing her hands then drying them quickly on a small towel folded neatly at the side.

She threw the towel down straight away, though, as she saw Alice's face begin to contort again as the next pain hit her. It looked stronger than the last and Alice cried out a little with the effort of it. Maud could only stand by her friend's side and hold on to her, telling her to breathe, to breathe in and out, just breathe. She knew that breathing like this always helped her in theatre when she was feeling anxious and she had seen the doctor with the chloroform tell patients to do it too.

'We can do this,' said Maud, sounding resolute. 'We can do this together.'

Marie was soon back with one of the other women. They brought in a pile of towels and a cupboard drawer lined with what looked like a sheepskin and a soft, fleecy blanket neatly folded. The woman with Marie stood wide-eyed for a minute watching Alice as another pain hit her, seeing how Alice's body was consumed by all that was happening to her.

'It's all right, Lizzie,' said Marie, placing a reassuring hand on the woman's arm. 'You can get back now. I think there's a fella waiting for you, but listen out, will you? I'm going to stay in here and I'll holler if we need anything else.'

'Right you are,' said the woman, her eyes still wide. 'I'll let all the others know as well.'

'We're all set now,' said Marie steadily as Alice clung on to Maud. The pains were definitely lasting longer and Maud sensed that the labour was progressing very quickly indeed.

'That was a big one all right,' said Alice breathlessly as, at last, the pain began to subside.

'We might be getting close now,' said Maud steadily.

Maud saw Alice look terrified and she felt a glimmer of that inside herself as well but bit it down hard. 'It's all right, everything will be all right,' she said, as much to herself as to Alice. Nevertheless, she knew that she was still listening out for the sound of Eddy coming. Why was she taking so long with her family? The labour was progressing at a very rapid rate and by this stage Maud was forced to accept that neither Eddy nor Stella would get there in time. Her legs felt a bit weak at this realization, and she had to make an almost physical effort to silence the voice screaming in her brain, telling her that she didn't know what she was doing.

'Alice,' said Maud gently, 'I think we need to help you take off that big skirt and remove your underclothes. Can we just slip these off then, Alice, before the next pain?'

'And before she sits back down,' said Marie, 'let's put some towels under her, on the seat, and some on the floor, like that. That's it, now it feels like we are ready ... Whoa, there she goes again.'

Alice had to remain standing for this one and lean forward on the kitchen table again. Maud stood next to her, a hand on her friend's back. She could see that Alice had got herself into a rhythm with the breathing and she was so proud of how she was managing.

'You're doing so well, Alice,' she whispered as she saw that the pain was beginning to subside, and then Maud started swiftly unbuttoning her cuffs and rolling up her sleeves.

But before she could get very far another pain came on top of the last one and something sounded different.

Alice was making a grunting sound, a guttural

sound that came from deep within her.

'It looks like she's ready to push,' said Marie. 'We'd best get ready.'

Maud picked up a clean tea cloth and mopped her friend's brow, but now it seemed like Alice had gone to a different place and she didn't seem to notice what Maud was doing. She was still making that noise, though, and then she started to yell, 'Aaaargh!' with the sheer effort.

'Sit back down in the chair,' said Maud, trying to help her friend back.

'Get off me,' growled Alice. 'Get off.'

Maud knew that she would have to take control so she stated more firmly, 'Alice, sit down. I need to check.'

She remembered when Lil was giving birth how some sticky mass had emerged and then the baby was about to be born.

Alice still didn't move and Marie came closer. 'Sit down now, Alice. Sit down on the chair,' and this time Alice did as she was told.

Maud lifted up Alice's shift and she could see that everything was starting to bulge down there. She glanced up at Marie, her heart racing. 'I think it's coming,' she said, and Marie nodded.

'Right then, Alice,' said Maud, remembering what Sister Pritchard had said to Lil at this stage, 'when the next pain comes you push. Push as hard as you can.'

It was only seconds before Alice was yelling out again but this time she was pushing as well — she couldn't stop herself — and she pushed as if her life depended on it.

Maud could see the sticky mass getting bigger

very quickly and then, magically, she saw a tiny face appear. The face was a bluish colour but it was beautiful, the most beautiful face that Maud had ever seen, and in that moment she was in awe at being the first person, ever, to see that new face coming into the world. She felt a lump in her throat and tears started to well up in her eyes and then, in the next moment, she was panicking inside: oh my God, oh my God, I hope it's going to be able to breathe. She knew that they needed to get the little one out as fast as they could, and make sure he or she was breathing.

'Now with the next contraction, push, push,' she urged Alice. 'Keep pushing.'

Alice pushed very hard and the baby shot out of her body on a stream of blood and watery fluid. It shot straight out so quickly that it was a good job Maud stood ready because she had to catch the tiny thing. It was all slippery and so small that she was terrified that she was going to drop it. But she had the baby firm in her grasp and she could see it was a little girl. She felt the tears come to her eyes then and she couldn't stop them. 'It's a girl, it's a girl,' she cried to Alice, holding up the tiny human being for her friend to see.

Alice smiled but then she started to cry. 'She is so beautiful, so very beautiful, but is she all right? Is she breathing?'

Maud had already seen that so far the baby girl was not breathing, or even looking like she was trying to, and her alarm grew as she saw the baby's skin looking quite blue.

Laying the tiny baby down on to the stack of towels on the floor, she had to answer the question. 'She's not breathing yet, but she will,' she said determinedly. Looking down again at the scrap of life there in front of her, Maud knew that she had very little time to make a difference, that what she did right then was the most important thing she had ever done in her whole life. She felt her heart pounding but she was strangely calm. She needed to stimulate the baby in some way, give her encouragement to take a breath, so she took the towel and she gave her body a bit of a rub, only gently, but the baby still lay there lifeless. She rubbed a bit harder this time and then she turned her over on to her side, like she'd seen them do with unconscious patients in theatre. She rubbed her again even more vigorously. Time was ticking on, there was everything to lose now, and she simply had to get the baby to breathe. She held her breath, gritting her teeth, rubbed again and then she heard a tiny snuffle. She felt some movement and she could see that the baby was starting to move her tiny hand. Then she moved her head and opened her mouth, and at last she let out a tentative cry.

Maud felt a surge of pure joy go through her body; she had never felt anything like it. She wrapped the baby in the towel and held her up for Alice to see, tears streaming down her face. Instinctively Alice held out her arms for the baby and Maud reached up with her and let Alice have her. The cord was still attached and dangling down, but as far as Maud could see it didn't seem to matter. The thing that needed to be done was to hand the baby to her mother and that is exactly what she did.

All she could do then was stand and watch Alice and the baby, her head singing, her heart racing. When she looked down her hand that was resting on the kitchen table was stained with blood and something sticky, but none of that mattered. The baby was breathing! Alice's baby was alive! Then Maud took a deep breath and collected herself, remembering what Sister Pritchard had said about the afterbirth. She knew that she needed to take charge again. 'Alice, when you feel the urge to push again, push as hard as you can. We need to make sure that all of the afterbirth comes away.'

But Alice didn't seem to be listening. She was just gazing into the tiny face of the baby in absolute wonder, and Maud could see that the baby's hand, her tiny hand that had perfect fingernails, was grasping the end of Alice's finger.

'Look at her wispy hair,' she marvelled. 'It's light brown like her father's hair, like Jamie's hair, just the same.' Alice's eyes filled with tears and she looked back at her little girl, telling her, 'He doesn't even know anything about you, does he? He might never know.'

'Do you need to push?' reminded Maud, starting to feel anxious again and seeing that there was a trickle of something on to the towels on the floor and some bleeding.

'I don't know, I think so,' said Alice.

'Right, Alice, push if you can,' said Maud, noticing more bleeding and trying to keep the rising concern out of her voice. She had remembered something that Eddy had told her a few weeks ago about some woman on the lying-in ward dying of a haemorrhage after the baby was born. She could not allow that to happen.

'Push, that's it, push,' said Maud, and then to her great relief, the afterbirth started to appear and she grasped it and wrapped it in a towel. There was still some bleeding but it wasn't gushing out or anything, and Maud was happy with Alice's colour. They were always checking a patient's colour in theatre. Alice was nice and pink and the baby was much less blue-looking now. Her hands and feet were still blue but that was all. Maud was glad that they were in the kitchen next to the range so that the baby wouldn't get cold.

Then the kitchen door burst open and a dog with long legs and a thin tail came bounding in, closely followed by Harry Donahue. 'Jeez, what the — ' said Harry, instantly withdrawing as Marie shouted, 'Get that dog out of here.' Maud had never seen anyone move so fast. Harry was gone from that room in an instant.

Maud and Marie exchanged glances and Marie shook her head, muttering something about bloody men . . .

Then the door started to open once more and they both stood ready to tell Harry to make himself scarce again. Maud nearly collapsed with relief when she saw it was Eddy in her big hat with the bright-red silk flower pinned on the side, a look of shock and wonder on her face.

For once their friend was speechless. She stood with her mouth dropped open, looking from Alice to Maud, then from Maud to Alice. 'What the blazes has been going on here?' she said at last, moving straight over to Alice and the baby with tears in her eyes.

'Will you look at that?' she said. 'It's a tiny, tiny baby. I've never seen a live one that's so small, and she's perfect. She's a bit underdone, but look at her tiny hands and her fingers. Oh, Alice, she is *perfect*,' said Eddy, starting to cry but smiling at the same time.

'She is, isn't she?' said Alice, beaming.

'And you, Maud, you've done all of this?'

Maud nodded. 'With some help from Marie here, but yes, I had no choice, did I, Alice?'

'None at all,' said Alice, looking down at the baby and gently stroking her face. 'This little one was coming and that was it. There was no way round it, was there?'

'Well, I never,' said Eddy, removing her hat and laying it aside.

Then seeing Maud standing by Alice, still holding the afterbirth wrapped in a towel, Eddy rolled up her sleeves. 'Now let me get that cord tied off and separated for you. It's the least I can do.'

Maud was so glad to see her friend take over that she suddenly felt completely drained of everything and slumped down on one of the kitchen chairs. Eddy put a hand on her shoulder and said, 'You have done an incredible job here, Maud, you have for sure. We'll make a midwife out of you yet.' Eddy took some string and a pair of scissors from her pocket.

She must always carry them with her just in case, thought Maud, feeling amused but way too tired to say anything except, 'Being a midwife is not for me, Eddy.'

Maud watched as Eddy expertly got on with all that needed to be done, even bringing a bowl of hot water and the soap over to the table for Maud, so that she could sit there and wash her hands. She still felt like she was in a dream as she plunged her hands into the water. It was a bit too hot for comfort, but that made Maud smile, remembering the first time that she had worked with Eddy on the ward and she had been so enthusiastic about applying those leeches. Then, as she slowly washed her hands and she could see the blood mingling with the water and her hands coming clean again, she started to feel some strength come back into her body.

Marie had brewed a huge pot of tea and she was busying herself getting out some slabs of bread and butter and some cake. The kitchen was warm, the baby was making little snuffly noises and to Maud, just then, this small world at the heart of a brothel seemed to be the most perfect place on earth.

'Put her to the breast, Alice,' said Eddy. 'See if she can suckle. She might be a bit small so don't worry if she can't. We can express your milk and feed her with a teaspoon at first.'

Eddy is so good and so clever with all this stuff, thought Maud, seeing how interested her friend was in the baby and knowing how hard she would work to make sure that she was fed and therefore would stand the best chance that she could get. Looking again at the child, Maud had no idea if a baby so small and so early could survive, but she knew that she, Eddy and of course Alice would do everything that they could to make that happen. She felt the fire of it burning in her belly already: she would do anything for that baby.

There was a gentle tap at the door and all the women looked up at once. They heard a muffled voice — a man's voice — and Marie went over to answer. Looking back from the door to Alice she said, 'It's Harry. He's asking if he can come in and have a look at the baby. He says he understands if you don't want him to but he would love to have a look at the little girl.'

'Of course he can come in,' beamed Alice, riding on the crest of a wave now.

'And the dog?' said Marie.

'Yes, yes, let the dog in as well.'

So they both came through: Harry, with the dog trotting after him. Maud saw how eager he was to see the baby. He looked straight over to Alice and then she saw how his face glowed with tenderness when he saw the little one. 'She is perfect,' he said, his voice not much more than a whisper. 'I have never seen one so tiny before. She is a very special little girl, aren't you, aren't you, little one?' he said, stroking the baby's face so, so gently.

Maud felt herself groan inside as she sensed the hard lump of feeling that she had from the night before start to melt inside her. What woman would have been able to resist the sight of a big hulk of a man like Harry Donahue stroking the face of a tiny baby with a finger skinned at the knuckle from a fight? The whole room was drawn to the sight of it, all watching him.

Then he looked up straight at Maud and she felt it in the pit of her stomach, as if he had sent out an invisible arrow straight across the room to her. For goodness' sake, she thought to herself, oh for goodness' sake . . . but she knew in that moment that, as far as Harry Donahue was concerned, she was completely lost.

The door opened again and Stella bustled in holding the hand of the woman with the red hair that Maud had met on their first visit to Stella's all those months ago. They were both a bit breathless and, of course, surprised by the kitchen full of people and a brand-new baby. Marie was clearly glad to see Stella's friend. She went over and hugged her, saying, 'Laura, Laura,' over and over again.

Stella saw everyone looking and said, 'It's a long story. We will tell you all, but first, let's just have a look at this special little person. I hope it's a girl.'

'She is,' said Alice, 'and I was thinking of calling her Stella, but then I thought that might all get a bit confusing with us living here, so I thought I'd call her the nearest thing. I'd call her Victoria, like the queen, like our queen here in this house, our Stella.'

'Thank you for that, Alice,' said Stella, overcome for just a second, her face flushing bright red with pleasure.

'Well, I don't know where we would have been without you, Stella, and your generosity. I might well have seen my baby born in the workhouse and not be sitting here now in your warm kitchen with all these people, so she will have a queenly name, after you.'

'Here's to Victoria,' said Harry immediately, raising his cup of tea in the direction of Alice and the baby. 'And to Stella, our own queen.'

'To Victoria and to Stella!' cheered the whole room as one, and then Harry sidled over to stand behind Maud and he watched as she reached out a hand to give his dog a stroke as it stationed itself beside her chair.

19

Let each person tell the truth from
his own experience.

Florence Nightingale

Maud and Eddy made sure that Alice was well
padded up with cushions and that the baby was
lovely and warm snuggled right up to her mother
before they sat down at Stella's kitchen table
with a ready supply of hot tea. There was a sense
of a very special bond in that room. It felt like no
one wanted to leave, to break the spell. After
Marie had brewed yet another pot of tea, she
came back to the table and put a hand on her
daughter's shoulder.

'So what happened to you two tonight?' she
said.

Stella waited for Marie to sit back down at the
table next to Laura and then she said, 'Well, it
was as we thought. Laura here was picked up off
the street by the police and taken away by them.'

Marie pursed her lips and shook her head,
reaching across for Laura's hand.

'Is it all right if I tell them what happened to
you, Laura, or do you want to tell them?' said
Stella.

'No, no,' said Laura. 'You tell them, Stella.'

'Well, a few nights ago, Laura was on an
evening off and she'd just come out of the pub.

Two policemen in plain clothes came out of the shadows and were there by the side of her straight away. They didn't give her any choice. They grabbed her and bundled her into a carriage and took her straight up to the Lock Hospital.'

Maud whispered to Eddy, 'That nearly happened to me one night.'

'What?' whispered Eddy. 'They nearly took you, of all people?'

Maud nodded grimly.

'Well, I won't go into the detail of what they did to Laura up at that hospital, but we all know what's been goin' on up there with women brought in off the street. They accused her of carrying infection and they told her she'd need treatment — weeks of treatment with mercury — and she would be locked up in there until the doctor was satisfied that she was no longer a danger to men.'

The whole group tutted and sighed, and Marie put an arm around Laura's shoulders.

'Well, Laura here, and all of our women, we all make sure that we keep ourselves clean. It's a risk of this work — the men spread it around — you have to be very careful, and we are. So, for a start, there's no grounds for holding Laura in the hospital against her will, and that treatment that they give is damaging. Women have died from it and some women just disappear off the street and are never seen again. Anyway, fortunately I have an acquaintance at the Infirmary. Some of you might know about Ada Houston, my half-sister. Well, I went to see

Ada and she was on to it straight away. Although Ada doesn't have any jurisdiction at the Lock Hospital, for many weeks now she has been working steadily to make various contacts with the nurses there and I can't really tell you any more except to say that, well, my half-sister is an absolute marvel. She managed to get into the Lock Hospital. She went in there herself and she brought our Laura out with her. I don't know what she said to them in there but she came marching out with Laura and that's all that matters to us.'

Maud felt a glow of pride. She had always liked Miss Houston — all the staff did — but to learn that she would get involved with rescuing a woman from the Lock Hospital made her realize just how special the assistant superintendent must be. Alice was looking over to her mouthing, 'Miss Houston?' but Maud was not surprised one bit.

'Three cheers for Ada Houston,' said Harry, holding up his cup of tea. 'Hip, hip, hooray . . .'

'Hip, hip, hooray,' shouted the group. Then they all looked over at Alice, still sitting cradling the baby and starting to look a bit tired.

'Right, you lot,' said Stella, 'our lass here is looking like she could do with some rest and although we all feel like we could sit round talking I think we'd best call it a night.'

Maud was the first to stand up. She wanted to make sure that they did the right thing for Alice and she knew that she and Eddy would need to get back before the door to the Nurses' Home was locked.

'We'll sort Alice and the baby out,' said Stella. 'No need to worry, we'll look after both of them. So say your goodbyes, you lot, then out through the door.'

Marie had already moved over to take the baby from Alice so that she could say her goodbyes. Immediately she held her arms open to Maud and Eddy and they both came over to be hugged. There were hardly any more words that Alice could say in her exhausted state but as she hugged Maud tears came to her eyes and she quietly said, 'Thank you.'

Out in the street Maud felt the exhaustion hit her and she was glad of Eddy linking her arm and helping her along.

'Come on then, Miss Midwife,' said Eddy. 'Let's get you home, and just to say once again, what a good job you did in there. I would have been worried about taking that one on. With the early ones there's so much that can go wrong. What you did was perfect, though, Maud. It was nothing short of a miracle.'

Maud just held Eddy's arm a bit tighter and snuggled up to her as they walked, still feeling the gentle glow of happiness go through her whole body. She couldn't think of anything to say in reply. She was too exhausted to speak but she knew that she would always remember what had happened in Stella's kitchen that night.

'We'll have to keep a close eye on the baby, though,' continued Eddy. 'There's plenty of full-term babies that die in the first year, never mind a little scrap like that. I'll be going down there each day and spending as much time as I can. I've already left instructions with Alice and the women about keeping the baby warm — tiny ones like that, they soon get cold — and I've told her to wash around the cord with warm water and soap once a day. They don't want to be bathing her, not for some time yet. It would be too much of a shock to the system. And Alice was worrying about the feeding. The baby had a bit of a suckle but not much, so I've showed her how to express milk and then they can feed with a teaspoon, only very small amounts at first, but regular. Most of those women in that house want to help with baby Victoria. They said that they'll take turns with feeding her and make sure she gets a few teaspoons of milk every two hours, and they'll help Alice put the baby to the breast as well. She couldn't be in a better place, that baby . . .'

'You know so much about all of this already,' said Maud. 'You really are very clever, Eddy.'

'Nah, I've just been in the right place at the — '

'Hold up a minute,' shouted a man's voice, and Eddy didn't finish her sentence but looked straight at Maud with her eyebrows raised. Despite her exhausted state Maud felt a tightness in the pit of her stomach and her heart beat a bit faster as Harry Donahue caught up with them.

'Just thought I'd bring the dog to escort you ladies back to the Nurses' Home,' he said, looking straight at Maud.

'Of course,' said Eddy, 'of course you can do that.'

343

'And I just wanted to tell you, Maud, that I've been out looking for your boy. I'm getting to know that woman on the pots and rags stall but she isn't giving anything away. I've seen him as well, that sweep. Shifty-looking bugger; wouldn't trust him as far as I could throw him.'

'Thank you,' said Maud, turning to him with a grateful smile, hoping that he was going to be able to find Alfred, and soon. She had not been confident that he would take on the search for Alfred so wholeheartedly. But it seemed he was really trying. Maybe, just maybe, she didn't really know much about the real Harry Donahue after all.

Once they were outside the Nurses' Home, Eddy made some excuse and dashed straight in, leaving Maud at the bottom of the steps with Harry and the dog.

'I just wanted to say, it was, well . . . ' he stumbled on his words. 'What you did in there with that baby, well, it was just grand.'

Maud looked down at the ground.

'That's all I wanted to say. I know I've not always come across to you as somebody who you want to spend any time with, but I'm just hoping that you might be able to change your mind. That you might be able to give me a chance.'

Maud smiled and then she looked up to find that Harry was now gazing at the ground and the dog, Rita, was the one looking up at her.

'I might give you a chance,' she said softly, and Harry looked up straight away, a huge grin spreading all over his face as he reached out and put an arm around her. She could sense that he wanted to pull her close but she wasn't having any of that just yet, so she put a hand on his chest, making sure that he kept at a respectable distance.

As she prepared to say her goodbyes, Maud saw a figure pass by to the side of them, and there was no mistaking who it was: Nancy. She stopped in her tracks for just a moment and looked across at them with such a mix of fury and misery on her face that Maud couldn't help but feel a little sorry for the woman. She knew what Nancy was like, she knew how ruthless she could be, but in that moment, seeing her standing there looking lost and bruised, she couldn't help but let her heart go out to her just a little, especially since Harry didn't even look in Nancy's direction. Maud could sense that he knew she was there, but he just ignored her. Nancy put her head down and moved past them and up the steps into the Nurses' Home.

Maud knew that she would never like Nancy — not after everything that had happened — but she simply couldn't rejoice in something that made another person look so lost and miserable, even if that person had seemed to set against her right from the start. It simply wasn't in her nature.

Then, as Harry smiled down at her, she followed her instinct straight away, something that she rarely did. She turned her face up to him and, still keeping one hand on his chest, she kissed him on the lips. It was just one simple kiss, but she felt it reach down all through her body. She could smell that special musky smell

345

of him mixed with clean sweat and tobacco, and as she drew back she could feel his body tense and the thumping of his heart under the hand that still rested on his chest. It sent a thrill right through her.

She pulled back away from him, saying, 'I need to go in before they lock the door.' And she left him there with his dog, watching her climb the steps and disappear inside the building.

★   ★   ★

It was hard for Maud and Eddy to go back to work on the ward the next day. They just wanted to return to Stella's place to make sure that Alice and the baby were all right. Stella had said that she would let them know at the hospital immediately if there was anything amiss but, even so, they were desperate to see for themselves. By the time the afternoon came they were both restless. It was a good job that the ward was busy so they had no real chance to stop and think.

Miss Houston had been down to see them on the ward. Somehow she had got to know about Alice's baby. Maud had, of course, been all set to go at the end of the shift to give her the news, but she already knew. Ada was full of concern, of course, especially for the baby, coming so early, and she brought with her a small knitted hat. She said that her clerk, Emily, had been knitting them for the babies in the workhouse and she'd asked for the smallest one that she had, but it still looked way too big for baby Victoria.

'Still no news on the boy, then?' said Miss Houston, and Maud shook her head. Despite all that had been going on, she still had Alfred very much on her mind and always carried that gnawing anxiety about him in the pit of her stomach. She hoped that Harry would come up with something soon.

'Well, no news is good news,' said Miss Houston, but Maud was not sure about that at all. From her fruitless journeys through the city she knew full well that a boy might just disappear and that they might never see or hear anything of him again.

'Anyway, please let me know how Alice and the baby get on,' said Miss Houston.

As Maud and Eddy walked together down the corridor at the end of their shift, Maud saw a ragged figure on crutches coming towards her. It was a man with a beard and long hair, someone she thought she recognized but couldn't quite place at first. As he drew closer she realized exactly who it was. It was the army veteran, that friend of Stella's, who had been in the next bed to Alfred on the ward all those months ago. It didn't look like he had taken one scrap of Sister Law's advice about getting away from Liverpool. If anything, he was thinner and more unkempt than she remembered him, his beard matted and his clothes dirty. As he passed her Maud felt pity for the man. He had fought for Queen and Country out there in the Crimea — he must have been a proud man back then — but looking at him now she got some idea of what that war must have done to him and she didn't know how he could live out there on the streets.

It looked like he was heading away from the Male Surgical ward; he must have been admitted again, she thought. She could tell by the way that he was walking he had pain, a lot of pain, in that bad leg. She wondered if she should speak to him, if he would remember her, or maybe, she thought wildly, he might even have seen Alfred somewhere out in the city. But as she drew level with him she saw the hostile look that he gave her and thought better of it. I do hope he makes it away from the city this time, she thought. She remembered how Stella had looked at Alfred and told him not to end up like 'this fella'. Maud had felt at that time that there was absolutely no chance of that happening. But for all she knew the boy could well be living in squalor somewhere, thin and ragged, with no hope of rescue. Maud pushed the thoughts away, she had to. Harry was out looking for Alfred every day and she did the same on her walks through the city.

All Maud could do was get on with her work day by day and try to stay hopeful, but it was hard. It helped her to go to see Alice and the baby, which she did every single day. The baby was still tiny and completely swamped by the knitted hat that Miss Houston had given for her to wear, but she was feeding from the breast now and sleeping in a proper crib that one of the women had brought in. They'd put the sheepskin in there to help keep her warm, not that she spent much time in the crib. There was always somebody who wanted to hold her or rock her to sleep. Alice was happy about that so long as they kept her baby close enough, where she could see her or hear her. But the good thing was Alice had such good support because Victoria was spending a lot of time with all the women at Stella's place and she seemed to be thriving on it.

Maud was also glad to see how radiant Alice looked. She glowed with something that you couldn't quite put a finger on. It was so nice to see how settled she was at Stella's place as well, and they had even started talking about her going back to work when the baby was bigger, with Stella and Marie offering to look after baby Victoria if Alice wanted to complete her nurse training. Alice wasn't ready for that yet, though, mainly because all the probationers had to live in the Nurses' Home, but it was definitely something to think about for the future.

The gentle pattern of life continued and Maud saw Harry at Stella's most evenings. Harry spent most of his free time out in the city with the brown sock in his pocket and the dog trotting by his side, keeping an eye on Market Street and actively searching for Alfred. Harry had more free time now because, since he'd been knocked down that night in the park by the big fella, he'd been far more wary of getting hurt or permanently damaged and so he'd almost given up the bare-knuckle fighting. He said that he remembered seeing Maud's face that night, then bang, he was out like a light, and he couldn't remember what had happened afterwards. He hadn't gone to hospital, though he probably should have done, but somebody had looked after him that time.

Maud knew exactly who had looked after Harry after that fight but she didn't say. She knew by the way that Nancy kept looking daggers at her every time their paths crossed that Harry had no interest whatsoever in Nancy now.

Maud was feeling increasingly drawn to Harry. She couldn't help herself, seeing him at Stella's, watching him making a fuss over the baby, seeing a different side to him, and doing his best to help her with Alfred. He had asked her to give him a chance and she was doing more than that now. She was walking out with him through the city on a regular basis, backwards and forwards to the Nurses' Home and then on their trips to look for Alfred. She was happy to take Harry's arm and feel him lean against her and then she would let him in closer as he embraced her, and the kissing, the kissing was going very well indeed.

Harry was very hard to resist and one night when they found themselves alone, sheltering from the cold Liverpool rain in the doorway of a grand stone building, he pulled her to his body and all she could smell was his damp hair, clean sweat and tobacco. He felt so warm against her and she snuggled in even further and then she gasped and instantly drew back.

Harry cracked up laughing and she scowled at him and tried to stop her face from flushing red.

'Ooh, what's that?' he teased.

'I know exactly what that is,' said Maud, taking another step back from him. 'I have seen a man's penis before, you know,' she said, a shade too forcefully.

He laughed loudly again and then said, 'I don't even know what that is. If it's what I think it is then round here we don't usually call it a pee nis.'

Then he grabbed her again and she couldn't help but smile. 'Look, you may have seen one in the hospital but I bet you've never seen one like this . . . '

'Harry Donahue!' Maud almost shouted, instantly drawing back, breathless and flustered.

'Look, Maud, round here we celebrate this kind of thing, we follow our hearts. Just think about it . . . no, don't think about it. Look . . . no, don't look, just come here . . . just relax and be glad of what we have right now, between the two of us.'

But Maud shook her head, stepping back even further before grabbing his arm and pulling him determinedly out into the rain. She knew exactly how far she would go and, even though she was sorely tempted, she was determined that there would be no improper conduct between them. Maud knew full well that if she took one step in that direction she would be lost. Knowing what had happened to Alice after just one night with Jamie, she didn't want anything like that to happen and risk not finishing her training at the hospital. She had been spending more time in theatre, she knew what she was doing, she wanted to qualify as a nurse and then get some more experience. She couldn't let it all go to waste, not now.

20

'A superintendent over all her nurses,
should be able to tell, at all times,
where her charges are . . . '
Florence Nightingale
(from a letter to William Rathbone, 1860)

One day, whilst Maud was busy on the ward, a small figure approached the hospital. It was a boy with bare feet, just walking along beside a man and his dog, reaching over every now and then to pat the dog as they walked, as if it was the most natural thing in the world.

At the door of the hospital, the man, who was wearing a dark-green jacket, bade farewell to the boy and gave him a pat on the head and then he watched carefully to make sure that the boy knew exactly where he was going and he was moving safely inside the building.

'What you doin', young man?' said Michael Delaney at the head of a stretcher as they carried a patient to the Male Surgical ward.

'Don't we know you?' said Stephen Walker, at the foot.

'I think we do,' said Mr Delaney, and the boy smiled at them.

'What you doin' back 'ere? You best watch out. Sister on this ward will be after you with a cat-o'-nine-tails,' he said as they all went as one

352

through the door of the Male Surgical ward.

'What's that?' said Sister Law, scowling at the orderly as he came through the door. 'What was that you were saying about Sister?'

Michael Delaney couldn't speak. He was, as always, momentarily struck dumb by the sight of Sister Law, her feet planted square, her chest puffed out and the white starched cap knotted firmly under her chin.

'Where do you want this patient, Sister?' said Stephen, taking the lead for once.

'Over there,' she pointed. 'And look sharp about it.' Then her expression softened, completely softened, as she caught sight of the boy who had walked in by the side of the stretcher.

'Well, well, young man,' she said. 'It's Alfred, isn't it, young Alfred? I think that you have been missing for quite some time.'

As Sister Law walked through the corridor with the boy she kept glancing down at him. She had never come across anything like this before. He had just walked into the hospital, calm as you please. Goodness knew what he must have gone through out there in the city, but he looked calm and he had asked to see Nurse Linklater, please. He had said 'please' all quiet and polite. Sister Law had never known a boy like this one. They were usually little scallywags, the whole lot of them, but this one was different. He was very special.

She knew that Nurse Linklater was working on Female Surgical. She knew because she had regular contact with Sister Pritchard, who had been so thrilled by Nurse Linklater's progress.

She was, according to Sister Pritchard, simply the best probationer in theatre that there had ever been. Even though she knew that Pritchard could get a bit carried away sometimes with regard to some of the probationers, Sister Law also knew from when Linklater had been on her ward that she had shown real promise. But as with all things related to nursing or medicine, the probationer would need to work really hard and get more experience if she was to truly become the marvel that Sister Pritchard predicted.

Anyway, Sister Law had seen how Nurse Linklater had taken to this boy, this Alfred. After all, she had been the one who had brought him into the ward and she had visited him every day. Sister Law would never forget someone who dared to sneak into the sluice without permission. She had admired Linklater for that, she had to admit. The girl was very quietly spoken but she had held her ground that day for sure, and the young lad obviously thought a great deal of her to come straight back to her here.

Sister Law stood on Female Surgical with the boy beside her, waiting to get some idea of where she should head. She knew that Sister Pritchard was an excellent and very experienced nurse but she didn't exactly run what might be called a 'tight ship'. There were nurses up and down everywhere, chatting away. She even saw one smiling. How could a ward function in this manner? She would never have stood for that kind of thing. And the chatter of the women, the patients on this ward . . . For goodness' sake, there was so much tittle-tattle and chitchat she felt like she was drowning under it and still she couldn't see any sign of Nurse Linklater or her ward sister.

So, reaching down, she took the boy's hand, and told him to, 'Come with me,' and as they walked together down the ward, that's when she saw the person she'd been looking for. Maud was just smoothing the sheet on a bed, and my word, the corners on that bed linen were perfect, Sister Law noticed that immediately. Nurse Linklater still had her back to them so Sister looked down at Alfred and put a finger to her lips so they could wait for Maud to turn round.

'Nurse Linklater,' she said softly, and Maud turned, instantly recognizing the voice and wondering what on earth she could have possibly done to bring Sister Law all the way from Male Surgical. She turned with a certain amount of dread but when she saw Alfred standing beside Sister, his face beaming, she cried out with sheer joy, 'Alfred!' and the boy ran into her outstretched arms.

Maud swept him up and hugged him and hugged him, saying thank you, thank you . . . over and over again to Sister Law, who was smiling — actually smiling — at them. And then Sister Pritchard was coming down the ward and Eddy was there and everything was absolutely wonderful.

When Maud was able to release Alfred from her embrace for a few moments she held him at arm's length and had a good look at him. He looked absolutely fine: he wasn't thin, he was reasonably clean, his hair wasn't matted, he was smiling at her and his blue eyes were shining.

'Where have you been?' she said, not able to let him speak properly because she just wanted to hug him over and over again.

'A man kept me in a room,' he said, the sound muffled against Maud's shoulder.

'A man? Was it Mr Greer?' said Maud, immediately afraid and holding Alfred away from her body so that she could hear him speak. 'Did he hurt you?'

'No, no,' said the boy, 'nobody hurt me. They just kept me in a room with the door locked.'

Maud hugged Alfred again and then held him away once more so that she could see into his face and hear him speak.

'But was it Mr Greer?'

'I never saw him,' Alfred said, and Maud saw a fleeting shadow cross the boy's face before he continued. 'But Mrs Greer took me from the school. She said I'd best come quietly or else you wouldn't be finishing your nurse training.'

'Oh, Alfred,' gasped Maud, 'I am so sorry that they used our friendship against you. Did they harm you? Where did they put you?'

'She took me to a house. I think it was somewhere near Greer's place. There was a man and his wife there and they pushed me into a room with one small window high up and locked the door. I think Mr Greer had sold me to them or something. I heard the man say that he was going to make me climb chimneys again and that made me feel afraid. Then one day I heard them talking outside the door after they'd been in with

356

some food. They were saying that they'd have to leave it a bit before they could put me to work. The man said that he'd seen some notices up round the city with my description and they didn't want to risk anything so they'd have to wait.'

Maud heaved a silent sigh of relief and gave thanks to Miss Fairchild for sending out those notices.

'Then ages later I heard them again, the man and his wife. They were angry and shouting, and she said that they would never be able to use me now and they'd have to get their money back. It took a while after that, but today the woman came to me and she pulled me out of the room and marched me to Mr Greer's house. I tried to get away from her but she had me held tight with a leather strap around my wrist.'

Maud glanced down and she could see a bright-red mark and the beginnings of a bruise around Alfred's left wrist. Tears sprang to her eyes and she lifted his small arm to kiss it better.

'It's all right, Maud, it doesn't hurt much.'

'It hurts me,' said Maud, 'to know that you have been held against your will and treated so cruelly.'

Alfred reached up and wiped the tears from her eyes with his small hand and then calmly continued his story. 'Well, she went up to Mrs Greer on that stall and they were shouting and screaming at each other and almost ready to claw each other's eyes out when Mr Greer came out of the house and gave the woman some money and she handed him the leather strap. So then Mr Greer was shouting at Mrs Greer and then he said something about taking me straight down to the docks to see if one of the ships needed a cabin boy. He thought he might be able to get some money for me like that.'

Maud now had tears streaming down her cheeks. She couldn't bear to think what might have happened.

'Well, he was dragging me along and by that time I was really starting to struggle and trying to get free and I was shouting out as well. I thought I had nothing to lose. So we were pushing through the people on the street and they weren't taking any notice and Mr Greer was still dragging me. Then, from out of nowhere, a dog came bounding through, straight at Mr Greer and it was growling. It came right at him and he tried to bat it away but it went behind and bit him on the backside. He screamed out and let go of the leather strap and I ran as fast as I could after the dog. Then another man grabbed me and at first I kicked and struggled, but then he mentioned your name and pulled this out of his pocket . . . '

'What?' said Maud, as the boy fished in his own pocket and then held out a single brown sock.

'That was Harry. So it was him that found you in the end,' cried Maud. 'His dog sniffed you out.'

'Kind of,' smiled Alfred. 'The man, Harry, said he's been looking for weeks and you had told him to keep an eye on Market Street. He had been letting the dog sniff the sock as well, but

Rita hasn't much idea about tracking. Then as soon as he saw me with Greer, he knew who I must be straight away and he told the dog, 'Go get 'im,' and she did. Oh, and Harry said to say sorry that he couldn't come in with me, because of the dog, and he'll be waiting outside the Nurses' Home at the usual time.'

'Oh, Alfred,' said Maud, hugging him again and never wanting to let him go, 'I have been so worried about you, and Miss Fairchild has as well. I can't wait to tell her that you are home safe. Now I don't want you out of my sight again, ever, do you hear?'

⋆   ⋆   ⋆

Sister Pritchard had made it clear that Maud was free to go as soon as she was ready, and she gratefully accepted the offer once she'd finished her immediate duties, taking Alfred with her. The whole ward had rejoiced after hearing the news. All of the patients had wanted to hear the story and even Sister Law had not been able to stop smiling before beating a retreat back to Male Surgical, where she was sure that the staff and the patients would be running absolute riot without her governance.

Alfred had tagged along with Maud and he'd had his hair ruffled and been kissed and hugged many times. He'd even been given sugar mice by one of the patients. Even Mr Jones and Dr McKendrick had been given the whole story as they made their way through the ward to check some new equipment in the theatre. Mr Jones had picked up Alfred and swung him round, so delighted was he by the whole outcome. It was simply overwhelming, especially for Maud, who just liked to get on with the work and make sure that she quietly blended into the fabric of the ward. So that was another reason that she was glad to accept Sister Pritchard's gracious offer to leave early, even though it meant walking by the stretcher as Michael Delaney and Stephen carried Alfred in triumph through the hospital.

'Yes, that will be fine, Michael,' said Maud quietly as she insisted that they leave Alfred at the main entrance and not carry him down the street to the Nurses' Home. 'That will be absolutely fine. We can manage very well from here, thank you.'

Stephen Walker looked very disappointed not to be able to continue the journey with the boy. Maud had never seen the man so animated, but still she held her ground and the two men made do with ruffling Alfred's hair a final time and then heading off to their quiet corridor for a cup of tea and a smoke.

As soon as the orderlies were gone Maud looked down at Alfred's feet. 'Oh, but you've no shoes,' she said. 'Maybe I should have let them carry you after all.'

'Oh, no, Maud, don't worry about that,' said Alfred. 'I've walked all the way through the city like this. I will be fine.'

'But your poor feet,' said Maud, almost on the verge of tears. Before she could say any more, however, or let the tears flow, Alfred had taken her hand and started to walk with her the short distance to the Nurses' Home.

As they came in through the entrance to the building Miss Mary Merryweather and her sister happened to be leaving the office. They both stopped in their tracks and were also delighted to see Alfred.

'Is this the boy that went missing?' said Miss Elizabeth, with a wonderful smile.

'Yes,' said Maud, wondering how they knew. As far as she could remember she had never spoken of Alfred to either of the sisters.

'This is a very happy day indeed,' said Miss Mary, reaching into her pocket to find a shilling to give to Alfred.

'Yes, it is,' said Maud. 'I just need to take him up to my room so that I can get changed. I know you don't like — '

'Boys are welcome in here,' said Miss Mary. 'It's just the full-grown men we try to keep out.'

Maud didn't tell the Miss Merryweathers that she was due to meet a 'full-grown man' outside the building in about an hour, but then they probably knew all about that as well. After all, they seemed to know everything.

Harry was already waiting with Rita at the bottom of the steps when Maud stepped out through the door, closely followed by Alfred. She saw him turn and he beamed a smile, and the dog started frantically wagging her tail.

'Hello again, young man,' said Harry as Rita bounded up to the boy and licked his face.

'That's a good sign,' said Harry. 'Rita doesn't like all that many people. I've never seen her greet anyone like that before. As you know, me

361

and Alfred are already acquainted.'

'Thank you so much,' said Maud, grabbing hold of Harry, and in that moment not caring who saw as they stood outside the Nurses' Home. 'I can't bear to think what might have happened to Alfred if you hadn't been there.'

'Well, you told me where to look,' said Harry, 'and I just kept looking. Besides, it's all down to Rita really; she's the one who saved the day. I was as shocked as anyone to see how she flew off like that. She's never bitten anybody before but she went straight for Greer and bit him right on the arse.'

Maud laughed. 'I would have loved to have seen that.'

'He was like this,' said Harry, breaking away from her and running with his hands on his backside, yelling, ''Keep that beast away from me!' The good thing is as well,' he continued as he came back towards them, 'is that Mr Greer doesn't know me from Adam, so there's no way that he would link Alfred's rescue to you. I told him I was going to report him to the police for child cruelty under the Chimney Sweepers Act. I shouted that at his back as he was running down the street. He glanced round so I know that he heard me. He looked petrified. Anyway, so long as the lad keeps well out of the way, I don't think you'll hear any more from the sweep or his missus.'

'Thank you, Harry,' said Maud, grabbing hold of him again and smiling up at him.

Harry pulled her closer to him and whispered in her ear, 'You'll have to marry me now, Maud.

Will you marry me?'

Maud pulled back straight away and she was instantly looking around to make sure that no one had witnessed her moment of abandon, right outside the Nurses' Home.

'So that's a no, then,' said Harry quietly.

'I'm sorry,' said Maud as she stood holding his hand, 'I just don't know how we could do that right now. I would have to leave my work, you know I would. And I can't, I just can't.'

Seeing how forlorn the man looked, Maud knew she had to do something so she put her arms around him once more and said, 'Look, Harry, you know how I feel about you. Just give me some more time, will you?'

Harry pulled her close again. 'I will,' he breathed. 'I will.'

'And right now, Harry,' said Maud, stepping back from him again, 'I want you to help me take Alfred to Devonshire Square. Miss Fairchild needs to know straight away that he is safe and she has always said that as soon as he turns up he can stay there with her. They can find him some work as a boot boy or something, just until proper arrangements can be made.'

'Right,' said Harry, still staring at her.

'He has no shoes; his feet are bare.'

'Right,' said Harry.

'Harry, you need to carry him.'

'Of course I do,' said the man at last, sweeping the boy up into his arms and setting off very purposefully.

'Not that way,' said Maud, laughing. 'Just follow me.'

Maud's final placement as a probationer took her back to Male Medical. As always, she was not as comfortable working with the men, but at least she was grateful to be nurtured in the bosom of Sister Cleary's ward. After all, she'd been lucky: Mr Jones had put in a special request for her to extend her time on Female Surgical so that she could continue to gain experience in theatre. So, fair enough, it was right and proper that she move on now. She was a probationer and she needed a full range of experience. Eddy had, at last, been given Female Medical and the dreaded Sister Fox, but she was making the absolute best of it, even saying occasionally that 'old Foxy' wasn't so bad after all, only to be miserably late off the ward the next day because she'd been kept back to give all the bedpans an extra polish.

Nancy was riding high on this, her last placement. She had been given Female Surgical and Eddy swore that she could already tell that Nancy Prancy thought she was the queen of surgery.

One day, while Maud was fighting to apply a bread poultice that had been made with a little too much milk to a nasty skin infection on a patient's leg, Miss Houston appeared at the bottom of the bed. Seeing that Maud was struggling with the sticky bread mixture she came around to help support the leg and then held it steady whilst Maud applied a bandage. Once they had together settled the patient and made sure he was comfortable, Ada took Maud aside.

'I need a word, Maud. Can you come up to my room? I've spoken to Sister Cleary so she is fully aware.'

Maud felt stricken; this was completely unexpected.

'Don't worry,' said Miss Houston. 'Go and wash your hands and then come up. I'll see you there.'

Standing outside Miss Houston's door took Maud right back to when she had been there after Alfred went missing, and then when she had stood with a tearful Alice.

'Come in,' called Ada after she had knocked lightly on the door.

It made Maud feel a little sad not to be greeted by the dog, Bob, or see him stretched out on Ada's bed. But there was still a nice warm fire lit in the grate and a lovely smile from Miss Houston. Whatever it was, at least Maud knew that Miss Houston would be kind and fair.

'Sit yourself down, Maud,' said Ada before slipping into the chair opposite. 'I'll come straight out with it. I don't wish to pry, but it has been brought to my attention that you are involved with a young man who has been a patient at this hospital.'

Maud felt winded. She'd had no clue what Ada was going to say and for a split second she wondered how she could have found out. But then, of course, it was obvious. It had to be Nancy who had told.

'Yes, it is true,' said Maud, feeling her face

start to burn, not with embarrassment but with anger. She knew that Nancy had been furious when Maud was given extra time on Female Surgical and she had gone around telling everyone that it wasn't fair. She had been her usual spiteful self and there was no getting away from it: for whatever reason, Nancy hated her.

'Now, Maud,' said Ada, reaching over to take hold of her hand, 'I need you to know that, unlike some of the senior staff here at the Infirmary, I understand that sometimes life takes over and we nurses need other things apart from our work, but you do need to understand that if you become engaged or married there are those here who would not tolerate your continued employment as a nurse.'

'I am aware of that,' said Maud, looking up to give Ada a small smile and then staring into the fire.

Ada withdrew her hand and sat quietly, waiting for her probationer to say more if she needed to.

When Maud looked up her voice was quiet but steady. 'I've tried so hard for this not to happen. He's asked me to marry him twice and I've refused him each time for that very reason. I don't want to leave nursing. I love my work.'

'I'm so sorry, Maud,' said Ada quietly. 'I am sorry that these are the rules and, personally, I don't know why they are enforced so cruelly. How can any human being have control over love? It is impossible to control.'

Maud looked up and as her eyes met Ada's she saw a connection there and she knew in that

366

moment that they had complete trust and understanding.

'I don't know what I can do, and that's the truth. The man that I'm involved with was the person who found Alfred. Since that day he and the boy have been very close . . . we are all close and we've even been talking about going to New York.'

'I have no easy answers for you, Maud, and, like I said, I fully understand that there is nothing that you can do about your feelings for this man and the boy.'

'He has a dog as well,' said Maud quietly, 'and I even like the dog.'

'Ah, well, you are definitely lost,' smiled Ada. 'But all is not beyond saving as far as I see it. We just need to find a way of working around the system. We can't defy it, we can't change it, but there might be a way to work around it.'

Maud looked up again with some hope in her eyes now.

'This might not be feasible, but with the work in New York, if you were to go there, then that might provide us with an answer.'

'In what way?'

'Well, although they haven't yet fully embraced Nightingale nursing in America, they are forging ahead in other ways and there is a sense that women over there are freer in some ways. That means that they might not be asking as many questions about your personal life.'

'Do you know anyone who's gone out there?'

'Not personally, but I've heard about a Nightingale nurse called Ann Reading, who went out to nurse the troops in the Civil War. She even married one of her patients. Look, leave it with me. I have a friend, Dr Lampeter, who has worked in New York. I'll write to him and see if he has any contacts. You once mentioned the Infirmary for Women, is that still something that would interest you?'

'Yes, definitely,' said Maud, smiling.

'Right, Maud, leave it with me,' said Ada, getting up from her chair. 'There has to be a way around this, though I'm not saying it would be an easy choice. You will be away from all that you know and it will be challenging.'

'I understand,' said Maud firmly.

'But you know what?' said Ada, taking hold of Maud's hand again as she stood up from her chair. 'You have the backbone for this, Nurse Linklater, and I know that you will work hard and grasp every opportunity. We can't lose a nurse like you simply because you want to be married. New York could be exactly the right place for you, Maud.'

As Maud walked back through the hospital she had a sense of everything starting to fall into place and it gave her a spring in her step. She hadn't realized to what extent the whole thing about her work and the relationship with Harry had been weighing her down. In a way, although Nancy — and she was sure that it was Nancy who had supplied the information — had clearly wanted to make things difficult, she had in fact done her a favour. Far from being dismissed from the hospital in disgrace, she was now being given support and valuable advice.

As she walked by the door to Female Surgical Maud glanced in and, strangely, Nancy was right there, staring straight at her. Maud just gave her a big, beaming smile and continued on her way.

Epilogue

'The true marriage — the noble union,
by which a man and woman become
together the one perfect being — probably
does not exist at present upon earth.'

Florence Nightingale

Liverpool 1871

Maud looked into the oval mirror that Eddy had given her months ago, after Alfred had been found. She brushed her hair back from her face and fastened it tight with a clip, before placing the white, starched cap exactly square on her head.

Today was an important day. She would be going to the Boardroom with the rest of her group to receive their certificates and qualify as nurses. Eddy had promised that she would be ready on time and Maud could hear her crashing around in the room next door. What was she doing in there?

They needed to be off so she glanced down to her apron one more time to make sure that it was perfectly clean and straight. Then she went to knock on Eddy's door and haul her out of there if necessary. Out on the landing she could see the others starting to emerge from their rooms, some smiling, others looking nervous.

There was a buzz of excitement in the air and as she stood for a moment outside Eddy's room all of the doors on both sides of the landing started to open. All except one: the door opposite, Nancy's door. That stayed firmly closed but, as always, Maud could sense that Nancy was in there. She could feel the too heavy silence behind that door and it started to make her feel unsettled. She needed to break the spell so she knocked firmly on Eddy's door and then went straight in. Eddy claimed to be all set but Maud still checked her over, straightening her apron and then asking her to remove her cap so that she could knock it back into the proper shape and make sure that, just this once, it wasn't sat skew-whiff on her head. When they emerged on to the gallery they joined the group who were descending the stairs and walked together over the now very familiar route that led to the hospital.

However, this morning they weren't going to the wards. They turned in the opposite direction down a corridor that led to the Boardroom and there, standing at the door and holding it open for all to enter, was Miss Houston.

'Come on, you two,' she said as Maud and Eddy came through into the grand room with its high ceiling and smell of polish.

Maud felt a small shiver run through her when she saw Nancy already there. She must have slipped out of her room whilst she was in with Eddy, because she was standing with a couple of probationers that she had recently acquired. Nancy didn't look in her direction but Maud could sense that she knew that she was there. Anyway, Miss Houston was organizing them into alphabetical order, which meant that magically she was next to Eddy on one side and Nurse Langtry on the other, so at least she wouldn't have to sit anywhere near Nancy.

Maud wasn't sure if she was excited or nervous but her heart started to pound when she saw the line of senior people standing in front of the shiny, wooden table: Mr Jones and Mr Fawcett; a man wearing a dog collar who must be the new chaplain, the Reverend Seed; and the Miss Merryweathers.

Miss Houston quietly explained that Miss Mary Merryweather would make a short speech and then the nurses would be called up one by one to be presented with a certificate. Then they would stand to the side until the ceremony was brought to a close before going straight to the wards to resume their duties.

As soon as Miss Houston stepped back to stand in line with the senior staff, the large clock that hung on the wall chimed the hour and all went quiet except for Miss Merryweather clearing her throat to speak. At that moment Maud heard the door squeak open as someone came into the room behind them and slipped into a chair. Strangely, Mr Fawcett looked suddenly like he'd seen a ghost. Maud knew in that moment who had just come into the room. It was Alice. She'd said that she would try to come and she would be the last person that the good doctor would want to see today; someone who had seen him at the brothel.

Miss Merryweather gave a small smile and then cleared her throat again. 'Now, you nurses,' she said, 'I am sorry that our Mr Rathbone cannot be here today to share this achievement with you all but he is currently in London. He is in fact visiting Miss Nightingale, so I'm sure that we can excuse him just this once.'

Miss Merryweather looked along the line of probationers and smiled. 'It is good to see so many of this intake come through the full twelve months. Despite those who inevitably fell by the wayside for want of moral character, at least this time we have had only one death, and that was from typhus. So it is good to see such a nice group of you here today. I don't want to take up too much of your time on such an important day so I will be brief. You women who have come through this year together are a very special breed. You have been able to display the requisite sobriety, determination, steadfastness and gentleness. You have shown that you are, for the most part, of the correct temperament to undertake this important work of nursing: you know how to be attentive, patient,' and then she paused and gave Eddy a steely glance, 'quiet and punctual. But this is just the start of things for you. You must go forth and do good work. All of you probationers have done well. I congratulate you . . . and now I will present the certificates.'

Maud saw Miss Merryweather take the first certificate off the stack on the long table and then Miss Houston began to call out names. Maud watched as her fellow probationers got up one by one and she felt her stomach tighten when it was Nurse Langtry's turn. She hadn't got to know Millicent Langtry all that well but she did know that whatever she did was thorough but slow. Today she seemed to move more slowly than ever as she took the certificate from Miss Merryweather and then walked along the line shaking hands. It seemed to take for ever and by the time she was finished Maud could feel her heart pounding fast.

'Nurse Maud Linklater,' called Miss Houston at last. As Maud got up from her seat her legs felt weak. Once she was moving, however, she managed to steady up and she started to buzz with energy. Miss Houston shook her hand first and as she did so she whispered, 'My protegee,' and gave Maud a big smile. Then Maud was receiving the piece of parchment from Mary Merryweather and moving along the line of handshakes. My word, Mr Jones has a very strong grip, she thought, and wondered for one moment if he was going to clap her on the back. Once back and standing to the side, Maud waited and watched the others make their own journey. Eddy was next, of course, and moving so fast that Maud almost missed her and she had to stifle a giggle when she saw how vigorously Eddy shook hands with everyone. It looked for one moment as if Miss Elizabeth Merryweather might be lifted off her feet.

As soon as Eddy was finished she came to stand by Maud and they held hands and both looked at Alice as she sat there smiling. They were so pleased that she had managed to sneak into the ceremony. But Maud couldn't help but feel sad for Alice. She should have been standing there beside herself and Eddy.

Nancy was next to last to pass along the line. She held her head high and moved gracefully, offering a small smile and a careful handshake to all concerned but, as far as Maud could see, there seemed to be little joy in her demeanour and her blue eyes were cold as usual. When she walked to the group she held Maud's gaze for just a few seconds and there was an unmistakable look of triumph seeping from her that made Maud feel uncomfortable.

'Now, nurses,' said Miss Merryweather, 'just one more thing. We are very proud of you and you should all be proud of yourselves, but remember, the piece of paper that you hold in your hand does not make you a nurse. There is a lifetime of learning that you still need to do . . . Now back to the wards for duty as usual and when you get to your rooms this evening you will find the uniform of a trained nurse ready and waiting.'

Maud linked arms with Eddy and Alice, and they were just about to leave the room when Miss Houston called to her.

'I'll see you both later,' said Maud, instantly peeling away and walking with Miss Houston back to the Boardroom table.

'I just want to say my own congratulations to you, Maud. You have proved me absolutely right. I knew when I saw you that day on the ward that you would make an excellent nurse.'

Maud felt her face flush with pride.

375

'Now, about the other issue.'

Maud glanced back over her shoulder to make sure that the room was empty and it was safe to talk.

'I've had word back from Dr Lampeter and he has direct contact with Dr Elizabeth Blackwell at the Women's Infirmary. I hope it's all right but he said that he would get in touch with her straight away, and yesterday I heard from him again.'

'And?' said Maud, hardly able to contain her excitement.

'And . . . they are very keen to take a theatre nurse trained under the Nightingale system and all they need to know is who will supply a recommendation. I will of course be happy to do that. Oh, and the only other thing they wanted to know is, when can you start?'

'Really?' said Maud, breaking into a smile as she stood clasping her certificate.

'Really!' said Ada, grabbing hold of Maud and crushing her in an embrace.

★　★　★

That evening as Maud walked steadily down the steps of the Nurses' Home and out through the city to meet Harry at Lime Street Station, she could feel her heart beating like a drum. After speaking to Miss Houston she felt sure of herself and she knew exactly what she needed to do, but when she saw him, standing in the usual spot, her breath caught and she paused just for a moment to look at him. As always he seemed casual, nonchalant amongst the crowd, leaning against the brick wall with a smoke in his hand and the dog sitting at his feet. However, a man like Harry could never blend into a crowd and even as she watched she could see some of the women who passed him giving him a glance or a smile. That's how it was for Harry and the attention just seemed to run off him like water.

As soon as he saw her he smiled and stood straight and Rita got up and shook herself. Then he ground the smoke under his boot and in the next moment she was in his arms and she could smell him and feel his body against her.

Maud had thought that she would wait until they were in a quieter spot but she couldn't contain herself for one moment longer so she drew back from him as they stood amongst the crowd outside Lime Street and told him there and then.

'Miss Houston has found a position for me at that hospital in New York. Please say you'll come with me? And Alfred, too? I know we need to find money for the passage, but can we try?'

'Of course we can,' cheered Harry, grabbing hold of her and lifting her off her feet. 'And of course I want to come with you. Just try stopping me!'

'And there is one more thing,' said Maud once he'd set her down, breathless. 'Will you marry me?'

'What?' he said, and the dog pricked up her ears as well.

'Will you marry me?' Maud almost yelled.

'Yes!' he shouted and then he grabbed her

again and they were dancing round and round with the dog barking at their feet.

★ ★ ★

Three months later Maud was looking into her oval mirror again. It was her last day on the ward at the Liverpool Royal Infirmary. Tomorrow she would be married and then she would be boarding a ship to cross the Atlantic Ocean for New York.

You're still all face and forehead, she thought with a wry smile, but even though your face is a bit long, I don't think you look so bad, not any more. And I mean, who'd have thought that you could have ended up with a man like Harry Donahue?

Moving her face a bit closer to the mirror, scrutinizing herself, she still couldn't believe it. Tomorrow they would be married. Eddy had presented Maud with a white silk flower to wear in her hair, and there it sat on the chest of drawers, accusing her of turning frivolous.

It was important for Maud to be married and she had always hoped that she would find a suitor, but the more years that she'd spent as a housemaid and the more time went by without her finding anyone, well, she had begun to believe what she'd always been told: that she had a plain face, that she would always be plain and that it was unlikely that she would marry. But back then she had never thought that she would be anything other than a housemaid; she had never dreamt that she could be a nurse, a trained nurse, and that she would capture the interest of a man, a very handsome man, at that. None of this had ever seemed possible until she started the new life that she now had at the Infirmary.

Despite her new life, however, some things remained steadfast for Maud: she held fast to the promise that she made to herself when she and Harry first started 'walking out' together. She had promised that she would never go any further with him than kissing. She had stayed true to this promise even though it had been very hard at times to be so close to him and smell that smell he had and want him so much. But once Maud's mind was made up, that was that. She had been clear with him from the start that she would not change her mind.

Her absolute insistence on this had been causing some trouble because Harry wasn't the sort of man who liked waiting. Her impression was that he'd thought once Maud had proposed and he'd accepted then it would all fall into place and it wouldn't matter. But he had been wrong. She had been clear: they would be waiting till after they were married and that was that. He had seemed to understand, and given that he'd been taken up by their plans to go to New York, perhaps the waiting time had been made easier for him. Given that they were bound for America and a whole new life of which she knew nothing, she was hoping that she wouldn't fall pregnant for some time anyway and she would be using the birth control sponges that Eddy had got for her. Yes, she did want children of her own eventually — even though she had

Alfred, she definitely wanted others — but she had done so well to get the offer of work from New York and she couldn't waste an opportunity like that.

They were all set to go, and young Alfred would be coming with them. He'd really taken to Harry. Maud knew that it would be very hard for Miss Fairchild to part with Alfred now but she was all in favour of him making a new life for himself and having a fresh start in America with Maud and Harry, as long as they were married, of course. Not only that, she'd offered to pay for the passage to America, not just for the boy but for all of them in their own cabin. Maud had said no at first: it was too much; they couldn't accept it; she'd been saving up her own money as well. She thought she would have enough, maybe not for a cabin but definitely for the passage. But in the end Harry had managed to persuade her that they should accept Miss Fairchild's offer. After all, Maud was like family to her. So Maud gave in and Miss Fairchild even arranged for them to take the dog as well, because she knew that it would have broken Harry and Alfred's hearts to leave Rita behind in Liverpool.

Maud was excited and so happy that she and Harry and Alfred would be travelling all together to America like a decent married couple with a son on board that ship. All together in their own cabin; a proper family.

She had not been prepared, though, for how very sad she would feel on her last day on the ward. She'd gone back to Female Surgical after she qualified, working mainly in theatre, and she really enjoyed the work. Now, as her last day had arrived and she thought about what she was embarking on — a marriage, a sea voyage and starting work across what felt like the other side of the world — she was feeling much more nervous than she thought she would be. If it hadn't been for Miss Houston coming on to the ward to see her and give her some reassurance, she might even have got herself to a point where she could have cancelled everything and stayed put in Liverpool. But Ada had set her straight. She never really talked about her experience in the Crimea but it was there with her anyway, it was part of who she was, and she seemed to have a different perspective than other people.

Whilst Sister Pritchard had been fretting away every time that Maud told her about her plans, Ada came and made everything seem calm and manageable. She made Maud feel that all she needed to do was take everything in her stride and then it would all fall into place.

But that didn't take away the sadness that she felt on her last day on the ward, to be leaving the Infirmary and the Nurses' Home, and most of all to be leaving Alice and Eddy, and baby Victoria, of course.

Now the day had come and she had completed her final shift on the ward, there was nothing left to do but take off her uniform for the final time, pack all of her stuff and then spend one final night in her single bed at the Nurses' Home. She soon had everything packed. There wasn't much more in her room than she had brought with her, except the mirror that

Eddy had given her, of course, a new dress that she had bought for the wedding, and a couple of new shifts and a chemise for that first night that she would spend with Harry — in a small cabin on board ship, sharing with Alfred and the dog.

Maud tossed and turned in her narrow bed that last night. She kept waking to find the new gown that she'd bought for the wedding, and which she had carefully hung up, looming down over her like some ghost. She was used to seeing the dark shape of her uniform, but the new gown was a very light grey colour and it shone out in the darkness. Every time she opened her eyes it gave her a bit of a fright.

She was awake even earlier than usual the next morning, and she was soon dressed in the new gown, slipping the mirror into her bag and placing the now dog-eared copy of *Notes on Nursing* carefully on top. Then Maud picked up the white silk flower between finger and thumb before slipping it into a small, drawstring bag. She would only wear the flower at the church, for the ceremony, to please Eddy more than anything.

At last she was all set. She'd already made the bed, neatly folding the corners, and she'd made sure that there wasn't one speck of dust left behind in her room. So, having picked up her bags and taken one last look around, she made herself go straight out and close the door behind her. Pausing on the gallery, remembering that first morning when Miss Merryweather had called up from the ground floor and Eddy had bounded along to say hello, Maud felt again the sadness of leaving. Even though Eddy was gone now, out in the district to nurse, and she lived on another floor, and Alice of course was long gone from the Nurses' Home, it still felt as if this was their special place. Maud tried not to look across to what had been Nancy's room. She still got that unsettled feeling when she looked at that particular door, even though there'd been a new probationer in that room for quite some time. And typically, no one seemed to know anything about what had happened to Nancy after they had all qualified. She had simply disappeared, melting away into the city.

Anyway, it was time to get going so Maud straightened her back, took a firmer grip of her bags and walked down the stone stairs into the space below for the final time. She had promised herself that she would spend a few moments gazing up to the skylight and that's exactly what she did. As she stood she could almost feel Miss Merryweather beside her, looking up to the light as it streamed through the glass. Maud had already said her goodbyes to the superintendent and her sister, and Miss Mary Merryweather had been thrilled that Maud was venturing out of Liverpool and would be spreading the Nightingale philosophy across the Atlantic. She wanted to know everything about it and made Maud promise to write to her.

Outside the sky was blue, and as Maud opened the door of the Nurses' Home for the last time and walked steadily down the steps carrying her bags she felt the warm glow of the sun on her skin. As she walked away from the beautiful building that she had grown to love so much, she felt as if it was trying to draw her back. So much so that she had to turn round in the street and look back at it. She could see herself on that first day in her new uniform coming down those steps, thoughtful and unsmiling and completely unprepared for what she would find on the wards. Then she pictured Alice with her pale, worried face walking carefully down after her, and Eddy, tearing out of the door with her hair all over the place and her cap askew. They were all still there together, all three of them, they always would be, following along behind the groups of eager probationers who had gone earlier and leading the way for the new nurses that still had to come.

Maud's little group would always be part of the Liverpool Royal, and that made her feel glad and more sure of what she was setting out to do now. No matter what happened in her life, her marriage or her work in New York, she knew that this place would always stand firm and remain in her heart alongside the people that she had grown to love like family. And when she was ready she could always come back and walk through that door and stand in her own space and look up to the skylight above.

We do hope that you have enjoyed reading this large print book.

Did you know that all of our titles are available for purchase?

We publish a wide range of high quality large print books including:
Romances, Mysteries, Classics
General Fiction
Non Fiction and Westerns

Special interest titles available in large print are:
The Little Oxford Dictionary
Music Book
Song Book
Hymn Book
Service Book

Also available from us courtesy of Oxford University Press:
Young Readers' Dictionary
(large print edition)
Young Readers' Thesaurus
(large print edition)

For further information or a free brochure, please contact us at:
Ulverscroft Large Print Books Ltd.,
The Green, Bradgate Road, Anstey,
Leicester, LE7 7FU, England.
Tel: (00 44) 0116 236 4325
Fax: (00 44) 0116 234 0205

Nettie's Secret

Dilly Court

London, 1875. Thanks to her hapless father, Nettie Carroll has had to grow up quickly. While Nettie is sewing night and day to keep food on the table, her gullible father has trusted the wrong man again. Left with virtually nothing but the clothes they stand up in, he's convinced that their only hope lies across the English Channel in France. Nettie has little but her dreams left to lose. Even far from home trouble follows them, with their enemies quietly drawing closer. But Nettie has a secret, and it's one with the power to save them. Does she have the courage to pave the way for a brighter future?

Shipyard Girls in Love

Nancy Revell

Sunderland, 1941. With a brief break in air raids providing some much-needed respite from the war, things are looking up for head welder Rosie, who has fallen head over heels for Detective Sergeant Miller. But how long can their romance last in such uncertain times? Life remains full of challenges for Gloria, who must face her abusive ex-husband and confront her own guilty conscience about baby Hope's real father. The secret is tearing her apart but if she admits the truth, she will risk losing everything. Both women are determined to keep the most difficult of promises, but nothing is as simple as it seems . . .

The Sewing Room Girl

Susanna Savin

1892. After her beloved father dies, young Juliet Harper and her mother, Agnes, are left to fend for themselves. When Agnes lands a job as a live-in seamstress with a well-to-do family on the Lancashire moors, things begin to look up. But their new life brings new challenges, and Juliet soon finds herself defenceless and alone. Without her mother to protect her, Juliet becomes the victim of a traumatic incident. She flees to her estranged family in Manchester, and her formidable grandmother, Adeline Tewson. Setting up her own dressmaking business, she discovers someone is out to destroy her. Is it Adeline . . . or could it be an old enemy from the past?